LOVE AND THUNDER

GENTLY Granger kissed her temple, her cheekbone, then the quivering corner of her mouth. She turned her head, and his warm lips covered hers.

Lisha's eager kisses matched Granger's own as she pressed nearer to him. Thousands of stars exploded in her being until she felt she would surely go mad. He engendered a blaze in her soul that matched the raging tempest outside.

The love Lisha felt for him threatened to devour her. She thought her wildly beating heart would burst. Now she knew she was meant to belong to this man, belong completely.

She yearned for him to ease this burning new to her, this throbbing he alone could satisfy.

Diamond Books by Sherry Roseberry

TENDER DECEPTIONS
LOVE ONLY ONCE

LOVE ONLY ONCE

SHERRY ROSEBERRY

DIAMOND BOOKS, NEW YORK

This book is a Diamond original edition,
and has never been previously published.

LOVE ONLY ONCE

A Diamond Book / published by arrangement with
the author

PRINTING HISTORY
Diamond edition / August 1993

ISBN: 1-55773-924-2

Diamond Books are published by The Berkley Publishing Group,
200 Madison Avenue, New York, New York 10016.
The name "DIAMOND" and its logo
are trademarks belonging to Charter Communications, Inc.

PRINTED IN THE UNITED STATES OF AMERICA

10 9 8 7 6 5 4 3 2 1

Acknowledgments

I'd like to thank my writing friends for their help and encouragement, especially Pat Tracy for her great insights.

And I'd be totally remiss if I didn't salute those at Taylor Maid: Jean, Vic, Sandra, Chris, Marina, Vicki, Tina, and Trena. They're a hoot!

Prologue

March 1862

The black night camouflaged the steamer that hugged the shoreline of the Gulf of Mexico. The ship's hull, painted the color of fog, blended with the brackish tide. Waves, breaking on the shore, drowned out the noise of its powerful engines. The anthracite coal burned clean producing no telltale smoke—a sure giveaway for blockade runners.

Captain Mercer eased the shallow-draft speedster along the numerous sounds, bays, and inlets that dotted the coast, navigating as much from memory and instinct as from the use of the sextant. He'd made this trip five times before for the insatiable Clayborne and had never been caught. The captain intended to keep his spotless record, knowing each run raised a greater risk than the last. Now even more so, from the inside information Clayborne had sent him.

Through his connections, Clayborne had discovered that the Federals would soon be executing a plan to capture New Orleans. No matter, they'd find other avenues into Harrington's property, or rather, what the foraging Mississippi had left of it.

The captain snorted. Wouldn't the Federals give their eyeteeth to get hold of that portion of the cargo hidden among the crates of cognac, silk, perfume, arms, and ammunition? Even his crew had no idea what all they helped to smuggle past the blockade. If they did, they'd have demanded a share, or worse yet, insisted on handing the lot over to the Confederate Government.

Clayborne intended to deliver a good portion of the cargo to

the Southern states while keeping the rest for future sales.
Being ruthless businessmen, they knew that in a half year's
time they could get twice as much for the goods they
smuggled. And Clayborne proposed, with the obliging help of
the war, to fleece as much as he could from both sides. On
occasion they had toasted to the war's long and continued
prosperous life.

"Cap'n, gunner a hundred yards away, passin' on star-
board."

The sudden announcement jerked him out of his musings.
"Prepare the crew."

"Aye, aye, sir."

The men of the *Apparition* silently watched the gunboat
draw abreast of the steamer. Each one held his breath, hoping
the vibration of the enemy's engines would drown out the noise
of theirs.

Captain Mercer swore. There weren't supposed to be any
Federal ships patrolling this area. The frigate that usually
scouted these waters had headed back to a Union-held base for
supplies. Where had this gunner come from?

The gunboat slowed its pace. Suddenly a flare brightened the
skies above both ships, and the crew of the *Apparition* sprang
to life. Their only hope anchored in outrunning the Federal
ship. The *Apparition*, built for speed, could clock up to
eighteen knots. They had no choice but to make a run for it, no
matter how dangerous that could be. At all cost, the Federals
mustn't get hold of their cargo. Questions would ensue, then
eventually answers.

The speedster began to pull ahead when the crew heard the
roar of guns. Because of the violent pitching of the ocean, all
of the balls but three missed their target. One shaved the bow
of the steamer; one toppled a smokestack; the third crushed the
side paddle wheel as if it were kindling wood.

Sweat trickled down Captain Mercer's forehead. His mind
raced. The *Apparition* couldn't outrun the Federal ship, not
now. Not only that, but with the use of flares the speedster
could be seen. But what if the men on the gunner couldn't see
them? What if their view was blocked?

An incredible idea formed in his mind, one so farfetched that it just might work. On his last run to Nassau his contact had refused to take his whole shipment of cotton, because England's storage houses were already bulging. As the war progressed, the need for it would mushroom, but for now there was no demand. Grumbling, he had returned with several bales. He didn't know it then, but those bundles just might be the edge they needed.

As he barked out orders, sails magically unfurled, buckets of coal dust appeared topside, and the crew lined the stern with bales of cotton. Men hurried about dumping the tiny particles of coal on the cotton, and, at a given word, set fire to the lot.

A dense screen of black smoke ballooned to veil the moonlit night shrouding the steamer. A shout rose from the crew. They heard the guns fire again, but the cannon shot missed their ship completely.

Protected by the vaporous cloud, the *Apparition* made a dash for the North Pass of the Mississippi River, free to make yet another run.

Chapter
❧ 1 ❧

Granger Hawks signed the hurriedly scrawled letter in a flourish, then flipped it aside with the tip of his finger. His actions smacked of distaste. What he planned, in his opinion, was a necessity, an arrangement of convenience beneficial to both his four-year-old daughter and a spinster by the name of Elizabeth Ann Johnson.

He settled back to the creaking of the timeworn chair and stared impassively at the crisp paper. A face, vibrant and full of mischief, materialized without warning. The image was that of a lovely woman with golden-brown hair and velvety doe eyes, dark and enticing.

With an oath, Granger reached for his coffee cup, trying to dispel the mental picture of his late wife. But he found the liquid cold and slapped the tin mug down on the desk with a clatter.

"Juanita, bring me some fresh coffee."

His booming voice eventually brought the Mexican girl from the kitchen bearing a steaming pot of coffee. Granger watched Juanita pour the dark liquid into his cup and wished for the hundredth time that she was more responsible, more educated.

"Can I get you anything else, Señor Hawks?"

"No!"

The girl nodded briefly and left him to his uninvited thoughts. Granger knew he had sounded curt. He hadn't much patience since the night his Julia died. She had succumbed, like so many others, to that terrible epidemic.

4

Wearily Granger rubbed his tired eyes. How Julia had loved their deep brown hue, flecked with green. "Beautiful," she had whispered on many long, sultry nights. "Too beautiful to belong to a man." He would retaliate by tickling her until she'd begged for mercy, then—

And then . . .

Granger groaned inwardly. If only he could hold her once more, smell the freshness of her hair after she'd come in from the cool of the evening, kiss the stern look from her face after he'd walked on her clean floor with mud-caked boots—if only for a moment.

It would be two years this fall since he'd lost her. Almost two years! Would he ever become whole again? He doubted it. Even his short stretch in the Union Army couldn't ease the hurt. Months spent in a makeshift hospital had only allowed him time to dwell on the past.

There could never be another Julia. Hence this final correspondence with a company based in St. Louis, whose main purpose was to find "suitable brides for lonely men living out West. Men who outnumber women twenty to one."

A suitable bride was not what he wanted. A suitable mother was more to his liking. The problem was he couldn't have the latter without the former; leastwise, not in this vast wilderness.

Granger had answered the advertisement, briefly stating his preferences for a "bride." She had to be at least twenty-five, trained in the social graces, educated, and have religious convictions—preferably Protestant. He had emphasized that he needed a mother for his daughter, Serena. And he had warned that his ranch was in the territory of New Mexico, a good two hours from the nearest town. His last request, though, was somewhat unusual: He preferred the woman to be plain and unassuming.

But *plain* seemed too generous a word, Granger thought dryly as he picked up the black and white likeness of Elizabeth Ann Johnson. A portly woman somberly stared back. The fleshy folds of her face overpowered her snub nose and small chin. A softness about her eyes offset thin lips pressed into a colorless line. Her dark hair, severely pulled back, was, no doubt, in a large bun resting on the nape of her stocky neck.

The woman's bearing reminded Granger of a skittish animal poised for escape at the least provocation.

There would be an adjustment period before the proposed wedding, time enough to assess the woman's character and maybe time enough for a bonding friendship. Granger felt sure of one thing. He needn't worry about becoming emotionally *or* physically involved with Miss Johnson.

To an appealing woman, he could offer his body but never his heart. Or he could seek relief from women in town, as he had a few times. But he would not permit a lustful bond with a woman who might become Serena's mother. Desire could sour, and what kind of home life would that create? Things would be so much easier if he could love again, but he was just like his father. They were the type of men who could love only once.

Reverend Hampton had tried to talk him out of his absurd plan, insisting that Juanita or her mother, Maria, could take care of his daughter. The reverend had hoped to convince Granger that one day his wounds would heal, and he would find another woman to love.

Granger tossed the tintype aside and reached for the letter he had just written. No matter what others might think, this was the best solution. He wanted a woman who could educate his daughter and present a permanent mother figure, a role that neither Juanita nor Maria could fill. As for finding someone in town, Granger dismissed that idea. Better to keep this a business arrangement, hence avoiding any interference from relatives.

He gave little consideration to how the future Mrs. Hawks might react to the ranch's isolation. After all, there were worse things in New Mexico: heat, Indians, smallpox . . .

At the thought of the menacing virus, Granger crashed his fist down hard on the desk. Damn! Why did such a dreadful disease have to plague mankind? Why did it have to take Julia?

Granger stuffed the letter inside an envelope along with some currency and crammed it into his breast pocket. Leaping up, he grabbed his hat and stalked out the door, leaving the anxious face of Elizabeth Ann Johnson to stare silently from her photo.

St. Louis, April 1865

The strong odor of liquor, charred wood, and the stench of burnt flesh curled Falisha Harrington's lip. The noxious smells crowded inside her nostrils and stuck to her throat, leaving a rancid taste. Heat diffused from the cobblestone street and brick buildings, generating a sense of suffocation. Puddles, formed during the water brigade, vaporized into an ethereal mist. The constant yapping of a dog droned in her ears, followed by a sharp command, a sudden yelp, then silence. A glowing ember stung her bare hand, and she quickly brushed it away.

Lisha had assisted her uncle several times, but not in the capacity the doctor now expected. She reined the mare to a halt and jumped from the buggy, praying fervently that she would be able to handle the responsibility.

Nervously she smoothed the coil of her braid. Serving as a substitute nurse was not the only worry that plagued her. She scanned the crowd milling about the saloon's smoking ruins, straining for a glimpse of her father. Apprehension knotted her stomach. Although it wasn't the finest bar in St. Louis, the Lucky Lady had been his favorite drinking spot. She prayed he hadn't been inside when the fire had roared to life.

Someone cried out in pain, and Lisha's attention riveted on the robust form of her uncle, kneeling over a young man writhing in agony. She gathered her skirts and hurried over, splashing muddy water onto her high-topped boots and black stockings.

"Uncle John, what happened?"

Dr. John Calder rubbed a sleeve across his sooty face, then motioned to the man at his feet. "It seems this young fellow voiced his thoughts about President Lincoln's murder. He said the only mistake Booth made was not doing it sooner. You know what kind of fervor that would cause. You can see the results."

"Are there many injured?"

"Enough to keep us busy for a couple of hours," he said, rising to his feet.

"Uncle John"—her voice faltered—"have you seen Papa?"

Dr. Calder rocked back on his heels, centering the bulk of his weight. Dabbing at his receding hairline, he studied his favorite niece. She was so much like her mother in appearance with her silvery-blonde hair and blue-gray eyes—yet so different when it came to inner strength. Too many times Lisha acted on impulse, while Brooke never acted at all.

"No, Lisha, as far as I can see, Edward's not here." John Calder heard her sigh of relief and grimaced his annoyance. "There's no time to dwell on your father. I need your full attention here."

With help they managed to get the wounded inside a nearby restaurant, where they laid them on tables. At the bark of Dr. Calder's command, a boy scurried from the room and returned minutes later carrying a crate filled with first-aid supplies, including four bottles of whiskey.

The doctor sorted out a few items, placing them at each table. To the volunteers, he quickly explained how to treat the minor wounds. That done, he motioned Lisha over to where the young man lay half-conscious.

"His thigh's cut pretty bad," her uncle said, rummaging through his black bag. "I've given him a good dose of laudanum to ease the pain. I need your help to cut away his clothes and clean the wound."

Lisha stared at the man's blood-soaked trousers. The bright red edged into a muddy brown. Panic swelled, threatening to take over. She felt a light touch on her arm. Turning, she looked into the understanding eyes of her uncle.

"I wouldn't ask it of you," he said solemnly, "if I didn't think you could handle it."

His trustful gaze gave Lisha courage. She arranged atop the table scissors, needles, and horse hair needed for suturing.

With scissors in hand she began to cut away the trousers, then hesitated. She had never seen a naked man before, even when helping her uncle with his patients. Just the sight of a man's bare chest took getting used to. How, in all that's decent, could she lay bare a stranger?

A tormented groan escaped the young man's throat. Lisha

knew his well-being weighed more importantly than her inbred sense of modesty. Taking a deep breath, she cut away the rest of the blood-caked fabric.

A warm tide crept up her neck and face. She lowered her head, hoping no one would notice. While her uncle applied pressure to the laceration, she prepared the needles and horse hair. Under his curt instructions, and her own misgivings, she lit a candle and held a knife to the blue flame.

Her uncle poured whiskey on the wound. The man struggled, screaming in pain, and Lisha tried to pinion his legs with her body. Uncle John picked up the white-hot knife and began to cauterize the gash. Lisha quickly averted her head. The young man's body shuddered from the burning pain, then fell limp.

Rancid fumes clogged Lisha's throat. The scorched flesh made her ill. She fought to keep from vomiting. Again and again her uncle applied the blistering steel to the open wound until she was sure she would faint. Finally he laid the blade aside.

"I'm going to make a nurse of you yet, girl. In fact, I'll let you finish."

"You mean sew him up?" Lisha squeaked out.

"You can do it. You've watched me plenty of times." With that he turned his attention to another patient.

Uneasy, she took the needle and knotted her first suture. Struggling to keep her nausea down, she stitched her second and her third. By the time she bandaged the patient's thigh, he had regained full consciousness, and she instructed some men to help get him home.

One by one the wounded received the care they needed and were then sent home. Eventually the only evidence of the night's work showed in the bloody clutter left by makeshift doctors and the nagging ache across Lisha's shoulders. She rolled her sleeves down, frowning at the striped design created by the folds of material exposed to the soot.

"Now," her uncle said, giving her an exhausted glance, "I'm going to prescribe a good night's sleep, what's left of it, for the both of us. Do you hear? I want you to follow doctor's orders."

"I will, Uncle John, but first I have to—"

"Find your father?"

She looked away from his steady gaze.

"You know, Lisha, you can't coddle him out of his habits any more than your mother could."

"I know, but since Mama died, Papa has changed. He seems so . . . lost."

Lost in his cups, John Calder wanted to say, but he couldn't upset his niece any further. He studied her smudged face, noting the pinched skin around her nostrils and the worry clouding her large eyes.

"I'm sure Edward is somewhere sleeping it off. He'll be home come morning."

"You're probably right, Uncle John. It's just that this time I have a feeling something is wrong."

Her uncle rubbed a veined hand across his mouth and stubbled chin. "Lisha, don't worry—"

"Uncle John, you know these premonitions come to me, and most of the time they turn out to be true. I sense that something is terribly wrong with Papa. I can feel it."

"Lisha, if you're apprehensive, it's because of tonight's fire, and because Edward visited the Luck Lady more than any other place. Yes, you do have a form of second sight. Lord knows I can't dispute that, but I know too well that you also have a dramatic nature with a highly active imagination. Take my advice, go home and get some rest."

Lisha knew the futility of trying to make her uncle understand her fears. Where her father was concerned, John Calder stuck to his opposing attitude, like a hatchling to its nest, feeding it with negative gossip about Edward Harrington. She knew her father and his weaknesses, but she had also felt his love and intense pride in her.

"All right, Uncle John." Lisha smiled and gave him a quick hug. "You win. I promise to be in bed as soon as I can."

"Make sure you do, young lady."

Lisha picked her way around the smoking rubble and climbed into her buggy, reassuring herself that she really hadn't lied to her uncle. She *did* intend to get some sleep—just as soon as she made one more stop.

The clip of the mare's hooves on cobblestone echoed in the stillness. The gas street lamps lit Lisha's way. Hardly a person could be seen, and she guessed it was sometime after midnight. The cool night air sent a chill down her spine, and she gripped her cape tighter about her shoulders.

When she pulled alongside her lawyer's office, Lisha reined in the mare. Gathering her soot-smudged skirts, she hurried up the steps and anxiously rapped on the door. She waited, shifting her weight from one foot to the other, and knocked again. As she had driven up, she'd seen a faint light in the back, and she hoped Weston Clayborne might be in. She prepared to knock a third time when she heard the opening of a door, hushed voices, then footsteps.

Someone, holding a lantern, walked to the front of the office while a soft light danced in the windows. A key jangled the lock, and the door swung open. Light spilled out onto the boardwalk, casting Lisha in its glow.

"Falisha, what on earth are you doing out at this time of night and alone? And why are you covered in soot?"

Lisha gazed up at the dark shadow created by the kerosene lamp. She warmed at the concern in Weston's voice. "The Lucky Lady burned down. I've been helping Uncle John, but now I'm looking for Papa. Have you seen him?"

"Not since dinnertime. He was with his friend, Forister. I wouldn't worry. He'll be all right."

"I hope so."

"It's not proper for a young lady to be out alone this time of night. I can't understand what must be on your uncle's mind to let you go about unescorted. Give me a moment. I'm going to see you home."

"Please don't bother. The boardinghouse isn't far."

"No, I insist. I'll be just a moment."

Weston turned and strode toward the back room. He tapped lightly, then opened the door. A man with shaggy white-blond hair and a long droopy mustache instantly appeared.

"Who was that?" His rough voice matched his seedy appearance.

"Falisha Harrington. She's worried about her father."

The man's half-cocked smile betrayed a hint of maliciousness. His watery blue eyes gleamed at a private joke. "Is that a fact? What did you tell her?"

"The truth. Harrington's with one of his friends. Look after things while I take her home. And, Jackal," he warned, "I don't want any stupid mistakes while I'm gone."

"Well, now," Jackal said, smirking, "I think that's right sound advice for us both, huh, Clayborne? No more stupid mistakes."

Weston felt the involuntary twitch of a muscle. He knew that no bond existed between himself and this man, no loyalty that money couldn't buy. If, at this late date, everything exploded in their faces, his so-called assistant would grow vicious, maybe even turning him in for a reward.

But what could he expect from a heartless jackal? The man was good at his job as a bounty hunter, almost too good. His specialty had earned him his name.

Lisha patiently waited in the buggy for Weston Clayborne to reappear. Although she was not afraid of being out alone, she had to admit that she liked the idea of Weston seeing her home.

She tried to brush away the film of dust covering her skirts but failed miserably. Even so, when she thought of the short time she would spend in Weston's company, she felt a surge of excitement tickling her stomach.

Almost three years ago she had realized he thought of her as more than merely a client's daughter when his manner toward her had changed from polite boredom to intense interest.

She had just turned sixteen, and the knowledge of his attraction unnerved her. Her mother had been too ill to teach her the ways of a man and woman, the games that were usually played, and the stakes involved. Weston's initial interest had frightened her, and his attentions had slackened—until recently.

But this time she was better prepared. She felt that with a little encouragement, Weston Clayborne would declare his intentions. She could hardly make a better choice for a husband.

A revered lawyer known for his generosity, he came from a wealthy family, and ambitious mothers touted him as the most eligible bachelor around. Women of all ages pined for his attentions. And yet knowing all this she still hesitated.

Did Weston's social prominence have anything to do with her growing feelings, her enchantment with love? She didn't want the power he represented to cloud her judgment. So she took her time. But deep inside she knew there was more to her hesitation, much more.

Once when a dirty boy had run headlong into him, she had seen a hateful mask slide over Weston's features. The sudden collision knocked stolen apples from the boy's grubby hands. He scrambled after a few, then ran off before the store proprietor could catch up with him.

Lisha concerned herself about the boy having to steal to stay alive. Weston's concern centered on rapidly brushing the dirt from his otherwise immaculate attire. He scowled at a faint stain on his white cuff, at the new crease rippling his smudged shirt, and at the smattering of dust dulling his shiny boots. His face grew red with fury.

When he noticed her startled expression, the ugly mask instantly disappeared. He smiled disarmingly, although his movements were stiff with rage when he had taken her arm and guided her across the street.

Lisha had never seen that part of his character before or since, and she had often wondered what other aspects of a rash behavior hid inside the extremely poised and meticulous man.

Weston stepped out on the stoop, interrupting her thoughts. He locked the door and pulled on calfskin gloves, fastidiously sliding them down the length of each long finger. Rearranging his flat-crowned Stetson, he descended the steps. He eased himself into the buggy, careful not to let her soiled dress touch his tailored pants.

"I hope you didn't tire waiting for me."

Lisha saw the flash of his wide smile, the teasing glint in his dark brown eyes, and a thrill pivoted in her heart. She pushed aside her doubts.

"I didn't tire. I enjoyed a chance to calm my nerves."

"I hope not all of them. I'd like to think that being with me causes a few flutters."

Weston winked at her, making her smile. She enjoyed the

short ride spent with him. He kept his distance physically, but emotionally he charmed himself a tighter nitch in her heart.

Later, when Lisha let herself into the boardinghouse, the warmth of Weston's masculinity stayed with her. She thought about how his hat fit enticingly above his disarming eyes. Dark eyes that could enthrall her one second, then remind her that he thought her a desirable young woman the next.

She slipped silently through her bedroom door and felt her way toward the lamp on the oak nightstand. The kerosene flame sprang to life under a match, and her glance rested on the tintypes of a couple on their wedding day.

Her attention turned from the picture of her father to that of her mother. People had told her often enough, as she grew up, that she looked just like Brooke Harrington. She gazed at the prominent cheekbones, square jawline, hollowed cheeks and eyes that had been the color of slate rimmed with black. The similarities ended there.

Instead of the long black lashes of Brooke Harrington, hers resembled her father's: dark brown, thick, and short. Her mother's chin held a fragile look while her own shouted defiance. Next to her mother's pale complexion, hers held a darker, healthier hue. Her mother's delicate mouth made hers seem overly large. And Lisha, standing a good four inches taller, possessed fuller curves than her petite mother.

Lisha pulled the pins from her hair, letting the braid fall loosely to her waist. She brushed the platinum mane until the tresses sparkled with silver, springing into curls. This luxurious birthright came from the Calder family, the only inheritance she would ever receive from her grandparents.

Fingering the cameo engraved on the back of the brush, she remembered how she and her father had once pretended the brush had belonged to a long-lost princess. With a sigh she crawled into bed, telling herself that all was well with her father.

By one o'clock, Weston unlocked the back door to his office and let himself in. As he made his way to the musty attic room, Lisha's lilting laughter continued to haunt him. He vividly remembered the soot smudging the delicate ridge that framed her full lips. Lips that had been imprinted on his mind for the last three years; lips, soft and innocent, hinting at the naiveté he had dreamt of stripping away while he slowly acquainted her to his own brand of lovemaking.

Oh, he could teach her all right, and if things turned out as he'd planned, that time would come sooner than even he had hoped.

"Well, it's about time, Clayborne. I thought you might've stopped off at Etta's for a little nightcap."

Weston's throat constricted. Finger by finger, he stripped the gloves from his hands. Jackal knew very well that he always saw Etta *before* she began her evening's work.

"How's our guest?"

"Rather uppity. He don't seem to want to cooperate much."

Weston tapped his gloves against his thigh in a deadly rhythm. He had worked too hard for his plans to disintegrate now. No one, not even a stubborn little man, was going to hinder him in his bid for political power. He had spent too much time, taken too many risks running Yankee blockades. Even if it took all night, he intended to find out where the smuggled gold was hidden. No matter the cost.

"We'll see about that."

Weston walked into the dark alcove, and Edward Harrington slowly raised his head.

Chapter
🌿 2 🌿

"Good morning, Tilly."

A cherub of a woman looked up from the mail stacked on her desk. When she caught sight of Lisha, a smile dimpled her pudgy cheeks.

"Good morning, dear. Did you sleep well?"

"Better than I thought I would. Have you seen Papa?"

Tilly paused in her work and squinted over her wire-rimmed glasses. "Now, Lisha, you're worrying too much again. You know how your father is. He'll come home at the most unexpected time."

"You're right, he always does." Lisha nodded toward the pile of letters. "It looks as if you have some new customers."

"I do at that." Tilly shifted her glasses to the tip of her round nose, making the knob appear smaller, and scanned some of the yellowed envelopes. "They seem to come from all over. This one is from Montana."

Lisha settled in her usual chair. "I hope there are enough 'brides' to go around."

"We don't need to worry about that, dear." Tilly looked underneath a ledger. "Thanks to the war, there are plenty of eligible women anxious for a husband." She shuffled through the dozen letters, then scanned the floor by her small feet.

"Tilly, what are you looking for?"

"My money purse, but I can't seem to find it."

Lisha chuckled. "Did you forget to get it down again?"

Tilly ceased her frantic search. "Oh, my, I guess I did."

16

Lisha watched the woman scurry over to the bookshelf lining one wall and pulled out a leather-bound book. Tilly's busy motions, her diminutive size, along with her snow-white hair, combed into a loose bun at the top of her head, had always reminded Lisha of what a pixie might look like.

Clicking her tongue, Tilly opened the book with hollowed-out pages and retrieved a black purse. She untied the strings and peered inside. Lines waffled the skin around her blue eyes.

"Empty. Well, at least I remembered to put the money in the bank."

Affection warmed Lisha. She loved this dear little woman with all her heart. Tilly had opened up her arms to Lisha and her father after the Mississippi flooded Kingswood, their estate five miles outside St. Louis, and she had been family ever since. Even to the point of refusing what little money Lisha had tried to give her for recompense.

So in order to repay Tilly for taking them in Lisha kept her mail-order bride business organized. Once Tilly almost sent a mother with three children to a man who had especially requested a woman who had never been married.

Tilly sat down at her letter-strewn desk and picked up the first envelope. "Here is a Mr. Brant. He writes that he wants a healthy 'bride,' one who possesses good teeth, and she needs to be strong in order to help with the farm work in between caring for five motherless children."

"What does he want, a wife or a beast of burden?"

"Sometimes the men sound blunt, but most of them mean well. A frail woman would never survive the harsh realities of the West." Tilly rearranged her glasses on her short nose and glanced down a list of names. "Now, I think Miss Helene Gray might be interested in this one. She helped her mother run their little farm during the war until they lost it, and she loves children. Remind me to write to her."

Lisha nodded, recording the woman's name, and Tilly picked up the next letter. A half hour later she came across a stained envelope. "My, this one shows signs of hard travel," she mused, slitting it open. "Oh, it's from that nice widower in New Mexico."

She pulled out the currency with the accompanying note. A

frown ribbed her brow. "Oh, dear. I think we might be in a little fix. Mr. Hawks wants Elizabeth to come to New Mexico as soon as possible. He has to drive cattle to Fort Sumner, and he needs her to care for his daughter while he's gone."

"Why is that such a problem? Wouldn't Miss Johnson have enough time to get there before he leaves?"

"That's not what I'm worried about. I talked Elizabeth into this match. I thought it would be good for her to get away from that domineering mother of hers, and frankly, what other possible way would she have to snare a husband? But I'm afraid she's backed out. Now that she's had time to ponder the idea of living with a man underfoot, the prospect has almost given her a permanent case of the vapors." Tilly peered at Lisha over the rim of her glasses. "To tell you the truth, the poor dear just couldn't cope with the idea of a marriage bed."

Lisha remembered the widower and his strange request for a bride. She had often wondered what kind of a man he was—and why his odd petition?

"Personally, I don't think Mr. Hawks wants a wife in that respect. In fact, I think what he really needs is a governess."

"I believe you're right, my dear, but it's not my place to alter his request. Now I'll have to find someone else whom he'll be satisfied with and send her off in time to meet him."

"Won't that be cutting it close?"

"He says here that he'll be in a town called Cibola the third week in May. So there'll be time enough. What we have to worry about is finding another bride."

They continued with their work. As the morning passed, Lisha began to pay more attention to the lateness of the hour than to Tilly. All of a sudden the front door banged open, and a freckled-faced boy bounded through. Thomas was in such a hurry he almost tripped in his oversize boots.

"Thomas, what's wrong?"

"Dr. Calder says to come quick. It's your pa. He's—" The boy didn't have time to finish before Lisha dashed through the door.

John Calder looked at his pocket watch again. Fifteen minutes had passed since he'd sent Thomas after Lisha. It seemed like hours. He began to walk the length of his office.

From the moment Edward Harrington entered their lives, he had caused the Calder family nothing but pain. John's sister, Brooke, had heatedly argued with their parents over her choice of a mate, causing an unbridgeable rift in their relationship.

Because of him, Brooke's notions of a hero in gleaming armor lay trampled, along with her childish dreams. Because of him, she'd died a premature death. And because of him, Lisha would be stricken with grief.

He hadn't wanted his sister to marry Edward, because he knew firsthand of Edward's weaknesses. But Brooke would not be dissuaded. She insisted her love would heal her "Eddy." If it hadn't been for inheriting Kingswood from their maternal grandmother, Brooke wouldn't have had a place to live.

John looked in on Edward. His brother-in-law lay on a narrow bed, his breathing shallow, almost indistinct. He'd made him as comfortable as possible, though with Edward's cracked ribs, bruises, and lacerations, it hadn't been easy. At first he'd hardly recognized him, his face was so swollen and bloodied. Again he wondered why.

Maybe some ruffian decided to have fun at his expense, and it had gotten out of hand. Maybe a few Southern sympathizers strongly objected to Edward's boisterous gloating, and they took their anger out on him. Maybe . . .

John sadly shook his head. Speculations would be all they would have. Edward lay unconscious, and the probability of him coming to was virtually nonexistent.

The bell on the door jangled sharply, and Lisha rushed into his office. John hurried from the examining room to place restraining hands on her shoulders.

"Uncle John, what's wrong? Where's Papa?"

"Lisha, I have to tell you it's not good. . . . I'm sorry."

She brushed past him and ran into the back room. Seconds later her pain-filled cry twisted his heart.

"Oh, Papa, what happened?"

John found her sitting beside her father. Tears flowed down her ashen face. She had dipped a cloth in a nearby bowl of water and was tenderly applying it to Edward's forehead. John refrained from telling her that her efforts were fruitless. With her experience, she already knew that.

"I was taking inventory of my supplies when he stumbled through the door." He answered her silent questions in a voice sounding as hollow as an empty cavern. "I saw no one else about, so he must have got here on his own. I have no idea what happened or when. He tried to say something before he passed out, but I couldn't understand it."

Lisha remained silent, scarcely nodding her head. John left her alone with her father. There wasn't much more they could do now but wait. He hoped Weston Clayborne had Edward's affairs in order. And he hoped his brother-in-law had done something right for once and had taken care of Lisha's future.

John saw Thomas swinging on the hitching post and stepped out to talk to him. The boy should have been in school, but more often than not, he played truant.

"Thomas, you know Weston Clayborne, don't you?"

The boy swung upright on the smooth post. His boot almost slipped off his foot. "Sure do. You want me to get him?"

"Yes, go to his office. Tell him it's urgent that he see me. If you can't find him there, try to track him down. Now, hurry."

Thomas tumbled off the post and headed down the street almost before the doctor had finished speaking. John heaved a sigh. In the last four years he'd thought he had grown immune to death. But when it involved someone he cared for, his emotions always surfaced.

Weston Clayborne swept his leather gloves across Etta's dressing table, savagely knocking over her collection of lotions, powders, rouges, oils, and perfumes. He yanked the pearl combs from her brassy red hair and scraped her bangs off her high forehead. Leaning down, he pressed his dark head next to hers and peered at the images they made in her gilt-framed mirror.

"How many times must I tell you that I want your face clean, that I insist you rid yourself of any hint of your line of work?" As if to emphasize his words, he placed punishing hands on Etta's shoulders, his fingers digging into her exposed flesh. "I pay you good money, and I intend to get what I pay for."

Etta bit her tongue against the sharp pain jabbing across her shoulders and down her arms. Weston was late, extremely so, and she'd assumed he wouldn't come. However, she knew better than to argue. She did that once; she'd never do it again.

"Yes, Weston. I-I know. I'm sorry." She tried to steady her voice. "Give me a few minutes while I wash."

Etta blinked back the tears that threatened to spill down her freshly tinted cheeks. She knew how he hated a "sniveling" woman, how he hated weakness of that sort in any person. But most of all, he hated to be told of his mistakes.

He released her. A smile warmed Weston's perfectly sculptured features. His eyes deepened in color, sparkling with new life, but Etta had grown immune to his seductive charms.

She no longer thought him too pretty to be a man. She no longer wished for his love and his name. She no longer loved him. Two years ago Weston Clayborne had become just another client.

Clayborne sat in a gaudy red chair, drew out a cheroot from his breast pocket, and settled back to enjoy his smoke. The fumes mingled with the heavy scent of perfume, the smell of liquor coming from the saloon below them, and the unmistakable odor of human passion long since exhausted.

All the while Clayborne's gaze never left Etta. He scrutinized every move she made. A corner of his mouth twitched. He knew it unsettled her to have him watch her so closely. But he liked to keep women off balance. They were easier to control that way. And he had to be in control.

A sharp rap on the door disturbed his thoughts. Angrily he waved Etta aside and answered the door himself. The kitchen maid cowered when she saw Weston's black look.

"What is it?"

"'Scuse me, sir, but a boy brung an urgent message from Doc Calder. He wants ya ta come ta his office right away." The girl picked up her frayed skirts and fled down the hall.

Weston's anger gripped his gut. What would that interfering old man want with him? Then, with a sinking feeling, he thought about Falisha. Suddenly he became afraid that something terrible had happened to her.

"I'll be back," he called over his shoulder to Etta. Grabbing his hat and gloves, he hurried from the room, knowing perfectly well that he wouldn't be returning until the next day.

When Weston entered the examination room a short time later and saw Edward Harrington lying on the bed, he felt the blood drain from his face. He quickly glanced from him, to Falisha, to the doctor, then back again to Edward. A thousand questions whirled in his brain, and Jackal had better come up with the right answers.

Edward Harrington fought to regain consciousness. His eyes fluttered open. He saw Weston hovering above his head, and fear leapt into his eyes. No one seemed to catch it but Weston.

"Papa?"

Edward's attention centered on his daughter.

"Oh, Papa, what happened?"

Edward's lips moved, and little more than a breath of sound could be heard. Falisha leaned over her father. Weston strained to catch the strangled words before Edward sagged against the sheets.

"No! Papa, no!"

Falisha's anguished cry filled the room. She kneeled by the bed, clutching the sheet in her fists, and pressed her cheek against her father's stilled chest.

"Papa . . . Papa, we're having your favorite tonight, chicken and dumplings. You know you love it. Papa, please."

Weston pulled her to her feet and cradled her against his chest. Anything to stop her blubbering. Her salty tears stained his monogrammed silk vest. He'd have to discard it, of course. Pity. It was his favorite.

"Papa, please don't leave me, *please!*"

"It's all right, darlin'," Weston soothed, "things will turn out all right."

He *had* to find out what Edward Harrington said to his daughter . . . no matter the cost.

Lisha clutched the edges of her worn velvet cape in her pale hands. Her fingernails took on a blue cast against the indigo material. The steady drizzle from the dull afternoon sky caused chills to invade her body. She stared at the mound of freshly turned earth, the smell of the pungent loam filling her senses. The ground covering of leafy mulch almost hid the dirty shovels lying nearby. Squabbling ducks, nesting on the muddy banks of the river, echoed along with the minister's droning voice.

Her uncle stood beside her, and she glanced up at him. A grim look set his round face. Lisha knew he came out of respect for her, not her father.

She heaved a tormented sigh. More's the pity that the Calder family refused to see Edward Harrington's good points. They had never seen the lighthearted play, never felt the spontaneous hugs, never heard the shared fairy tales and nursery rhymes. Maybe her father hadn't been a good provider or an upstanding pillar in the community, but he had showered his wife and daughter with love and attention.

Curly-locks, Curly-locks.

The words danced in her mind. Her father's pet name for her were the last words he had uttered before he died. He hadn't called her that for a long time, not since she had grown too old to climb the live oak trees that gave Kingswood its name.

Curly-locks had been her favorite nursery rhyme. Her dear papa used to sit with her and read from her small collection of books. Then, under his tutelage, they would act out the stories. She accused him of being a frustrated thespian—for he loved the theater. But he'd never had the nerve or the faith in his acting ability to join a play company. So they made up their own, passing many a peaceful afternoon playing to the giant trees that towered above the gardens.

Curly-locks, Curly-locks, wilt thou be mine?
Thou shalt not wash the dishes, nor yet feed the swine;
But sit on a cushion, and sew a fine seam,
And feed upon strawberries, sugar, and cream.

Once again her father's dramatic voice echoed from Lisha's past. She thought she had cried herself out long ago, but hot tears brimmed over and scorched a path down her taut face.

Instantly Lisha felt a protective arm. Again, she gave thanks for the strength Weston Clayborne possessed, thanks for his help and kindness.

As their underpaid lawyer, Weston had taken over the management of Kingswood. Lisha had thought they would lose their beloved land to taxes, but somehow the lawyer had figured a way out. Not only had he found a way to pay the creditors, he had come up with enough money to provide Brooke Calder with her expensive medicines, besides funds for food and clothing.

Lisha suspected that Weston had eventually used some of his own money to pay their expenses. How else could he have wrung any more from Kingswood and still kept it?

Weston could fight the creditors, but he couldn't hold back the elements that ravaged their land. He found room for Lisha and her father at Tilly's boardinghouse. There was no sense in them staying in their big, empty house. A house full of haunting memories. A house too far from the saloons.

The minister cleared his throat and finished his speech with a solemn "Amen." The small party left the gravesite and silently rode home, each with his own thoughts.

"You know how I hate to bother you with this, Falisha, so soon after the burial, but hopefully you can see the reason."

A ghost of a smile lifted Lisha's lips. She knew Weston had tried to ease her pain, and she knew he wouldn't ask her to come to his office if it weren't important.

"Yes, I realize there are probably a lot of things that need clearing up. Papa wasn't the best manager when it came to business."

"That's not exactly why I asked you here." Weston shifted in his chair. New leather creaked when he moved. "It concerns your father's will."

"A will? I didn't realize there was anything left of value except the house, and Papa always said that Kingswood would be mine."

"Yes, that's right, but there's more to it. I'm afraid that everything I've been able to raise from selling off pieces of the land is almost depleted. There's enough money left to pay

taxes for a couple of years, but that's all. Eventually you'll
have to sell Kingswood or marry someone who can take over
the responsibilities.''

"I don't want to sell. Not just yet." She studied the
thoughtful look on his face. "I've a feeling there's something
more.''

"There is." He leaned forward. "Your father was worried
about how you would be taken care of in the event of his death.
He arranged for a guardian until you come of age or marry.''

"A guardian? Who?"

"Me.''

Lisha stared at the man sitting across from her. His shy smile
endeared him to her heart. "But, Weston, you can't."

"I can't? Why not?''

"Money. There's nothing left to pay you for the work
you've already done, let alone to cover my living expenses. I
can't let you pay my debts from your own pocket. I've lived
too many years off other people's kindnesses."

"I understand your feelings, Falisha, but don't act on
anything too hastily. I have some ideas that might enable you
to keep Kingswood and have enough money to live on."

"You do? What?''

"Give me time to smooth the rough edges, then I'll present
my proposition, something I'm sure your father would have
wholeheartedly agreed to.'' He patted her hand. "We don't
have to settle a thing, though, not for a while."

At his reference to her father, Lisha felt a jab to her heart. No
matter what she said or did, the ache always stayed with
her—reminding her of all she had lost. Sighing, she stood.

"Thank you, Weston, for all you've done for me and Papa.
I'm sure your plans will be for the best."

Weston leaned over her extended hand and brushed it with
his lips. "I assure you, they will be."

He walked her to the door. The makings of a smile creased
his face. At a different time Weston would have argued that a
future husband had a moral right to lavish a wife-to-be with
anything money could buy. But out of "seeming respect" for
the deceased, he would wait to propose to Falisha. Of course,
she would gladly become his wife. And he'd be free to search

Kingswood and the surrounding gardens, using the excuse of refurbishing the grounds.

Edward's death just complicated things for a while, that's all. Soon there'd be nothing to stop his political bid for power. He had taken steps to see that some influential men would pledge their support to him. The few who couldn't be persuaded were already cold in their graves.

"Falisha Harrington, how many times must I tell you to think before you act?"

As Lisha determinedly made her way to Tilly's office, Edward Harrington's voice traveled from the past to chastise her.

She had made up her mind and didn't have time to think about it anymore. The idea had taken shape on her way home from seeing Weston. She knew as well as he did that the avenues of squeezing money from Kingswood were long since past; and she couldn't accept any more charity—no matter how much love came with it.

Besides, she needed time away to sort out her true feelings toward Weston. Was she merely grateful for his help, or did she truly love him?

Lisha saw her elderly friend sitting at her desk. Tilly resembled a fragile doll lost in the copious chair. The lonely ache riding Lisha's heart increased.

"Tilly, have you found anyone to take Elizabeth's place?"

Tilly raised her cotton-topped head from the letter she was composing and pushed her glasses back against her face. "No, dear, I haven't. Why?"

"Because I want to go."

"You?" Tilly sputtered in a high voice.

"Yes, me. I decided that I could be of great help to Mr. Hawks."

"But . . . but he's expecting a bride."

"I know that's what he thinks he wants. However, I intend to change his mind. I have no intention of marrying him. . . . I mean to become his daughter's governess."

"But what if he sends you packing the minute he sees that you're not what he's asked for?"

"He has to drive a herd to Fort Sumner, remember? He needs someone to watch after his daughter. He'll have to let me stay—for the summer, at least. What else can he do?"

"My goodness!" Tilly flopped against her high-backed chair. She anxiously patted her chest with a tiny hand. "You seem to have this all figured out."

"I do."

"What will Mr. Clayborne say?"

"He'd try to talk me out of it, if he knew."

"*If* he knew?"

"I don't intend to tell him. I'll write him a letter explaining everything, but you're not to deliver it until the day after I leave. In fact, I don't want you to tell him where I've gone. I don't want him to know for a while."

"But, my dear, your life is here, with us."

Lisha heaved a sigh. "Yes, I'm well aware of that, extremely so. But if I stay, I'll have to live off your generosity, yours and Weston's. I can't do that anymore. My family has been living off others for too many years now. It's time I earned a little respect for the name of Harrington, even if it is in some remote town called Cibola." Her voice lowered. "But mostly, I need time to sort out my feelings for Weston. Will you help me?"

Tilly rose from her chair and hugged her. "You don't need to do this because you feel like a burden on those who love you, my dear." Her voice bubbled with emotion. "But I do understand why you feel you have to go. I guess, if it came right down to it, I'd do the same thing."

Lisha wrapped her arms around Tilly. She would miss the little woman, miss her terribly.

"Mr. Clayborne, thank you so much for taking time to see me," Tilly said, kneading her clutch bag with her fingertips as if it were a wad of dough. "My goodness, I know how busy you must be." Her cape slipped from a narrow shoulder, and she gave it an anxious tug.

"Not at all, Mrs. Ward." Weston smiled one of his most charming smiles. "I'm never too busy when it comes to Miss Harrington's friends, particularly you."

Bright red splotches appeared on Tilly's cheeks. She looked all the more like the clown she was. Didn't the stupid woman realize her shawl was twisted in the back? Not any more than she realized what a joke she was. When Felisha became his wife, this ridiculous woman would be the first of her so-called friends who would no longer be welcome company.

"Now, what can I do for you, Mrs. Ward?"

"Lisha asked me to give you this." Tilly fished inside her bag and brought out a letter. "But she asked me to wait until today."

"Until today?" Weston hesitantly reached for the badly creased envelope. "I don't understand."

"She wanted to be well on her way before you found out she'd left town."

"Left town!"

Weston ripped open the letter and read.

. . . and you know as well as I that Kingswood cannot sustain me any longer. And I, in all good consciousness, cannot live off my friends, especially you, dear, dear Weston. I need time to think, to sort out my life and feelings. Please, don't worry about me. I'll be all right, I promise. I'll write soon.

Falisha Harrington.

The neat penmanship blurred before his eyes; the words echoed in his brain. Falisha gone? Up and gone without so much as a "please" or "may I?" Weston clenched his jaw until his teeth hurt. His hands clamped together, squeezing the stationery. She would regret this action, sorely regret it.

"Where is she?"

Tilly's eyes widened at the deadly tone of his voice.

He cleared his throat, trying to gain composure. "Please excuse me, Mrs. Ward, you must know how worried I am."

Tilly pulled her shawl back onto her shoulder. "It's all right, Mr. Clayborne, but you have no need to fret. Lisha will be fine."

"When did she leave? This morning?"

"Two days ago."

"Two days!" Weston slapped his palms against the waxy edge of his desk and pushed himself to his feet. "I can't believe it! I can't believe she'd run away like this. . . . Mrs. Ward, I need to know where she took off to."

"I can't tell you."

"Can't or won't?"

Tilly stood. "I'm sorry, Mr. Clayborne, truly I am, but Lisha entrusts me to keep her whereabouts secret, and I cannot break that trust."

Weston barely heard the door closing behind Tilly. All he could think about was Falisha running out on him. *Him!* Well, she wasn't going to get away with it. He'd hunt her up, hunt her up like the whore she proved herself to be.

Chapter
3

May 1865

Granger leaned against Mario's Barber Shop and watched the passengers descend from the four o'clock coach from Santa Fe. The brim of his felt hat shaded his narrowed eyes. A young woman alighted. He straightened, then cursed softly. Granger could plainly see she didn't bear any resemblance to Elizabeth Ann Johnson.

He bristled. There had been enough time for Miss Johnson to arrive, *if* she'd planned to. He was a fool for swallowing that ad. Shrugging, he lifted his hat to run a hand through his sweat-dampened hair. He didn't have time to brood over lost money.

Across the way Lisha stood between her valises, her bone-jarring fatigue temporarily forgotten. The magic of Cibola enthralled and delighted her. As with most New Mexico towns, this one boasted a central plaza with a water fountain fashioned from stone. Cottonwood trees shaded the marketplace, and an array of flowers added color.

Lisha watched the other passengers enter the hotel. No one stepped up to introduce themselves as Granger Hawks—the rancher with odd specifications for his bride. And why should he? He wasn't expecting someone who looked like her.

"'Scuse me, miss, but are you needin' help?"

Lisha turned to a boy not much younger than herself. She could tell by his awkward movements that he hadn't grown accustomed to his latest spurt of growth.

"Could you tell me where I might find a man named Granger Hawks?"

The boy stared at her for a few seconds, then a grin spread across his blemished face. "Oh, yes, ma'am. He's right over there by the barber shop."

Lisha saw a tall man striding over to a nearby wagon filled with supplies. He swung effortlessly up onto the wooden seat.

"Mr. Hawks," she called out, hurrying to him before he gathered up the reins. "I'm Falisha Harrington. Tilly sent me in place of Miss Johnson."

The rancher turned and stared down at her. Instantly her attention riveted on his rugged features. His thick brows arched over sensuous brown eyes. Dark sandy hair, streaked with strands the color of aged wheat, curled behind his ears. His oval face sloped to a strong chin shadowed with fine bristles. A small Adam's apple centered in his tanned neck.

Granger Hawks's masculine bearing was strong enough to make her hesitate. Poor Elizabeth would have sunk well out of her puritanical depth if she had decided to come after all.

Lisha didn't expect to see a welcoming smile, but she hadn't anticipated his barbed look, either.

"Mr. Hawks?"

"I heard."

She felt uncomfortable under his hard stare. His eyes seemed to darken from anger. She noticed, too, that his thick eyelashes were a warm brown at the lids, then gradually lightened into curly blond tips. His upper lip had the looped curve a woman's might possess, only definitely more masculine.

"Mr. Hawks, I realize that I'm not exactly what you had in mind for a bride, but—"

"You're not *anything* like what I had in mind."

Granger's inspection transferred from her flawless skin smudged with dust to her brown traveling suit and pelerine caped over her shoulders. Both were wrinkled from long hours of jolting about in the stagecoach. The cut of the tweed dress was simple in design, but the conservative lines did little to hide the young woman's soft curves.

He knew she must be tired, yet her eyes—the color of the sky gathering strength for a storm—fairly sparkled. The wisps of hair curling out from her lacy bonnet could tempt a monk to release the tresses from their confining quarters, to languish for the feel of the silvery mane. Her lips, full and moist, could respond easily to a man's domination. No, she was definitely *not* what he had in mind.

She made a motion to tuck in the strands from around her face, then stopped the nervous gesture. Straightening her shoulders, which he guessed were sore from the tedious trip, she stared back. Her obvious resolve not to cower under his fixed gaze amused him.

"Mr. Hawks, I'm not one of your prized mares to be ogled in the middle of town."

"Was I ogling, Miss Harrington?"

"You were."

"Pardon me, but as a rancher I've gotten into the habit of checking over all my purchases."

"That goes both ways, Mr. Hawks. I would also like to examine the other half of the agreement. After all, *you* might not be suitable for my requirements. I think we could complete our inspections easier over an early dinner. Say, in an hour? Good day." She nodded curtly, then headed toward the hotel.

His insensitive remark was meant to rankle, but it only succeeded in piquing her apparently defensive nature. His irritation fading, he watched her cross the plaza, intrigued by the graceful sway of her hips. The lady had spunk. After leaping down from the wagon, he tied the reins to the hitching post. He would have to hone his wits in order to spar with Miss Harrington. The rest of the afternoon promised to be very interesting, and he wouldn't miss it. Even though, he reminded himself, he would be sending her back on the next stage.

Lisha carried her bags into the hotel lobby and paused by one of several high-backed chairs. The rug spotted with yellow and blue flowers bordered in Indian-brick covered the middle of the hardwood floor. Velvet drapes hung at the arched windows. Pieces of stitchery adorned the chinked walls. Even though the rug had worn in the line of traffic and the window dressings were faded, the foyer still held a feeling of grandeur and emitted a sense of peace.

A willowy woman bustled in from the dining area, buttoning

the sleeves of her stiff cotton dress. Her black hair, salted with gray, was neatly combed into a bun at the base of her neck. The woman glanced up, surprised to see Lisha. Her dark eyebrows, fanning over the thick bridge of her nose, generated the illusion that her eyes were too close together.

"I'm sorry," she offered hurrying forward to take Lisha's bags. "I hadn't realized there were any more passengers."

"That's quite all right. I just came in. I had to see someone first."

"Then you plan to stay elsewhere for the night?"

"I hope so. I mean, I think so." Lisha smiled at the confused look on the proprietor's face. "I was wondering if you might have a place where I could freshen up a bit before dinner."

"Why, certainly. What's the name?"

"Falisha Harrington, but my friends call me Lisha."

"They call me Martha—friend or foe." She removed a key from a wooden hook and, with a valise under each arm, started up the curving staircase. "Do you have relatives living in Cibola?"

"What few relatives I have live in St. Louis."

Martha made no comment. She unlocked the first door to the right of the landing. Obviously, she was curious as to whom Lisha knew in town, but she was too polite to ask.

The door opened to a cheery room with lacy pink and white curtains at the window. A flounced checkerboard comforter enveloped the bed, and a multicolored braided rug covered most of the gleaming floor.

"What a lovely room."

A ready smile formed on the woman's narrow lips. "Thank you. I only put women in here. The men don't appreciate the work that goes on in making a place homey." She deposited the bags on a chair. "I'll fetch some warm water." Martha hurried through the door almost before Lisha could utter a thank-you.

The window overlooked the street. Lisha could see Granger's wagon, but he was nowhere in sight. At least he hadn't started out for his ranch. He had every right to be angry, every right to leave her stranded in Cibola. She smiled, glad that he hadn't. Something about the man interested her, and she looked forward to their dinner.

Lisha was pulling a dress from the larger of her two carpet bags when Martha tapped on the door, then entered with a teakettle full of hot water. Steam curled up from the copper spout. She placed the kettle by a porcelain bowl and a matching pitcher full of cold water.

"There. Now, will you be needing anything else?"

"I don't think so. Thank you, Martha. I appreciate your help."

The woman's dark blue eyes wrinkled at the corners. "My motives aren't all that innocent. It's not often that we have visitors as lovely as you in Cibola, and if I make a good impression, maybe you'll decide to stay awhile."

Lisha sighed under her breath. "I wish Mr. Hawks felt the same way."

"What?" A multitude of emotions crisscrossed Martha's round face. Her animated voice rose an octave. "Did you say Mr. Hawks?"

"I did. But don't—"

"*You're* the one he's been waiting for?"

"Well, in a way. I—"

"Why, that scamp! Word got around about what he was up to." Martha gave her a quick hug and joyfully looked her up and down. "He didn't tell us that his expected bride would be so pretty."

"Martha, there's a problem. You see, Mr. Hawks is not too happy to see me. He expected someone else. Someone quite different from me."

"I would think taking one look at you would change anyone's mind, even Granger's. My goodness," she said, clasping her hands in front of her spotless apron, "I'm so excited. After Julia died, Granger just withdrew from life. For a while he hid in his whiskey bottle until Rena—you know, his daughter—forced him to think of something else besides his loss.

"Until now, he hasn't had any interest in any other woman besides Julia. I was afraid he'd take up with . . . Well, I don't approve of such activities, but what can a body do about some men's thinking? What Granger needs is a good Christian woman." Martha smiled. "From what I can see, you're perfect for him, an' I'm going to exert all my energies into making him see it, too."

She glanced at the dress Lisha held over her arm. "Here, let me press that for you. We'll just see if that man don't change his stubborn mind." With the gown cradled in her arms, Martha scurried out before Lisha had a chance to comment on anything the woman had said.

Lisha had finished toweling herself dry and started to dress when Martha knocked. At Lisha's bidding, she entered with the freshly ironed frock.

"Here it is, as good as the day it was stitched." She laid the dress over the arched back of the chair. "I saw Granger heading this way. Take your time. A man puts more value on things harder to come by." With a parting wink, she vanished out the door.

Lisha was drawn to the window. She could easily pick out Granger's form from the rest of the men on the street. She watched him make leisurely strides toward the hotel. The wide brim of a black hat kept the sun from his eyes. The rolled sleeves of his brown checked shirt displayed the sinewy bulges on his forearms. Trousers, lightened with age, disappeared inside calfskin boots.

Granger glanced up, scanning the windows. Lisha pressed back against the curtains even though she knew he couldn't see her.

After securing the last pearl button on her bodice, Lisha tied a dark blue ribbon around her midriff. The sash contrasted smartly with the pale blue flowers printed on the creamy background of the dress. The gauzy material, fairly floating over silk petticoats, weighed less than the tweed suit. Even the design of the frock raised Lisha's spirits.

Martha's pleased smile assured Lisha that she looked her best. The woman showed her into the dining room. Patrons paused from their eating to watch Lisha cross to Granger's table.

Granger stood, aware of the curious stares, the sly smiles, and the murmurs Miss Harrington had caused the moment she appeared in the doorway. Word had gotten around town that the lady he waited for had arrived, and suddenly every chair in the dining room became occupied.

He seated her, conscious of every watchful eye noting his stiff attitude toward his prospective bride. Martha didn't help matters any by anxiously hovering about.

"What do you suggest, Martha?" he asked.

"I suggest you leave the ordering up to me."

"You're the expert."

"At least that's one thing you'll admit to." She nodded at Lisha, then hurried from the room.

Several conversations resumed. The light buzzing grew in intensity. Utensils clanged against crockery, and Lisha no longer felt the object of blatant curiosity.

"I had no idea so many people ate dinner this early."

"Sometimes they do when Martha has a special entrée," Granger said, the corners of his mouth twitching.

Lisha glanced around at the grinning faces turned her way. "And by the looks of things, they're all enjoying the main dish. Let's hope, Mr. Hawks," she murmured, leaning slightly forward, "that you fare as well."

Granger's grin grew wide. Chuckling, he settled back against his chair. "All right, Miss Harrington. A truce."

"I think that would be wise."

Granger studied her, comparing her with his dead wife. They were as different as daisies were from roses. Julia's short frame had fit under his arm. Her golden-brown hair had hung straight, reaching beyond her slight shoulders. Her dark eyes had seemed too large for her V-shaped face.

Miss Harrington, on the other hand, had hair almost as pale as a dandelion gone to seed; hair that curled profusely around a square face boasting of prominent cheekbones, a straight nose delicately bridged, slate eyes, and a wide mouth. The contrasts of their outer appearance were obvious, yet he wondered if both women harbored the same sensitivity.

"Mr. Hawks, I get the impression that you're inspecting me again."

"No, just comparing."

"You must mean with Miss Johnson."

"Miss Johnson? I—"

"I know you expected her," she rushed on, "and I hope my being here in her stead won't be too disappointing."

"What happened to Miss Johnson?"

"What happened? Well—"

To Lisha's relief, Martha chose that moment to reappear, setting before them plates heaped with pot roast, buttered carrots, and mashed potatoes smothered in dark brown gravy.

A stocky man shorter than she had followed, toting a tray laden with thick slices of hot bread, a pot of coffee, and saucers of butter, strawberry jam, and golden honey. Martha quickly added the items from the tray. Lisha realized how long it had been since she had last eaten.

"Martha, everything looks so good."

"You eat up, now. I don't like waste. Remember, I have an apple cobbler for dessert."

"You can't possibly think I can eat all this."

"My wife's cooking has a way of coaxing people to have one last bite," the husky man said. "I was forty pounds lighter before I married Martha."

Lisha laughed. He had a somber face to match his monotone voice, but his brown eyes twinkled.

"Now, hush, Jim. You know as well as I that you've enjoyed earning every ounce. Come, let them eat in peace."

Martha scurried away, pausing a moment at a table before going into the kitchen. Jim trailed behind, visiting with his friends as he went. The two reminded Lisha of a racehorse and a turtle.

"They sure are opposites, aren't they?"

Granger picked up a slice of wheat bread and liberally coated it with butter and jam. "Speaking of differences, you never did tell my why Miss Johnson changed her mind about coming."

Lisha had taken a bite of a carrot, which she slowly chewed while her mind jockeyed around for a truthful answer. How could she tactfully tell him that the intimacies of marriage horrified Elizabeth? She sipped her coffee, then cleared her throat.

"When it came down to it, Elizabeth didn't feel she could

leave her family. And because my father recently passed away, I decided to come in Elizabeth's place.''

"Don't you think marriage is a strong antidote for mourning?"

Lisha finished spreading her bread with honey and set the knife down. A nagging doubt surfaced. What if Granger Hawks didn't agree to her plan? What would she do then? Sounding more confident than she felt, she plunged in.

"I really wasn't contemplating marriage, Mr. Hawks."

"Oh?" Granger's thick eyebrows rose, creasing his forehead. A teasing chuckle lifted his voice.

Lisha's cheeks warmed. "No, you misunderstand me. When Tilly received your last letter, we thought what you really needed was a governess. So I came in hopes I could convince you of that."

"Miss Harrington, I don't think—"

"If you're worried about my competence, I assure you I'm well qualified. I went to the best schools that St. Louis could offer, graduating with high marks. I know how to play a harpsichord, and I can do needle point. I . . ."

> *"But sit on a cushion, and sew a fine seam,*
> *And feed upon strawberries, sugar, and cream."*

"Miss Harrington . . . Miss Harrington, are you feeling ill?"

To Lisha's embarrassment, her eyes filled with tears. She blinked rapidly several times. Gradually her father's teasing voice faded into the background.

"No. No, I'm fine."

Thoughtfully Granger stroked his chin. "Look, Miss Harrington, I know you mean well, but you don't know anything about my situation."

"Mr. Hawks, I'm aware of the business you have with the government and your predicament with your daughter. When you get back from Fort Sumner, if you decide that the arrangement isn't turning out as it should, then I'll make other plans."

Granger remained silent. He only glanced at her a few times while he cut off a piece of meat and ate it.

"Well . . . what do you think of my proposition?"

He paused with his fork poised above his plate. Setting it down, he settled back in his chair. His dark scrutiny seemed to take in everything about her while he apparently mulled over what she had suggested.

"I have a feeling that I'm going to regret this, but I have no other choice. You're hired, Miss Harrington, for the time being. Now, what excuse do we give these good folks when . . . if," he amended, noticing the determined look on Lisha's face, "we decide you're to leave? I'll bet Martha has already begun to hum the wedding march."

"We'll just tell them I couldn't take country life and decided to go back to St. Louis."

"That will hold. It takes a special breed of woman to help tame this territory. We haven't had much of a problem with the Indians during the war, but that doesn't mean we won't."

"Have you had many problems with Indians before?"

"A few times, but luckily all they wanted were a few head of cattle."

Lisha listened while Granger told of the skirmishes he'd had with raiding Apache. She liked the rich baritone of his voice. The honeyed tones did strange things to her stomach. The rise and fall of his Adam's apple enthralled her, and she had to force herself not to stare at it.

Martha interrupted by bringing hot apple cobbler topped with thick cream. Lisha was surprised at how much she had already eaten, and how readily she accepted the pie. After Martha delivered the dessert, true to her nature, she hurried on to the next project.

"Tell me, Mr. Hawks, has Martha's appetite for life been inherited by any offspring?"

Granger shifted in his chair. "No, she and Jim were never able to have children, but they make up for it by acting as aunt and uncle to every child in Cibola."

As they ate, Lisha kept Granger talking. She didn't want to give him a chance to change his mind and decide to send her packing after all. When they finished, he escorted her from the dining room.

"Did you two eat your fill?" Martha asked, walking them to the desk.

"And then some, Martha." Lisha sighed. "Thank you, it was delicious."

"Well, I bet it wasn't anything better'n you can whip up, was it, Lisha?"

"I can do a lot of things, Martha, but I'm afraid that cooking isn't one of my best talents."

"Oh."

"Shot her down the first round," Granger whispered, lowering his head so only Lisha could hear.

His breath fanned her ear, creating tiny rivulets of pleasure. She suddenly realized that Weston had never affected her quite like this.

Undaunted, the woman pressed on. "What kind of talents do you have?"

"Talents? Well, I don't know if it's a talent, but I've done a little nursing. My uncle, who's a doctor, often said he didn't know how he ever got along without me."

Lisha felt Granger stiffen at the same time Martha's smile faded. What did she say that could have produced such a frigid response?

Martha cleared her throat. "Have you decided if you're going to stay with us, Lisha?"

Lisha glanced at Granger. A scowl had replaced the humor on his face.

"She's coming home to watch after Rena while I'm gone. Tell me where her bags are."

"Room one."

Lisha watched Granger disappear up the stairs, then turned back to Martha. "What did I say?"

"You said you were a nurse."

"What's so upsetting about that?"

"Julia . . . did what she could, here and there, to help sick friends who couldn't make the long trip into town for the doctor. Two years ago smallpox broke out. The doctor was worn ragged and asked her to help. Granger begged her not to

go, but she went anyway. She'd never gotten sick before, and
she believed she wouldn't this time, either. Several of her
friends were among those ill, and she said she had to be there.
Julia had such a giving heart. . . . She died two weeks later.''

"I'm so sorry."

Lisha began to understand Granger's reasoning for answering Tilly's ad. He still mourned his dead wife.

Granger descended the stairs, gripping the handles of each
bag. Lisha's pelerine was slung over his shoulder. Setting the
bags down, he fished in his pocket for some coins and slapped
them on the desktop. He then helped Lisha on with the cape
and silently ushered her out the door.

For the next half hour Granger maintained his dark silence.
They traveled northeast out of Cibola, toward the Sangre de
Cristo Mountains barricading the distant horizon. A flush of
lavender at the base of the range filtered into royal blue.
Silvery snow capped the jagged peaks, and glistening white
clouds with gray underbellies embroidered the darkening sky.

Lisha soaked in the artistic scene. She had grown up
surrounded with rolling plains, and the rugged mountains awed
her. Fleetingly, she wondered if becoming acquainted with
Granger Hawks would be equally as awe-inspiring. She mentally shook herself and decided to ask questions to take her
mind off such unladylike thoughts.

"How far is your ranch?"

"About a two-hour wagon ride. Shorter if you're on
horseback."

"Tell me about it."

"Not much to tell. The Pecos River lies to the east and the
Sangree is on the north. I raise cattle."

"Alone?"

"No, I have help. My foreman's been with me for three
years now. Jackson's talked about starting a spread of his own,
but he's never gotten around to it. Maria and her daughter,
Juanita, take care of the cooking and housework. Maria will be
leaving for Santa Fe to spend a few months with her aunt soon
after you arrive."

His impatient flick of the reins told Lisha that he was

through answering questions. They rode the rest of the way in silence.

Sturdy cottonwoods dotted the landscape along with a few pine and aspen trees. Longhorn cattle grazed on the grassy hillside. The road swerved to the east, and eventually Lisha spied a two-story house of whitewashed adobe.

The team pulled the wagon under heavy arches and onto the bricked courtyard. A little girl, too anxious to wait on the porch, ran toward them. Her sun-bleached braids bounced against faded bib overalls.

Granger stopped the horses and jumped down to swoop the child into his arms. Rena squeezed him around the neck, then placed chubby hands on his bristled jaw. She forced him to look at her pixie face, her freckled nose inches from his.

"Oh, Daddy, I missed you."

"I missed you, too, Pumpkin." He chuckled, tickling her.

Giggling, Rena brushed a few strands of hair away from her dark eyes with the palm of her hand and glanced over his shoulder at Lisha. Her mouth gaped open.

"Is she my new mommy?"

"No, she's not. She's going to be your teacher, and she'll take care of you while I'm away."

"Oh-h. I like her better'n the one in the picture. She's prettier."

"Young lady, how did you know there was even a picture?" Granger made his voice sound stern, and Rena's childish laughter pealed out.

"Daddy, how do you think? I sneaked a peek when you were gone."

Lisha couldn't help but smile at the precocious child. Rena grinned back. Granger placed his daughter on the wooden seat between them.

"Rena, this lady is Miss Falisha Harrington."

"Feesha?"

Lisha laughed. "You may call me Lisha. That name's not as hard to pronounce."

"Good, and you can call me Rena. My name's really Ser-e-na, Serena. But, I can't 'nounce it berry well."

Granger glanced down at his daughter, surveying the plain

cotton shirt, bib overalls, and the sandals on her tanned feet. "With a costume like that Miss Harrington wouldn't know you were a little girl unless I told her."

"Oh-h, she knows. I got long hair."

"Indian boys have long hair, too. Are you an Indian?"

"Daddy, you're silly."

The child's infectious giggle warmed Lisha's heart, and she couldn't resist hugging her. Rena raised her shoulders, ducking her head to one side, and glanced out of the corner of her eyes. A shy smile tugged at her lips.

Granger clicked his tongue, and the horses pulled the wagon to the house where Maria waited with her daughter. The Mexican woman bounded down the porch steps, waving her heavy arms, but Juanita hung quietly back.

"Señorita Johnson," she proclaimed in her thick accent, "we are so happy to have you with us. Little Rena has been running 'round like chickens with no head, waiting for you. I bet you are so hungry, you could eat many horses."

"Oh, she's not Miss Johnson," Rena piped up before Lisha or Granger had a chance to reply. "She's Lisha, and she's pretty."

Marie stopped short of the wagon. A broad smile cut dimples in the woman's pudgy cheeks. "Welcome, Señorita Lisha. You are a sight for red eyes."

"Why . . . thank you, Maria."

The woman nodded, acting pleased that Lisha knew her name. She called Juanita, and together they helped unpack the wagon, then carried an armful of supplies into the house.

Lisha laughed, lifting out one of her valises. "Maria's a colorful woman."

Granger hefted a bag of flour onto the steps. "She is that. Now you can see why I needed someone for Rena. Maria can give my daughter love, but she can't teach her the ways of a proper young lady."

"I can see that."

At Rena's insistence Lisha let her carry one of her bags into the house with Lisha following through the heavy paneled doors.

Granger's home had been built with the sensitive eye of an

artist, and Lisha wondered who that artist was. The house
consisted of two parts separated by a patio. The rear section
served as the kitchen, storehouse, and an informal eating area.
The living quarters in the front were built into a two-story
structure.

The tiled floor and hearth of the recessed fireplace gleamed
a waxy, tobacco brown. Textured stone walls raised to an
arched ceiling of salmon-pink brick supported by wood beams.
An overstuffed settee rested on a rug with colorful geometric
designs of dark blue, brown, and brick red.

Raised steps led to the dining room, where the walls were of
the same chinked whitewashed mode as the living room. Doors
opened to a patio and flower gardens enclosed by masonry.

The house's rugged styling, bold design, and strong colors
told of Granger's character more than anything else could. She
didn't really know what she had expected. Certainly not an
adobe hut with dirt floors and squawking chickens, but neither
had she expected such grandeur in the middle of nowhere.

While he was undoubtedly comfortable on the dusty range,
Lisha could tell that Granger Hawks took great pleasure in the
soothing symmetry of his home.

She guessed that he was an intriguing blend of textured stone
and fine silk, a blend she suddenly wanted to know more about.

Passing a small room that harbored an old desk and chair,
Lisha followed Rena up the stairs to the bedrooms. The room,
which had been prepared for the bride-to-be, faced the back.
An array of colors was repeated in the crocheted afghan, the
braided rag rug, the patchwork quilt, and the frilly curtains. A
door opened onto a veranda.

Lisha stepped outside. Cattle and horses grazed on rolling
plains flecked with green grass and red clay. The fast-growing
cottonwoods intermingled with aspen, pine, and fir. The trees
gradually grew thicker until they clothed the rocky sides of the
distant mountains. She breathed deeply, savoring the fragrant
smells from the flower garden below.

All at once a spark flared in the gathering dusk, and Lisha's
attention riveted on a small grove of aspens. A dark figure of
a man stood silently, smoking a cigarette. She had the odd

impression that he was intently watching her. Her apprehension grew.

Lisha heard Granger enter the bedroom with the last of her things. "Mr. Hawks," she softly called to him, "please come here."

He instantly appeared by her side. "What's the matter?" She heard the alarm in his voice.

"There's somebody down there by that grove of trees," she whispered, glancing up at him, "somebody watching me."

"Where?"

She scanned the aspens but failed to see the lone figure. "I'm sure he was down there. I saw him."

"It was probably someone I hired to help with the cattle drive. Don't worry, they're all good men."

Lisha readily believed his explanation, but something inside—an ability she had been born with—told her she had cause for her uneasiness.

Lago shrank farther back into the trees and studied the girl on the veranda. He could tell she and Hawks searched the grove—for him no doubt. After taking a long draw on his cigarette, he slowly exhaled.

The second she'd stepped off the stage, he knew she was perfect for Chavez. But it wasn't till he'd gotten a good look at her in the hotel dining room that he had realized just how perfect.

He couldn't believe his good fortune. She'd bring an excellent price, all right; one he couldn't pass up; one he wouldn't have to share with the others. He'd keep a close watch. One way or another there'd come a chance to get his hands on her. He spat on the ground. One way or another.

Chapter
𝕏 4 𝕏

The next morning Lisha parted her bedroom curtains, binding each half with a tasseled rope. Dewdrops glistened like fragile gems under the lacy web of the early morning rays. She walked out onto the terrace conscious of the fresh smell of foliage, wet dirt, and bark.

She heard the rapid drumming of a woodpecker and tried to pinpoint the bird's whereabouts. Her gaze rested on the grove of aspens where she had seen the disquieting man from the night before. Goose bumps shivered on her arms, and the muscles on the back of her neck tightened. She blamed her chills on the cool air, refusing to think that they might be caused from something else.

The aroma of percolating coffee, frying bacon, and sourdough pancakes teased her taste buds. Setting aside thoughts of last evening's visitor, she hurried downstairs, blaming her growing appetite on the high altitude.

Maria slapped a pile of pancakes onto a pewter plate and set the food in front of a black man deep in conversation with Granger. The man paused long enough to top the stack with softened butter and thick syrup.

"Señor Jackson," Maria lovingly chastised, shaking the spatula at him, "you keep eating us out of home and houses."

Jackson laughed. "Maria, I could never eat all the food that Hawks has stored away." His rumbling voice sounded as if it came from the depths of an empty well. "Besides, I'm still a growin' boy."

Lisha stood quietly in the doorway observing Granger's

foreman. She had to smile. A growing boy indeed! If the man grew any larger, he wouldn't be able to get out of his chair. She'd never seen such a huge man, all bone and sinew. Every thing about him appeared big, from his large head, thick neck, and massive shoulders, to his tightly coiled arms. Even his hands resembled leather mitts with wagon wheel spokes for fingers. Jackson glanced up and saw Lisha. His cheeky grin vanished.

Granger twisted in his seat, his gaze following Jackson's stare. "Good morning, Miss Harrington," he said, jumping up. Taking her by the arm, he propelled her in front of his foreman. "I want you to meet Jackson, my right hand. Jackson, this is Miss Harrington."

The giant of a man stood, scraping the legs of his chair across Maria's polished floor. Lisha had to crank her head back to look up into his coarsely chiseled face. The hard scrutiny of his wide-set eyes penetrated into hers, as if assessing her character. She matched him stare for stare. After a moment his broad lips formed a grin around even white teeth.

"I'm very pleased to meet you, Miss Harrington." Her extended hand disappeared into the callused folds of his. "It's about time Hawks did something to decorate the place."

"Thank you, Jackson."

Maria brought her a plate of food, and she sat down. Without so much as a "pass the butter," the men resumed their seats and continued their breakfast in silence. What had happened to their easy banter? Lisha felt as if she'd stumbled across a shy boy attempting his first kiss and missed his mark. She cleared her throat.

"Do you have all in readiness, Mr. Hawks?"

"Readiness, Miss Harrington?"

"For the cattle drive. There are preparations, aren't there?"

Granger sat back in his chair. "Aside from branding the cattle, I can't think of any."

"Won't it be hard going for them?"

"Not as taxing as it will be for the Texas herd."

"You mean there's a herd coming from Texas?"

"Yes, and I don't envy the trail boss. He has to skirt the staked plains, crossing ninety-six miles of semidesert. Which means they'll be three days and nights without water. Then he'll have to turn the cattle north following the Pecos River on up to Fort Sumner. The whole trip will take them two months.''

"And you won't have to travel the distance?"

"Nor will I have the hardships."

The ice was broken, and Granger easily discussed last-minute details with his foreman until Jackson pushed back his chair and stood.

"Best get to work, or those longhorns'll never get to the fort.'' He plopped a battered hat on top of his close-cropped hair, nodded toward Lisha, and strode out the door. The tune he whistled grew faint.

"I'm sorry if our ranch talk bored you."

"But it didn't," Lisha reassured him, blotting her lips with a napkin. "Learning about new things is never boring."

Granger's attention rested on her mouth. His undistracted gaze caused a warm flush to spread throughout her body. Maria clattered dishes into a tub of hot soapy water, breaking his concentration.

He raised his gaze to Lisha's, and she caught vibrant messages. Messages that she had neither experience nor resistance to ignore. She searched for a safe subject to talk about.

"How long have you known Jackson?"

Granger reluctantly pulled himself away from his vivid thoughts, thoughts of passion-warmed kisses on a lazy spring evening. Suddenly he realized how far his mind had wandered, and the extent disturbed him. He snatched the neutral line Lisha fed out.

"We met while in the army almost two years ago."

"How did he happen to come here?"

"He had nothing to go back home for, so he took me up on my offer to help me run my ranch."

"He had nothing? No family?"

"No. I guess it was mutual circumstances that drove us to enlist. I had lost a wife, he'd lost his wife and two boys."

"What happened?" Lisha asked, almost afraid of the answer.

"Some men used the war as an excuse to butcher. They

didn't like the idea of Jackson being a free man, let alone more educated. So they took their anger out on the one thing he cherished the most, his family.''

Lisha heard it in Granger's voice. Grief, not only for Jackson but for himself. Deep absorption worked the muscles of his face. Expressing her condolences would not have helped, and except for the first exclamation of empathy, she remained quiet.

Maria concentrated on washing the utensils, and Lisha became acutely aware of the woman's contented humming. The knives and forks clinked against the metal washtub in steady beat with her lively tune.

"Well," Granger suddenly said, changing the topic and the tone, "feel free to take a look at the ranch. If I find I've a few moments, I'll show you around."

"Thank you. I think I will."

Granger plucked his aged hat from a spike next to the back door. He positioned it low across his brow, casually touched the brim, and disappeared out the back, the door clanging at his heels.

"Are you wanting more, Señorita Lisha?"

Lisha looked up into Maria's pleasant face. Her well-defined cheekbones eased the fullness of her plump cheeks, and her double chin sloped down to her collarbone, disguising the original contours of her short neck.

Lisha shook her head. "Your cooking is so good I'm tempted to have seconds. But I'd better not."

Maria smiled, revealing crooked eyeteeth. Her black eyes sparkled. "You have no problem. Now, me, I have a problem!" She chuckled, patting her fleshy sides. Her bright blue skirt, gathered at the waist, accentuated her rotund hips.

"Maria, you would be special no matter how much you weigh."

The woman blushed, waving the compliment aside with a flick of her wrist, but Lisha could tell it pleased her.

After Lisha helped Maria clear the table, she grabbed a dishtowel and began to dry the dishes. "Where's Rena this morning?"

As if on cue, the urchin vaulted through the back door

carrying a basket of eggs. Bits and pieces of straw stuck not
only to the white and brown eggs but also to her. Juanita trailed
behind. The instant she spied Lisha, laughter died on her lips,
and she stood quietly aside.

"Here," Rena's lilting voice rang out. She struggled on
tiptoe to slide the worn basket atop the cupboard. "I found
some in the barn again. I wish those ol' hens would just lay
eggs in the chicken coop. Morning, Lisha."

"Good morning, Rena."

"I get to help Jackson fix the corral."

"You do?"

"Yup. I get to pick up all the nails he drops." With that
announcement Rena ran out, followed by her sulking shadow.

"Rena must really be a comfort to Mr. Hawks."

"Sure. She is big help to her *padre*. For long time he at
untied ends, lost in sinking ship with no paddle, when Señora
Julia died. Rena bring back laughter in his eyes. Now," Maria
ordered, taking the dishtowel from Lisha, "I finish here, you
go rake hay while sun is shining."

With no say in the matter, Lisha found herself outside.
Sunshine filtered through graying clouds. The lazy morning
instilled a peace within herself that she hadn't felt for a long
time.

"Curly-locks, Curly-locks, wilt thou be mine?"

"Oh, Papa," she whispered longingly, "I wish you could be
here to enjoy this with me."

Wandering about the grounds, she thought of Julia Hawks.
The woman must've been very special for Granger to mourn
her all this time. At that moment Lisha envied the woman. She
wondered what it would be like to be cherished so much.

Without realizing it, she had made her way to the flower
garden she'd seen from the dining room window. When she
caught sight of the lovely arrangements, her wistful thoughts
vanished.

The little alcove presented the onlooker with a pageant of
beauty. Of all the flowers she sought out the roses. In the first
stages of bloom they grew in splashes of color around the
enclosed brick patio. Lisha knew this would become her
favorite spot during the coming months, an easy access from

the veranda above. This was the perfect place to bring Rena for her lessons.

Continuing on her self-conducted tour, Lisha ignored the blackening sky. She stopped by a grove of quaking aspens, realizing it was the group of trees where she'd seen the spark of a match the night before. Moving the dead leaves with a booted toe, she studied the ground. Finally she spied the object of her quest nestled in the crook of a rock and bent to pick it up.

"At least I wasn't seeing things."

"Do you always talk to yourself?"

She turned at the sound of the masculine voice, knowing very well whom to expect. "Not always, Mr. Hawks. Only when I've positive proof that I haven't been seeing things."

"Oh?"

"When I went to bed last night, I wondered if I really saw that man." Lisha opened the palm of her hand to reveal a used match. "As you can see, I did." She caught the twinkle in Granger's eyes. "I know what you're thinking, Mr. Hawks, but you're wrong. The match looks too clean to be very old, and the tip is still in one piece, not eroded by the elements."

Granger chuckled. "You impress me, Miss Harrington. If I need any detective work done, I'll keep you in mind."

She inclined her head. "If I decide to start my own agency, I'll certainly let you know."

They both laughed, then an awkward silence engulfed them. Lisha searched for something to say, and she impulsively blurted out the first thing that popped into her mind.

"I used to climb trees bigger then these."

Staring in astonishment, Granger erupted into laughter. "Excuse me, Miss Harrington, but somehow you don't strike me as the sort who occasionally dangled from a tree limb."

"Well, I was, and I became pretty good at it, too. Why, I could even beat Freddy to our tree house."

"Who?"

"Freddy. He was a boy who visited me every time his father made a run down the Mississippi."

Granger thought of her skirts hiked well above her ankles while she scaled the branches and wondered if in reality Freddy wasn't so slow after all. His devilish thought must have shown on his face, for Lisha's expression became stern.

"Mr. Hawks, I do believe you're letting your imagination run away with you. To ease your mind, I wore a pair of my father's trousers whenever I climbed to my tree house."

Instantly the mental image of drab cotton dropping over a slender calf invaded Granger's vision. He sobered, trying for all he was worth to hide his amusement.

"I'm afraid it is. I apologize . . . but only a little," he added quickly.

Lisha laughed. He liked the musical lilt of her voice, liked the way laughter deepened the blue in her eyes, liked how he could tease without her pretending to be offended, as so many other women would do. *Face it, Hawks, you're beginning to like her, like her very much.*

"Where did you peruse this unusual pastime?"

"Kingswood, where I lived until . . ."

Granger saw the light fade from her face and the intriguing smile evaporate from her lips. "Until?" he prodded.

"Until the Mississippi flooded its banks and rerouted its course, destroying much of our property, until . . . until my mother died, and we moved to St. Louis."

The rain finally came. A drop fell on the slender bridge of her nose, as if to emphasize what she'd just revealed. Granger gently wiped it away. He found he liked the feel of her silky skin, and guessed she'd be just as soft all over.

Granger's light touch, and his strong presence, brought Lisha's biting memories to a halt. She had a strange feeling that this man, this time, and this country would come to mean more to her than all the heartaches and joys of her past. Suddenly she feared the future. Her instincts warned her to run. Then instantly she felt a flaming desire to turn around and embrace it. What powers did her future hold to bring out such conflicting emotions?

The rain padded on the foliage surrounding them, dampening the red soil mulched with bark and dead leafage. A light breeze fantailed through the aspens, conducting the silvery leaves in a whispering sonata. Fresh air evaded their secluded grove, filling her senses.

Lisha thought of another grove of trees which guarded a gravesite and the last time she'd been caught in the rain. She remembered the thrusting pain in her heart. But this time was different. This time she felt a sense of peace. She wondered if Granger Hawks perceived the change in the atmosphere.

"You'll find as many dangers here in the desert as you'll find back in Missouri," he murmured softly, as if reading her mind. "Some come from nature, some from man."

"Such as?"

"Such as in nature—when it rains around here, it can cause life-threatening flash floods." He reached out to finger a curl. "Such as in man—when he sees a beautiful woman he can't help but—"

"Daddy, Daddy," Rena called, running toward them, glee evident in her voice, "come see what Saber's doin' in the rain."

The child propelled herself up into her father's arms. Her surprising interruption dissolved the pregnant mood between her father and Lisha. Lisha wondered if he was as disappointed as she.

"What's Saber doing, Pumpkin?"

"He's actin' awful funny. He stands still, then shakes all over, and races around the corral."

"Who's Saber, your dog?"

Rena giggled at Lisha's question. "Saber's Daddy's horse." She squirmed out of her father's hold and tugged at his fingers. "Come see, Daddy. Hurry."

Lisha followed after them. As soon as she left the protection of the trees, she realized how hard it was raining. She hadn't realized how sheltered they'd been. But, then again, she'd had other things on her mind to pay any attention to a spring rainfall.

Rena raced to the corral and leapt up onto the first rung. Inside, a magnificent stallion pranced about the enclosure; his golden coat glistened with rain; his black tail and mane flowed with each powerful movement. The buckskin paused a moment before furiously shaking his great head.

"See, Daddy? I told ya. Saber likes the rain."

"Only if it isn't a downpour."

At the sound of Granger's voice, the buckskin nickered softly and trotted over to his master.

"Ah, Daddy, now he won't do it anymore."

Lisha watched the unspoken bond between horse and man. "He's a beautiful animal. Is he very friendly?"

"Pet him and see," Granger offered.

With little hesitation Lisha reached out and stroked between Saber's ears. When she started to pull away, the horse bobbed his head, nudging closer. She smiled her delight and caressed the buckskin's velvety nose.

"I can see he likes to be petted."

"I don't blame him."

Granger freed scores of fireflies in Lisha's stomach. She hazarded a glance into deep brown eyes and caught a mischievous sparkle.

Without so much as a warning, red mud splattered a trail across Lisha's ivory skirts, distorting the blue flowers.

"Oh, oh!" Rena was hunched down by a leaking watering trough with a telltale stick clutched in her hands.

"Serena Hawks, apologize to Miss Harrington."

Rena brushed the palm of her hand across her cheek leaving a streak of dirt. "Sorry, Lisha. I was diggin', like this."

She dug in the pliable soil with the end of her stick, and again flipped mud on Lisha's dress. The child grimaced, sucking air through the spaces between her small white teeth.

Granger looked from his daughter's forlorn expression to the stunned look on Lisha's face and tried for all he was worth to stifle a chuckle.

As best she could, Lisha scooped the mud from her skirts and bodice. Her eyes narrowed dangerously at Granger's muffled snickers. Without warning, she threw the wet clay at her new employer. Gleefully Rena followed suit, obviously delighted with the new game.

Granger stopped laughing. He stared at the mud clinging to his checkered shirt and faded jeans, then at Lisha. Under the steady rainfall the clay slid an red-orange path down his chest.

Never taking his eyes from hers, Granger stooped, carefully molding a mud ball. Too late she realized the impact of her hasty decision. Would she ever learn?

"Oh, oh, Rena, I'm afraid it's every woman for herself."

Gathering her skirts, she turned and raced for the ranch house with a giggling child hot on her heels. A mud ball splattered at their feet, but they didn't stop running until they were safely inside.

Lisha dried the last spoon and surveyed the pile of clean dishes on the table. Maria had developed a sick headache before they'd finished eating their evening meal, and Lisha persuaded the housekeeper to lie down. Juanita was supposed to help, but the sulking girl had slipped away before the table had been cleared. Now Lisha wondered exactly where to put everything.

"If you hold your breath, wish real hard, and turn around three times, they'll disappear."

Lisha looked up at Granger. His teasing smile curved his sensuously bowed lips. She couldn't help but return it. "Does that work for you?"

"No, but Rena swears by it."

"Well, since she isn't here to weave her magic, I'll just have to guess where they belong, unless you could tell me."

Granger raised his hands in defeat. "Sorry."

"Somehow I expected that."

Lisha did her best to put everything in its usual place while Granger poured a cup of coffee and settled himself in a chair. He wasn't much help, but she liked his company.

"Did you leave any family behind in St. Louis?"

Lisha juggled the last pan in the cupboard. "Just Uncle John."

"There's no one else?"

"My grandparents, but they would rather I didn't exist. You see, they didn't approve of Papa."

"I'm sorry you lost your father." Granger's voice softened.

Once again she remembered her loss. She stilled her actions a moment before reaching for a coffee cup. "Thank you. It's much easier for me to recover from his death here. I'm not faced with it every day as I would have been in St. Louis."

"What about your home?"

"Weston is taking care of Kingswood."

"Weston?"

Lisha joined Granger at the table, cradling the cup in her hands. "Weston Clayborne. He's our lawyer, and friend, and now my guardian."

For a fleeting moment Granger protested inwardly at how the tone of her voice caressed the name of this man. He chided himself for his momentary brush with envy. He wouldn't call it jealousy, telling himself that he hadn't known her long enough to feel that emotion.

"What does Claybeard think about you coming way out here?"

"Clayborne. I don't know. I didn't tell him."

"You didn't? Why?"

"Because as my guardian he would have tried to stop me."

"Is that so bad?"

"In a way, yes. You see—Papa and I—have been living off the charity of friends for the past three years, and I couldn't stand living that way anymore. I needed to do something where I could earn my own way. I found out about the problem with Elizabeth Johnson, and I took advantage of it."

Granger nodded his head. He knew very well what she meant because he also needed to prove he could make it on his own. People had always referred to him as Ben's boy, to where he couldn't stomach it anymore. He had wanted to be known as Granger Hawks, the rancher. So he'd left Iowa, migrated to New Mexico Territory, and carved out his own niche. When he had done all he'd set out to do, he'd sent for Julia, his childhood sweetheart.

Thinking of his wife reminded Granger that Lisha had recently lost someone she loved. "Tell me about your father."

A sad smile tugged at her lips. "Papa was the kind of person who could find beauty in an obnoxious weed. He was a dreamer—an unforgivable trait to my grandparents' way of thinking. We read a lot together. Sometimes we would act out the stories, taking different parts. He called me Curly-locks, from a favorite poem he used to recite. In fact, that was the last thing he ever said to me, Curly-locks."

"How did your father die?"

"From a beating. We have no idea who did it or why."

The despair shadowing Lisha's face pulled at Granger's heart. He suddenly had the immense desire to wipe away her sorrow.

"Please forgive my asking. I didn't mean to bring up unpleasant memories."

"I'm glad you did. It helps to talk about it."

"I've a feeling, Miss Harrington, that you could tell me quite a lot of things."

"About what?"

"Your childhood. I already know your favorite hobby was beating Freddy to the tree house." Lisha laughed. He liked the way she laughed.

"On the contrary, I had many favorite hobbies to fill my somewhat unrefined childhood."

Granger raised a brow in mocked astonishment. "You mean you participated in more than tree climbing?" She nodded. "What did your father say about that?"

"Sorry to disappoint you, but I'm afraid Papa encouraged it."

"Give an example."

"Let's see . . . one time he smuggled me into what a women's club had labeled a scandalous performance by a troupe of traveling actors. Afterward, he took me backstage to meet the leading lady."

"Shocking. And did you bump into the town's most reputable citizen trying to slip unnoticed out the back?"

Again, she burst into laughter. "Almost. We caught Grandfather Calder coming from the dressing room."

"Something tells me he and your father never got along."

"They didn't. Grandfather disowned my mother when she married Papa. I'd never met him until that night. He didn't say a word. He just looked me over very carefully, glared at Papa, and walked away."

As they talked, Lisha realized she liked sharing part of her past with Granger. She felt he really listened to what she had to say, unlike Weston, who was always too preoccupied to ever give her his full attention. He usually seemed to have his mind working on his next project while summing up a current one.

When she thought of the lawyer, Lisha mentally calculated

how very different he was from Granger. Weston would
chuckle now and again, but she had never heard him laugh, not
really. In fact, she doubted he had ever allowed himself to be
relaxed enough to enjoy the comical pranks life might bring.
And with his fetish for cleanliness, he most assuredly would
not have joined in on this morning's antics.

Thinking about the spontaneous play, Lisha smiled wickedly
at the thought of the handful of mud she'd thrown and
Granger's surprised expression. Thank goodness he possessed
a sense of humor.

"What are you thinking of now?"

"That I'm terribly sorry for what happened this morning."

"I'll just bet you are."

Granger had to chuckle at the effort Lisha took to appear
contrite. He found he really enjoyed her company. She was
easy to talk to and laugh with, easy to grow a liking for. There
was only one other woman he'd ever felt this comfortable with:
Julia.

Chapter
🌿❦ 5 ❦🌿

"Lisha, are you coming with us to watch Daddy brand the cows?" Rena asked, sliding the basket of eggs onto the table.

Lisha began to wash off the eggs. The idea of watching Granger at work suddenly appealed to her. "Do you think I could?"

"Sure, if we don't get in the way, huh, Juanita."

Without taking her eyes from her bare dusty toes, the Mexican girl reluctantly nodded. Her long-limbed, shapeless figure reminded Lisha of how she'd looked in her adolescent years. She remembered the painful frustrations of being an awkward schoolgirl, sure she'd never become any better, and felt a kinship toward Juanita. She was going to befriend the girl whether she wanted it or not.

"Give me a few minutes to change my clothes."

"Oh, boy!" Rena exclaimed, racing for the door. "I'll get Shag-shag ready."

After changing into a navy blue skirt and white blouse, Lisha ventured out to the corral, where Rena stood beside an oversize burro. The little girl held on to a battered bucket filled with oats. Chewing briskly, the animal raised his shaggy head, then foraged inside the pail for more grain. The force of his search almost pulled the crooked handle from Rena's tight clench.

"I have to give Shag-shag some oats or he won't go."

"Go? Go where?" Lisha asked, swatting at an insect flying too near her face.

The apparent answer to her question nettled the back of her

59

mind even before she'd asked it. Both girls snickered at her obviously dumb question, acknowledging her misgivings.

"To the cows." Rena giggled, loosing her grip on the bucket. The container fell to the ground with a crash. "How else do you think we'd get there?"

Lisha stared at the animal. He pushed the empty pail along the ground with his muzzle, rooting around for more feed. "I didn't stop to think about how we'd get there. Least of all by donkey. Since all of us can't ride him, I'll volunteer to walk."

"Can't."

"I can't?"

"Nope. Takes too long. You have to ride Ginny."

Rena motioned toward the corral, where a horse stood quietly, swishing away flies with her tail. Lisha forced a stiff smile. She watched Juanita bridle the mare and throw a sidesaddle across her back. At least the saddle resembled the kind she'd learned to use.

Riding had never been her strong suit. No matter how hard she'd tried, she could never set her mount to the satisfaction of her strict teacher. Each morning she'd cringed at the thought of her riding class and her forever-criticizing instructor. She could do nothing right. Eventually the course had ended with profound relief for both teacher and student.

Juanita led Ginny over to her and silently held out the reins. Lisha nodded a thank-you. Placing a booted foot in the stirrup, she hoped no one around the ranch had been tutored by Leopold VanDeusen.

She mounted, a little awkwardly, and secured herself in the saddle, sitting, she hoped, with back straight. Automatically tensing, she waited for a fault-finding reaction. To her surprise, Rena clapped her hands. A begrudging smile played on Juanita's lips.

Rena giggled. "Wait till I tell Daddy he's wrong." She pranced about the barnyard, her pigtails flying.

"Tell Daddy he's wrong about what?" Lisha asked sweetly, knowing she wouldn't like the answer.

"He said he doubted you could tell which end of a horse was which."

"Oh he did, did he?"

"Yup. He said city females don't know nothin' 'bout ranchin' 'cause they're too busy with pretty clothes and parties and such."

"He did? What else did he say?"

"He said you wouldn't go watch 'cause you'd be afraid of stepping in somethin'."

The thought of backing out had crossed her mind, but not for the same reasons that Granger Hawks had guessed. Now nothing could keep her away.

"Sometimes daddies can be wrong," Lisha said, hoping she managed a melodious lilt to her voice. "Let's prove to yours that not all 'donkeys' have four legs."

"Huh?"

"Never mind. Your father will understand."

Lisha urged Ginny forward, and the girls scrambled up on Shag-shag's back. They'd gone only a few yards before Maria burst through the doorway. She held a basket in one hand and furiously waved a blanket in the other.

"Wait! I fix you a good picnic. You gets hungry as bears in no time."

She trotted up to them, the short sprint leaving her breathless. Smiling proudly, she handed the quilt and their lunch up to Lisha.

"Thank you, Maria."

"I thinks you want to stay. I thinks you no come back soon."

"You may be right. Come on, girls, lead the way. The sooner Granger Hawks eats crow, the sooner it can digest." She grinned at Maria's puzzled expression.

The rhythmic sway of the prodding horse relaxed Lisha, and she found herself enjoying the ride. The vast countryside, bathed in bright sunlight, appeared virginal. The clear blue sky stretched on for miles without the interruption of a single cloud.

Grassy hills sheathed with trees, rocks, and dead timber rolled to a flat stretch of red ground, only to lunge up into craggy inclines. A warm breeze played tag in the leaves of the aspens. Lisha breathed a contented sigh. A person could get used to this kind of territory, this kind of creation.

Lost in her own thoughts, she steadily fell behind the girls.
Suddenly the sensation of being stalked caused chills to race
down her spine. She instantly reined Ginny to a standstill. The
mare shook her great head and stretched down to nibble at the
tufts of grass alongside the crude trail.

Lisha shielded her eyes, carefully scanning the saw-toothed
crests that surrounded her. She failed to spot anything that
could have given her such a start and wondered if Granger's
ranch was a wild habitat for fierce animals. Yet, her mount
hadn't sensed danger. The only danger the horse faced was
overeating. Pulling up on the reins, she eased Ginny forward.

Soon she heard the sounds of bawling cattle, men's shouts,
and shrill whistles. She set aside the eerie feeling of being
hunted and guided Ginny around the rocky bend.

Lisha gaped at the longhorns filling the landscape. She'd
never seen so many cattle in her life. Several men hog-tied
cattle and applied the searing branding irons against their
flanks while others cut out the dodging yearlings from the rest
of the herd.

One man sat ramrod straight in his saddle while his
surefooted buckskin started and stopped, swerving quickly to
edge out a stubborn calf. The broad brim of the black hat
shielded the man's eyes from the relentless sun while he kept
a steady vigilance on the yearling.

Lisha sensed the sinewy power beneath the leather chaps
while man and horse worked as one. The man had to be
Granger Hawks.

Lisha urged the mare after Shag-shag. The small group
followed the winding trail down toward the pasture. Rena
stopped the donkey by a huge flat rock and slid from the
animal's back.

"We like to watch from here," she announced, plopping
down on the edge of the rock.

Lisha could see why. The spot was high enough on the hill
to watch the men at work and far enough away so they
wouldn't be underfoot. Juanita took the picnic basket from
Lisha's outstretched hand and silently joined Rena. Lisha sat
down beside her. The girl hardly moved a muscle.

Red dust swirled around pawing hooves, whiffs of smoke

drifted from singed hides, and snatches of voices intertwined with the bellowing longhorns. Enthralled, Lisha gazed at the multidimensional scene displayed before her. This was something new to learn about, to soak up.

Granger cantered toward them, dismounted, and quickly covered the short distance between them. The spurs on his high-heeled boots jingled against the rocky ground. His eyes sparkled in merriment.

"Hello, Miss Harrington." He chuckled, pulling off his hat to reveal a line of demarcation in his wet hair. He wiped the sweat from his brow with the crook of his arm. "I really didn't expect to see you here."

"So I'm told."

"See, Daddy," Rena exclaimed, scrambling up into her father's arms. "You was wrong."

He plopped his dusty hat down on her head, forcing her to raise her chin in order to see out from underneath the brim.

"I was, huh?"

"Yup. Lisha came with us. She's not afraid of getting her feet dirty."

"I can see that."

"She knew where Ginny's head was, too."

"So I gather."

"And she wants to show you Shag-shag's legs."

"She wants to show me what?" He looked from Rena to Lisha.

"What Rena's trying to say is," Lisha explained primly, a corner of her mouth curving slightly, "I wanted to show you that not all . . . donkeys . . . have four legs."

Granger coughed, and his daughter gently patted his back.

"Do you understand, Daddy?"

"I believe I do."

"Lisha said you would. She also said we had to hurry so you could eat a crow. Daddy?" Rena asked, the brim of her father's hat slipping over her eyes. "Don't you want to have a picnic instead?"

Granger set his daughter down. He looked at Lisha and cocked his head in a mock bow. "Yes, I would, if it's all right with Miss Harrington. I've eaten enough crow for one day."

"It will be perfectly all right with me, Mr. Hawks, so long as in the future you remember how fowls taste."

"Oh, I think that once learned, a man never forgets. I'll look forward to dining with you ladies at lunchtime." He donned his hat in a rakish manner, mounted Saber, and rode away.

Juanita watched the receding horse and rider with something akin to hero worship, and Lisha realized what was bothering the girl. She suffered the distress of a schoolgirl crush—a crush that would never be reciprocated—and she hated Lisha for coming, for representing everything she had yet to become.

Through experience, Lisha knew how gauche and unattractive Juanita felt. The summer months were a long time to spend with someone who disliked her. Now, more than ever, she'd have to find a way to bridge that resentment.

Rena absentmindedly kicked a pebble off the flat rock. "Can we go rock hunting, till it's time to eat?"

"I guess, if you don't go too far away."

"We won't." She skipped off, with Juanita following along behind.

Lisha watched the two girls scour the ground, stopping now and then to pick up a rock and herald their find or discard the useless object before moving farther on up the hill.

The large rock Lisha sat upon became increasingly uncomfortable, and she searched for a softer spot to sit. She spread out the blanket Maria had given her. The steady hum of insects along with the warm sun made her drowsy. Stifling a yawn, she permitted herself to lie down. She'd never fully rested from her rigorous travels. Maybe she could take a short nap. For only a moment, she promised herself before she drifted to sleep, listening to the girls' constant chatter.

Lisha's eyes flew open. She didn't know how long she'd slept, but she no longer heard Rena and Juanita looking for their treasures. The men continued their work in full force with no signs of stopping for lunch. Before they did, she decided she'd better find the girls.

Turning, she noticed that Ginny had also wandered off. She hadn't thought to ask if the horse needed to be tethered. Only Shag-shag remained in sight, grazing on anything edible.

Lisha started up the hill, heading in the same direction she'd last seen the girls. Periodically she called to them, waiting for an answer. None came.

Winding her way through a maze of angular slopes, she entered a gully, catching sight of someone's shadow disappearing behind a boulder. She hurried her steps but found no sign of the girls.

The rock formations that surrounded her gave no sign of life. Yet she could have sworn that somebody had walked past moments before. Shrugging her shoulders, she blamed the reflection on the bright sun and pressed forward.

The terrain steadily grew rougher until she realized that she'd gone too far. Ginny certainly wouldn't have come this way—not enough grass. And the girls had more sense than to stray so far away from the pastures.

So what does that make of you, Falisha Harrington? The girls probably know exactly where they are. Do you? Although there's nothing to worry about. Just go back the same way you came.

To her relief faint sounds of childish laughter drifted in about her. Unsure of the direction they'd come from, she cocked her head, listening intently. She heard nothing except nature's harried hum.

Choice words formulated in her mind as she thought of the little talk she'd have with the girls when she caught up to them. Sighing, she scanned the nearby boulders. When she made a broad sweep of a rugged structure twenty feet to her left, she thought she saw an object glinting in the sun. She placed a shading hand above her eyebrows and retraced her visual search of the area. The shiny apparition had vanished.

A shiver skirted down her back. For the second time in the last ten minutes she was sure she'd seen something only to find herself mistaken. And the laughter—did she imagine that also?

Suddenly the crooked rocks appeared threatening. Their rough-hewn forms seemed to press down on her. A quick scan of a hill to her right reinforced her idea of something she wouldn't care to tackle, but anything was better than mentally chasing phantoms. Besides, what could she see from down here?

She anchored her toe inside a shaley fissure in order to scale up the knoll for a better view. Her foot slipped, and she banged her leg against a rock. Hissing air through clenched teeth, she rubbed her shin, sarcastically betting on one solid bruise. The morning had started out so fine. Why did she have to end up foraging trails? Again, she tried to ascend the steep rise. This time she grasped hold of the exposed roots of a dead tree for pulling leverage. When she reached the top, her spirits waned. Strewn about her were higher slopes to climb.

With a disheartening sigh, she sank down on a boulder. How did she ever get herself into such a mess? Better yet, how would she get out? She had to admit that she was definitely and unreasonably lost.

"Now, Miss Harrington," she muttered to herself, "you may panic."

Perspiration trickled around her ears, and she mopped her forehead and neck with a handkerchief she'd had sense enough to tuck into the pocket of her skirt. She studied her surroundings, trying to set her bearings.

Bearings, hah! Who was she trying to fool? Herself? She'd never been very perceptive at figuring out the directions in something as familiar as home. So what did that make her in these hills?

Illiterate, that's what. Confusion had set in from the start. How on earth could she ever unravel her way out of this one?

"Well, young lady"—she sighed—"are you just going to sit there feeling sorry for yourself, or are you going to do something about it?"

All of a sudden she was thrown into shadow, as if something momentarily blocked the sun's path. A dislodged pebble rolled down from the jagged peak behind her.

Her heart quickened. She whipped around, craning her neck to see above her, but found nothing. Tiny hairs on the back of her nape rose. The shadow had been real. She didn't imagine it this time as she had done down in the gully. But did her mind really play tricks on her then?

She remembered her leisurely ride and the odd perception that someone or something watched her intently. Now the same feelings rushed back, the alarming anxiety of the hunted. Her breathing stilled.

Don't just sit there. Do something!

Lisha slowly stood and stretched. She began what she hoped looked like a casual descent down the bluff. With every laden step she felt as if a pair of eyes scorched a hole in her back, as if their owner had materialized inches behind her.

Rising panic hastened her paces. She heard loose shale slide down the cliff behind her, and her throat contracted. The blood pounding in her temples seemed to crystallize.

With a strangled cry she raced down the hill. She was too paralyzed to look over her shoulder to see what pursued her. Automatically she ducked her head, expecting an attack any second.

Slipping over a ragged edge, she half ran, half slid down into the ravine. Her breath came in hot gasps. Her heart beat a terrorizing pace against her burning chest.

The rough ground skinned the palms of her hands. Dried grass and twigs worked their way through her stockings, pricking her tender skin. Unruly strands fell away from the loose bun jouncing on the nape of her neck, eventually followed by the rest of her waist-long hair.

Suddenly a hand grasped a firm hold on her bruised elbow, and a shrill scream died in her throat.

Chapter
❦ 6 ❦

"Lisha! Lisha, what's wrong?"

Lisha jerked in the direction of the familiar voice. Her eyes focused on Granger's concerned expression, and she almost swooned. She threw her arms around his neck as if deathly afraid he'd disappear.

Her spontaneous action must have taken Granger by surprise, for he stiffened. After a few seconds he wrapped his arms about her.

"What happened?"

"S . . . something was after me. Maybe it's still there."

"Whatever it was, it's gone." He pressed his cheek to the top of her head. "There's nothing to harm you now."

She relaxed against Granger's solid torso. Her breathing calmed, and her heart slowed to regular beats. As her fear faded she became aware of the hand slowly massaging the length of her spine, aware of the steady breath fanning the top of her head. She noticed how well she fit in Granger's embrace, how protected he made her feel, how his presence chased away phantoms. And she found she liked it.

When did his tender strokes change from consoling to electrifying? She couldn't even guess. She only knew that each caress heated her blood. Granger's heart thumped against her cheek. Something animated coursed between them, a force so strong, so overpowering, that she could scarcely breathe.

Granger's hand stilled on the small of her back. He clutched a hand full of her hair, fingering the strands. She slowly lifted her head; afraid to look into his eyes, afraid of what she would find there, afraid of her response.

Her gaze locked with his, and she heard his sharp intake of breath. His vivid brown eyes held her transfixed, and she sank in their hypnotic, fiery depths. Tiny lines extending from the corners of his eyelids appeared white in contrast with the ruddy hue of his skin. For the first time she noticed a hairline scar that slanted downward from his right cheekbone, and she wrestled the urge to stroke the ridge.

Never before had she been so painfully aware of a man. Nor had she harbored such blatant ideas where Granger was concerned. He had said there was nothing to harm her now. Wasn't there? She nervously moistened her lips.

Granger groaned. His Adam's apple bobbed in his throat. Gently he rubbed the back of his hand against her temple, across her cheekbone and down her jawline, resting his fingertips lightly on the side of her neck. The pressure of his finger coaxed her chin to rise, as if she had no will of her own, as if she were mesmerized by his touch.

With a growing hunger too strong to resist, she wished his lips on hers. He must have read her mind, for he lowered his head, his mouth barely grazing hers. The tender kiss shot a thrill through her heart. But it wasn't enough. She wanted more, much more. Without a second thought to her actions, she folded her arms about his neck.

Moaning, Granger pulled her closer and applied pressure; pressure to her lips, her body, her heart. Then, slackening off, he ran his hands from the sides of her breasts, down to her waist to tarry there awhile, and back again. She could get oh, so used to this kind of attention, this—

Abruptly a horse's whinny snagged their delicately woven spell. Granger's head shot up. She gave a guilty start and stepped back. Ginny stood several yards off, her reins caught in the gnarled limbs of a scrub bush.

Lisha raised a shaking hand to her face. The heat radiating from her skin astonished her. She breathed deeply in an effort to calm her thudding nerves. The potent emotions evoked from Granger were something she'd never encountered before. She ran from what she thought a life-threatening incident only to hurtle herself against a powerful force even more dangerous. A force so powerful it could sweep two people away, melting their hearts, entwining their bodies, blending their souls.

"I . . . ah . . . I was looking for Ginny."

"Looks like we found her."

Granger's thick voice mirrored her own. Whatever affected her had affected him, too. She became acutely conscious of their surroundings: A light breeze tugged at her hair, swirling the strands about her face; a fly buzzed close to her ear; the sun glinted on the rocks underfoot, reflecting glistening veins of color; and an eagle called to his mate from somewhere overhead. Then, to her dismay, she realized that grass and straw stuck to her hair and clothing.

"I must look a sight."

His lazy scrutiny surveyed her. She felt as if he caressed her with his haunted eyes, causing her blood to again race a heated path through her body.

"No," he answered, reaching out to pull a twig from her hair. "No. You look anything but 'a sight.' "

"I set out searching for the girls. I'm afraid they're lost."

"I left them eating their lunch. You're the lost one."

His deepened voice triggered an intoxicating warmth in the pit of her abdomen. "How . . . ah . . . how did you find me?"

"Wasn't hard. You sounded like a crazed bull crashing down that hill."

"I thought something was after me. In fact, I'm sure of it. I . . ."

Daring to look into his face, she saw a craving mirrored in his green-flecked eyes. She felt her cheeks flush. Did that same hungry flame smolder in hers? She tried brushing out her crinkled skirt. The action seemed to bring a little bit of sanity to her thoughts.

"We . . . ah . . . we'd better get back, or they'll think we're both lost."

"I 'spect you're right. We'd better get back. But not because they'll think we're lost."

Granger's words made her heart tip. She caught his meaning and knew he was right. To keep her mind from her heart's resounding crescendo, she started walking. He grabbed Ginny's reins and fell in beside her.

"Mr. Hawks, it's the same as this morning. I really did feel as if something was stalking me."

"This morning?"

"When we rode here, I could have sworn I was being watched. Do you have the kind of animals around here that would do something like that?"

"A cougar might. . . . Just make sure you're never alone."

She had detected a pause when Granger spoke and thought she caught a false ring to his voice as if he himself didn't believe what he'd said about a cat. But she was keenly aware of his muscular form inches from her own, and she wanted any sort of conversation going on to ease her mind.

By the time they reached the girls and their half-eaten lunch, Lisha had recoiled her hair and managed to pick off most of the twigs and grass that stubbornly clung to her clothing.

Rena jumped up and ran toward them. The changes that had occurred between her father and Lisha passed over the child's head. But when Juanita stared at them with a reproachful look, Lisha guessed that she had indeed picked up on the transformation. Raising her nose, the girl turned away.

Maria's glorious array of food failed to tempt Lisha and Granger, but they made the pretense of eating while Rena regaled them with stories of her rock hunting.

Juanita remained quiet, somberly watching their interaction. The girl had several years to grow before she fully matured, but she was old enough to know that something happened back in those rocky hills. Lisha could tell she didn't like the results. Once in a while Lisha glanced her way, and Juanita rudely averted her head.

"Well," Granger eventually said, setting aside his plate, "I bet by this time Jackson's thinking about deducting my pay."

"And he'd have good cause," Lisha teased, gathering everything up. "If I were him, I wouldn't pay you to loaf around."

"He wouldn't." Granger laughed, hefting Rena up onto Shag-shag's back. "He's been too well taught."

"Are you coming home with us, Daddy?"

"No, Pumpkin, I still have work to do."

"Can it wait? I want you to take us fishing."

"Can't today. We have work to finish up here."

"Are you going to be late again?"

"Afraid so. Maybe you and Juanita can take Miss Harrington fishing. I'm sure she'd enjoy that . . . with the worms an' all."

His words and his casual smile baited Lisha. She could handle this side of Granger Hawks. Relief spread through her. She'd rather fence words with him than maneuver heated debates of the heart.

"I'd love to go fishing," she said, acknowledging his challenge with a slight bow of her head. "Worms an' all."

Rena's eyes widened. "You mean worms don't make you squeamish?"

Lisha thought of the nursing she'd done for her uncle, the death she'd seen, and the bloody results of the war. It would take something more than worms to make her squeamish.

"No, those wriggling little creatures won't make me squeamish."

"My goodness!"

Granger helped Lisha up onto the saddle and gave her the reins. "If you ladies catch enough fish, have Maria fry up a batch for supper, will you?"

"We will do our best, Mr. Hawks."

"I'm sure you will."

Granger watched while the three rode from sight. He reflected on the kiss and the emotions that nearly overpowered him while he held Lisha in his arms. All too vividly he remembered how he had felt as he gazed into her face. A face so innocent, yet so wise to the ways of feminine seduction. How could she be such a child, yet so versed in the womanly art of lovemaking?

Then he remembered her fear of being chased. There was no mistaking the terror in her voice. He had scanned the direction she'd come from. Nothing in sight could have reduced her to such panic. But from what little he knew of her, she was not the kind to crumple over just anything. He made a mental note to have Jackson scout the area and turned to the business at hand.

* * *

All the way home Lisha made a conscious effort to keep her mind on things other than the few glorious moments spent in Granger's embrace. Whenever she forgot her resolve, tiny charges played tag throughout her system. Maybe it was a good thing Ginny had interrupted them. Maybe it was best not to start anything she couldn't finish.

When they reached the barn, Rena raced to gather up the fishing gear. She wanted to make sure everything would be ready for their afternoon fishing expedition. Chuckling at the child's excitement, Lisha picked up the picnic basket and blanket and carted them into the kitchen.

"Having good time?" Maria asked, vigorously kneading a big batch of dough.

"As a matter of fact, I am. I've learned a great deal."

The back door slammed shut, and Juanita passed through on her way upstairs. By the cloudy look in the girl's eyes, Lisha figured Juanita thought she knew just what kinds of lessons Lisha had taken to heart.

Maria punched the bread down into a large bowl and covered it with a dish cloth. "I not letting no flies sit on me, too." Chuckling, she washed the sticky dough from her stout fingers. "I get many chores done before I go."

"Maria, something tells me that even if you weren't planning a trip, you would busy yourself at something."

"Maybe so," she answered with a pleasant smile on her face. "Maybe so."

Granger squinted against the glaring sun. He watched as Jackson raced toward him. His friend had been gone for a considerable amount of time, which meant that he must have found something worth investigating.

A subdued expression set the foreman's face. Jackson halted his horse and dismounted. He held out a big hand, revealing a partially smoked cigarette nestled in his callused palm.

"Someone was up in those rocks. No doubt about it."

Granger picked up the cigarette, frowning at its crooked shape. Instead of grinding the butt into the ground with the heel of a boot, as most men did, someone had just bent it in half.

"Any ideas who?"

"Only that he isn't one of us. All of our men are working."

"I want you to ask around and see if anyone has spotted any strangers."

"To be on the safe side, don't you think we ought to send Miss Harrington back to St. Louis? From what I can see, someone is mighty interested in her comin's and goin's."

Granger rubbed his temples. He remembered the talk he had with Lisha and her inbred need to prove something to herself. "I don't think she'd go. She's here for a purpose."

"Then it looks like I'll have to stay and keep an eye on her while you handle the drive."

"She's my responsibility. I'll stay."

Jackson absentmindedly thwacked the reins against the calf of his leg. "She might be that, all right, but it's best that you go. Remember, Commander Brigs don't cotton to anyone whose skin's a darker shade than his."

Granger brooded. A few moments passed before he nodded. "You're right, Jackson, but don't let her out of your sight. If it weren't for the livestock left at the ranch to take care of, I would pack everybody off and settle them in at Martha's."

"Are you going to tell Miss Harrington about what I've found?"

"No," Granger said, dropping the cigarette butt and crushing it into the dirt. "No use in scaring her any more than she is. With you watching her, she'll be safe."

Chapter
🌿 7 🌿

"Keep hold of him, Lisha. Don't let him get away!"

Rena's excited shrieks broke Lisha's concentration. For a fraction of a second the taut line slackened, enabling the plucky trout to escape the deadly hook. The fish landed on the edge of the creek, flipping his way toward water and freedom.

"Get him, Lisha, get him!"

Lisha stared dumbfounded at the fish. Without much thought to the consequences she lunged, falling to her knees, and scooped the trout up from the shallow water, tossing it over her head. In doing so she lost her balance and tumbled face first into the cold stream.

Instantly she shot up, gasping for breath.

She struggled from the creek, her ankle-high boots squishing with each labored step. Soaking wet clothes conformed to her body. Her hair was plastered to her face.

Rena cradled her stomach and rolled helplessly on the spongy ground. Juanita leaned against a bowed cottonwood, laughing until her sides must have ached.

Seeing the comedy of her hasty act, Lisha's own giggles made it hard for her to walk straight. She knew she resembled the men she'd seen reeling from the Lucky Lady.

"Please stop laughing," she pleaded, gripping her sides. "You make it hard for me—"

An odd raspy sound jerked her to attention, and she glanced about. Four feet away coiled a rattlesnake. His pointed tongue flickered in lethal irritation. Lisha's pleas died on her lips.

Frozen with fear, she kept her eyes trained on the deadly
serpent.

"Rena . . . Juanita. There's a snake." The frightened
tremor in her voice silenced the girls. All that could be heard
was the steady hiss of the reptile. "Juanita, what do I do?" she
whispered hoarsely.

"Stay still. Don't move!"

Lisha could scarcely breathe. Oozing mud sucked at the
heels of her boots, wedging them deeper into the soggy ground.
Water dripped from her hair, followed her neckline, and angled
its way between the swells of her breasts. Roving clouds
blocked the warmth of the sun. The breeze that had seemed so
refreshing before now rebelled, and a shiver laced sharply up
her rigid spine.

The involuntary shudder vexed the rattler. It writhed in its
exotic dance, intending to strike, and Lisha was powerless to
do anything about it. As the reptile dived, a gunshot reverberated in the air. Stunned, Lisha watched the snake's head
vanish. She stared at its limp body before looking up to see a
lone rider silhouetted against the sinking sun. He held a rifle in
his grip.

Sobbing, Rena jumped up and ran to Lisha, throwing her
pudgy arms about her waist. Caressing the child's head, Lisha
watched Granger ride down to them. As he slid the rifle into its
scabbard, he eyed the dead rattlesnake and how close it had
come.

"Looks like I wasn't a mite too soon," he observed softly,
swinging effortlessly from his saddle.

"You could have been sooner."

"I was too busy chuckling to notice you had company."

"Well, I hope you were adequately amused."

Granger pushed his hat back from his sweaty forehead. He
surveyed her from the haughty tilt of her dripping wet head to
the waterlogged skirt molding her hips and thighs. His smile
came slow.

"I was at that."

Her fright quickly turned to anger. "Rena, Juanita, please
gather up your fishing poles. We've enough trout for supper."

The girls collected the meager equipment and went in search

of Shag-shag and Ginny. Eager to get as far away from
Granger Hawks as she possibly could, Lisha haughtedly
flipped back her wet hair, gathered up her skirts, and almost
tripped over her feet because her boots were deeply wedged in
the mud. Granger stifled a chuckle.

With a glare she silently dared the man to speak. Mustering
all her strength, she tugged up on her right foot to free it from
the mire, lost her balance, and fell against Granger, toppling
him to the ground. With a cry she landed squarely on top of
him. Trickles of water dripped from her hair to alight on his
startled face. Her embarrassment deepened.

"Tell me, Miss Harrington," he said dryly, "do you always
approach everything in life so passionately?"

"I beg your pardon?"

She stared into a face inches from her own. A lazy grin
spread across Granger's gently curved mouth.

"Miss Harrington," he drawled, flipping her over, pinning
her against the earth. "From the first moment I met you and
from what I've gleaned of your past, you attack everything
with an unquenchable appetite. It makes me wonder how you
would embark on the universal games played by a man and a
woman."

"That, Mr. Hawks, is a mystery you'll always wonder about.
Now, would you please help me up? I do believe your daughter
is coming."

"You win," he threatened under his breath before pulling
her to unsteady feet. "For now."

Rena came into view with Shag-shag plodding along behind.
The child half led, half pulled the donkey. Juanita followed,
shepherding Ginny. She stared at Granger, then at Lisha. Lisha
knew the girl couldn't help but notice that insufferable grin on
Granger's face, his wet shirt, and the dried leaves and grass
sticking to them both. Juanita almost threw the reins at her.

"You ride Ginny, Juanita," Granger intervened. "I think it
best that Miss Harrington go with me."

"Go with you?" Lisha's voice rose incredulously. "Why?
I've got perfectly good transportation with Ginny."

"Look at you. You're soaked to the skin."

"So?"

"Around here the days are pretty warm, but it can get awfully chilly toward evening. And"—he made another sweeping glance of her—"I'd hazard a guess that you're not prepared for the drop in temperature."

"But what has that got to do with riding with you?"

A corner of Granger's lips curved. "Think, Miss Harrington. How are you going to keep warm?"

"Keep warm? I . . ."

Realizing what he'd had in mind, she almost choked on her words. Granger's grin spread, and his eyes sparkled, causing her cheeks to burn. Blast him! How dare he make such a suggestion, then laugh at her flustered state? She squared her back.

"No! Thank you. I'm not the least bit chilly."

As if on cue, her body trembled, acting out the part of a traitor. She groaned inwardly, knowing she was cold and becoming more so by the second. Sobering, Granger pulled her toward his horse.

"Enough said. Your lips are turning blue, and your hands could chill an Eskimo. You girls hurry home and tell Maria to heat water on the stove. I imagine Miss Harrington will want a hot bath."

"Ok, Daddy, we'll tell her."

Granger began to unbutton his shirt, snatching Lisha's attention away from the disappearing girls. "This isn't much, but at least it might give you a little warmth. We're not far from the ranch house, or I'd build a fire to dry you out."

He shed himself of his shirt and handed it to her. Her gaze riveted on the mat of sandy curls that covered his muscled chest, and she blushed all the more, if that were possible. She thought she'd gotten used to seeing a man half naked, but those men had been patients of her uncle, and they didn't possess this man's virility.

For some odd reason the sight of his bare torso unnerved her. She felt the greatest urge to stroke the silky strands, to lingeringly draw her fingernails across his tight muscles. Shocked by her blatant fantasies, she averted her gaze and her hot face to don his offering.

He gripped her arm. "You can't put that on over your wet

blouse. What good would that do? The idea is to put something dry on for warmth—not to see how fast it can soak up water."

His casually uttered words shocked her. "You don't mean—"

"I seem to keep unhinging you these past few minutes. Yes, I do mean. And if you don't hurry and change, I'll do it for you."

"But I—"

"Turn around, I'll hold out my shirt so you can trade. . . . Now!" he barked, holding up her screen.

Hesitantly turning her back, she unbuttoned her blouse, vowing to keep on her chemise no matter what he might threaten. Quickly she slipped the damp garment from her shoulders and unlaced her corset as a series of shivers consumed her body. She struggled into his shirt, grateful for its warmth.

When Granger turned to pick up his hat, she couldn't help but notice the soft brushing of hair at the small of his taut back, disappearing underneath his leather belt. Again she felt the urge to stroke the sandy curls. Again, her inward reaction embarrassed her. She turned to wait quietly by Saber.

All the way to the ranch house she was vividly conscious of her back snuggled against Granger's bare chest, of the welcoming heat flowing from his body, and of a sinewy arm wrapped tightly about her waist.

Cool air laced with the smell of burning pine lingered on the shirt she wore. As did Granger's own scent mixed with leather and soap. The stirring combination kept the memory of his half-clothed body alive.

Her stimulated mind brought to life the earlier memory of Granger holding her close with his lips on hers. Somehow she knew the kiss had just begun and wondered what would've happened if Ginny hadn't interrupted them. Oddly, she felt cheated.

"*The Lord shall scourge the land of evil, the lust of flesh that can lead a good woman astray. And nowhere will the sinners be able to hide.*"

The blistering lecture from Beatrice, a sanctimonious patient of her uncle, echoed in her mind, and she winced. If the woman knew of Lisha's thoughts, she'd say they housed the devil. But that didn't stop her from enjoying the ride. She settled back against Granger. It felt good, almost too good, like she belonged there.

She'd never felt this comfortable with Weston, this relaxed. There had always been a stiff reserve about the lawyer. She doubted that he had ever allowed himself the joys of childhood or the fantasies of optimistic little children. Even as a boy he probably starved the vital child deep within, while Granger still nourished his.

"What else did you and Freddy do besides climb trees?"

Granger's teasing voice broke into her reverie, and she gave a guilty start. "What made you think of Freddy?"

"I thought that if you climb trees as good as you fish, then you must surely have other talents he's taught you that you're keeping from me."

Lisha liked the lighthearted tone of his voice. "I know how to swim thanks to Freddy."

"That's useful. What else?"

"One summer we built a raft."

"And did you spend many lazy hours floating down the Mississippi?"

"No. We couldn't keep from running it aground."

Granger chuckled.

"What's so funny?"

"The thought of you with mud splattered all over your breeches. Or did you wear a dress?"

"I wore trousers and a big cap."

"To cover your hair? Why?"

"So the others wouldn't know."

"Others?"

"Three boys who didn't care for Freddy."

"Why? Were they jealous because he had a little girlfriend and they didn't?"

"No. They didn't know I was a girl, at first. They teased Freddy unmercifully because he had a clubbed foot."

Granger's arm tightened about her midriff. "When did they find out?"

"One day they knocked Freddy down, and my hat fell off when I got mad and . . ."

"And?"

"I . . ."

And? How could she tell him that Freddy also taught her to fight? Dirty. How could she tell him that she'd swung out with her elbow, catching the bully on the windpipe, and when he doubled over, she'd kicked him in the groin?

"Well?" he prompted.

"If I told you everything, I wouldn't have any secrets, now, would I?"

Granger's laugh came easy. "Too bad. I've a feeling it would've been one whale of a story."

The adobe house came into view, but Lisha wished the ride could go on for hours. It wasn't the actual ride she wanted to prolong, but the proximity with Granger and their easy harmony.

When Lisha walked into the warm kitchen, she saw Maria pouring boiling water into a large tub. The metal sides rocked from the force of the scalding liquid merging with cooler water. Hot steam rose from the kettle's spout. A thick towel, draped over the back of a chair, lay alongside a blue robe. Maria glanced up from her work and grinned.

"You are back," she stated simply as she placed the blackened kettle on the stove.

"Yes, I am back, and I hope that bath is for me."

"It is for you. The girls told me about your fishes and your snakes."

Lisha shuddered. "Don't remind me about the snake. I want to pretend it never happened."

"You get in tub and forget."

"But what if someone comes in?"

"No one dares," Maria answered, setting her face in mock anger. She picked up a cast-iron pan and wielded it like a club. "I get my frying pan if they do."

"Maria, you're a gem."

The woman screwed her eyes half shut and cocked her head to one side. "You thinks so?" she asked. After a pause her black eyes gleamed. "I thinks so, too."

Laughing, Lisha disrobed and gingerly settled in the tub. Even though the hot water raised goose bumps on her chilled flesh, she found the prescribed soaking delightful. A bar of soap and a washcloth were within reach. All she needed was more time.

"This one's yours?" Maria asked, holding up a fish.

Lisha contemplated the "catch" that no self-respecting fishermen would admit to netting. She eyed the nice-size trout lined up on the cupboard.

"I don't suppose Rena would claim it?" Maria rudely shook her head. "Then I guess it's mine."

"You try fishing pole next time. Get bigger fish."

"I don't know about a next time. This one seems to have satisfied any curiosity I might have about the sport."

The second Lisha shrugged into her wrapper, Rena banged on the kitchen door. "Lisha, are you through yet? Can I come in?"

"Yes, Rena, I'm—"

Before Lisha had time to finish her sentence, Rena impatiently rushed in, dancing a two-step around the oval table. Her braids bounced in rhythm against the back of her overalls.

"My fish is the biggest one, an' I get to eat it."

"You do, do you?" Lisha asked, gathering up her clothes.

"Yup!"

The child grabbed Lisha's blue skirt, wrapped it around her tiny shoulders, and strutted about. As Lisha fondly watched Granger's daughter, she thought of a solution that could solve two problems.

"Rena, how would you like to come help me choose something to wear?"

"Can I really?"

Lisha grinned at her eagerness and thought how unfortunate that adults couldn't maintain some of that zest for life. She led the way while Rena followed with an exaggerated sway of her hips.

As they passed Rena's room, Juanita emerged from putting away the clothes that Maria had darned. Curiosity must have gotten the best of her, for she casually brought up the rear, easing through the doorway to Lisha's room.

Rena dropped the skirt and rushed over to the white wardrobe. She gleefully rummaged through Lisha's clothes. "I like this one!'' she announced as she pulled on the hem of a muslin gown the color of eggshell blue. ''Wear this dress.''

''Don't you think it a bit fancy for a fish fry?''

''Kinda,'' Rena admitted, although somewhat reluctantly. ''But it's still pretty.''

''Do you like the color?''

''Oh, yes!''

Lisha took the dress from the wood hanger. Draping the skirt across Rena's shoulders, she turned her around to face the mirror. The light blue cloth brightened the child's complexion, setting off her dark eyes and softening her sun-striped hair.

''Oo-o. Is that me?''

''It sure is.''

With wide-eyed innocence Rena bent forward, peering into the mirror. She smoothed the material with a pudgy hand. ''Am I pretty?''

''You are very pretty. Would you like me to make you a dress from material that same color?''

''Do you know how?''

''I sure do. When we take Maria into Cibola to catch the stage for Santa Fe, we can buy the cloth and make the dress in time to surprise your daddy when he comes back home. How would that be?''

''Oh, my!''

Rena whirled, wrapping the skirt about her face. She would have tripped if Lisha hadn't been holding the bulk of the gown. The child's contagious giggles pealed out, but Juanita didn't laugh. Envy pinched the girl's angular face.

Lisha stepped over to the closet and pulled out a white day dress trimmed with rose-pink ribbon. She fashioned the gown on Juanita just as she had done for Rena. Juanita stared at the resulting image of a young lady.

''How about you? Would you like me to make you a dress? I would be happy to.''

Juanita could only nod. Her reflection kept her mute.

''Except,'' Lisha continued more to herself, ''red ribbon would be better than pink. Your olive coloring will glow against vivid colors.''

Lisha viewed Juanita in the mirror. On impulse she reached

out and twisted the girl's waist-long brownish-black braids on top of her head. Lisha studied the finished picture reflecting in the mirror. Her gaze locked with Juanita's.

"You're a very pretty young lady, Juanita, with the makings of a real beauty."

Flushing, the girl lowered her eyes to stare at the braided rug. "Don't tease."

Lisha placed a firm hand on her chin, forcing it up. "I'm not teasing," she replied softly. "You might not believe it now, but you will grow into an attractive woman, becoming more beautiful with age."

"How do you know?"

"I know because of your bone structure. You also have beautiful eyes, a lovely oval face, and a glorious head of hair."

"But my nose," Juanita wailed. "It's not small like yours."

"Your nose isn't as big as you think. Look at my mouth. When I was your age, I thought it covered my whole face. Eventually I matured, my face filled out, and suddenly my mouth didn't seem quite so large. Smaller mouths are more the fashion, but I can live with mine. Now," she said, changing the subject as she laid the white dress on the bed, "you two go help Maria put supper on the table, and I'll be down soon."

Rena bounded from the room, but Juanita took one last look in the mirror. She viewed her face on one side, then the other. Sliding her finger up and down the length of her nose, she stopped at a small bump. She stared at her profile, gave a resigning shrug, and headed downstairs.

Pleased with the results of her first real effort in winning Juanita's friendship, Lisha dressed in the white frock. She vigorously brushed her hair and pinned it at the nape of her neck. After stealing a last glance in the mirror, she hurried to the kitchen, determined to enjoy a fish that had nearly cost her her life.

Lisha sat a cast-iron skillet full of fried potatoes and onions on the table just as Granger strode through the kitchen door. With a worldly air Rena sashayed up to her father, rolling her shapeless hips. Her lips were pulled into a haughty smirk.

"I'm pretty, and I have a surprise."

Confronted by his playacting daughter Granger tried hard to

keep a serious face. "A surprise? What kind of surprise would a pretty lady have?"

Raising her freckled nose, Rena gazed out from under lowered lashes. She rested the fingertips of one hand on her hip, the other on an imaginary parasol. The haughty imitation perfectly fit a few women Lisha had had the unfortunate duty of administering nursing care to.

"I can't tell you—then it wouldn't be a surprise."

Granger rubbed his bristled jaw with a weathered hand. He controlled the muscles in his face, but he could not master the telltale laughter in his voice.

"Well, I guess you'd better keep it to yourself. All pretty ladies have secrets."

Granger looked over at Lisha. An impish gleam shone in his eyes, and a lopsided grin tugged at his lips. Straightening her back, Lisha defiantly lifted her chin and stared back.

"If it weren't for a woman's little secrets, Mr. Hawks, I'm afraid there wouldn't be any challenges for a man to uncover."

Granger made a sweeping glance of her anatomy. "Oh, I wouldn't necessarily say that."

Blushing, Lisha realized the folly of her statement. He had taken something she had said in innocence, twisted it, and come out with a whole new meaning.

"Is it ready yet?"

Jackson's rumbling voice interrupted their verbal foreplay. He stomped his booted feet at the back door. His shirtsleeves were rolled up to his elbow, and traces of water glistened in the black hair that framed his wide forehead.

"Maria, them trout and fried potatoes have been hauntin' me for several hours now. So much so that I came in early. When do we eat?"

Maria had just placed a big pot of savory beef stew next to a platter of hot biscuits and with a mock sigh of exaggeration planted her hands on her rotund hips. "Eat, eat, eat! That's all you thinks about. Sit or I throw it out to the roosters."

Grinning, the foreman complied. "You sure don't have to tell me a second time."

The best restaurants in St. Louis would never have served Maria's combination of dishes. But the food tasted better than any Lisha had eaten. Lisha suspected that it was as much due to the family atmosphere as to the good cooking. She enjoyed the light banter between Granger's housekeeper and his foreman, the spontaneous giggling of his daughter, and the easy smile of the man himself.

She carefully watched the interaction between father and daughter. In most of the households she'd known, children were not allowed to eat with the adults. Here the bond was wonderfully different, and she liked that difference. Granger chuckled softly while Rena performed a childish rendition of Lisha's fishing techniques. Once again Lisha pined for the special relationship she'd shared with her father.

Eventually the dinner talk turned to the impending cattle drive. An unexpected sense of loss settled over her when she heard that the trek would begin in two days. Why? she wondered. Was it because when the herd left, so would Granger? She knew all along that this situation would be temporary, but somehow that knowledge failed to ease her sudden feeling of emptiness. Before Rena could finish the dessert of custard pudding, her chatter slowed to a stop, her swaying head drooped, and her eyelids lowered. Granger tenderly picked up his child. Startled, she opened her eyes, then smiled and snuggled against his shoulder.

"*Mi nena*, my baby girl," Maria crooned. "Here, I put her to bed."

"No, Maria. I'll do it. I won't be seeing her for some time." Nestling Rena closer, Granger carried her upstairs.

The sight of Granger Hawks cuddling his sleeping daughter injected a pang of envy into Lisha's heart. She found herself longing to be a part of a family, maybe one just like theirs.

Moonlight shimmered through the open window, mantling Lisha's room in a mystical haze. She refrained from lighting the oil lamp, preferring to prepare for bed in the silvery glow. Her nightdress fell in gauzy folds to her ankles. The white material felt deliciously cool against the warmth of her skin.

She fastened all but the top two buttons, choosing to leave the high neckline undone. Pulling the pins from her hair, she freed the tresses, then brushed them until they crackled.

Cool air seeped in underneath the windowpane, interjecting a fresh bouquet. Breathing deeply, she set aside her brush and stepped out onto the veranda. She leaned against the banister, listening to the steady drone of the night. The evening's concerto dulled her senses. Faint snatches of bellowing cattle wafted in from the distance. The twinkling softness of the stars added to the wizardry of the night.

She knew the hour grew late. But she was not in the mood for sleep. She refused to let her mind dwell on just what she was in the mood for. Thinking about the gardens below, she gingerly walked the veranda along the length of the house and descended the side stairs onto the lower patio.

The bright moonlight helped her navigate about the garden as she stopped now and again to smell the sweet fragrance of a rose. The unseasonable hot weather had hastened their growth. Unable to resist, she picked one fragile bud, careful not to prick her fingers with its thorny stem. Once more she inhaled the scent of the red rose before anchoring the flower in her hair.

A shiver encased her backbone, reminding her of the coolness of the night, her bare feet, and the thin cloth of her nightgown. "You could have grabbed your wrapper before venturing out." She chastised herself as she rubbed her arms to quell the goose bumps. She turned to leave and knocked over a watering pitcher that had been resting precariously on the edge of the adobe steps. The pail clanged loudly against the red brick flooring.

Grimacing, Lisha picked up the pitcher, hoping that the sudden noise hadn't disturbed anyone. She hurried from the garden only to run straight into an unyielding pair of arms. Startled, she looked up into Granger's surprised face.

"Out for a walk?"

"As a matter of fact I was. I hope I didn't wake up anyone else."

"I wasn't asleep."

Lisha couldn't think of anything more to say. Her thoughts zeroed in on Granger's tight grasp. She watched as his close scrutiny roved from her shadowed face to the flower perched jauntily behind her ear. His grin came easy.

"I seem to have caught a flower-poacher red-handed. Do you know the penalty for poaching in this territory?"

"I have a strange feeling that I'm about to find out."

His dark eyes narrowed. "It depends on whether the thief can pay for his misdeeds," he said, lowering his voice menacingly.

"And if he has no purse?"

"Then payment is extracted at the discretion of the owner. He decides what punishment fits the crime. I'm the owner, so that must make you the thief."

She fell prey to his lighthearted goading. "I beg, kind sir, that you show mercy. I happened upon this lovely garden and fell victim to its charm. I must confess . . . I plucked a rose."

Granger watched the moon's rays glint on Lisha's platinum hair, making her waist-long mane appear to be laced with silver. The shafts of light diluted the darkness of the confined garden, contouring her face in a dusky glow. Sobering, he stared at her softened appearance, then at the flower. Reaching out, he stroked the budding flower.

"Tell me, fair maiden, are you also a thief of hearts? Like the rose, do you harbor prickly thorns?"

Chapter
🎋🎋🎋 8 🎋🎋🎋

Lisha opened her mouth to utter a light retort, but no sound came. The husky timbre in Granger's voice heightened her awareness of his taut frame so close to hers. His fingers, still grasping her upper arms, sent a surge of heat tingling through her body. Thoughts of chills, her bare feet, and the gossamer nightdress faded into the background. She was only conscious of the potent aura of this man.

His eyes deepened to a tobacco-brown, binding her with their fervent gaze. He placed both hands alongside her throat. His thumb deftly stroked a pulsating vein.

When he lowered his head, she forgot to breathe. He lightly brushed her quivering mouth with his own, and her heart pirouetted deep within her chest.

"I see you have no thorns," he whispered, his lips teasing her sensitive skin. "Or are they hidden like a cat's claws, ready to strike?"

He wrapped his arms about her, pulling her close, and molded her soft form to his. With a guttural sigh, he slowly massaged her mouth with his. He teethed her lower lip, before dusting kisses down her cheek and along her jawline. Resembling fermented leaven, his slow torment increased when he nibbled at her earlobe. His heated breath pivoted shivers down her spine, then he meticulously retraced his way back again. Her mind reeled.

When he finally captured her mouth in a crushing embrace, her senses cried out in delight. Her hot blood drummed a primitive beat in her temples, and a ravenous flame licked at the sentient parts of her body. So this was what it was like, this native force that seemed to demolish everything in its burning path.

Her emotions whirled. She felt she would swoon from the fervent impact of his kiss. By the time he released her, a suffocating buzz seemed to fill her being. The tempestuous force that had engulfed them rendered both of them breathless.

Granger ran shaky fingers through his thick hair. "I didn't mean for that to happen."

"Are you sorry?"

"No." His laden voice echoed his craving. "Are you?"

"No."

He intently scraped the pad of his boot against the adobe patio. Shifting his weight, he stared over her head before centering his gaze back to her flushed face.

Never, since Julia, had a woman twisted her way inside his heart like Lisha had. Wasn't this what he'd been afraid of all along? The last thing he wanted was to get tangled up in the thoughts of another woman, any woman. Nothing good could come of it. He was sure of that. Yet . . .

The growing silence comforted Lisha rather than caused her to feel awkward. She searched Granger's ruggedly handsome face, the planes and contours already etched in her mind.

She liked the way his blond-tipped lashes curved above expressive eyes that could tease one moment, then mirror the depths of his inflamed soul the next. She liked the way his finely bristled jaw sloped to a strong chin, a chin which sometimes hinted at stubbornness and integrity. She liked his sensuously peaked lips that, when pressed to her heated skin, could make her forget everything but him, her, and the electricity they generated.

She had memorized the angle of the hairline scar on his left cheek. Reaching up, she ran a fingertip down the tight ridge. She could feel a muscle twitching in his jaw.

"How did you get this?"

"I'd been chasing an ornery bull through some trees. He swerved, leaving me to ride straight into a branch."

"That must have stung."

"It did. A lot."

Grabbing her fingers, he turned her hand over and plied her palm with kisses. She could feel her reserve slipping. His attraction waxed strong, and at times it overpowered. To keep control of her senses she uttered the first thought that popped into her mind.

"It's . . . ah . . . it's a good thing the cut wasn't very deep. It would've had to be sewn. I helped my uncle one night after a fight, and he made me sew up a laceration. I . . ."

Granger stiffened. He dropped her hand as if it were offensive to him. The rigidity of his stance invited no more familiarity. His warm gaze turned cold, and she suddenly faced a stranger.

What did she say to cause such hostility? With an inward groan she remembered. Julia had assisted a doctor. And because she had, she died.

"Granger, I—"

"Having you here was a mistake from the start," he growled under his breath. "But what just happened between us is a bigger one. When I get back from the cattle drive, I'll expect you packed and ready to leave." His dark stare made a sweeping study of her person before he turned on his heel and disappeared into the night.

She watched after the angry man. Why did she have to remind him of his loss by talking about her own work as a nurse? But what did it matter to her if he backed off because of something that gave her so much satisfaction? She wasn't about to give up nursing for any man.

Besides, she only wanted to be friends, didn't she? What did she care if he refused to let his feelings grow because he thought she might catch some deadly disease? But if she *didn't* care, then why did she feel so empty?

The light breeze captured strands of her hair and whipped them about her face. Shivers, working up her spine, reminded her again of her thin nightgown. With a deep sigh she turned. From the corner of her eye she caught a slight figure framed in a nearby window. Taking a second look, she found nothing but a blank windowpane. She could have sworn she'd seen Juanita.

* * *

Lisha saw little of Granger the next day. When he was nearby, he ignored her. A strong case of melancholy settled in when she realized that he wasn't going to allow her to be alone with him. But what if they were? What would she say that could change his mind about her? Caring for the sick was in her blood, and she wasn't about to change.

Furor charged the air. Rena's excitement concerning the next day's drive kept Lisha occupied. She swore the spirited girl had told her the planned route half a dozen times in as many hours. Did Rena really understand that her father would be gone for most of the summer? Two months seemed a relatively short time for an adult, but it could mean eternities for a child.

Juanita, on the other hand, stayed in the background, looking sour. Lisha had noticed a definite change in the girl's attitude toward her. Juanita refused to respond to friendliness of any form. Maybe Lisha hadn't been mistaken. Maybe the girl had watched while Granger made love to her in the moonlight.

Maria began to make ready for her Santa Fe trip. Besides the job of preparing her own clothes, she insisted on making sure that the garments of those left behind were mended and in order. Maria's contagious humming spread, and Lisha couldn't help but feel lighter even though unresolved emotions grew within her, along with thoughts of passion-spun nights and warm, demanding lips.

"Maria, I'll feed the chickens and gather the eggs," she volunteered, hoping the chore would keep her mind on safer ground. "Rena's been so preoccupied with the cattle drive that I'm afraid she'll bring back nothing but the makings of scrambled eggs."

The woman looked up from her scrubbing board and solemnly studied her.

"You sure?

"Sure I'm sure. What's so hard about that?"

"Clara."

"Clara? Who's Clara?"

"The meanest chicken on God's earth. She should be in the pot pies long ago, but she's a good layer. One ill-tempered chicken sitting on the nest is worth two in the pan, I always say."

Lisha smiled at the gravity in Maria's voice. "How can one little hen possibly stop anyone from gathering eggs?"

"Let's hoping you don't find out."

She took the egg basket from Maria's outstretched hand, ignoring her staid countenance. The woman's habit of exaggerating caused Lisha to believe only half of what she'd told her.

Coming in from the bright sun, Lisha's eyes had to grow accustomed to the barn's dimness. Thin shafts of light streamed in from small cracks in the walls, magically transforming dust particles into a steady glint of floating diamonds.

Her nose distinguished between the smell of hay and leather and the fresh odor of animal dung. The latter reminded her to watch where she stepped on the thick layer of straw that covered the dirt floor.

Currycombs and brushes hung on one wall next to a hand plow, plow shears, and saws. Horse blankets draped the edge of one stall, and three sawhorses bore the weight of saddles. A burlap sack, half full of dried corn, flopped against the planked wall.

Lisha dug into the bag and brought out a battered pan full of chicken feed. She stepped outside, tossing handfuls of corn about the barnyard.

"Chick, chick. Here chick, chick."

The sharp, broken cries of the chickens rose in a frenzy while they fluttered about. Their necks arched again and again toward the ground. Dust rose under flapping wings and scratching talons.

Suddenly déjà vu gripped her. She saw herself as a toddler squealing with delight at the feathery creatures pecking at the ground under her feet. Vaguely she remembered reaching to touch a red comb, and her mother's hand darting out to stop her.

"No, darling. Mustn't bother the chicken."

Forgotten voices and memories from the past faded into the back of her mind. An overwhelming sense of hunger for her mother washed over her. Yet, after a moment of torment, she felt at peace. She felt as if she'd finally come home.

With a light step Lisha reentered the barn. She quickly canvassed suspicious-looking mounds of straw for eggs before moving onto the henhouse. Going to the last pile, she reached for an egg nestled inside. Suddenly a shrill cluck halted her course of action.

"Clara!"

Whirling, she saw an angry chicken swoop down upon her with wings furiously beating the air. The hen landed at her feet, and she quickly stepped aside before the sharp talons dug in.

Clara's neck arched with rage. Her high-pitched cackling drowned out all other noise. Her wings whipped dust, bits of straw, and red feathers into the air.

No matter which way Lisha pivoted, the hen's pointed beak came within inches of her ankles. The only escape route she could see was the hayloft. Dropping the basket in front of the hen, she scooped up an armful of skirts and scrambled to a nearby ladder. Just as she cleared the first three rungs, Clara flew to her feet, pecking at the heel of her boot.

Lisha stopped halfway up, thinking that if Clara had gone, she could go back down. She turned as much as she dared to see the bird strutting about below. The hen appeared calmer, maybe calm enough that Lisha could get past without much of a problem. Rung by rung, she slowly descended. As Lisha neared the bottom, Clara flew at the ladder amid squawks and a flurry of feathers.

"One of these days, Clara," Lisha warned, scrambling up into the loft, "I am personally going to see that you fit into a great big pot!"

From the safety of the loft she eyed the militant hen. The scene would have been a comical one like those portrayed at the Merriam Theater in St. Louis except she had the feeling that Clara would demand top billing.

The hen arched her neck and ruffled her feathers before pecking in the straw on the barn floor. Lisha groaned. How would she ever get past that squawking guard? She couldn't sit here, waiting for help. To be caught in this position would be mortifying. She looked around for another way out, preferably as far away from the bad-tempered chicken as possible.

Light filtered in around the splintered edges of the loft door. Maybe that could be her way of escape. Ignoring the hay sticking through her cotton stockings, she made her way around the yellow-green piles and yanked the door open.

A tightly coiled rope threaded its way through a pulley and ran the length of a pole where both ends were anchored on the side of the barn. If farmers successfully used this contraption to lift hay up into the loft, then why couldn't she use it to lower herself down? How difficult could it be? The landing would be somewhat soft with the residue from the last crop of hay strewed about below.

She scrutinized the pole and the pulley. How hard would it be to hold on to the rope and lower herself down? She was physically strong enough to handle the strain, and heights didn't bother her. After all, hadn't she used to climb trees higher than this loft? Besides, she'd never been one to quake in a corner.

She stubbornly refused to think about what would happen if her idea failed to materialize as she'd planned. She had to escape the situation without being found out.

The thought of Granger with his herd gave comfort. At least he wouldn't be around in case anything went wrong. And what if something did go wrong? That wouldn't be a big problem. She would take steps to ensure everyone's silence.

With thoughts of future blackmail invading her mind, she untied one end of the rope to check the ease in which it slid through the pulley. Satisfied, she gripped it and anchored one leg over the edge of the opening, then the other. She unsteadily balanced herself and counted to three. With a deep breath, she lunged forward, swinging clear of the barn.

At first, as the mechanism easily lowered her, she felt suspended in air. Gloating, she mentally patted herself on the back. This would be something to tell Tilly.

All of a sudden she felt a hard jolt, and for a fleeting second she hung in space, floundering a few feet above the ground. Seconds later she plummeted unceremoniously to earth with her dress billowing out like a parasol.

   She barely had time to cry out before landing squarely on her
bottom. A shocking amount of white pantaloons jutted out
from under yards of frothy pink and lace that fanned about her
hips.

   Reaching back to steady herself, her shaky fingers grasped
hold of the scuffed toe of a boot. Her heart sank. Groaning, she
sent up a hopeful prayer before twisting her body to face
Granger Hawk's stunned expression.

   "Tell me, Miss Harrington, is this your version of manna
from heaven?"

   She let out an audible sigh. Why, of all people, did she have
to land in front of him? Couldn't it have been someone from a
foreign country who couldn't speak one syllable of English,
much less understand it? Someone from Mongolia perhaps?

   "May I ask what you were doing?"

   "Praying!" She didn't like the amused tone of his voice.

   "Was it answered?"

   "Not that I can see."

   Chuckling, Granger clasped her under the arms and raised
her to her feet. She tried shaking straw from the folds of her
dress before turning to face him. His amused glance swept
from the barn and the pile of rope at her feet to her disheveled
appearance. The corners of his mouth twitched.

   "I can hardly wait to hear it."

   "Hear what?"

   "Your explanation for your unusual form of transportation."

   "It's because of your guard . . . animal."

   "My what?"

   "Clara."

   "Clara?"

   "She chased me up the ladder and wouldn't let me out of the
loft."

   Granger stared at Lisha. Her excuse for swinging in midair
at the end of the pulley clearly dumbfounded him. Then, much
to her annoyance, laughter rumbled from deep within his chest.
His tanned face took on a red tinge. He helplessly shook his
head every time he looked at her.

Affronted, she raised her chin. "I don't see what's so funny. I could have broken my . . . something."

"You don't understand," he said, taking a calming breath. "Clara doesn't like me, either. Once she tried to corner me in a stall."

"Corner you? What happened?"

"Rena casually picked her up and took her outside. Good layer or no, if that bird weren't a pet of my daughter's, we would've boiled her long ago. In fact, Jackson and I would have fought over who got the honor of dispatching her soul to purgatory."

"Jackson? *He's* had trouble with Clara?"

Solemnly Granger knodded. "Twice she flew down at him from the loft. Believe me, it's not fun to have a chicken land on your head when you're not expecting it. Scared the he— Well, it scared him." He cleared his throat, trying to dispell the laughter bubbling just beneath the surface.

More than anything, Lisha wanted to hang on to her justified anger. How dare he be amused? But, whether she wanted to or not, she began to see her downward plunge from Granger's point of view. Despite how hard she tried to remain placid, a grin tugged at the corners of her mouth.

"I must have looked like a large pink albatross diving to earth."

It was the wrong thing to say. Granger's jaw twitched, and once more his laughter echoed about the barnyard. Eventually her sense of the ridiculous won out, and she was consumed with laughter.

Trying to get control of herself, Lisha sat on a mound of hay. Averting his gaze, Granger followed suit, and Lisha became deliciously aware of the man lingering beside her. She loved his easy manner, his ability to see the humor in things, and she felt strangely comfortable with him, secure.

"Granger, I'm glad I have you for a friend."

"Friend?"

"Don't deny that you are."

"No. No, I don't deny it."

Her hand stung, and she rubbed her palm against her thigh.

The burning sensation grew stronger until she forced herself to inspect it. The rope had left its mark embedded in her skin.

"Rope burn," Granger stated flatly, taking her stinging hand in his. "Come, I'll put some salve on it." Turning, he left her to follow him to the tack room at the back of the barn.

The strong smell of leather and sawdust filled the room, and she decided that she liked the pungent odor. Bridles, hackamores, and harnesses dangled from nails on one wall, while a mallet, hammers, and saws hung on another. Wagon wheels, in various stages of repair, were stacked against a leg of a workbench. Saddle soap, sheep tallow, and a can of Balm lined the bench. Lisha immediately relaxed in the orderly atmosphere of Granger's private domain.

He grabbed the horse liniment and indicated for her to sit. "Are you familiar with this?"

"Believe it or not, I am."

A lopsided grin pulled at his mouth. "At this point, if you told me that you've scaled the Himalayas, I'd believe you." A frown worried his brows. "You haven't, have you?"

She laughed. "No, I haven't. But, actually, I've given a thought to mountain climbing."

"Somehow I'm not surprised."

Granger took her hand and gingerly applied the salve on her scraped palm. Her flesh tingled at his touch, and not just because of the rope burn. He parted her fingers and gently rubbed the areas between. His light strokes slowed to a deliberate caress. Swallowing hard, she looked up to meet his steady gaze.

Without a word he raised her quivering hand to his lips. One by one he nipped at her fingertips. All the while he intently eyed her.

Forbidden pleasures branded messages in her hazy brain. Her shallow breathing throbbed in her ears. How long must she withstand this calculated erosion of her frayed senses? How long must she wait to feel his arms about her once again?

A wistful sigh escaped her throat. With a groan Granger swiftly gathered her into a crushing embrace. His lips captured hers in a final assault against her austere upbringing. Guilty pleasure ebbed through her body, and she matched him kiss for kiss.

Seconds, hours later Granger straightened. "Lisha, this won't work." His laden voice threaded through to her consciousness.

"Why?" Her question fluttered on the breath of a whisper.

"Because you have your home and friends . . . your . . . work in St. Louis, and I . . . I can't give you the love you deserve. It's better that we stop this here and now before someone gets hurt."

He cupped her face, fragile with heated emotions, in his big hands as he seemed to imprint every curve, every angle in his mind. He leaned over and planted a kiss on the tip of her nose.

"Goodbye, Miss Falisha Harrington."

Granger left her then, left her to sort out this tangled web alone. He hadn't wanted anyone hurt. But what if somebody's pain had already begun? She hadn't intended to, but she felt she was falling in love with him. Else why did his words lance her soul?

Lisha caught only glimpses of Granger throughout the rest of the day. Everything was in readiness for the drive the next morning, and he chose to spend the last few hours with his daughter.

Rena took advantage of her father's afternoon off and planned a picnic for the two of them. The child insisted on fixing the food herself. With a ghost of a smile Lisha hoped he liked honey and watercress sandwiches with dried apples for dessert. Maria wisely saved him some dinner.

When father and daughter returned, Lisha kept to her room. She couldn't bear to see Granger again; she couldn't trust herself to behave as a lady should.

Eventually she heard his light tread up the stairs when he carried his sleeping daughter to her bed. Moments later he paused at her door. She held her breath, listening, wondering what she'd do if he knocked.

He retreated to his room, and her breath expelled in a rush. All night long she listened to the night sounds of the country. She couldn't sleep knowing that the man she grew to love lay so close . . . yet so far away.

* * *

Granger struggled with his unsettling thoughts, insisting to himself that the magnet pulling him toward Falisha Harrington was purely physical. He hadn't been able to keep his mind on Rena's endless prattle during their picnic because the face of a woman, who could be so vexing at one moment and so tantalizing the next, tortured his mind.

He tried to ignore her inner force that made up such a vital part of her nature. If he weren't as strongly opposed to possessing her, as he was, he knew she would have conquered him long ago. Jackson would have called it a streak of "plain stubborn," but Granger didn't agree.

The problem was that Lisha had exquisitely lovely features. The problem was, she carried that loveliness inside. The problem was, in many ways, she reminded him too much of Julia.

"Damn!"

For the hundredth time that night he hammered at his feather pillow and flipped onto his bare back. But the vision of a silvery-gold mane and deep slate eyes continued to haunt him. He had almost lost his resolve once tonight. He had almost knocked on her door. But he sadly realized that he'd better not. . . .

Chapter
❦ 9 ❦

"Well?"

Weston's impatient voice greeted Jackal the second the bounty hunter strolled into the lawyer's squeaky-clean office. Jackal slapped the dust from his thighs, ignoring Weston's scurry to avoid the fallout, and idly planted himself into a chair. He swiped at his brow with the leathered edge of his hand, disrupting the low perch of his hat.

"This heat's going to be the death of me."

"*I'm* going to be the death of you," Weston roared, "if you don't stop hedging and tell me what you found out about Miss Harrington."

Jackal's watery-blue gaze held the cunning of a badger, and badgers never stalled. They just bided their time. "Nothing," he tossed out. "I found nothing that'd suit you."

"You couldn't trace her?"

"Oh, I traced her all right. Tracked her clean to the Arkansas Territory. That's where I lost her. As far as anybody can figure, she just disappeared."

"Are you sure you didn't overlook something?"

Jackal pulled himself to his feet. "You'd have to go some to find anybody better'n me at trackin'," he said, nestling his hat onto his white-blond hair. "Believe me when I say there ain't no sign of her."

No sign of her. Weston had never known such anger as he'd had when he'd read Falisha's parting letter. Now it seemed that she had evaporated along with his plans.

* * *

"Lisha! Are you hurry'n or not?"

Rena's impatient voice reached Lisha's ears. She hadn't settled down from the instant she knew they were going to Cibola. Since Granger had left the day before, the child had reminded Lisha several times of the promised frock of eggshell blue. She'd insisted that Lisha wear her dress to make sure they found material to match. And it had to match exactly.

Lisha secured the ribbons to her straw hat under her chin and grabbed her handbag with the remainder of the money Granger had sent to St. Louis. She couldn't think of a better use for it than buying the cloth for the girls' new dresses.

As soon as she stepped outside, Rena let out a war whoop and skipped to the wagon. Maria sat on the seat, and the girls settled themselves on a soft bed of straw and quilts in the back.

Jackson stood by the wagon, waiting to help Lisha up. She hadn't understood why he'd stayed home from the drive to watch after them during Granger's absence. She thought they'd have no problem taking care of themselves.

When Jackson caught sight of Lisha, his smile deepened in appreciation. "No wonder Hawks hightailed it out of here like the devil himself was after him." His black eyes sparkled. "He's trying to outrun his future, and he don't even know it. If I had a woman like you around, I'd just sit back and let tomorrow settle softlike over my head."

"Jackson, you don't know what you're talking about."

"I do, sure as I'm standin' here." His low chuckle rumbled from his diaphragm. "I'm just waitin' till *he* figures it out."

The foreman helped Lisha up into the wagon seat. She smiled at the girls. Rena grinned back, hugging herself with excitement, but Juanita sharply averted her head.

The long ride to Cibola pleased Lisha just as much as the ride to Granger's ranch. She'd never seen scenery that could peacefully lull a person with its green foliage and languid sloping hills, then fill them with awe with its craggy red cliffs and deep crevices all at the same time.

Jackson must have felt the same emotions as she had, for he kept a constant vigil on the surrounding area, especially the rock formations. They seemed amazingly lifelike, and a few times he acted as if he'd expected someone to step out around them at any moment.

In Cibola, Jackson reined the team to a stop in front of the hotel and proceeded to help the ladies down. The door to the hotel burst open, and Martha rushed out. The corners of her dark blue eyes wrinkled in delight, and her smile lit her face.

"My, it's good to see you people. Lisha, I've been dying of curiosity. I want to know if anything good has happened. Maria, I see you're ready for the big trip." She took each by an arm and propelled them toward the door. "Come, come, we have lots to talk about, and you're just in time for chicken and noodles."

"Oh, boy," Rena chimed in, bobbing about in a circle. "That's my favorite. I hope you have plenty of chicken."

"If not," Lisha commented dryly, "I have a great candidate for the pot."

Jackson watched as Martha ushered them to the lobby. No one noticed the man leaning against the stuccoed front of the hotel, but he had. The man's very stance reeked of insolence from the one bent knee with the sole of his worn boot planted on the wall that supported him, to the cigarette he sucked on with agonizingly slow draws.

He needed a haircut, shave, and bath. His clothes were so stained that a person could hardly tell he wore the uniform of the Confederate Army. He had the look of a deserter—a man worth keeping an eye on.

Jackson's brows furrowed. He couldn't put his finger on it, but something about the stranger bothered him. His gut instinct told him that under the man's cool exterior boiled a private battle.

As he turned to leave, he saw the man casually flip aside his cigarette. The glowing butt landed at Jackson's feet. It was bent in half.

Maria handed the stagecoach driver her valise and hugged Juanita, giving her last-minute instructions. At one point her daughter interrupted the rapid Spanish, obviously not wanting to do what her mother had ordered. Maria's voice rose in a chastising tone, and the girl threw Lisha a hateful glare.

With dimples creasing her cheeks, Maria advanced on Lisha, clasping her to her massive breasts. "I tell Juanita to keep good eyes on you. I think you stay when I get back."

"I wouldn't be too sure about that."

"I know. You just right for Mr. Hawks. And for *mi nena* here." She bent over and scooped Rena up into her arms. The child placed pudgy hands on Maria's face.

"I will miss you, Maria."

"I miss you too, *mi nena*, but I no worry. Señorita Lisha take good care of you." She put Rena down and turned to Jackson. "And you, you no longer a growing boy," Maria warned with an admonishing finger. "You no eat all the foods!"

"I no eat all the foods." He chuckled, handing her up into the coach.

Lisha watched the stage rumble down the street and round the corner. She felt Juanita's stare and heard her mutter something that sounded distasteful. Jackson threw the girl a disapproving frown, and she stalked off in a huff.

Turning to follow, Lisha glimpsed a flash of gray and vaguely saw a pair of hands shoot out before she felt them plant a steadying grip on her shoulders. Embarrassed, she raised her head to apologize for not watching where she was going.

A pair of cold gray eyes penetrated her sense of dread. The shaggy hair beneath the man's hat framed his face of sharp angles and planes. His long chin carried the strength of his features; his hard mouth curved in a mocking smile. Her apology froze on her lips.

"Excuse me, miss," he drawled, his chilly gaze washing over her. Lazily he touched the tip of his hat and sauntered on down the walk.

Lisha felt as if she'd been mentally caressed by a reptile, and she shuddered. Her sixth sense screamed caution. She watched the man's receding back. His drab clothes and frayed hat matched the dull aura that surrounded him. Somehow she knew that he enjoyed alarming her, that he would enjoy harassing any woman.

For reasons she failed to understand the encounter frightened her. But she knew she couldn't let Rena see how upset she was.

So she pasted on a smile and entered the mercantile, determined to keep up the happy facade.

"Look, Lisha, look at all the pretty cloth." Rena bobbed around two tables laden with bolts of material. "Where's a blue one? Remember I want blue."

"I remember." Lisha rummaged through the bolts and found a piece of fabric a shade darker than her own dress. "How's this one?"

"Oooo. I like it. Don't you like it, Nita?"

Nudging over, Juanita looked at the material as if she were inspecting an angleworm. "It's all right if you like blue."

Some of Rena's excitement dimmed. "Well, I like blue, and it's pretty. You're just sour."

"Why don't you pick something out, Juanita," Lisha encouraged in an effort to stop a quarrel before it began. "This white piece with the tiny red roses would look lovely on you."

The girl screwed up her face as if she'd been told she had to eat the worm. "I hate it, and I hate you. I wish you'd never come here. You've ruined everything!" Choking down a sob, she turned and disappeared behind a rack of dresses.

"Juanita, wait."

Lisha hurried after her, only to see the Confederate soldier. His abrupt presence stopped her cold. She felt the blood drain from her face.

"Having problems, ma'am?"

"I . . . no."

She could hardly speak past a lump of fear, and her hand flew to her throat. His icy stare followed her action. A corner of his mouth twitched.

"If I can be of help, I'm at your disposal." He brushed the rim of his hat with a ragged fingernail and ambled out the door.

"Was that man bothering you, Miss Lisha?"

Jackson's sudden appearance gave her strength. "Juanita was angry, and he asked if he could be of any help."

The foreman grunted something unintelligible and became absorbed with a display of hunting knives a few feet away.

"Lisha, can I have this?" Rena held out a tightly woven ball for her to inspect.

"Well . . ."

The child dimpled. "Please."

"I guess it would be—"

"Oh, boy! Jackson, look at the ball Lisha's going to buy for me."

Lisha knew she spoiled Rena, but who could have resisted that pixie face? After she paid for her purchases, she stepped outside with Jackson following close behind. Glancing across the street, she locked gazes with a pair of gray eyes. Seconds later the stranger became preoccupied with his tobacco pouch. But she still felt his intense scrutiny. Her heart sprinted.

Throughout the afternoon she caught glimpses of the man, but she also noticed that Jackson always found some excuse to stay within speaking range of her. His motherly behavior seemed odd, but she was eternally grateful. She felt safe around the big man.

At one point she'd toyed with the idea of sharing her fears with him but decided against it. He would probably explain it away as her imagination, just as her uncle would have. But, imagination or no, she sought his comforting presence.

Resting under a tree, she watched Rena toss the ball into the air. The magic of Cibola had captured her. She dearly loved this quaint little town and its people.

She took off her straw hat to tuck in a few strands of hair when suddenly she caught sight of Juanita running down a side street toward them. Red dust rose under her churning feet. Tears streaked down her smudged face, and her sobs came in hard gasps. Her ripped bodice revealed mud caked under her collarbone.

Jackson was the first to reach her. He placed his hands on her exposed shoulders, forcing her to look up at him.

"What happened, girl?"

Wincing, she shrugged out from under the pressure of his big hands. "That man . . . he . . . he dragged me behind the livery stable."

"What man?"

"The man in the army. The one who bumped into Lisha."

"Did he hurt you? . . . Girl, did he *hurt* you?"

Juanita covered her face with her skinned hands. "No, I . . . I hit him with a rock. I think I killed him."

"Stay here."

"No! I . . . I mean I have to go with you. To show you where he is."

"You said he took you behind the livery stable."

"He did, but you don't know where. He could attack you if you're not looking."

"All right."

Lisha stepped forward. "I'm coming, too."

"No," Jackson said. "Better stay with Rena."

He followed after Juanita. They pressed through a small crowd of people that had formed, and everybody headed across town to the stable.

Lisha wondered how the girl had come all this way in her disheveled state unnoticed. Surely someone would have given her aid before she'd gotten this far. When Lisha had insisted on coming, Juanita's eyes turned cloudy. Was it a different kind of fear? And for some reason, the girl looked relieved when Jackson had told Lisha to stay behind with Rena.

"Lisha, what's the matter with Nita?"

With a guilty pang Lisha realized she'd forgotten about Rena. The worried child clung to her skirts. Threadlike lines creased her baby-soft forehead.

"Did that man hurt her?"

"No, Pumpkin. Not really. Why don't you play with your ball?"

"Can't. I losted it."

"Then go look for it. It can't be very far away."

Bending slightly, Rena gave the impression of carefully searching for her lost toy. "I throwed it too high, and when the ball came back down, it rolled over by the walk. I looked, but it isn't there. Darn ol' ball anyway."

"It probably rolled down the alley."

Straightening, Rena bit the inside of her cheek. "I don't like alleys. Bears can hide in there, 'specially behind the pile of crates."

"Do you think your papa would let me bring you to town if there were bears living in the alley?"

Rena trailed her toe in the dirt. "'Spect not. He'd shoo them all away. . . . I guess I'll go look."

Smiling, Lisha watched Rena make a big display in coughing and timidly enter the alley. No self-respecting bear would stick around after all that noise.

Lisha glanced down the street and wondered if Jackson had found that man. The effect of the man's attack on Juanita worried her. Nightmares would probably haunt the girl for some time.

"Lisha!"

The terrified scream rose into a sharp pitch, then abruptly stopped. *Rena!* Lisha's stomach lurched. The hair on the nape of her neck stood on end.

With a strangled cry she raced down the alleyway. A band of fear cinched her chest. She should never have let the child come this way alone. Rena had to be all right. She just had to be.

Seconds after she rounded the corner of the feed store, someone threw a stinking horse blanket over her head and tossed her across a saddle like a sack of corn.

Chapter

🌿❦ 10 ❦🌿

Lisha gripped the blanket; its coarse material chafed her arms. With tremors racking her body, she huddled close to the fire. The evening had grown cooler after the sun went down, but she knew the shivers skating around in her back were more from fear than the night air.

Silently her captor offered her a dish of beans. She shook her head, not being able to think of food, much less eat. Shrugging, he sat down to his late supper. As he ate she tried to think of something else besides his spoon scraping the bottom of the tin plate before each mouthful, or the precise way he chewed his food. She wanted answers, but he seemed in no hurry to give them. Eventually he laid down his platter, rolled a smoke, and struck a match. Suddenly she knew.

"It was you, wasn't it? You were the one watching me."

Turning slowly, he probed her with his hard gaze before shifting his attention back to the fire.

"'Spect so."

"Why?"

Like before he didn't answer immediately. She guessed it wasn't in his nature. His type looked over any situation before jumping in. Too many men have gotten themselves killed because they neglected to consider all the angles.

"Money."

"Money? What money? If you mean ransom, I know of no one who could pay."

"Lady, you're worth more to me than a few hundred dollars in ransom."

"For what?"

As if in a trance, he stared at the cigarette he held in his hand. Methodically he rolled it in his slender fingertips with agonizing slowness. Then, almost tenderly, he brought it to his lips and inhaled. The tip of the cigarette glowed. Smoke curled up from his nostrils. He leisurely let out his breath.

A queasy lump settled in the pit of Lisha's stomach. What kind of a human was this? She had the horrible feeling that under his maddening calm, he harbored a violent anger ready to explode.

"Look, mister—"

"Name's Lago. Pure and simple."

Pure and simple? She could strongly debate that but not with him. "Whatever you call yourself, I've a right to know what you want with me."

Lago finished his smoke, bent the butt in half, and flicked it aside. "Suppose it'll do no harm to tell ya what's in your future"—he chuckled—"so's you can look forward to it."

Her breath caught at the hollow sound of his voice, and she shrank deeper within the horse blanket. She sensed that Lago worshiped evil, and he intended to use her for scripture.

"Me and my friends take 'merchandise' and sell it down in Mexico."

His words and the way he uttered them brought her lurching heart to a sudden halt. She didn't like what her gut instinct whispered in her ear.

"Am I supposed to be that merchandise?"

"Just a part."

"What do you intend to do with your . . . merchandise?"

"Sell it to work the silver mines, mostly."

"Is that why you abducted me? For the mines?"

"Men are sold to work the mines. I'm selling you for somethin' better."

The amused tone of his voice and his cruel smile chilled her to the core.

"You"—her voice cracked—"you intend to sell me?"

"To a very rich man who ordered a girl with your coloring.

When I saw you arrive in Cibola, I knew you more than fit the bill.''

Lisha tried to get a hold of herself. "How much am I worth?" she asked dully.

"Two thousand dollars, and an extra thousand to the man who brings in his order . . . untouched."

The impact of his words stunned her. Could he really carry out such a barbaric plan? Fear dissolved into anger. She squared her shoulders. No matter what Lago planned, he would have quite a chore on his hands for the next few weeks. She'd see to that. Mexico lay a long way off.

At least, she surmised, he didn't intend to harm her. Apparently virgins brought in more money. But what Lago failed to realize was that Harringtons were survivors.

"They will send people after me, you know. You can't fight them off alone."

"By the day after tomorrow I won't be alone. A few of my friends are joining us."

This must be a dream. Some horrible nightmare, and soon I'll wake up in my room.

But she knew she wasn't dreaming. The nippy air, the smoke rising from the fire to dissolve in the starry night, and this man named Lago were, indeed, real.

He stood, throwing the remainder of his coffee on the fire. "Better get some sleep. You're going to need it."

"Rider, comin' up fast."

Granger glanced up from the strays he'd gathered. He should have seen the horseman before now, but he'd had his mind on blue-gray eyes and a soft yielding mouth. Warm thoughts persisted, day or night.

A red bandanna covered the lower half of his face. The wind seemed to catch the dirt, shuffled up by two thousand hooves, and blow it all right into his face. Already his eyes burned, and the day had just begun.

He squinted at the oncoming man. If he hadn't known better, he would swear that the rider looked like Jackson. With a jolt he realized it *was* his foreman. His stomach formed a hard knot. Had something happened to Rena—or Lisha?

He spurred his horse forward, cutting the distance between them, and reined to a stop amid a dust cloud. Dirt caked Jackson's face. The sides of his horse heaved from exertion.

"What's wrong?" Granger barked, yanking his scarf from his face.

"Miss Lisha's been kidnapped."

"Kidnapped?" Granger felt as if a battering ram caved in his chest. "Who would kidnap Lisha?"

"The same man nosin' about in the hills. He's a deserter. From what I can gather, he and other deserters teamed up with Javier's band."

"That cutthroat?"

Granger's heart twisted with pain. He whipped off his hat and wiped his sweaty forehead. Thoughts began to torment him. Thoughts he couldn't erase, and the panic began to rise.

"If they hurt her, Jackson, so help me—"

"Maybe they won't. Women like Miss Lisha are worth a lot of money in Chihuahua. Javier's too greedy to let his men have her."

"I hope you're right. . . . But we both know the Comancheros are a bloodthirsty lot. Fill me in while Jess packs me some grub," he said, his voice dropping to a steely monotone. The tone men had backed away from. "Who's this deserter?"

"The blacksmith knows him as Lago. They were in the same regiment. He said Lago had a mean streak wider than the Rio Grande. He'd caused almost as much havoc in their company as the Yankees did on the battlefield.

"After he'd deserted, reports filtered in that he made raids on isolated settlers with a man named Sloan. Eventually they teamed up with Javier."

"True to nature, venomous snakes slither after their own kind," Granger spat out, stuffing his saddlebags with provisions. "How did Lago get his hands on Lisha?"

Air expelled from Jackson's lungs. "With Juanita's help."

"Juanita?" Granger spun around. "Juanita helped Lago? That dosen't make any sense."

"Guess it does to a jealous girl."

"Jealous? Jealous of Miss Harrington?"

"Lago's smart. He made use of it. Juanita was more than willing to help him until he roughed her up some. Guess he'd wanted to make sure she could fool us. He'd warned her that if she didn't come through, or if she told, he'd kill her. Or worse, he might even think about selling her.

"Seems Juanita had changed her mind about getting rid of Lisha but didn't dare go against Lago. After I made no bones about telling her what happens to women in the hands of the Comancheros, she finally blurted out the whole story."

Granger tied the flaps of the saddle bags down and mounted Saber. Blood pumped behind the scar on his left cheek. He imagined it stood out like a smoke signal against a storm-blackened sky. The same kind of storm that boiled in his gut.

Knowledge of the outlaws—a deadly mixture of outcast Mexicans, army deserters, and renegade Indians—hammered him. The notorious band had blazed a trail of pain and havoc from the territories of Texas and New Mexico down into Mexico. They robbed, plundered, and violated. Their favorite sport was robbing small wagon trains traveling the Santa Fe Trail. Thoughts of what Comancheros did to the women and their families cut through Granger. He gripped the reins until his knuckles whitened.

"Hawks," Jackson said, his voice revealing more emotion than Granger had ever heard from his foreman, "in the Holy Bible it says 'Justice is mine, saith the Lord.' But I think this is one of those times the Lord might be willin' to sidestep that order."

Granger looked at the black man he considered his brother. During the war he'd come to rely heavily on him. More than once they had covered each other's back. Only this time he worked on his own. He placed a comforting hand on Jackson's shoulder.

"Don't whip yourself over this. You couldn't have known that Juanita was up to tricks. I'd have reacted the same way."

Jackson nodded. Nothing more needed to be said. Granger urged Saber forward, leaving Jackson in a cloud of red dust.

While Granger kept his horse at a steady lope, Jackson's words reverberated in his brain. Of all that his foreman had reported, Granger felt relieved about one thing. Martha was taking care of Rena and Juanita.

When he thought of the Mexican girl, he stiffened. If it weren't for her unfounded jealousy, Lisha would still be in Cibola under Jackson's watchful eye.

Granger tried to keep his mind off what Lisha might be suffering. Fear and anger gnawed at his gut. He had to get her back. After all, wasn't he responsible for her? Wasn't it his letter that had brought her to New Mexico, no matter how inadvertently?

His primary obligation, as he saw it, consisted of rescuing Miss Harrington and seeing her safely on her way back to St. Louis and this man named Clayborne. Cursing all females with silver-streaked hair, he headed to the south.

Dusk found him leading his horse over rocky ground. The way had been agonizingly slow and arduous. Scanning the half-hidden trail, all he could see was bunch grass, jagged cliffs, boulders, and a few yucca plants. He squinted into the shadowed evening but saw no signs of Lisha or her captor.

Earlier he'd been positive two riders had passed this way. Now he wasn't so sure. He'd bet money that Lago would've taken Lisha through the White Sands before traveling down into Mexico. That was the fastest route, and the one least likely to be followed on.

He rubbed the muscles in the back of his neck, trying to relieve the tight cords. Suddenly a wisp of blue caught his eye. Pushing his hat back from his forehead, he dropped to his haunches for a closer look. His tired muscles protested against the strain.

Then he saw it. A prickly weed had snagged a patch of material in its naked limbs. Granger tore it off. He couldn't swear that the cloth came from Lisha's dress, but the odds were strong enough to point that way. What other woman, besides her, would be in this wild country? Acting on his hunch, he pushed on.

An hour later he came upon a recently abandoned camp. Someone had tossed out coffee grounds and leftover beans. The coals, buried under charred wood, were still warm to the touch. He looked around but found no signs of a struggle, no signs of Lisha to prove that he'd followed the right trail.

A pale object arrested his attention, and he stooped to retrieve a cigarette butt that had been bent in half. Blood pumped in his temples. He rolled the butt between his fingers, deliberately crushing it in his rough hand. Tobacco and bits of paper fluttered on the breeze.

He scanned the darkening horizon. The hot lick of anger filled his being. Since there were no signs of a struggle, he'd permit Lago to say his prayers before he took pleasure in killing him. The deserter would soon be meeting up with the rest of the band, but Granger intended to overtake him first.

Dawn splashed various shades of pink and maroon across the morning sky. The gray light created eerie apparitions with Granger and his horse; he slumped in the saddle and Saber wearily plodded along.

Granger closed his eyes, feeling their burn. His sore muscles painfully nagged at him. He knew he had to stop and rest, not only for himself, but for his horse. Rage, causing temporary insanity, had kept him moving, but wisdom returned with each long mile. He knew if he didn't stop soon, he wouldn't be of any use to Lisha, and Saber wouldn't be of any use to him. The distance he'd traveled failed to satisfy him, but tracking a man who hadn't intended to be found proved tedious.

Searching for a likely spot to camp, he chose a knoll under a cliff for protection from the coming sun. The spot lay several yards from a watering hole. He uncinched the latigo and pulled the saddle from Saber's glistening back. The buckskin nickered, shaking his head, and trotted to the grass growing around the natural spring.

Granger gathered wood to build a fire. He'd nursed the idea of sleeping before he ate anything but decided against it. After a few hours of rest he wanted to be on his way and didn't want to have to stop and prepare something.

He chewed on a dried biscuit, the last of several that Jess had packed. Coffee boiled in a tin pot. The bubbling rhythm meshed with the growing whine of the countryside.

After swallowing a bit of hard tack, Granger tried to take a sip of coffee and immediately spit it out. With an oath he tossed out the remaining brew. Why couldn't he ever learn to make coffee that a man didn't have to eat with a spoon?

With immemse relief he nestled his aching head against his saddle and covered his face with his hat. He drifted off to sleep with a light hand resting on the butt of his rifle lying beside him.

It seemed only moments before a sharp whinny cut into his dreamless sleep. Opening heavy eyelids, he jerked up only to find the barrel of a cold pistol shoved against his nose. He stared unblinking into a man's grinning face. Another man with a scarred eye stood behind him, cradling a rifle against his chest. Granger groped at his side for his gun.

"Looking for this?" The man chuckled, holding up Granger's rifle. "Now, we don't cotton to inhospitable people. We're friendly like. Be obliged for your company."

Chapter
❦ 11 ❦

"Hold it." Lago's threatening voice bit into Lisha's purposeful stride. "Where do you think you're going?"

She raised her chin. "To the creek."

"Not without me, you ain't. I told ya not to go anywhere without askin' first."

"Where, pray tell," she asked sweetly, "would I be taking off to way out here? I haven't tried to escape so far, have I?"

Lago remained silent. With a curt nod she turned and headed for the stream knowing her abductor wouldn't be far behind, but she didn't care. She'd refused to react like a docile little lamb. Slaughter or no slaughter.

Sitting on a rise above the creek, she dangled her hot feet in the stream fed by the snow-capped Sierra Blancas. Her muscles were sore from riding astride her mount, and her stomach begged for decent food. Still Lago had treated her well enough. It could have been a lot worse.

Wishing she could have a soothing bath, she contented herself by splashing the frigid water onto her arms and legs. Unbidden memories reminded her of the last time cold water raised goose bumps on her flesh, and how Granger ended up keeping her warm. . . .

Granger.

Did he know of her abduction? Did he care? Was he searching for her? Was anybody?

"Well, well, well. Looky what we have here."

Startled, Lisha turned to see three men on horseback. She

scrambled up, covering her bare legs with her rumpled skirts.

"Seems the little lady is bashful, Sloan."

The one called Sloan dismounted. His gaze lingered long and hard over her soft curves. He sauntered toward her, his Spanish spurs scraping stone.

Remembering Freddy's advice on cat fighting, Lisha waited, ready to defend herself. She hadn't the chance to put up much of a struggle with Lago, but she wasn't going to let this overstuffed peacock lay one finger on her. His rounding stomach, a vulnerable spot, informed her of his leisurely life.

"No need to be bashful, little lady. We're all friends here."

"Don't tire her out too much, Sloan," the second one drawled in a boyish lilt. "Be obliged if you leave something for me." Angry scar tissue slanting from his left eye to his cheekbone was the only blemish that marred his otherwise handsome face.

"Don't worry, Tyler," Sloan tossed over his shoulder. "By the looks of her she has enough for the both of us." Anticipation gleamed in his close-set eyes.

"She's a luscious one, all right," Tyler agreed, leaning an arm across his saddle horn. He spit tobacco juice on the ground. "But don't you think she's a mite too tall for you to handle?"

"You know I like my women big and sassy."

Sloan took another step. Instantly a bullet split the ground at the point of his toes. He jerked around to see Lago glaring at him, a smoking pistol casually cupped in his palm.

"Lago—wondered where you were."

"Did ya, now?"

"Sorta hopin' you took a long walk."

"Well, I didn't," Lago growled. "An' for future references, I ain't plannin' on takin' any."

"What're you so all fired protective of her for? She's just a piece of skirt. Same as any other female."

"Take another look, Sloan. She's worth three thousand dollars to me . . . all in one piece."

Sloan turned his attention back to Lisha. He studied her with something other than his loins. "You mean she's for Chavez?"

"Exactly, an' I'll stop *anyone* who tries to git between her . . . and me." Lago leveled his gun at his partner's chest.

The third man released an audible sigh. For the first time Lisha zeroed in on him. The familiarity of the breadth of his shoulders, his black hat, and his buckskin horse hit her all at once. When she recognized Granger under a week's growth of beard, her heart leapt.

She took a step forward, her hands outstretched, his name on her lips. Then she noticed the stolid expression chiseled on his rough features. His gaze flickered over her, giving her a slight nod. Then he turned his full attention to Lago, as if imprinting the man's image on his brain.

Granger's indifference dumbfounded Lisha. Why had he acted so callous? Why hadn't he tried to stop Sloan? She couldn't think of any reason unless . . . unless he did it on purpose. Whatever he had in mind, it'd better be good. She glanced at the other men.

"When did ya get him?" Lago asked, waving his gun toward Granger.

"Yesterday."

"Do ya know who he is?"

Sloan shrugged. "Some drifter."

The line of Lago's lips curved into a brittle smile. "Well, I know who he is, an' he ain't no drifter. He's a rancher by the name of Hawks. He has an interest in the mail-order bride here. A personal interest, from what I can see."

Granger pushed his hat back from his grimy forehead. "The only interest I have in this woman is being a temporary guardian for my daughter. After the cattle drive I intend to pack her back to St. Louis."

"That so? Then why did ya come hightailin' it after us?"

"I wasn't. I didn't even know you had taken her. Before your buddies interrupted me, I was on my way to pick up a small herd of cattle from a widow needing ready cash. I promised her I'd sell her stock along with mine in Fort Sumner."

Lisha was puzzled. He'd never mentioned anything about a widow. And why did he sound so unfeeling when he referred to her?

Lago spat on the ground. "You expect me to believe that?"

"I don't care what you believe. I have no future interest in this woman. She doesn't fit in with my ideas of a wife, and the sooner she's on her way, the better I'll like it."

Lago glanced at Lisha. A callous expression set his features. "Well, now, I'll sure do my best to set her on her way, an' I don't mean to St. Louis. But I'm curious—how come you're so anxious to have her gone?"

"Simple. Appearances are deceiving." Granger turned his attention to Lisha. His bold gaze roved over her. "Under that beautiful shell lies a heart as frigid as that stream. So much so that I don't intend on forcing my husbandly rights on her every time I get the urge. A man don't need that kind of irritation, especially from a *bossy* woman."

Finally Lisha realized what Granger was attempting to do. Until she knew why, she'd continue his charade. Giving thanks for Beatrice Dodd's pious sermons and the hours playacting with her father, she narrowed her eyes and pressed her lips into what she hoped was a condemning line.

"Mr. Hawks," she bit out, "as I see it, you're not any better than these three men. At least *they* don't hide their carnal lust under the guise of matrimony. You men are all alike—you're nothing more than rutting animals that we women have the unfortunate duty to endure."

Sloan whistled. "She reminds me too much of my own wife. Sure can see why ya want to get rid of her, Hawks."

Lago's thoughts worked the muscles in his face. "Yeah," he said quietly, "but if what they say is true, why did she come out here in the first place? Heard she came to marry you, Hawks."

Lisha snorted, tossing her hair. "I wondered that myself, after I had arrived at the ranch. In his letter Mr. Hawks had stated he wanted a wife in 'name only,' someone to take care of his daughter. I thought the situation perfect because I'd be able to raise a child but be spared the marriage bed." She wrapped her arms about her chest. "But I was rudely awakened. The further away from him, the better I'll like it."

Sloan chuckled. "Sorry, lady. Can't oblige. I figured Hawks would be of great help to the people in Chihuahua. So he'll accompany us. Even though at first he didn't seem to want to come along. We had to 'convince' him some.''

For the first time Lisha noticed the stiff way in which Granger carried himself, and the dried blood on his shirt.

"Help Mr. Hawks down."

Three startled sets of eyes focused on her. She rested her hands on her hips and stared back. A ghost of a smile passing over Granger's lips did not escape her notice.

Sloan shifted his footing. "Now look at who's givin' the orders.''

"No, you look!" she commanded, advancing toward the men. "That man needs attention."

"We all need attention, darlin'.'' Chuckling, Tyler leaned over to spit tobacco juice on the ground. "What makes him so special? Are you sure you didn't have something going on before Lago broke up your little party?''

"Don't be crude," she flared. "The only interest I have in this man, or in you three for that matter, is purely medical. I don't care for him any more than I care for you. But I am a nurse, and I intend to help him. If any of you object, I would strongly suggest that you seriously think about changing your minds. You can never tell when one of you will need my assistance. Besides, how much money will you get for a dead man? Now"—softening her voice, she smiled sweetly—"will one of you gentlemen please help Mr. Hawks down?''

The two men plainly didn't know what to think of her outburst. Tyler shifted in his saddle, and Sloan scratched the back of his head.

"Come on," Lago barked, shoving his pistol inside its holster. "I've been with her long enough to know we won't get any peace unless we do what she asks. Bossy as hell.''

Lisha tried to keep a placid face as they pulled Granger from his saddle but knew she failed a few times when Sloan shouldered him to the creek. By the way Granger reacted, it appeared he had a few cracked ribs and riding for so long hadn't helped his condition.

"Does anyone have a can of salve?''

She looked expectantly at the three men. No one moved. Finally Tyler shrugged and fished in his saddlebags for the

Balm. Lisha lifted her skirts, took the hem of her slip, and ripped out a lengthy piece.

"Here," she said, holding the bandage out to Lago. "If you're just going to stand there, roll this up."

Lago stared at the frayed strip of cloth in Lisha's out-stretched hand. His passive look migrated to her face. A steely shade of anger glossed over his wide-set eyes before he turned and stalked away.

Lisha refused to dwell on Lago's hostile mood and offered the crude bandage to Sloan. Ducking aside, he threw up his hands.

"Not me, Nurse Lady. I faint at the sight of blood, especially if it's my own." Shrugging apologetically, he saw to his horse.

Lisha turned expectantly to Tyler. She decided he was the best prospect, besides being the last one.

"All right," Tyler mumbled, giving in, "let me have it."

He rolled the bandage while Lisha helped Granger ease out of his bloodstained shirt. Carefully she spread the salve over the scrapes on his side.

She touched his chest, remembering when she'd had the sudden urge to draw her fingertips across his back, to know the feel of it beneath her skin. Now that she had the chance, she was more concerned with the way he winced at her light touch than her own shameless curiosity. With Tyler's help she bound up his cracked ribs.

"Thank you, Tyler."

"Anything for a pretty lady," he said, spitting at her feet. "But don't get me wrong because of my good nature. If I had to, I could put a bullet through that pretty head of yours without blinking an eye."

Lisha looked up from Granger's neatly bound chest. Tyler's words neither shocked nor frightened her. "And don't get *me* wrong, Tyler. I might be a woman, but I'll do what it takes to survive."

The glint in his eyes dulled. He seemed to mull over what she'd said, then grinned. "We understand each other."

"We understand each other."

Tyler turned to leave, then hesitated. "Since you're got a fair amout of savvy, I want to give you a piece of advice. Don't bait Lago. He won't stand for it, money or no.''

"Thank you, I'll keep that in mind.''

When Tyler strode from earshot, Granger grabbed hold of her wrist. "Lisha, are you all right?" Worry edged his voice.

Her breath expelled in a rush. "Lago's treated me better than I'd have expected. I'm terrified, though.''

"Could've fooled me. You act as though you're made of iron.''

"I'm not, but I don't want them to know. I'm not going to make things easy for Lago.'' She turned her back, tore another piece of fabric from her slip, and sloshed it around in the creek. "Why did you say all those things about me?''

"Gut instinct,'' he whispered. "I don't want to give them any more leverage than they already have.''

"I don't understand.''

She wrung out the excess water and turned her attention to the blood caked in Granger's hair. When she pressed the wet cloth to his head, he flinched.

"I mean they play rough. Sometimes they terrorize people by taking out their sport on a member of their family or on somebody they're fond of. I had to convince them there is no affection lost between us. Thanks for jumping in when you did.''

Appalled, she stilled her work. "Lago might do that, but—''

"Lisha,'' Granger hissed, "listen to me. We're not playing games here. These men don't work alone. They're scouters for an outlaw named Javier and run with the most ruthless pack of dogs imaginable. You'll do well to remember that.''

"Was there really a widow?''

"No.''

"Then you really were looking for me?''

"Yes.''

His simple answer spoke volumes, and her heart tipped. Sooner than she would have liked, she finished cleansing the wound. Already, she yearned for another excuse to be near him, another excuse to touch him. Gently she applied salve to his cuts, hesitating at the split on the corner of his mouth.

She remembered one moonlit night when his lips had played

havoc on her usually calm senses. A warm flush spread over her body. Thoughts of him filled her being. She would give him her heart and soul if he would but take them.

"Is . . . is Rena all right?"

"She's fine."

"And Juanita?"

"Better than she deserves to be."

"She's a confused child who needs our understanding."

"Understanding isn't quite what I had in mind for her," he said in a tight voice. "More like a good—"

"Hey, Lago says you've taken long enough. No need to waste any more time on Hawks. There ain't no parties where he's goin'."

Sloan's sudden appearance startled Lisha. If she hadn't been reaching for the lid to the tin of salve, she wouldn't have been able to camouflage her guilty start.

"Tell Lago I'm not taking any more time than need be." She picked up Granger's stained clothing. "Mr. Hawks, do you have another shirt?"

"In my saddlebags."

"Good, I want to soak the blood out of this one."

Sloan scratched under his ear. "Lady, I doubt Lago would like that."

Because of Granger's warning, she studied Sloan in a new light. The man wasn't the simpleminded person he'd made out to be, she could tell by the shrewd gleam in his eyes. He worked hard on his facade, and she would have fallen for it. In the coming weeks, or however long it would take Granger to get them out of this mess, she would never let her guard down.

"Why on earth would he object?" she asked, trying to sound shocked. She doubted if Lago knew that water could be used for bathing, let alone doing laundry. "I'm sure if he were in Mr. Hawks's situation, he'd like clean clothes, too." She headed toward Saber with Sloan trailing along behind.

"Ya see, lady, Lago don't like nobody doin' nothin' less he says so."

"I found that out."

When she reached for the ties to the saddlebag, Sloan clamped a leathery hand onto her wrists. "What say we go off somewhere so's you can give me a little bit of your personalized attention, and I'll forget tellin' Lago about your laundry service. . . . I can hardly believe you're as cold as Hawks says your are." He chuckled. "Maybe you just need the right man to take the chill off."

Lisha cocked her head, hoping she gave an air of confidence she didn't feel. "I've a better idea. What say you forget to tattle on me, and I'll forget to tell Lago that you were willing to ruin his chances at getting three thousand dollars for a little of my time. I don't know what you pay your whores, but I'll hazard a guess it's considerably lower than that."

The cocky smile dropped from Sloan's face. Any form of friendliness faded. Maybe she had gone too far by threatening him. Much to her relief, he grinned.

"Lady, you've got guts. I always said that I liked my women sassy. I'm going ta enjoy watchin' Lago try to work while havin' his hands full with you. It'll be interesting ta see if he gets you ta Mexico at all. It's for those reasons I'm willin' ta let things pass. But"—the reflection in his eyes hardened—"if somethin' happens to Lago, I'll be there ta finish his job."

"I'm sure you will."

Lisha pulled Granger's extra shirt from his saddlebags. By the time she helped him on with it, Sloan had started to gather wood for the evening's fire.

Clustering stars flickered overhead in a sky of midnight blue. Crickets added their steady rhythm to the ripple of the creek. Sloan began to snore. At one point his loud snorts woke him up. Disoriented, he glanced about, then turned over, taking up his snoring where he'd left off.

The smoke from the dying fire meandered into the crisp night air. A cool breeze teased the curls around Lisha's face, and she burrowed into her blanket. The stiff material still chafed her neck and face, but at least it smelled better since she had thoroughly soaked it in the creek.

She lay, listening to the crackle of the fire. Tyler got up from his perch and kicked a half-burnt log with the toe of his boot. Red embers sputtered into death. He added another piece of wood. The flames shot up, licking hungrily at the dried bark.

In a way hungry flames licked at Lisha. She thought of Granger lying so close to her, so close. During the rest of the day she had hardly glanced in his direction because she'd wanted to keep a stiff distance from the men, and that meant ignoring Granger.

Had he slept, or had sleep evaded him as it did her? Did thoughts of her occupy his mind?

At dawn the aroma of coffee drifted in the air. The rising sun softly brushed Lisha's eyelids, and they fluttered open as if having a mind of their own. Sometime during the night the ground underneath her bed had grown rocks. Wincing, she stretched her cramped muscles and sat up. The men had already gathered their bedrolls, and she could see Granger down by the creek, washing.

"Morning, Nurse Lady."

Lisha glanced at the man standing by the fire. "Morning, Sloan. May I have a cup of that coffee?"

"If you want somethin' with a little kick."

Clutching the blanket around her bare arms, she took the tin mug eagerly. At least in their relentless diet of beans, hardtack, and jerky, this was something she could stomach. The welcome heat radiated through the metal and warmed her hands. The air was nippy, but she knew how fast it would warm up once the sun came out.

"Lago wants ta pull out soon. Better get ready. He don't like ta wait once he's made up his mind on doin' somethin'."

With a sigh Lisha set the cup down. She couldn't imagine Lago in a hurry over anything. His character was too precise, too deliberate.

She sought a secluded spot near the creek to wash. The icy water revived her flagging spirits. As she patted herself dry with a portion of her slip, a twig snapped, sounding like the crack of a whip. Whirling around, she faced Lago's solemn stare and felt her insides coil.

Would she ever get used to the bold angles and deep clefts of his face? Even his straight nose appeared too long and narrow, his jaw and chin too square. Everything about his makeup hinged on the extreme.

Lago smiled. Not a smile boasting of warmth, but rather one an executioner might use before the ax fell.

"What do you want?" she demanded, angry at his unheralded intrusion.

"Come to tell ya we're leavin'."

"You could've called out."

"Wanted to make sure ya heard."

"I would've heard."

Even though he had far-ranged intentions, she didn't care for the sheen in his eyes. When she made to pass him by, he clamped his long fingers about the tender flesh of her upper arm. Grimacing, she jerked free from his hold.

"Don't touch me."

A muscle twitched in his jaw. "You'd better watch who's in position ta give orders. One day your sass is gonna backfire. An' I'm countin' on bein' there when it does."

With great effort she raised her chin, met his icy gaze, and walked past him. She hoped her control would last until she reached camp.

Granger looked up from filling his canteen and saw Lisha emerge from the willows. Moments later Lago sauntered out behind her in his usual lazy gait. Granger caught sight of the hard set of the man's protruding jaw.

He quickly turned his attention back to Lisha. There seemed nothing from the ordinary with her appearance. Lago hadn't touched her, Granger was sure of that. Yet, there was a hesitation in her stride, a venerable bend to her head.

Better watch your back, Lago, 'cause when you least expect it, I'll be there. No matter how long it takes, I'll make you pay.

Chapter
12

Lisha's horse plodded obediently along the rocky trail. The past week had been as hard on the animal as it had been on her. Lago was relentless with their travel. He wanted to meet up with the rest of the band by the first of next week, and they all showed the effects of the strain.

The three deserters had been at one another's throats for days now, and Lisha had enough sense to keep her saucy mouth shut, knowing this was not the time to be assertive. She'd also realized that Granger relaxed when he felt sure she would not purposely start up any trouble.

There was one consolation about the long days without any physical work. Granger's rib cage had begun to heal nicely. Finding excuses, she rewrapped his chest and checked his progress.

She hadn't allowed herself the luxury of gazing at Granger, but he was always in her thoughts. Ofttimes she felt someone staring at her, and she would glance up to see a familiar pair of liquid brown eyes gently probing, watching her every move.

Sometimes he would feign sleep and watch her from under his hat. She regarded this as unfair. The men would think he'd had something wrong with him if he hadn't taken notice of her, but for their sakes, she couldn't single him out.

To her, Granger's steady gaze felt completely different from the others'. Theirs smacked of indecency riddled with lewd connotations. His had a touch as light as a cobweb, as soft and smooth as the belly of a two-week-old puppy. Whenever she felt his silent caress, her heart beat a little faster.

Besides the nearness of Granger, the land they passed through played with her emotions. The changing scenery both awed and intimidated her. The northern part of the territory, which housed Granger's ranch, boasted of a variety of trees, majestic mountain ranges, and rich grazing land.

Here the landscape gave way to imposing mesas, rocky ground dotted with bunch grass, mesquite, and groves of the spiky yucca plant. Everywhere she looked, stocks, as high as ten feet, had exploded with a profusion of creamy-white blossoms.

Dormant seeds had taken advantage of recent spring rains and had sprouted into flowers, splashing the desert with yellow, white, and pink. The land in which Granger had carved out his home steadily wove her into its magic spell.

She thought she'd seen everything the territory of New Mexico had to offer until the weary group came upon a vast wilderness flanked by mountain ranges. Until she realized the country she'd so much admired changed into a deadly waste-land baked by heat and filled with countless acres of prickly pear and rabbit brush. Until she faced a glittering world of white. Reining in her horse, she stared at the hills of sand rippled in sun and shadow.

A scorpion's sudden scrambling for cover startled her. She shuddered at the sight of its nipping claws and the curving jointed tail with its poisonous sting. How many other desert creatures would she have the misfortune to come across?

"That's the San Andres Mountains to the west and the Sacramento Range on the east. . . . Sorta takes your breath away, don't it?"

Lisha pulled her gaze from the disappearing scorpion to look over at Tyler. "I can't begin to tell you what it does to me."

She stared at the leprous pockets of white sand and sparse vegetation. The sun glared down on the valley floor that heaved with shimmering sand dunes. Wind swirled gritty gypsum around the rabbit brush. The arid land seemed to ebb and swell before her stinging eyes. She felt so alone, so fragile, and at the random mercy of nature. Despondency overwhelmed her. She wished with all her heart she could be back home in her own room, back home on Granger's ranch.

A suffocating heat pressed down upon her. Perspiration trickled around her ears, angled along her throat, and ran down the gully between her breasts. She could have sworn that the hum of the desert spawned in her ears. Numbing feelers snaked their way from her fingertips and limbs to center in her buzzing head. Darkness shrouded her. As she pitched forward, a familiar pair of arms caught her.

"You have to quit pushing so hard, or you won't have anything left of her to sell."

Granger's angry voice threaded itself into Lisha's subconsciousness. Floating along in a land of shade trees and cool breezes, she gently settled down by a limpid pool. Her love came and sat beside her. Cupping his hand, he rained water on her face and throat and into her mouth. After a few swallows she focused on brown eyes flecked with green.

"How do you feel, Miss Harrington?"

Granger's worried question brought her out of her faint. Immediately she felt the desert heat crowd in, plastering her clothes to her skin.

"I'm so hot."

"You'll cool off soon. The sun is going down."

With Granger's help Lisha sat up. She blinked at the changing desert scene spread out before her. The San Andres, swathed in a misty veil of lilac shadows and purple hollows, blackened against the sunset. As the full moon emerged, the whispering wasteland she'd thought so grim and hateful before transformed itself into an austere gleam of coasting sands, a mystical portion of a long-ago fairyland.

"I didn't realize that anything so deadly could be so beautiful."

"There're a lot of things about nature that will surprise you."

"Yes, I know."

She glanced up at Granger. Her soft answer held a double meaning, and by the sudden twitch of his cheek, she knew he heard it, also.

"I'll get you out of this, Lisha," he promised under his breath. "I swear, somehow I'll get you out of this."

"Hey, Hawks," Sloan called from a growing pile of dead mesquite, "you know there ain't no use letting your guts get in an uproar over that girl. Better busy yourself by the time Lago comes back from huntin' us up some grub."

Granger pushed to his feet. Wincing, he placed a hand to his midriff. For a moment he studied Lisha's upturned face, then began to gather wood. Lisha stayed where Granger had put her. She still felt dizzy. A result accumulated by the endless sun, hours in the saddle, and a scant variety of food.

Soon an eager fire rushed at the wood. The dry crackle would have sung Lisha to sleep, but the mouth-watering aroma of roasting meat kept her awake. Lago had killed an animal and was cooking it. When the meat was done, Granger brought her over a plate. Without a word he left her to eat in peace.

Rabbit proved to be quite tasty. Or was it because she was so hungry? Just as she finished her last bite, Sloan brought over more food.

"Thought ya might like some more ta eat."

"Thank you," she said, taking a second helping. "Tell Lago he certainly has a way with rabbit."

Sloan's grin widened. "I'll tell him just that, Nurse Lady."

She heard Lago's laughter after Sloan delivered the compliment, but she didn't care. Some men were used to manners; some were not.

Lisha awoke to the dawn ferreting out the black shapes of the pines dotting the range. Lago sat by the fire drinking coffee, his tin mug gripped in his hand. Lisha got up to pour herself a cup. As she picked up the pot, she noticed the tail end of a rattlesnake beneath the remaining pile of mesquite.

"A snake!"

The pot slipped from her fingers and landed at Lago's feet. Scalding coffee splashed up on his thigh. With a tortured yell he jumped up, frantically plucking at his pant legs.

Startled from a deep sleep, Tyler vaulted to his feet. He clutched his rifle against his grayed long johns, blinking first in one direction, then the other.

Alarmed, Sloan hastened his barefoot way back across a dune, stepping on a dead bush. Letting out a bloodcurdling oath, he clutched his injured foot and hopped around on the other.

Only Granger took notice of where Lisha's reptile lay hidden. He kicked the wood aside to reveal a snake's head and tail.

As Lisha stared at what was left of a rattler, a sick understanding gnawed away at her stomach. Swallowing passed the lump in her throat, she placed a shaky hand to her forehead.

"Is . . . is that the remains of our supper?"

"I'm afraid it is."

Groaning, she closed her eyes. No wonder Lago had laughed at her compliment the night before. Thoughts of eating the rattlesnake, no matter what the circumstances, churned her insides.

"You mean to tell me I got burned 'cause of a dead snake?" Lago loomed up beside her. His shouting hadn't helped her upset stomach.

"Seems so." Granger's voice carried a hint of laughter.

Lisha's nausea kindled into anger, and she turned on Lago. "Well, if you'd brought back something else, you wouldn't have had so much trouble." His threatening look failed to temper her. "If you were any kind of a gentleman, you'd have warned me."

"An' if I had?" he asked in a tight voice.

"I wouldn't have eaten it."

"That's what I thought."

Glaring at the red-faced man, she realized why he was so concerned that she eat. "Oh, heaven forbid, if your valuable goods failed to reach their destination in prime condition."

"Miss Harrington, you're upset." Granger laid a warning hand on her arm. "Have a cup of coffee. It'll help calm you."

She looked from Lago's enraged face to Granger's tight mask. "I understand that ranchers lose money on their cattle if they aren't properly fed. I'd surely hate to see the same kind of thing happen to such a fine man as this."

Lago balled his hands. The veins on the side of his neck

stood out. Cursing, Sloan hobbled up, but catching sight of Lago's furious scowl, he clamped his mouth shut.

The pressure of Granger's hand tightened on Lisha's arm. He propelled her toward her bedroll and set her down. "If you don't keep your mouth shut," he warned under his breath, "I'll allow him to gag it. Don't ruin any chance we might have at all for escape. Please sit quietly and don't cause any more trouble. Or we'll both live regretting it. . . . Now, see what you can do to protect yourself from the sun."

Wishing again for her bonnet, Lisha followed Granger's instructions and covered her head with a scarf fashioned from a piece of her petticoats. After ripping off more strips, she tucked the cloth around the neckline and the sleeves of her dress.

"The lady's smart as well as beautiful," Tyler said, coming up to her. Nodding his approval, he fingered the edge of her scarf. His callused knuckles brushed her cheek, and she shied away.

"Where are we going?"

"El Paso."

"El Paso?"

"We'll skirt most of the white sands," he said, guiding her to her horse, "then head due south." He gave her a hand up. "You'll like El Paso."

"Care to bet?"

To shut her mind to the endless desert, Lisha thought of leisurely baths scented with perfume. Gradually a vision pieced itself together in her mind. She lounged in a porcelain tub with claw feet made from cast iron. Leaning forward, she pulled her shampooed hair over one shoulder and basked in the luxury of having her back washed.

Skillful hands soaped her down, lingering on the ticklish areas of her lower back and sides. They scooped up handfuls of soothing water to rinse her off. Like a mermaid breaking the ocean's surface, she rose from the tub. Her skin tingled with excitment. For what reason she didn't know.

A strong pair of hands seized her waist and lifted her out. Her bold gaze roved along muscled arms to the thick mat of

dark sandy hair centered on a broad chest. She scarcely
breathed. With each beat of her heart delicious heat coursed
through her. She tried to focus on the eyes that gazed down at
her, but the vision faded, and she could not call it back.

When the emotionally charged mood evaporated into the
desert heat, and the sinewy chest dissolved into Lago's stiff
back, Lisha felt an enormous sense of loss. She longed to be
with Granger. Would he be able to hold her in his arms again?

He rode right behind her, and often she felt his stare. Many
times she had stopped herself from glancing back. She thought
of his wrists, now bound to the saddle horn. How could he get
them out of this situation when he could barely move? For the
first time thoughts of never escaping chilled her.

"Make camp here," Lago ordered, reining in his horse at the
base of a cliff.

Relieved, Lisha slid from her mount. Granger reined up
beside her, and she released the rope binding him to his saddle
horn. Saber nickered softly and pawed the naked ground.

"What's the matter with Saber?"

"He smells water."

"Water? Where?"

"Most likely in the rocks. The rain leaves pools of water all
over the desert, especially after a flash flood."

"Hey, there's water over here." Tyler called out as if taking
part in their conversation. "Bring the horses."

If water collected in those rocks, wouldn't it be feasible that
other pools of water lay hidden from prying eyes? Craving a
chance for a bath even if she were only able to sponge down,
Lisha promised herself to make a search of her own when the
men would be less likely to miss her.

Spreading out her bedroll, she watched Lago disappear over
the bluff in search of game. Sloan lengthened the rope between
Granger's wrists in order for him to gather wood, and Tyler
occupied himself with the horses. Unobserved, she eased her
way past the horses and on up the side of the gorge.

With little difficulty she reached the boulders that Granger
had indicated, and to her delight she found that nature had
eroded a perfect bowl filled with water. Giving a delighted cry,
she hastily unbuttoned her bodice and toed aside her dress and

slips. The pool proved to be too small for her to use as a bathtub, but that wouldn't stop her from enjoying it.

As she began to unlace her corset, she saw a reflection in the motion of the water's surface. She had hoped the men wouldn't notice that she'd slipped away until she had a chance to wash.

Sighing, she turned to beg for a few moments alone only to stare into the fathomless black eyes of an Apache. The sun glinted off a wickedly sharp knife he gripped in his hand.

Chapter
🌿 13 🌿

Lisha's pounding heart promised to squeeze the breath from her throat. A savage grin broadened the Indian's glistening face. He stepped closer, forcing her back against the rocks. With all she'd worried about the past few days, her life ending at the hand of a Mescalero definitely had not crossed her mind.

The Apache gripped a handful of her hair. She quailed. Fear somersaulted in her stomach as he rubbed his thumb up and down the loosely coiled braid. Grunting his pleasure, he held the sharp blade to her forehead.

She felt the cold steel against her skin. Her cry for help suffered death in her dry throat. She closed her eyes, praying for a swift end. Then all at once she heard a whizzing sound, a soft thud, and a groan. The Indian slumped against her and bonelessly slid to her feet. She could hardly grasp the meaning of the pearl-handled knife protruding from his back.

Numb, she looked up to see Lago standing on the bluff above her. At that moment she'd almost rather face the Indian. The deserter half slid, half walked down the shale-covered side of the cliff, creating miniature avalanches with each step.

"Why ain't you in camp?" he lashed out, reaching the bottom.

"I wanted to take a bath."

"Was it worth the company? Another few seconds an' you wouldn't need a bath. Leastways not so's you'd know."

Bending, he jerked his bloodied knife from the Indian's back and methodically wiped the soiled blade on his pant leg before

136

he slid the weapon back into its sheath. "Don't even think about leavin' camp again," he warned in clipped tones. "You've caused me enough trouble. I don't want any more."

"Goodness, we certainly don't want any more trouble. I understand there's very little market these days for a scalped woman."

Lago grabbed her hair and yanked her against his chest. "Listen, lady, and listen good," he warned in a voice as rough as pumice. "You'd better not ruin my chances, or you'll be sorry as hell. Even if I have to take it out on someone else, you'll pay. Understand?"

He savagely twisted her braid to press home his warning. Tears sprinted to her eyes. She gave a short nod. With a crooked smile he let her go. For the first time since her ordeal, fear for Granger and little Rena choked Lisha. Lago must never find out about her feelings for them.

Suddenly an arrow whizzed passed her ear, and she instantly dropped to her knees. In one fluid motion Lago whirled, leveling his rifle. He fired at an Indian silhouetted against the cliff. With a cry the Apache tumbled off the jagged edge, flipflopped, and landed in a cloud of dust.

"Find cover and stay put!" Lago commanded. Not bothering to see that she obeyed his orders, he sprinted to the steep bluff and zigzagged his way up the side.

With no argument she squeezed behind the huge boulders and waited. The rough stone snagged her hair and clothing and scratched her tender skin. She didn't hear a sound save for the constant wind whistling through the jagged rock formations.

Sluggish time acted the enemy. Thinking she would surely go mad with waiting, she heard the roar of a gun, and the ping of a bullet striking stone. A few more shots rang out, then silence.

She buried her face in the crook of her arm. Her stomach twisted painfully. The mixed sounds of war whoops, gunfire, and a cry of pain wedged themselves into her brain. She clutched the ragged stone beneath her hand until her palms burned.

More shots were fired, more time elapsed. What was

happening? Who cried out in pain? Where was Granger? Thoughts of their hair hanging on a lodge pole made her ill.

"Lisha. Lisha!"

She jerked up. Someone called out her name. It sounded like a soft whisper. She strained to hear it again, but her efforts were only met with the wheezing of the incessant wind.

"Lisha . . . Lisha, where are you?"

This time the whisper sounded harsh, the timber strained. She recognized Granger's anxious voice, and her heart quickened. "Over here," she called softly, emerging from her limestone shelter.

Almost instantly Granger slipped his bound wrists over her head and hugged her to his chest. He quickly kissed her forehead, the tip of her nose, her upturned lips.

"Thank God you're all right," he breathed. "When I heard the shooting, I . . ." Not able to finish, he clutched her tighter.

She'd never known such joy. The man she loved held her in his arms. His actions and words expressed deep affection. Would he ever admit his feelings and declare his love for her?

"Grab your clothes," he ordered, acting as if he were reluctant to let her go. "There's no time to waste. We've got to get away while they're busy with our welcoming."

She bent to retrieve her dress and saw the Indian's knife lying a few inches from her petticoats. Swiftly gathering it up, she hid the weapon under the folds of her slips and followed Granger down the incline. Reaching the horses, he offered her a leg up. Only the sound of a cocked rifle stilled his motions.

"Goin' somewhere?"

Letting out a sigh of defeat, Lisha turned to face the three deserters. Lago's nonchalant stance belied the anger burning in his steely gray eyes. Tyler rolled the wad of tobacco to the side of his mouth and spat. The scarred flesh around his eye had grown tight.

"Looks like Hawks don't like our hospitality anymore."

"Yeah," Sloan intoned, "seems he wants ta leave and take the Nurse Lady with 'im."

Granger shifted his position, not cowering before the men.

"You don't think I'd be inhumane enough to leave her to the likes of you, do you?"

"Or maybe," Sloan added, "the sum of three thousand dollars clouded your thinkin'."

"Maybe."

"Cut the chatter," Lago barked out. He leveled his rifle at Granger's chest. "I'm going to teach you that a man don't stick his nose in where it don't belong."

Sloan stepped up, obstructing the line of fire. "Hold it, Lago. We're not disputing your claim on the lady here, and you're not butting into our plans for Hawks."

He meant his words as a warning, not as a means to clarify the situation. Lago well understood the barbed undertones. He glared at his partner, whose outer appearance gave the impression of calm, but willingness to do battle shined in his close-set eyes. Lago lowered his gun.

"All right, but see he don't interfere again, or I'll make sure of it."

"He won't have the chance," Sloan said, motioning toward Granger.

Granger grabbed his gear and followed the deserter without so much as a glance at Lisha. Lago then turned his attention to her. His hard scrutiny roved over her half-clothed body. He made her feel as if she already stood on an auction block, and he, a perspective buyer, inspected the merchant's goods. A sudden gleam heated his cold stare.

She stepped back, holding her dress protectively across her breasts. Was he about to change his purpose for her? To her relief, his eyes dulled, and he jerked his head toward camp.

"Get to your bedroll and stay put."

"May I step behind the horses and dress first?"

Lago pressed his lips together, making his jaw appear even larger. "Lady, anyone would think that you'd have the sense to stay closer to camp."

"I presume you've taken care of the Indians, or else you wouldn't be back."

His bored glance flicked over her. "If you make it snappy."

Uttering a quick prayer of thanks, she used the shield of the horses to splash her face and arms at the pool. The water cooled her heated skin but only momentarily. She knew she had the beginnings of a painful sunburn.

Maybe she'd be able to have a real bath and wash her clothes when they reached this town called El Paso. She scrambled into her dress and stooped to gather up her petticoats, careful to keep the knife hidden in the yards of material.

She saw no sign of Lago, but Sloan and Tyler busied themselves gathering wood. They'd left Granger tied to a mesquite bush. He sat too close, in her estimation, to its spindly thorns. She walked right up to him.

"Mr. Hawks, do you have a mirror and some Balm?"

Granger barely heard what she'd asked. With the sun hitting her back and no slips under her cotton dress, the shadowy forms of her long legs captured his thoughts. The wind whipped the diaphanous material around her ankles and her hair about her face, making her appear to be a mystical goddess glowing in silver and blue. Granger swallowed, hard.

"Did you hear me?"

Reluctantly he dragged his gaze away from her shapely thighs to concentrate on the corner of her mouth, which was drawn up into a saucy smile. The sparkle in her eyes glinted an enticing blue. Damn her! She knew darn well what she looked like. Her walking around half-dressed like that. Just what did she propose to accomplish by carrying her petticoats instead of wearing them? If it was a riot she wanted, she was bound to get one.

He pressed his lips together, trying not to let his eyes stray too far down. Eventually he noticed she concealed an object among the folds of her slip.

"I repeat, may I borrow your mirror and some Balm? I need them for my sunburn."

As Lisha talked, she partially uncovered an Indian knife. He stared dumbfounded at the wicked-looking blade before glancing over at their captors. The men paid them no heed. He looked back at Lisha's innocent face, which contradicted the amusement in her voice. She'd already hidden the knife.

"Ah . . . help yourself. They're in my saddlebags."

"Thank you."

From the corner of his eye he watched Lisha sit on her

bedroll. She fumbled inside his saddlebags, pulling out his extra clothing, a mirror, salve, and a bar of soap. Without so much as a nervous twitch, she rolled the clothes back up and returned them to the leather pocket. Only he noticed the knife she had ingeniously concealed in the folds of his shirt. His gear already searched, no one would think there'd be a knife tucked away at the bottom of his saddlebags.

Pretending to settle back for a little shut-eye, he watched Lisha struggle into her tattered slips. It galled him to think of her situation, and he wondered how the nightmare would end. He knew of several men who, in Lisha's circumstances, would plain give up and wallow in despair. Not so with her. She seemed to reject anything that might pull her down.

Lisha peered into the mirror, touched the bridge of her nose, and pulled a face. A corner of his mouth curved. The sun had tanned her creamy-white complexion. With a sigh she anointed her face and neck and rubbed the Balm into her hands.

Next she attacked her hair, trying her best to comb through the snarls with her fingers. How he longed to entwine his own fingers in that silvery mane, to kiss that perky nose, to . . .

Lisha picked up his bags and without hardly a glance at him placed them by his side.

Later that night he lay listening to Sloan's rhythmic snores and Lago's steady breathing. Tyler had taken the first watch. Granger could tell that long days in the saddle and short nights on the cold, hard ground wore on the outlaw. The man slumped by the fire, feeding it pieces of mesquite. He listed to the side, jerked upright, stood, and stretched. Grabbing his rifle, he began to circle the camp, a habit the man had gotten into to stay awake.

This was what Granger had waited for. Straining against the rope, he reached for his saddlebags but could barely touch them. Groaning, he tried again to get a fingerhold but failed. Lisha had set them too far away.

Think. He must think of another way. With both hands he worked away at a crooked limb of the mesquite, finally breaking it loose. Once, twice, three times he tried to hook his bags without succeeding. What the hell happened to three times the charm?

He hadn't much time left. Taking a calming breath, he slipped the limb through the folded bags and gingerly pulled. The makeshift pole held, and he inched his catch forward. Grabbing a solid grip of leather, he sat upright, and anchored the bags between his thighs. With a little difficulty he maneuvered his hands inside one pocket.

A burning piece of wood split in half and sent sparks shooting into the air. Sloan raised his head, glanced about with a blank look, and turned over. Soon sleep steadied his snoring.

Granger searched deeper, finding his shirt. With as little movement as possible he tried to unravel it. Bound wrists and time worked against him. Sweat beaded his upper lip. Finally he gripped the handle of the knife, pulled it free, and carefully slid the weapon inside his boot.

A dried twig snapped, signaling Tyler's return. Granger quickly settled back against his bedroll, breathing steadily as if in deep slumber.

Several yards away Lisha had lain wide awake, listening to Granger's subtle movements. Every fiber of her body had tuned in on his struggling efforts. When he'd eventually recovered the knife and hid the weapon on his person, intense relief had flooded her. Now hope rose to cradle her heart. They had a chance.

Lisha swayed with the motion of her horse. She had lost track of the long hours they'd traveled since breakfast. The sun seemed to have wiped away any sense of time.

Before they'd started out that morning, she had rubbed her face and hands with the Balm. However, she could still feel the penetrating heat. And what the sun failed to bake, the wind scoured. The desert landscape no longer awed her. All that this vast countryside meant to her now was mile after mile of baked wasteland, little water, and wind.

Lago suddenly jerked on the reins. His horse shied at his abrupt command. The outlaw leaned forward, listening. Then Lisha heard it, too, faint snatches of irregular gunfire. And laughter. She could swear she'd heard laughter.

The outlaws grinned at each other, and Lago whipped his horse into a canter. The second Lisha's mount took up the rhythm, her sore body made her cry out in pain. Were they insane running headlong into something they knew nothing about?

When their horses crested the ridge, she could see men milling about two covered wagons. All their contents had been dumped on the ground, and a man or two rifled through the piles. Some staggered about, waving what appeared to be bottles of whiskey in their hands. A couple paraded a woman's corset between them. One man threw what appeared to be china plates up into the air while others used them for target practice.

Three men on horseback circled a stumbling man, keeping him caged in with their animals. Anytime he tried to dart between their mounts, they would close in, taking potshots at his feet.

The whole scene made Lisha ill.

Lago spurred his horse down the rise. The closer they came to the Comancheros and the fear they delighted on breeding, the more Lisha's insides tightened.

In the mixture of Indians, Mexicans, and Civil War deserters, she concentrated on one man swaddled in his own flesh. Sweat and dirt stained his once white shirt. The transversely running strips of his jacket made him appear even larger. His breeches, too tight around his rotund belly, flared at the knees and barely covered the tops of his cracked boots. His sombrero shaded most of his splotched face.

The man squinted up at Lago. Recognition set in, and a smile rippled across his puffy face. Waving a whiskey flask in the air, he shuffled up to them, his Spanish spurs scraping the ground.

"Hey, Lago, you back? Come drink with us."

Laughter bubbled deep within his chest. He took a long swig. Liquor trickled down his heavy jowls, and he wiped it off with the back of a hairy hand.

"That's Javier," Granger whispered to Lisha. "He's the bloated maggot who runs this outfit."

The bandit spied Lisha and Granger. He screwed up his face, trying to focus his bleary gaze. His fleshy eyelids all but cloaked his red-rimmed eyes. Within seconds a light glinted in their black depths.

"You bring us somesing, eh, my friend?" Javier asked, inching closer to take a better look at Lisha. "You bring us somesing to amuse ourselves with?"

His grin widened, revealing yellowed teeth too numerous for his small mouth. Swiftly he grasped Lisha's arm and pulled her from the saddle. His hasty actions were none too gentle, and her scarf gave way under thick fingers. Her half-braided hair fell across his sweaty arm while he hugged her against him. The bullets, carried in the bandoliers that crisscrossed his massive chest, dug painfully into her breasts. She bit back the tears and the panic that threatened to topple her courage.

The Comanchero reached out a stubby finger to caress her cheek. Cringing at the sight of the dirt caked along its fatty creases, she averted her head. Her rejection failed to curb his growing appetite. He clamped his hand to her chin. Nausea overcame her. She knew he intended to kiss her, and she would do anything to stop him.

Abruptly she twisted her head and bit down on his index finger. His mouth fell open in surprise. With a curse he let go of her chin but kept the tight grip about her waist. Making a quick study of her rigid expression, he roared with laughter, rolling his head on a squat neck.

"You will amuse me for a long time, eh, señorita?"

His chilling words froze her heart. Lago had intentions to deliver her down into Mexico . . . all in one piece. How would he ever be able to stand up to this drunken beast intent on using her for his own purposes?

Chapter
❧ *14* ❧

Lago slowly stepped down from his horse. To Lisha, his movements seemed greased in tar. "No, Javier. She's not for you, or for anybody here. She's for Chavez."

"Eh . . . Chavez?"

Javier blinked a few times, as if trying to clear his vision. He peered at her through half-closed eyelids. Relaxing his tight hold, he fingered a portion of her hair.

"Ah, is color the likes I have never before seen." He tugged at her braid, forcing her head back. "And her eyes, they are like a cloudy day. . . . For Chavez, eh? Yes, she is perfect for my friend Chavez." Laughter barreled from his chest, and his arms dropped to his bulging sides. "My friend will be most grateful, most grateful, indeed."

"That's what I'm countin' on," Lago said. "I've heard of him parting with extra silver when he's pleased. And I'm bettin' he'll be *very* pleased."

Javier waved a hand at Lago. "Come. Let us celebrate."

They left Lisha to face the ogling Comancheros. Most of them were dressed the same as Javier and looked equally as clean. Low murmurs and a chuckle or two spread throughout the group. They viewed her as if she were a juicy tidbit, a delectable offering—and the ceremonies were about to begin. Well, there wouldn't be any ceremonies. Lago would make sure of that. She prayed he'd make sure of that.

Sloan ordered Granger down from his horse, and she followed them to the wagons, where Javier and Lago shared a

bottle of whiskey. The man that the Comancheros had terror-
ized with their horses sat by the first wagon, mopping his
balding pate. She guessed he panted as much from fear as from
the bandits' exhausting game. He looked up at her with a blank
expression.

"We won't live through this," he uttered in a flat monotone.
"You realize that? We'll never live through this. I told them
not to leave us stranded out here, but they didn't listen. We'll
never live through this."

"Who are they?" she questioned.

"The rest of the wagon train. My wife got sick and couldn't
travel any farther. I buried her yesterday."

"I'm sorry."

"There's no need. At least my Alice won't be in the hands
of these butchers. Not like Mrs. Radford."

"Mrs. Radford?"

Almost before Lisha could get the words out, she heard a
low moan coming from the wagon. The man continued to mop
his brow. By the looks of how much he perspired, that would
be a never-ending job.

"Who's Mrs. Radford?" she repeated in an insistent tone.

"She's the young wife . . . widow . . . of William Radford. They stayed behind with us because . . ." He faltered,
his face growing red, and he lowered his gaze. What he had to
say obviously dealt only with women, and it embarrassed him
to talk about it.

"Because she had a baby?" Lisha prompted.

"It's not her time. Her baby's too early."

"Are you telling me Mrs. Radford is in that wagon now,
suffering a miscarriage?"

The man ducked as if he'd been hit. "It seems so."

"And nobody is doing anything for her?"

"There's nobody around here that can do anything, even if
he'd let them." The man indicated Javier.

"Well, I'm here, and I can do something."

Lisha immediately headed for the wagon. She thought she
heard Lago shout her name, but she ignored his call and
climbed on the tailgate. The temporary home was barren,
except for the feather mattress and the woman lying on it.

Mrs. Radford sucked in her breath. "Will," she barely whispered, "they have come for me." She turned her head toward the canvas. Silent tears angled down her glistening face. A sharp pain gripped her weak body, and she stiffened.

"Don't fight it," Lisha cautioned, placing a hand to the woman's fevered brow. "It's best to ride with the pain."

Mrs. Radford blinked and turned to gaze at Lisha. "Are you an angel, then? Did my Will send you?"

"No, Will didn't send me."

"Oh. I'd hoped he'd found help." Her voice faltered, and she bit down on her cracked lip.

"I can help. How long has this been going on?"

"Since yesterday, I think. Maybe longer."

"Have you had trouble before?"

"Almost a month ago. . . . The pains . . . they stopped. . . . But I don't think they'll stop this time."

"How far along are you?"

"Eight . . . eight months." Her voice broke. She averted her gaze. Any expectant mother knew the chances of her baby living if he were born so early.

"Maybe your baby is strong," Lisha encouraged. "Maybe he's as stubborn as a mule and a real fighter." She smoothed the woman's damp hair, the color of cinnamon, away from her forehead.

"He'd never let me sleep on my right side. He'd kicked 'til I turned over. He was such a kicker."

Lisha stilled her actions. "What do you mean, was?"

"Always moving, always. He was so active, but he stopped moving over a month ago." Another pain gripped her body, leaving her panting.

Lisha didn't like the sound of things. She felt Mrs. Radford's pulse. The hours of labor had made her very weak. "I'll go see what I can find to help you feel better."

The woman latched on to her hand with surprising strength. "Don't go out there," she warned in a frightened whisper, her hazel eyes growing larger. "They'll kill you, like they did my Will." She dissolved into tears.

"No, they won't kill me any more than they'll hurt you. Try to relax. I'll be back soon."

Lisha had to pry Mrs. Radford's fingers from hers. When she did, she felt like a traitor, but she had to find something that could help. Just as she stepped down from the wagon, someone gripped her by the arm and hauled her about.

"Thought I told you never to go anywhere without my say-so!"

Lisha glared back at Lago. "You did, but there's a lady in there who needs my attention, and I don't have to ask permission to help her just to assuage your manhood."

She wrenched free and marched over to Javier. He sat in the shade of the wagon, regaling Tyler and Sloan with exaggerated accounts of the band's escapades during their absence. Granger sat a few yards away tied to the wagon tongue.

"I want to know what you plan on doing to help Mrs. Radford," she demanded.

When he realized she addressed him, Javier stopped spinning his yarn. He acted as if he didn't know what she was talking about, but then, of course, because of the stupor he steadily worked himself into, he probably wasn't acting.

"The woman in that wagon is trying to have her baby, and I want to know what you plan on doing to help her."

Granger cursed softly and bent forward to closely inspect the bare ground at the tip of his boot.

Javier shrugged. "What can be done? I know nothing 'bout these things."

"Sloan, Tyler—is there anybody, anybody at all, who might have something to relieve pain? Besides whiskey, I mean."

Sloan scratched his head. "No, not that I can—"

"What about the shaman?" Tyler cut in, spitting tobacco juice on the ground.

"The shaman?" Lisha queried. "What's the shaman?"

"An Apache medicine man. He lost his followers when the chief's favorite son died of a sickness he couldn't cure."

"I don't mean to be disrespectful, but what would he have that could help Mrs. Radford?"

"Herbs. He's always out digging up roots of one kind or another. Why, he even has something to wash your hair with."

"Then do you think he might have something for pain?"

Tyler shrugged. "Might."

"Would you go ask him?"

He hesitated, looking at Javier. The bandit took another drink and wiped his mouth. "Go, find the señorita what she wants. Maybe we soon have two women in camp, eh?" He dissolved into a fit of laughter before taking another swig.

Tyler pulled the brim of his hat over his brow, leaving his scarred eye in shadow, and sauntered out after the shaman. Avoiding Lago, Lisha went in search of anything she could use to help make Mrs. Radford more comfortable.

A small group of Javier's men milled around the contents from the wagons. The piles represented years of accumulation and hardship, and the men treated most of it as rubbish.

She picked up a discarded petticoat and placed it over her arm. She could rip it up into bandages instead of using more of her own. Besides, Granger Hawks could breathe easier.

Smiling, she remembered the look on his face when she had stood in front of him with the sun at her back. She'd never realized that without her slips a person could see her shadowed form through the folds of her dress. That is, not until she saw the earthy appetite spring into Granger's darkened gaze, the same craving she'd seen on a night a lifetime ago.

Bits and pieces of broken china scattered over the ground interrupted her thoughts. Why were these men so destructive? It was obvious there would be no reasoning with this savage bunch. They lived like animals, thought like animals, and sniffed about a woman's skirts like animals.

Carefully she stepped over to a barrel packed with kitchen supplies. She rummaged through it and found a tin bowl, three mugs, and several pewter plates. Coming across a few utensils, she added them to her growing pile. A fork dropped to the ground, and she knelt to pick it up. Without warning, a knife sliced through the air and in a flurry of red dust split the dirt between her fingers.

Automatically she jerked back her hand, her heart beating frantically. Then, her temper gaining control, she wrenched the knife from the ground and stood to face a Mexican. Her anger mirrored in his red face. The man erupted in a rapid string of Spanish.

"I don't understand you!" she yelled over his tirade. "Do you speak English?"

"He can, if he's a mind to," Tyler cut in.

"Ask him why he threw a knife at me."

"That's easy. You're stealing from him."

"Me? *I'm* stealing? Just what does he think he's done? All this happens to be Mrs. Radford's belongings."

"Doesn't count. This stuff belongs to him now."

She gave an exasperated sigh. "Can't I have these?" The man stubbornly shook his head. "Then may I borrow them, just until we reach Chihuahua?"

The bandit paused a moment. Shrugging, he reeled off more Spanish. Lisha looked to Tyler for an interpretation.

"He says they're yours only until we reach Chihuahua, then he gets them back with no argument. . . . They're for his mother."

"I'll bet," Lisha spat out, locking gazes with the Comanchero. He grinned sheepishly and hunched his shoulders. She turned to go when a flow of Spanish again stopped her. "*Now* what does he want?"

"His knife."

Stupefied, she glanced down at the weapon in her hand. Holding it out butt first, she spoke straight to the man. "Tell him that if he throws it at me again, I'll throw it back. And I'm not as accurate a shot, so I might hit something other than what I'm aiming for."

The Mexican took the knife and muttered something to Tyler. They both laughed, and the bandit returned to his friends.

"What did he say?"

"He says it's too bad that you're going to be wasted on Chavez."

She figured there was more to it than that but didn't press. "Did you find the shaman?" Tyler knodded. "Well . . . what did he say?"

"He says he has powerful medicine. Too powerful for a white woman."

She slowly inhaled in an effort to curb her irritation. "Will he talk to me?"

"Might."

"Please see if you can get him over to the wagon. I need his help." Not waiting for an answer, she turned on her heel and left Tyler standing there to stare after her.

To Lisha, it seemed like an awful long time before she climbed back into the wagon. So it must have felt like eternities to Mrs. Radford. The slightly built woman stared impassively at the canvas ceiling. She hardly moved a muscle to indicate she knew Lisha had returned.

"I have some water to sponge you down with, Mrs.—"

"Please . . . please call me Flora."

"Flora? That's nice. My name's Lisha, short for Falisha."

"Pretty name, Falisha." A pain gripped the woman, and she gasped.

Lisha stroked Flora's brow with a damp rag. "Try to relax. You'll need to conserve your strength."

She sponged her down, thinking that all Flora might need was rest, then her baby wouldn't be so impatient to be born. But even as she fantasized, Lisha knew it was not to be. But the woman was fast losing strength. She needed help. Maybe the shaman had something for pain. Because of her uncle John, Lisha knew a little about herbs.

When she thought of her uncle, her heart ached to see him and the dear friends she had left behind in St. Louis. Had it been just two months since she'd last seen them? To her, it seemed more like two years. How were they doing? And Weston? Did he understand her reason for leaving?

Her sorrow must have shown on her face, for Flora's brow wrinkled. Lisha smiled and continued to sponge her down, talking about anything except the baby, the heat, or the Comancheros holding them captive.

Suddenly the wagon swayed, and Tyler poked his torso inside. Flora sucked in her breath and grabbed Lisha's hand.

"It's all right, Flora. His name's Tyler, and he won't hurt you." Lisha patted her hand reassuringly and went over to the deserter. "Did the shaman come with you?"

"He's outside."

"Why doesn't he come in?"

"Because he believes . . ." Tyler's face grew red. "Well,

he thinks . . . ah . . . he thinks that if he touches a woman givin' birth, or . . . or gets . . . anything on him, then his joints will swell and become painful.''

''Crazy superstitions!''

She pushed aside the sailcloth and stepped out into the evening air. An Apache stood a few feet away. At first glance he looked like the Indian who had held a knife at her throat, and it gave her a start. His manner of clothing was the same—symbols painted on a white shirt, breechclout over leggings, and fringed buckskin moccasins. He even wore his shoulder-length hair the same—parted down the middle and held with a headband. But there the semblance ended. The proud tilt of the shaman's head reflected his regal bearing.

''Do you speak English?''

''I speak.''

''I need your help, Shaman. A woman in there is having a baby. The child may be dead. She's weakening fast, and I don't think she'll have the strength to give birth. Do you have any medicine that will help?''

The shaman studied her with his fathomless black eyes. She mustered up all her courage to look him straight in the eye and not recoil under his intense gaze.

''White women are known for their weaknesses. My medicine is very strong.''

His cultured tones made Lisha wonder if he'd once lived in a mission home. ''I've used strong medicine before with a doctor. I have seen how he does things. He trained me. If you don't want to give her the medicine, you could show me what to do.'' Inside the wagon Flora cried out in anguish, and Lisha stepped closer, her hands outstretched. ''Please, will you help?''

The shaman took so long in answering that she thought he hadn't intended to. His eyes seem to bore into hers, but to her relief he gave a curt nod.

''I find yucca plant. Leaves hasten birth.''

Lisha slowly climbed back into the wagon, praying he would take precious little time. Flora passed in and out of consciousness, and Lisha kept a cool cloth on her brow. For Flora's sake, she tried to maintain a serene facade, but inside she felt anything but calm.

"Hey," Tyler called out a little while later, punching the canvas, "shaman's here."

Lisha fairly flew from the wagon. "Did you find the plant?"

The shaman took a painted pouch from the scarf that belted his waist and opened it up. He pulled out a buckskin bag, a root of a plant, and what appeared to be four tightly rolled leaves. These he gave her.

"From yucca plant. Salt inside. Have woman swallow this, and baby will come." He handed her the root. "Boil in water. Wash her to speed healing." Last of all he opened the bag, caught up her hand, and emptied a small portion of the contents into her palm. Lisha stared at the whitish powder. "For pain. To much will kill." He turned and disappeared into the dusk.

With a prayer in her heart, Lisha followed the shaman's instructions. She found that the hardest part was convincing Flora to swallow the leaves. After she did, Lisha sat beside her and waited.

She didn't know how long it took before Flora's pains became more intense. The woman no sooner relaxed from one pain than another followed. Lisha ached for her. She had assisted in several births with her uncle, but most had ended happily.

"Lisha, why won't my baby come?" Flora panted, her face a pasty white. "How long must I suffer?"

Lisha bit her lip. "Flora, I'm not positive, but I think something's wrong with the . . . baby."

Flora's glazed eyes riveted on Lisha's face. "What do you mean!" Her voice choked on a sob.

"There's a possibility your child will be stillborn."

"What . . . what gives you the right to say that?"

"Because I'm a nurse . . . and, because you said your baby had been active until a month ago, just before you started into labor the first time."

Her words seemed to echo in the canvased silence. She was suddenly conscious of the outside noises: drunken men milling around the wagon, the crackling of the fires, the loud laughter, and the crushing of whiskey bottles against rock.

"I know what you're telling me is the truth," Flora finally whispered. "Deep down I knew something was wrong when my baby stopped kicking, but I didn't want to admit it." Tears ran down her cheeks. "Why? What . . . what did I do that was so wrong . . . to be punished like this? First my Will . . . now my baby?"

Lisha refrained from answering. She cradled Flora in her arms, her own tears angling down her face in silent empathy.

Three hours later Lisha held a tiny infant in her arms, a miniature replica of her mother.

"Please . . . please let me hold my baby."

Lisha handed Flora her stillborn daughter. The woman ran a shaking fingertip alongside a silky cheek and lifted a cinnamon-brown curl with a colorless fingernail. Finally exhaustion took over, and she fell asleep. Salty tears dried on her cheeks.

Lisha gently lifted the baby from Flora's protective arm. Then she wrapped the tiny body in a quilt she'd begged off one of the bandits and placed the infant inside a silk-lined chest.

By the heaviness in her heart one would think that it was her baby she was preparing to bury, not someone else's. Why had this loss affected her so strongly? She'd seen grief before. Why was *this* so hard to take? Was it because the harshness of the land painfully reminded her just how fragile their existence was? Or was it because she fully realized that anyone could be snatched away in the space of a sigh?

She stepped out onto the tailgate. Weariness seeped from every joint and muscle of her body. With a fist she brushed the hair from her aching forehead and repeatedly wiped away her tears.

Knowing the ache of losing a mother, she now knew the bitter taste of how it felt to suffer the loss of a baby. Mothers and children should be together. At that moment she wanted so desperately to be held by her mother, to be told that everything would be all right. She wanted her mother to dry her tears, to sing her to sleep once more with a lullaby. How she wished she were here!

Listlessly she walked behind the wagons. When she thought she was well out of hearing distance, she sank to the ground and gave into her grief. Uncontrollable sobs shook her body as she desperately tried to dig a shallow grave with her hands.

Close by Granger lay on the bare ground. He had listened to the moans of pain coming from the wagon and was vividly reminded of the night his beautiful Rena entered the world, pink, wrinkled, and all lungs. There had been no silence then as there was this night.

Fondly he remembered how he had sat by Julia's side as she cradled their baby in her arms, professing that their daughter was certainly the most beautiful baby ever born. He couldn't see it then, but it didn't take long for him to come around.

He had wondered how Lisha was holding up under the ordeal. Now he knew. Her muffled cries branded his heart, and he listened helplessly. She had given much to others in her short life, but when she needed comfort, where was he? About twenty yards away tied to the tongue of a wagon.

He strained at the unyielding ropes and cursed. He wasn't even in a position to retrieve the knife he'd hidden in his boot. The Comancheros never thought of a man's comfort. Or a woman's.

Finally he could no longer hear Lisha's weeping. He tried to pinpoint her whereabouts, but the night prevented it. He yearned to hold her in his arms, to soothe her aching spirits. During the past few weeks, he had come to think of her as a dear friend. And wasn't that what friends were for? To help each other through the rough spots? Granger angrily kicked at the ground. He hated feeling so damned helpless.

Flora leaned heavily against Lisha. She had told Lisha that she hadn't been able to officially say goodbye to her husband; nothing was going to stop her from doing so to her daughter. But Lisha guessed that Flora's grief-stricken mind could barely comprehend what was said.

"Flora, do you want to throw on the first handful of dirt?"

"What?" Flora stared numbly at Lisha. "Oh! Oh, yes, of course."

Reaching down, Flora clutched a small amount of loose red earth. The particles filtered through her fingers, thudding softly against her grandmother's chest. Lisha cringed at the forlorn sound. This was not how it was supposed to have been. This was not the happy future Flora and her husband had dreamed of.

Lisha carefully guided Flora back toward her wagon. She had dared to give her a small portion of the shaman's white powder, hoping it would ease her aching heart. The drug had helped a little. At least she had been able to sleep.

She helped Flora to her bed and made her comfortable. Sleep overcame the woman once again, and she slept somewhat peacefully. Although every once in a while heartache would crease her serene face.

After two days of lingering in one place, preparations to leave were under way. Lisha could hear Javier as he shouted orders and refereed some disputes among his men as to what items really belonged to whom. The bandit had decided to keep the wagons instead of burning them to the ground, at least for the time being, and he had given Lisha permission to stay with Flora.

Finally the company pulled out, leaving a cloud of red dust and a tiny grave behind.

Chapter
⊱ 15 ⊰

The third knock, in what seemed as many seconds, sent Tilly rushing to the front door. Curious as to who the impatient person might be, she swung the door wide.

"Why, Mr. Clayborne!" she exclaimed as she slid her spectacles back onto the bridge of her nose. "What a surprise! Do come in."

Weston swept off his hat without so much as disturbing a single strand of hair. "Mrs. Ward, may I have a word with you?"

"Oh, my, is there anything wrong, Mr. Clayborne?" she asked, ushering him into the parlor and showing him to a seat. "You seem awfully anxious."

"More concerned than anxious."

"Would you like some refreshment? Tea, perhaps?"

Weston's stomach tightened at the thought of swallowing anything this woman might prepare. "Thank you for offering, but no. . . . Mrs. Ward, I am truly concerned about Miss Harrington."

Tilly's worried expression changed to one of relief. "So it's Lisha who's got you so wound up."

"Pardon?"

Tilly waved a hand. "You don't have to play coy with me, Mr. Clayborne."

"Coy?"

"I know how one can pine for an absent 'friend.' You might not think it now, but the wait is actually good for us."

157

"Good for us? Mrs. Ward—"

"It clears away the cobwebs." She gave him a sidelong glance. "It makes people realize what they're truly missing."

Weston gripped the brim of his hat. "Mrs. Ward, I need to know the whereabouts of Miss Harrington!"

"Why, Mr. Clayborne. You're a tease!" Tilly chuckled in delight.

"A tease?"

"Of course. We both know a man of your standing would *never* expect me to betray a confidence. You're here for another reason."

Weston breathed a sigh of resignation. "And what is that, Mrs. Ward?"

"You miss Lisha more than you realized you would. Now, then, about those refreshments. I've just made a raisin pie. Although I ran out of raisins and had to fill in with prunes."

Raisin and prune pie. He had the impulse to accept. The way he felt, he might as well finish the job.

"Rio Grande ahead."

Lisha leaned forward, straining to see the river. Thick bushes, cottonwoods, and dwarf oaks grew along the banks, covering a few hundred yards in both directions. The days had been strenuous for both her and Flora, and the prospects of a dip in the water, no matter how turbid, held her in anticipation. Dabbing at her face and neck with a handkerchief, she could almost feel the river's tranquilizing coolness on her hot flesh.

The tight-lipped Mexican who sat beside her on the wagon seat watched her from the corner of his eye. She pretended not to notice, finding that the safest route. Since they'd started out, she'd found too many men watching her. Their sunbaked faces reflected their wishful thoughts, and she didn't want to attract any additional attention.

The wagon in front of them swerved off, and the horses were reined to a stop. A high-pitched voice suddenly rattled off a scathing retort, and a woman alighted from the seat. The driver followed, his laughter mingling with her tirade.

With a tired sigh Lisha averted her gaze. Scenes such as that had been going on since a few members of the band had caught up to them with three fighting women in tow. She felt bad for them until she'd seen one woman sidle up to Javier.

Confused and a little sick, she found an excuse to talk to Granger. He'd told her that they were whores on their way to California, but the bandits decided to give the women an opportunity to carry out their chosen profession with the Comancheros, whether they wanted to or not.

At least with those woman around the men wouldn't be so apt to come after her and Flora. She knew she should stick up for them, but she was forced to play the game of survival.

"Are we there?" Flora asked, poking her head out into the bright sunlight.

Lisha smiled back at her. "Yes, we're almost there."

The woman's progress pleased her. Flora had gained some of her strength back and a little of her faith. Her obstinate hair strayed in a lively profusion of cinnamon curls around her head, and a pink tinge had started to replace the waxy sheen of her heart-shaped face. Her hazel eyes, once dull and glassy, had begun to glow once again with life. She felt better, but she still refused to venture outside the wagon except when necessary. Lisha hoped the lure of a bath would cure that problem.

The wagon pulled to a stop under the stretching limbs of a tall cottonwood. The sudden shade felt deliciously cool. Grinning like a child on Christmas morning, Lisha jumped down from the wagon seat and rushed to the edge of the Rio Grande, awed by its quiet strength.

"The river's overflowing its banks because of the rain we've had this spring."

The speaker's honey-rich tones sent hundreds of static fissures to her heart. She hadn't seen Granger for two days, and thoughts of his nearness turned her bones to water.

Turning, she gazed into his deeply tanned face. She noticed how bright the green flecks were in his brown eyes, the dark growth of beard, the pale scar running along his cheekbone, and the sensuous curve of his lips. Flustered, she lowered her gaze to his bindings and gasped at the raw skin underneath the frayed rope.

"Look at your wrists!" she cried out, snatching up his

hands. "It's an outrage for them to allow this." The rough edges of the rope burn had turned a dirty red.

"It's not so bad . . . now."

"Still, something has to be done." She began to untie the knots.

"Lisha, I don't think that's a good idea."

"Good idea or not, I'm doing it." She managed to untie one wrist and had begun to release the other when she caught sight of Lago's angry advance.

"What in hell do ya think you're doin'?"

"What does it look like I'm doing? A child could see that I'm untying this man."

Lago clamped on to her arm. "I know what you're doing," he growled, digging his dirty nails into her soft skin. "You're sticking that pretty nose into where it don't belong."

Lisha winced at the biting pain. She knew she should have hidden her discomfort from Granger the second she saw the clench of his bristled jaw.

"Let the lady go," Granger said quietly. His narrowed gaze stressed the threatening tone that underlined his words.

Lago released her. A hard smile curved the corner of his mouth. He could not mistake Granger's meaning nor his rigid stance. The two men faced off, as if calculating each other's strength and weaknesses. Neither backed down.

"What is matter, eh?"

Ambling up to them, Javier gripped the butt of his gun. His interruption slackened the men's discord.

"I'm taking the ropes off this man's wrists," Lisha spoke out.

Javier's grin lost some of its luster. "Why you do that?"

"The rope has rubbed his wrists raw. They need attention. That's why I'm untying him."

"He is strong, no? He be all right."

"You're a smart man, Mr. Javier, and a smart man knows that a healthy person brings in more money. How much do you think you'd get for him if he ends up with gangrene?" The likelihood of that happening was nil, but she banked on Javier's ignorance.

"How you know that, eh?"

"I know because I had to help a doctor amputate a foot because of gangrene."

A thoughtful look shadowed the bandits' faces. Only Granger's held a ghost of a smile.

"You fix him up," Javier grunted, turning away.

Lago followed, but not before he shot a warning glance at Granger and an angry glare at Lisha.

After gathering the meager first-aid supplies, Lisha sat by the river's edge and tended to Granger's rope burns. She'd applied salve and begun to wrap his wrists when she noticed his teasing grin.

"What's so funny?"

"You."

"Me, why?"

"You might have fooled those two idiots, but I've known you long enough to tell you were lying about amputating a foot."

She secured one bandage with a knot. "How could you tell?"

"By the slight stammer in your voice."

"To be fair, it wasn't all a lie. We did have to amputate a toe because a young boy drove a wagonload of supplies over the patient's foot."

Granger's deep chuckle touched her heart and captivated her soul. She hadn't heard him laugh for such a long time. And she knew it would be a while before she had an excuse to talk with him again. So these few precious moments were very special.

All too soon she knotted the second bandage. After gathering her supplies, she dared to look into his face. She wanted so much to throw her arms about his neck, to proclaim the love that grew stronger each day. But she knew she mustn't. No one must know how she felt about him, especially Lago. Thoughts that he could cause them both pain would give him great pleasure.

Lowering her gaze, she dipped her hand into the muddy water, searching for something to take her mind off Granger's disturbing nearness.

"May we borrow your soap?"

"We?"

"Flora—Mrs. Radford—and I. We want to make use of this river while we're here."

"If you do, keep in mind the quicksand and the bogs." He stood. "Thank you, Miss Harrington. I appreciate this. And if you want to borrow my soap, you're welcome to it."

Confused at his sudden formality, she turned to see Sloan coming their way. "Oh, yes, of course. Your burns should be fine now. Mind, I'll have to be changing the bandages." She turned her back, not wanting to see him bound and led away.

Lisha skimmed the top of the cool water with the palm of her hand, spraying Flora in the process. The woman gasped, clutching her chest, then giggled. Lisha laughed, thrilled with her steady healing. The moments when Flora forgot her loss occurred more and more. Then she would remember, and grief would pull a muted shade over her eyes. Lisha tried her best to keep that dullness from her friend's stare.

At first she had taken the roll of Flora's foster mother. She comforted her, fed her, bathed her, and cried with her. But when Flora's nightmares dimmed, the relationship gradually changed. To Lisha, it felt like a decade since they'd first met. Now a bond existed between them, a solid bond of sisterhood.

"Come in," Lisha urged. "The water's wonderful."

Shaking her head, Flora continued to scrub Lisha's dress. "No. It's best that I stay here. It's too soon since—"

"Then I'll wash your hair after I wash mine," Lisha cut in, trying to distract Flora's thoughts. She lathered up with the pulp of the aloe plant that the shaman had pounded from its root.

After Lisha rinsed her hair, she washed her chemise and pantaloons. The task proved to be a little awkward since she still wore them.

A piece of toweling lay ready for her when she would, no doubt, emerge with wet cloth plastered to her body. She wouldn't leave anything to chance. They had chosen a secluded spot. The added height of the river formed a perfect little pool in a grove of cottonwoods and willows, but she knew someone watched them.

Snatches of lewd laughter and splashing reached her ears.

The other women bathed around the bend, and with what she could make out, they were not alone.

Lisha washed Flora's hair. The red-brown strands glistened in the filtered sun. She wondered if the woman realized just how lovely she was. A man would cherish someone like her, so beautiful and as fragile-looking as a porcelain doll. She thought about Flora's husband. There were a dozen questions she'd like to ask Flora, but she held back. There would be time enough to find out, time enough to talk and share confidences.

"Thank you, Lisha. I couldn't have done it without you."

"Oh, it wasn't that hard."

"I'm not just talking about my hair. I'm talking about . . . everything."

"I had ulterior motives," Lisha answered lightly, detecting tears in Flora's voice. "I wanted a friend to wash my clothes."

"Oh!" Flora scooped up a handful of water and showered Lisha's face with it.

Lisha was not one to ignore a challenge, especially a water fight. The best medicine was laughter, and to Lisha, Flora's welcomed giggles sounded like a tinkling aria. Sometime later she relaxed against a tree trunk, far enough from Flora's reach. Her stomach growled.

"I wonder what delightful cuisine we'll have tonight?"

"Whatever it is, there'll be beans in it."

They curled their lips at the thought.

Granger watched Lisha from under his hat. To his annoyance she had become the camp's doctor, taking care of their burns, lacerations, boils, and bruised ribs. The Comancheros rode together, but not all of them agreed with one another.

He was glad Lisha had something to occupy her mind, even if it was nursing the sick and injured. Grudgingly, he could see the good she did and saw the growing respect she'd gained from the men.

The wind snatched locks of her hair and whipped them about her face. He marveled at how lovely she looked even though dirt smudged her now freckled face and grime stained her blue dress. Her untidy appearance lent a wildness to her beauty.

He squirmed. Lately the sight of her—even the thought of

her—ignited a craving in him that proved hard to repress. Breathing an oath, he chastised himself for having these blatant urges, especially in their situation, and cursed her for triggering them.

Hell's fire, he thought, reaching with agitated motions for a dirt clod and crushing it until powder ran between his fingers. *A woman hasn't struck a spark in me without my consent for two years. Why now? Was this any way for a decent man to think about an innocent woman who happened to be his friend?*

He knew he should stay away from her, drive her from his tortured mind. Even so, he'd used the excuse of needing his bandages changed, used her nursing as a means to see her again.

An angry shout broke his concentration. About one hundred yards away the shaman argued with Lago about one of the whores. As near as Granger could make out, the woman had taken the Apache's medicine bag, and he wanted it back. Lago had stepped in and stopped the Indian from using force to get his property.

For over a week Granger had been keeping his eyes open, trying to spot weaknesses among the men. He'd hoped to use their shortcomings, their habits against them. It didn't take him long to realize Lago hated Apaches—the shaman in particular. The deserter purposely searched for ways to needle the Indian.

In one smooth motion Lago pulled out both a knife and his pistol. Grinning, he pitched his gun to Sloan and agilely tossed his knife from one hand to the other, taunting his chosen enemy. A knife flashed in the shaman's hand. A crowd gathered as the men circled each other, waiting for the right instant to make their move. The sun glinted on the sharp blades. Dirt swirled around their feet as they lunged, ducked, and sidestepped.

Lisha had picked up a roll of bandages preparing to wrap a man's blistered arm when she heard the commotion. Someone, usually Javier, suppressed such skirmishes, but this time no one tried to intervene. She had the sinking feeling that everyone had been waiting for this battle, which was destined to end in death.

With a pleased smirk a woman watched. Her dark hair blew

freely in the wind. The neckline of her blouse rested well
below her shoulders, exposing the swell of her ample breasts.
She'd drawn the hem of her skirt up and had tucked it in her
wide waistband. She cheered Lago on, acting as if the fight
were some sort of game. Everybody treated it as such, but it
wasn't. Any fool could see that. Didn't life mean anything to
anybody around here? Wasn't anyone going to stop this
madness?

Metallic sounds rang out as blades clashed and held. The
strength of each man was tested, but each held his ground.
Then, with a sudden spurt of energy, the shaman forced Lago
back. The deserter tripped over the edge of the fire where a pot
of chili heated for supper. Sparks fanned out. A burning log
rolled to a stop at the tip of his boots.

In one swift motion Lago flipped to his feet. He lunged at the
shaman. The Indian suddenly dropped to the ground, lodged
his feet against Lago's stomach, and pitched him over his head.
The deserter's weapon flew from his hand and landed by the
horses.

Lago slithered in the dirt, groping for his knife. The shaman
dived underneath a horse's belly and latched on to Lago's
boots, curtailing his progress. The startled animals shied. Their
frantic whinnies rose above the jeering crowd as the men
scuffled between powerful legs.

Losing ground, Lago tried to keep the shaman's knife at bay,
but his strength seemed to ooze from his muscles. Sweat
streaked dirty paths down his face and into his eyes.

An animal slashed out, kicking the shaman on the side of his
head. His body fell limp. A few seconds passed before Lago
rolled the Apache off him and staggered to his feet. He stared
at the unconscious man who had almost killed him. It it weren't
for the horse, he'd be dead right now. Wiping the dirt from his
lips with a fisted hand, he glanced about for his knife.

Lisha's mind raced. She knew what Lago intended when he
scoured the bare ground for his weapon. Wasn't anyone going
to stop him? Acting on her impulses, she wrapped her hands
with the bandages she held and snatched the cast-iron pot from
the fire. Heat nipped at her fingers through the cloth.

Granger shouted her name, but she ignored the alarm

straining the tone of his voice, knowing if she hesitated, even for a moment, the shaman would be lost. Lago had retrieved his knife and confidently swaggered over to the Indian. With a cry she let fly the hot chili just before the deserter knelt to drive home his sharp blade.

Lago roared in pain. He danced about, frantically brushing the beans from his chest, face, and hair, and raced for the river.

Lisha dropped the pan and bent over the shaman, conscious of the laughter going on about her, especially Javier's deep chuckle. The Apache glanced about, his eyes half closed in pain. Blood matted his hair, and she carefully wrapped his head with the bandage encircling her hands. All the while he kept muttering something about his medicine bag.

She glanced up, looking for the whore who had started the trouble. The woman stood off to one side. When she saw Lisha striding purposely toward her, she began to walk away. Lisha caught up with her, placing a firm hand on her bare shoulder.

"You have something that belongs to the shaman."

"I don't know what you're talking about."

Lisha knodded at the bulge on the side of her waist. "I know you have his medicine bag, and I want it. It doesn't look right for two ladies to fight, but if it comes down to it, I'll win. I promise you that."

The woman hesitated. Shrugging, she pulled out the leather bag. With a flick of her wrist she threw it to Lisha, then tossed her dark head and strutted off.

A ghost of a smile flickered across Lisha's lips. Edward Harrington would have applauded her performance. She turned back to the Apache and almost bumped into Granger. A mixture of fear and anger creased his face. She sidestepped past him and headed toward the shaman.

"What the hell do you think you were doing?" Granger ground out, falling in alongside her.

"I did what no other person attempted to do—I stopped Lago."

"You might have stopped him from killing the Indian, but you more than likely started something else."

She dropped to her knees and placed the medicine bag in the

Apache's hands. He muttered something unintelligible and closed his eyes.

"I might have started something else, but I couldn't stand by and allow him to kill a man in cold blood."

Granger followed her to where she'd left her first-aid supplies. "Why? Why are you so bent on *nursing*?" He used the word as if in a curse.

"Because I can't sit back and watch people suffer when I can help, any more than your Julia could. And I mean to do everything possible to give these people the care they need in spite of what they are."

"Do everything possible? That's just it. Lisha, you've got to bridle yourself," he pleaded in desperation. "You're too bullheaded for your own good. And you're on dangerous ground."

"And so will you be, if you don't stop following me about. Don't worry, Lago won't hurt me. The others will see to that."

"I hope and pray they do." He jerked against his bonds and turned sharply on his heel.

Lisha headed toward her wagon, but in the space of a heartbeat she was wrenched around to face Lago. Red blotches marked his face. Water dripped from his plastered hair and wet chest. A cold hatred filled his eyes.

"Lady, you've caused me nothin' but trouble since the day I met you."

"Then why don't you let me go?"

"That'd be too easy."

"For whom? You or me?"

Lago's features hardened, narrowing the sharp angles of his face. "What do you mean by that?" He tightened his hold.

Pain shot through her arm, working up her neck. "I mean you take the easy way out. Tell me, is that the way you win all your fights? Stabbing unconscious men?"

She knew she'd made a grave mistake the instant the sharp words slipped past her lips. Lago scarcely breathed, scarcely moved. His coloring paled, then reddened. She stared at him, but there seemed to be no response, no life behind those glassy eyes. To her it felt as if time dangled on the rickety blade of a guillotine, time turned against her.

Suddenly Lago yanked her up against him. "I'll make you pay for saying that." The threat in his voice sent a lead weight thudding to her heart. "I'll make you pay for everything."

Throwing her to the ground, he pinned her with his torso and tried to wedge a knee between her legs. His free hand groped at her skirt. She struggled beneath him and heaved with her body. They rolled on the ground, stirring up red dust.

Help . . . help!

Had she screamed the words, or had they died a choking death in her throat?

When she thought she could no longer keep Lago at bay, he was pulled from her. Thick hands, none too gentle, helped her to her feet. She saw three men holding Granger back. He fought against the added shackles, his face crimson from the struggle.

"What ya stoppin' me for?" Lago spat out, shaking free of the men who held him.

Javier's joyful mood had vanished. His black eyes sparked dangerously. "I think it best the lady goes to Chavez."

"Yea," Sloan cut in. "Ease your guts on someone else. You might not care 'bout the money she'll bring, but we do."

"She's gonna pay. She's . . ."

Lago's pinched mouth formed a slow grin. A warning flashed in the back of Lisha's brain. Again, she knew that something terrible was about to happen. He looked over his shoulder. She turned, following the direction of his gaze—the wagon. Her heart froze.

"No!" she screamed.

Throwing herself at him, she clawed at his face and neck, tearing the fragile tissue of his burns. Two men pulled her back, holding her tight while the deserter climbed into the wagon.

Hearing Flora's startled cries, she propelled herself forward, kicking out with her feet, then dropped her full weight against the hands holding her. Yet they held fast. Again she lunged. Again she was restrained.

She had worried about what Lago might do to Granger or Rena, but she had never given a thought to what he was capable of doing to her friend.

Lago dragged Flora from the wagon. He threw her kicking and screaming to the ground. Lisha saw the terror on her face, and she was powerless to help. Lisha found she had no room to breathe.

The taunting crowd cheered Lago on. He acted as if he played the lead in a popular play. Flora pummeled his chest with her small fists while her skirts and petticoats flew about her.

Stunned, Lisha could not tear her eyes away from the horrible scene playing before her. Why hadn't she let Flora die in the first place? Because of her, she lived only to be violated. Why couldn't she have left well enough alone?

Laughing, Lago managed to rip away Flora's skirts and lowered himself down. Lisha choked on a sob, all the fight wrung from her, and she sank to her knees. She could shut her eyes to Flora's torment, but she could not shut her ears to her anguish.

Eventually she heard nothing but the crude banter among the men. Numb, she lifted her head, unable to think. Surely nothing could be worse than what she had just witnessed.

"Hey, Lago. Let us have a try."

"Yea, Lago. Take a bow. It's our turn."

Lago raised up on his knees. Straddling Flora, he bowed over one shoulder, then the other.

Lisha had thought the pain couldn't twist any deeper. She was wrong. Must her friend go through this again and again? To everyone's surprise, Flora snatched Lago's pistol. The vulgar remarks ceased. The smirk vanished from the deserter's face. He backed off when she cocked the chamber and steadily aimed the gun at his groin. Her easy handling of the pistol made it quite clear that she could use it. Lago's scratched and bleeding face turned several shades paler in fear.

In the breath of a second the stricken woman pointed the barrel at her throat, and before anyone could stop her, she pulled the trigger.

Lisha's shrill scream followed her into a blackened abyss.

Chapter
❦ 16 ❦

"It's . . . it's all m-my . . . fault. If . . . only I h-hadn't made . . . him angry."

The minute Lisha and Granger were out of earshot from the camp, the misery inside her poured forth. Granger carefully laid Flora's body on the rocky ground and took the shovel from Lisha.

"Lisha, I know that what happened to Flora pains you a great deal, but it wasn't your fault."

"Yes, it was. I—"

"Listen to me!"

She whipped around at the roughness of his voice. A shaft of empathy pierced his heart at the sight of her swollen eyes. She had cried away most of the night, and he wished he could hold her in his arms to soothe her pain, kiss away her tears.

"Lisha, you've got to understand what I am going to say. Flora lived on borrowed time. What happened to her would've happened anyway, and there wouldn't have been anything you or I could've done to stop it.

"She's married. To these pigs that means used goods, which, if sampled, wouldn't hurt her selling price any. They were just biding time until she gained her health. Normally they'd have passed her around some night no matter what her condition, but they're a greedy lot. They waited until she was well on her way to recovery. After all, they can't sell a dead woman."

Lisha sank to the ground. "Oh, Granger . . . if only I'd let her die in the first place. None of this would have . . . happened.'' Mindlessly she sieved through the crusty dirt with trembling fingers.

Granger hunkered down beside her. He placed a rough hand on hers, stilling her actions. ''Even if you knew what would eventually happen, you wouldn't have been able to sit back and not do anything. You're a fighter, Lisha. It's not in your nature to let someone die.''

When she didn't comment, he tipped her chin up, forcing her to look at him. ''Lisha, you've been around these men long enough to know what they're capable of. Do you honestly think they would have let her be?''

After a pause Lisha shook her head. ''I knew I'd be safe, I just didn't think . . .'' Her low voice quivered with tears. ''I feel so bad. I know it's wrong, but I still wish I could've buried Flora with her baby. . . . If . . . if I had only known then what I know now, I would've gladly sacrificed the friendship I'd found with her . . . if she could have died a more peaceful way.''

As each chink of the shovel's sharp edge clashed against the rocky ground, Lisha's tormenting thoughts replayed themselves.

For the next two days she kept to herself, not talking, not acknowledging anybody. The Comancheros noticed the change and acted as if they preferred her gutsy side to the docile one.

She hadn't even stood up for the shaman when Lago demanded that the Indian leave. Maybe the real reason was that Lago couldn't force the Apache to do anything he didn't want to. The time had come for the shaman to go, and she felt a little sad. After all, he did help her once.

As they crossed the Rio Grande, the other wagon lodged itself in quicksand. She viewed the danger as if she were in a dream. The bandits transferred most of its contents to her wagon and redistributed the rest to the men on horseback.

Before, she had looked forward to the prospect of arriving at El Paso, of quenching her thirst for civilization. But because of her blunted senses, she didn't care when they finally reached the town, a fertile oasis sandwiched by barren country. Javier traded the wagon for pack mules and supplies. While there, they met up with more of his men who had "merchandise" to sell in Chihuahua.

The following day they ascended from the valley of vine-yards, orchards, and grainfields to the wild broken desert covered with greasewood and mesquite. She ended up luckier than some; she had a horse to ride.

She took no notice of the country they passed through. To her it all looked the same. They were traveling deeper into Mexico. That's all she knew—or cared to know.

The day wore on and so did the wind. Distant sawtooth crests appeared to totter in the shimmering heatwaves that rose from the sunbaked earth. A haze of dust turned the steep sides of the cliffs to a pale blue. Ribbons of sand skittered across the trampled road. The land looked as dead as she felt.

Before sunset they arrived at a dirty, stagnant pool. Not a blade of grass could be seen, and they were compelled to leave the trail for a patch to camp in.

Too tired to eat, Lisha passed up supper. She welcomed sleep even though she felt that the second she closed her eyes, she'd have to rise again and start another day of endless travel. Her last thoughts were of Granger. She knew he rode ahead of her, but she was never able to catch sight of him.

The company began to stir long before dawn. Men filled canvas bags, canteens, and water barrels at the pool. After the animals drank their fill, the band pulled out.

As the morning crept into afternoon, the silent group came upon mountains of shifting sand in need of a sea. The glaring sun sparked against the gritty particles, hurting Lisha's eyes. The hills were barren save for greasewood half buried here and there in the ever-changing landscape.

The road had disappeared, but the trail was repulsively marked by the remains of animals in different stages of decay. Insects steadily hummed around the rotting carcasses. Her throat contracted at the unbearable stench.

On one ridge she saw the upper half of a human skeleton protruding from the sand. The bleached bones nipped a shiver of realism into her own mortality.

The sand became increasingly deeper, and she climbed off her laboring horse to walk. She sank up to her knees and gave out a startled cry. Her sore muscles almost prevented her from moving. Up ahead she heard the frightened whinnies of the horses trying to maneuver through the sand.

A terrified pack mule bucked in and out of the dunes. His shrill brays broke the morning calm. The ropes gave way, and supplies flew into the air. Some dangled down the animal's sides and against his rump. Then Lisha heard it, a definite bone-crunching sound. With a shrill scream the animal dropped to the ground. He lunged with his head, trying to stand. A shot rang out, and the mule lay still.

Some men gathered the supplies, and the company continued on. As Lisha passed yet another sacrifice to appease the insatiable desert gods, she averted her head.

The land they covered that day was almost unbearably flat. The sparse plants, the stony ground, and the constant reflection of the sun glinting against the naked soil and pale vegetation gave a brittle look to the Chihuahua desert. She longed for a cloud to appear and filter out some of the sun's torrid rays, but she knew by this time that clouds were rare. So she pulled her scarf farther down over her eyes.

In some places they passed communities of runty creosote bushes. Their olive-green color relieved the monotony of the bland landscape. Suddenly a horned toad slithered off a rock, startling her mount. The surprised animal sidestepped into one of the bushes, crushing some leaves under its hooves. A pungent odor rose to assault her nose.

Toward sunset the band reached a muddy watering hole. She was too thirsty to care whether or not it housed clear water. All she cared about was that it was wet.

That night the men camped on a large plain covered with mesquite. She relaxed in the gathering twilight, relishing the opportunity to sit on solid ground. The cooling air became a welcome transition from the blistering heat.

"Here," Tyler said, striding over to her. "I brought you something to eat. The hardtack we had for lunch won't keep you going."

Lisha thought of the biscuits and took the tin plate gratefully. The spicy smell of the tortilla convinced her that she was hungry even though she was almost too weary to eat. Tyler turned to leave when she stopped him.

"What will it be like tomorrow? Will the trail be so rough?"

"It won't be so bad. Around noon we'll stop for water at a little place called Star Spring and camp for the night at a small lake."

"A lake? A real lake . . . with water?"

Tyler grinned at her childlike excitement. "A real lake . . . with ducks."

She could hardly believe her ears. Wouldn't it be wonderful to go swimming? How long had it been since she'd immersed herself in water? After she ate, she settled down in her bedroll and dreamed of water, birds, and Granger.

The next evening Lisha stared longingly at the lake Tyler had promised her.

When the men prepared to camp, she finally saw Granger. The man looked worn but in good health. After taking his saddle from Saber's sweaty back, he glanced up. His face brightened under his growing beard and mustache. Lisha thrilled at the warm look capturing his face, and she smiled.

He raised a hand in silent salute, and she saw that his wrists weren't tied. The bandits must have figured he wouldn't stray very far from the protection of the company. Others had tried it, and their bones bleached white under the dazzling sun.

Lisha knew he didn't make a run for it because of her. She remembered the Apache's knife he had hidden in his boot. She guessed he waited for the right moment to escape, a time that would give them the best chance.

Just before supper Lisha, along with the other women, bathed in the lake. When the newcomers first joined the main band, she hadn't the strength to get to know them, to risk another loss. She felt sorry for everyone, including herself. They all had a dreary future mapped out for them.

Lisha sat, sheltered in the willows. She'd stripped down to her chemise, corset and pantaloons and had washed some of the trail dust from her aching body.

"Having a good time, eh?"

Startled, she whipped around. The sight of Javier towering

above her made her skin crawl. She clutched her dress to her breasts.

"I—uh—yes, I'm enjoying myself."

"Good, because tomorrow you not be so lucky."

She didn't like the sound of that, but the next day she found Javier had been right. They traveled across a bare plain that seemed to boast of having no streams or lakes. They were forced to camp without water for the animals or wood for the fires. Lisha huddled in her blanket and prayed that this thirsting torment would end.

The next day fared no better. Eventually she spied a large body of water that stretched as far as she could see, but when she noticed alkaline covered the marshy ground, her excitement dulled. The brackish water contained salt, leaving a metallic taste in her mouth, but she didn't care. If it hadn't been for the rainy season, the water would've been unbearable to drink.

Throughout the next day, every time she took a sip from her canteen, she was reminded of the foul taste. No one was happier than she when they finally camped outside a small village named El Carmen, near a pretty little stream fringed with alamos.

At mealtime she ate her fill of frijoles and chili. For the first time in days she felt like eating. A rush of restlessness accompanied her growing appetite, and she felt the strong urge to stroll along the stream, to lull herself into thinking that this harsh desert had all been a bad dream. Even the increasing wind failed to deter her. She noticed that Granger watched her from under his hat. With a saucy grin she waved and disappeared among the trees.

Lisha soon found herself sitting with her back against the trunk of an alamo, a cottage standing in the background. The scene smacked of something fairy tales were made of, the same elements as those stories she'd shared with her father. Except the cottage was really an abandoned dugout and the wind had increased its velocity to that of a full-blown gale.

Moments before, she'd noticed a yellow haze had appeared in the distance, filling the lower part of the sky. She'd thought the wind had caused a small dust storm. Now her hair whipped unmercifully about her face, and gritty sand stung her eyes.

Trees bent under the gale's fury, and she thought she'd heard a sharp crack. The dust cloud had now turned brown and had risen high into the air. Her visibility diminished at an alarming rate, and fear pounded in her pulse. This was more than the usual afternoon wind, a lot more. Why couldn't she have seen that sooner?

She tried to stand but could hardly maneuver against the growing force. Her dress molded against her body and billowed out behind. Leaning into the wind, she tried to walk. For every two steps she took, she felt sure the gusts forced her a step back. Making it to camp would be impossible, but she prayed she'd be able to see the dugout long enough to reach it.

"Lisha."

She could've sworn someone had called her name. Yet, how could she have heard it with this constant howling? Eventually she saw a form working itself toward her. Each labored step seemed to take eons to complete. When the form took the shape of Granger, relief spread through her.

As soon as he came close enough, he shouted something, but the wind tore the words from his mouth. She frantically gestured toward the dugout. He squinted into the haze only to shake his head in confusion. Clutching his hand, she guided him in that direction. Moments later the huddled shape of the structure materialized.

Adobe steps led down to the door. Granger used force, opening the door wide enough for only her to slide through, but she refused to budge.

"Get inside!" he yelled, his words barely reaching her.

"No!" She shook her head for emphasis and began to push. "Not unless you come, too."

Resigning under her persistence, Granger leaned his weight against the door. After several hard thrusts the opening became large enough to admit him. Lisha stepped inside and turned to help him shut the door, when she heard an awful crack. With a protesting groan, a tree fell across the dugout. A limb struck Granger, and he pitched headlong into the crude shelter.

Alarmed, she bent over him, feeling for any broken bones. She found none, but her hand came away sticky and wet. Ripping off another piece of her ruffle, she bandaged his head.

With all the strength she could muster, she dragged him away from the open door and sat against the adobe wall with his head cradled in her lap. The roar of the wind drowned out his breathing. Gritty sand filtered through the cracks at a constant rate.

Eventually Granger groaned and lifted a shaky hand to his head. He tried to raise up, then sank back down.

"Lie still. You don't want the bleeding to start again."

"What happened?"

"A tree fell on the dugout, and a branch hit you."

"Oh, is that all?"

"You must be all right if you can joke about it."

"It helps to keep my mind off my headache. How long have I been out?"

"I really don't know. Maybe a couple of hours."

A strong gust increased the amount of sand seeping through the cracks, and the limbs of the downed alamos scraped against the framework of their shelter.

"Granger, why don't we escape to the village?"

"Because it wouldn't work. El Carmen isn't big enough to get lost in, and the people wouldn't dare hide us. Javier and his men would burn the town down to get at us, and he would probably kill a few of the villagers so it wouldn't happen again. I couldn't do that to them."

"Will there ever be a way out of this?"

"There's always a way. Don't get discouraged. Something will come up, and we'll have our chance."

"How is it that you came to look for me?" She leisurely began to comb the hair at his temples with her fingertips.

"I knew by the looks of the sky what we were in for, and realized that you wouldn't have any idea. So with everyone busy shackling down the horses, I slipped off and came looking."

"I'm glad you did. I would've hated to go through this by myself." Another gust rattled the roof, and she tensed. "Do you think this place will hold up?"

"Women are all alike." She detected Granger's grin by the tone of his voice. "First thing they want to know is if everything is safe. This place will still be standing when my great-grandchildren are old.''

She stilled her movements. "I wonder how Rena's doing."

Granger clamped a hand over hers. He pulled it down to his lips and softly kissed her palm. "She's all right. You don't have to worry. You know Martha's taking good care of her."

"I miss her."

"I know. So do I."

He didn't release her hand, and her heart quickened as each breath he took fanned her palm.

"After this is over, could she come to visit me in St. Louis?"

Granger took so long in answering, she thought he hadn't intended to.

"I suppose there wouldn't be a problem in that."

"Granger . . . Do you really think we'll get out of this?"

"I refuse to think otherwise."

By the tone of anxiety in his voice, she knew he was just as worried as she. She could no longer cope with the tensions she was forced to live with, and silent tears began to roll down her cheeks. She tried to brush them away, not wanting him to know that her strength had evaporated. A choked cry escaped her throat, and Granger pulled her down beside him. He cradled her shaking body in his arms while she sobbed out her anguish against his shoulder.

"Go ahead and cry it out," Granger said in low tones. "Heaven knows you've earned the right." His mellow voice soothed her, calmed her torment, until the tears no longer flowed. Only involuntary shudders controlled her body. He placed a finger under her chin and raised her tear-stained face.

Gently he kissed her temple, her cheekbone, then the quivering corner of her mouth. She turned her head, and his warm lips covered hers, forcing her to dwell on other subjects. Each peck of his lips kneaded her rousing senses.

She knew the instant when his reassuring kisses changed to those of an ardent lover. Breathing a contented sigh, she wrapped her arms about his neck in answer to his demanding caresses. Her eager kisses matched his own, bringing along their own brand of intensity. He kissed her salty cheeks, brushed his lips against her eyes, nipped a fiery trail down her jawline, and teethed her trembling mouth.

She pressed nearer to him, to feel his rapidly beating heart next to hers. Groaning, Granger nuzzled his face against her throat, kissing her soft flesh. His hand deftly stroked the small of her back.

Thousands of stars exploded in her being, heating sensitive areas heightened for the completion of their lovemaking. She thought she would surely go mad because of Granger's skillful fondling. He engendered a blaze in her soul that matched the raging tempest outside.

The love Lisha felt for him threatened to devour her. She thought her wildly beating heart would burst. Now she knew why the course of her life had brought them together. She was meant to belong to this man, belong completely. Then why not here, and at this time? If the Comancheros succeeded in damning her to the sort of life they joked about, then she wanted what little happiness she could find enveloped in Granger's arms.

She yearned for him to ease this burning new to her, yet somehow not foreign, a throbbing he alone could satisfy. She hungered for his light touch on her bare skin, for his flesh pressed against hers. She ached for release. Why must he torture her so? Why must he make her wait?

Granger could feel the urgency in Lisha's kisses, sense the wanting in her body as she pressed closer to him. He had dreamed of this moment almost from the day they had first met. His craving for her had grown in the past few weeks, and now, it seemed, his desire governed him. With her, he could weather any storm, succeed in anything. Not since Julia had he felt the emotions churning deep inside. Was that what these feelings were? Love? He almost gave in to them . . . until he remembered.

"No, Lisha," Granger moaned, "I can't do this to you!"

He collapsed against her, his body gripped in tremors. Burying his face in her bosom, he hugged her close until he gained control of his passions.

"Why?" she mumbled, confused at his rejection. She wanted feast in her life of famine, not scant nibbles. She wanted him to make love to her, to be the first one, not a man she'd never met. She wanted so much to tell him of her love. "Why? Don't I please you? Did I do something wrong?"

Her voice cracked, and Granger gathered her to his chest. He nuzzled her ear and brushed a kiss across her cheek. "No, you didn't do anything. I'm the one in the wrong. If I gave in to what I wanted to do, still want to do, then there would be nothing to stop those dogs from setting on you like a starving pack. I can't throw you to those vultures, make you pay for one night of pleasure."

"But, Granger—"

"No buts," he commanded, lightly placing a finger across her lips. "Remember Flora? I would kill you myself rather than let those pigs have at you."

She took a steadying breath to still her inflamed nerves. How could she ever be the same when fire had almost swallowed her whole? She knew he was right, but she was afraid there'd never be a night such as this. A night where a desert storm boiled outside, while inside they created their own tempest.

"Come," Granger coaxed, settling back down with her head cradled in his arm, "we'd better get some sleep. We're going to need it by morning when they come looking for us, demanding an explanation."

She snuggled against him, certain she wouldn't be able to sleep. But fatigue soon took over, and she dozed off.

Granger listened to Lisha's steady breathing. He wanted to keep her as contented as she was at that moment, contented and safe.

Two questions plagued him, keeping him awake. Was it love he carried for this "Nurse Lady" or the strong emotions one friend had for another? Not finding an answer that he felt comfortable with, he, too, eventually slept.

Chapter
❧ 17 ❧

Lisha heard them first, especially Javier's gruff voice, spewing out Spanish profanities. Stirring, Granger opened an eye to the sun streaming in through the cracks and shut it.

"Tell them to go away. I haven't had all my beauty sleep."

"How can you joke at a time like this?" she whispered. "We have to figure out something to tell them."

"Tell them the truth."

"What?"

"Sure. Tell them how I found you, and how we tried to break in here for shelter. Tell them about the tree. But it's too bad that it had to turn out the way it did?"

"What?" His words deflated her sweet memory of what happened—what almost happened—between them. "Are you making fun of me, of last night?"

Chuckling, Granger pulled her toward him and planted a kiss on the tip of her nose. "I'm talking about what happened to me. I've heard tell that some people act a little funny if they get hit hard enough."

"Oh . . . oh, I see."

Maybe Javier would believe an explanation as farfetched as that. She hoped so. What else was there? She stood and looked through the cracks. Two men gestured their way.

"Well, here goes," she whispered, settling herself back down in the dirt and nestling his head in her lap. "I sure hope you have a bit of the thespian in you. I'm finding it's come

181

in handy for me.'' She raised her voice. ''In here. We're in here! The tree's blocking the doorway, and we can't get out!''

A shout rang out, and she heard several men converge upon the dugout. ''Things fine in there, eh?''

She could visualize the huge Mexican, his mouth curved in that perpetual grin of his. ''I'm fine, but Mr. Hawks is badly hurt. The tree struck him on the head when it fell.''

''He is dying?''

''No. But he isn't acting right. He hasn't been himself all night.''

With that Granger trailed a finger up from her midriff and threatened to cup her breast. Shooting him a warning glance, she slapped his hand away. To her irritation, he broadly winked and closed his eyes.

Amid the sounds of grunts, limbs scraping against adobe, and passionate oaths, the bandits were able to pull out the tree until light flooded the passage. Almost immediately Javier blocked the sun with his immense weight. The Mexican studied them intently.

She hoped they passed muster. Dried blood crusted Granger's dirty bandage and stained the front of her dress where she held his head in her lap. With a satisfied nod, Javier stepped aside to let Sloan and Tyler in to help Granger. As they shouldered him out, he weaved and blinked his eyes, trying to focus.

When Lisha reached the top step, she saw a blur of movement and felt a hand clasp her on the wrist before Lago twisted her hard against him. His shaggy hair fringed out beneath his sweat-stained hat, and his anger deepened his ruddy face.

''What happened?''

Lisha glanced at Granger. He sat on the ground, mindlessly rubbing the design on his worn boot. He meant what he'd said about the band never having the chance to get their hands on her. The Apache's knife lay inches within his innocently roving fingers, a knife that would penetrate her heart if their little playacting was not believed. Lago's fingers tightened.

''Take your hands off me,'' she demanded. ''You can see

for yourself that Mr. Hawks was and is incapable of forcing his attentions on me. Your money is safe.''

"How did he happen to be here with you in the first place?"

Stiffening her facial muscles, she looked at him as if she'd eaten something distasteful. "Being a man, I could guess his reasons, but he ended up helping me into the dugout. Then the tree fell, and he was knocked unconscious. He has a concussion, and a loss of memory, among other things."

"You mean he's crazy?"

With relief, Lisha felt Lago's grip relax. She pointedly gazed at Granger. "You might call it that."

"How long will he be like this?"

"It's hard to tell. He could come out of it in a couple of hours. Or not at all. But isn't that what you people would like, a docile slave always ready to do your bidding?"

Lago studied Granger. "Hey, Hawks!" he yelled. "Look at me." Granger blankly stared about him. With an exasperated sigh Lago shoved his way past a couple of men. "Bring these two. We've wasted enough time. Javier wants to get to Encinillas by nightfall."

Camp had been pulled, and the company milled about, waiting. When Lisha started to gather her things, the three whores grinned knowingly. One woman jabbed another with her elbow.

"What's Miss High and Mighty been doin' all night?"

"Ain't nothin' different than what we do," the other one chided, "only we're smart enough to sell it."

When they caught sight of Granger, their catty laughter subsided a fraction. "Honey," the third called out with a sway of her hips, "you must've shown him a whale of a good time. Maybe you've got talents we don't know about. Care to share?"

Cursing, Lago swung out and slapped the woman across her mouth, knocking her to the ground. "Shut up, slut, and get ready to move." He stalked off issuing more orders.

Trembling, the whore pushed herself to her knees. She gingerly fingered the split at the corner of her mouth. Lisha grabbed a piece of cloth and knelt down beside her. The woman pushed the bandage aside and, with savage motions, wiped the blood away with the back of her hand. Red fanned across her cheek.

"If I ever want help from the likes of you, I'll ask for it." She struggled to stand, and her two companions helped her to the stream.

Within minutes the band headed out. Having no time to eat a hot breakfast, Lisha had to content herself with eating jerky and hardtack along the way. Thinking of Granger and the night they'd spent together made the day pass swifter. Thoughts of him and his lovemaking brought a warmth to her cheeks. She felt a stirring from the pit of her stomach to her heart.

Her uncle's patient, Beatrice, would classify what went on between them as evil. Lisha didn't, because she loved Granger with her whole heart and soul. Besides, what kind of woman would be able to keep her distance if she believed she'd never again see the man she loved? How many women would shrug and coolly walk away, and how many would seize as much love as they could?

Their trick had fooled Javier and Lago, at least for a while. Now the Comancheros wouldn't keep such a vigil on Granger if they thought the blow to his head made him an imbecile. She had to keep thinking there'd be a way out. Especially after last night. She wouldn't allow herself to think otherwise.

The party passed Apache villages on the plain walled by Sierras. The nearness of so many Indians didn't frighten her as it would've done before. She almost felt invincible because she knew Granger loved her. Oh, he wouldn't admit it . . . yet . . . even to himself. But he loved her, all right.

That night they camped among the banks of an arroyo, and Lisha fell asleep dreaming of Granger. Lying in his embrace, she languished in his skilled art of lovemaking. The delicious warmth he aroused flowed through her veins, bringing to life every nerve. She grew hotter and hotter. Reaching out for him, she found only sand, cactus, and rattlesnakes.

The heat pressed unbearably down upon her. Words refused to slide past her parched throat. The sun burned her skin and relentlessly drew out precious oils. What the sun left, the wind took. Blackbirds glided in the heat waves above her. With a shock, she knew she was dying. *Dying?* The word screamed in her mind, but she couldn't mouth it. A heaviness shrouded her, but she couldn't break free.

"No!"

Lisha bolted upright, throwing her blanket aside. Men turned to stare at her. She gazed back in a stupor. Perspiration beaded her forehead. In agonizing slowness her dream faded, and her bearings cleared.

Her heart beat wildly as she looked about her. Never had she thought she'd be glad to see her captors. But she'd rather be in the Comancheros camp than mindlessly wandering the burning sands. Even so, the realism of the dream buried itself just under the surface, ready to emerge anytime she allowed herself to think about its horror.

They would reach Chihuahua later that day. She relished the idea. As they rode through an immense flock of grazing sheep, she knew they weren't far from civilization, which meant decent food, clean clothes, and baths.

Tyler reined in beside her. "You ready for Chihuahua, a city of romance?"

"After the desert, I'm ready for anything."

Lisha didn't fully understand Tyler's meaning until the company rode into the town. Tall cottonwoods, grass, roses, and most surprisingly of all, a fountain graced the middle of a plaza facing an imposing cathedral and town hall. The rather wide main street had been paved with river cobblestones.

"The stones are washed down every morning," Tyler pointed out, "and workers sprinkle the unpaved street to keep the dust settled."

From the broad boulevards lined with colonial mansions to the narrower streets where thick-walled adobe houses stood, the people had taken extreme effort to protect themselves against raiding Apaches. They had barred their windows, turreted the roofs, and enclosed their courtyards.

The city's magic worked its wonders, and Lisha could hardly believe that such beauty and life existed in a desert of death. A desert where a man could die in a dry arroyo, only to have turkey buzzards and ants pick his bones.

They neared the central marketplace, where Mexican and American merchants from Santa Fe held a brisk trade. Brightly

uniformed men mingled with professional scalp hunters in
buckskin and moccasins. Weather-beaten immigrants in heavy,
rough clothing bickered with vendors about their high-priced
tobacco.

Black-clad padres rubbed shoulders with dark Indian slaves
whose futures were grim at best. Wealthy ranchers, wearing
wide-brimmed sombreros and clothes trimmed in silver, assisted their richly dressed ladies from carriages and into the
cathedral.

Dirty-faced children raced their siblings around fruit and
vegetable stands while others hid in their mothers' vividly
colored skirts. Young wives jostled fitful babies who needed
naps. The sounds of laughter, agitated arguing, and children's
cries mingled with rapid Spanish, creating an energy that Lisha
could feel.

A few people stopped their haggling to watch the party's
arrival. A little girl with a runny nose stared at Lisha. She
smiled back, and the child quickly ducked behind a fruit card
only to watch her through a split in a board.

The Comancheros began to spread out the wares they'd
stolen from their victims and were surrounded by buyers. Lisha
had little stomach for the bartering over Flora's prized posses-
sions. She studied the overzealous faces. Was this a good
example of the way it would be when humans were forced on
the auction block? The thought sickened her.

She felt an intense gaze and glanced up. A man stood a few
feet away, staring openly. His buckskin garb looked as
unkempt as his person. His light brown gaze lowered to her
breasts, lingered over her waist and hips, then back to her face.
Like a starving dog would drool over a piece of anticipated
meat, he almost slobbered in his lust, his eyes bright with the
emotion.

Lisha could tell that he knew exactly why the Comancheros
had brought her here, and she could almost see him mentally
counting the money he had to bid with. Javier shuffled up to
the hopeful buyer.

"You like my goods, eh?" His heavy jowls pulled into a
grin.

The scalp hunter's eyes gleamed. They bored into Lisha's.

He rubbed the palm of his hand on his grimy thigh. "A man's gotta be crazy not to."

"I have many to choose from."

"Not interested. This one'll do jist fine."

"But I have bad news for you, señor. This one is not for sale. She is already spoken for. You come to Spider's Web, eh? See what else I have."

Naked disappointment reflected on the man's face. He took a last hungry look at Lisha before he gave a curt nod and walked off. She had the feeling that she'd see him later. In fact, she guessed she'd see many more like him at this place Javier called the Spider's Web.

Within the hour Lisha, along with the other captives, followed Lago and Javier into the kitchen of the Spider's Web. The heavy scent of spices and onions almost overshadowed the potent odor of liquor. Gleaming copper kettles hung from sturdy beams above a butchering block. The wood floor squeaked as a white-haired woman rubbed lemon oil into the planks.

A light-skinned man advanced on them. What little hair he had left on his head curled into blond wisps. A cheery smile framed his puffy lips but failed to reach his deep-set eyes. He rubbed his hands enthusiastically.

"Ah, Javier, you have brought me more guests. How delightful." He put an arm across the Mexican's broad shoulders. "Come, have a drink. We can discuss business while Rosa shows our lodgers to their rooms."

With awkward motions the frail woman rose from her kneeling position. She silently turned toward another door. Using the butts of their rifles, two Comancheros prodded those at the end of the line, forcing everyone to follow her.

They crossed a small brick patio and entered the main building. Rosa led them down a narrow hall, reached out a veined hand, and unlocked the first door on the left. Lago motioned for the men to go through.

As they filed past Lisha, she spotted the man who had been with Flora and who had helped bury her baby. He looked sallow in spite of the long days he'd traveled in the desert. Dark circles mapped a path around his eyes and stained his hollow cheeks. His skin draped loosely on his bones. He hunkered into his frayed coat much like a turtle would seek refuge inside his shell. Lisha hardly recognized him. He wouldn't last long.

Granger obediently followed after the man. Plopping down in a corner, he raised his knees to his chest and began tracing the pattern etched on the top half of his boot. As the door closed, he glanced up and his gaze locked with Lisha's. All in one brief second he had reminded her of his concealed knife and to have faith.

Rosa unlocked another door and stepped aside, not looking at anyone, not saying a word. Lisha somehow knew she was past feeling and could not help them.

"All right, half of you inside," Lago barked.

A Mexican girl, Lisha guessed to be a year or two younger than Juanita, gripped the arm of a woman. She started to follow her friend into the room until Lago stopped them.

"Not you," he ordered, breaking the girl's tight hold with a stinging swat of his hand. "You go to the next room."

The girl's lower lip trembled, delighting Lago. Lisha had to look away. She couldn't bear witnessing any more of his brutal games.

"No, señor," the woman pleaded, trying to block the closing door with her knee, "please, let her come with me. She es so young. Please, señor! I beg of you!"

Lago jabbed at the woman's leg with the barrel of his Smith & Wesson and pulled the door shut. Rosa obediently locked it. Lisha could hear the woman's muffled pleas as they continued on down the hall. Her stomach rolled in a tight ball of fire. She had vowed not to get closely involved with anyone else again, but the tears flowing down the girl's dirty face changed her mind. Lisha's heart went out to her. The girl looked up, and she gave her what she hoped was a reassuring smile. Pent-up air rushed from her chest, and her body visually relaxed.

The three whores and the girl entered the next room. Lisha started to follow suit when Lago's arm barred her way.

"We've got another place for you."

The woman Lago had backhanded brushed her hair from her

eyes. Hate tightened her bruised face. "My, my, my, look who gets special treatment."

The girl saw that Lago prevented Lisha from going in. She pointedly stared at the tight-lipped whores then back at Lisha. Her face crumpled.

"Oh, no," another whore sneered, "don't tell me we have to deal with her. Do we look like nursemaids?"

Study your character before you speak, Lisha, and your part will sound more convincing.

Lisha raised her chin to a haughty angle and narrowed her eyes. "Well, *honey*, I'm glad it's you who has to listen to the sniveling brat, and not me." She was pleased with the arrogant flavor in her voice. "As far as I'm concerned, you're welcome to the dirty little Mexican."

The girl's jaw dropped at Lisha's definite shift in looks and voice. Lago stared at her. The dark-headed woman, who had stolen shaman's medicine bag, charged at Lisha. Lago was the only barrier between her and daggerlike nails.

"I've met women like you," she spit out. "High-class women who pretend ta be all heart till it comes to the finishin' line. Then they sing another tune." She shook free of Lago's hard grip and placed a protective arm about the girl. "We can't offer her much, but we can give her sympathy. That's more than you're obviously willin' ta give."

Lisha yawned. "Just shut her up, whatever you do. I don't want my sleep interrupted."

Lago closed the door to the woman's vivid descriptions of just what Lisha could really do, and Rosa moved on to the next room. Lisha stepped inside her musty "cell," which boasted of a small window glowing with sunlight, and casually glanced at the wood-framed bed. The door squeaked when Lago swung it shut. She heard Rosa insert the key and the clicking sound of the levers sliding into place, then receding footsteps.

Sobbing, Lisha gripped her midriff and felt her way to the bed. Remembering the wounded look on the girl's face, she buried her face into a pillow losing its feathers.

Her father would have been proud of her superb performance. She hated what she had to do, but those women would have made the girl's stay unbearable unless something dra-

matic changed their minds. And she had to give them that
reason. Now the frightened child would have some comfort
even though it would be at Lisha's expense. Exhaustion
eventually took over, and she slept.

A few minutes, a few hours later, a key jangled in the lock,
waking Lisha. The sun no longer filtered through the dirty
window, and she wondered briefly what time it was.

Rosa silently brought her a plate of tortillas, then left,
locking the door behind her. Almost before Lisha could
swallow the first few bits, the woman returned with a pitcher of
water and a rag. At least she would be allowed to clean up
before Lago threw her to her merciless future.

Eventually the levers in the lock rolled again, but this time
Lago stood in the doorway.

"You finished?"

"Yes."

"Come with me. I want you to enjoy this." He clasped the
back of her arm and steered her toward the barroom. His
secretive grin made her nervous.

Lisha heard the roused men long before she saw them. Some
lined the walls while others sat around tables, dirty plates by
their elbows and whiskey bottles at their fingertips. Smoke
curled up from cigarillos only to hover at the stained ceiling.

The dark-headed whore stood on a raised platform wearing
only high-topped shoes, slips and a corset covering. Her skirt
and blouse lay at her feet.

"Come on," she goaded the men, "is that all you think I'm
worth?"

Leaning forward, she gave her rapt audience a perfect view
of exposed flesh. With a teasing smile, she pulled one string,
then another, loosening the band on her petticoats. As the men
shouted out bids, she slowly wiggled the material past her hips,
down her thighs, and dropped it in a drab puddle around her
ankles. She kicked the petticoats aside and, bending, ran her
fingertips along her bare calf. The combined din of catcalls,
stamping feet, and whistles was almost deafening.

"At first, Lisha thought the whore's character truly fit into
that of alley cats in heat, but then she realized just how shrewd
she was. The woman had successfully raised the bidding so

high, the common man couldn't match it. Only the more wealthy men could bid. Knowing she could not escape the buyers' block, she must have decided to labor in luxury. The woman teasingly played the game of survival and was definitely winning.

A short, paunchy rancher finally outbid the rest, and he rushed up to claim his prize. The woman held out her arms. He swooped her up and carried her to the door. Just before they disappeared, she blew a kiss to her appreciative audience.

Lisha looked around but didn't see Granger. "Where are the men?"

"Gone."

"Gone? Already?"

"Doesn't take long for them."

"What happened to Mr. Hawks?" she asked, trying to sound blasé. "Did he ever regain his senses?"

"Not that I could see. He went right along with the others."

When Lago didn't offer any more, she decided to let the matter drop. Again the men raised a commotion. Searching through the crowd, she spied Sloan pulling the Mexican girl up to the front. She felt as if the air had been purged from her lungs.

"She's the last one . . . besides you. Thought you'd be mighty interested in findin' out what happens to the 'dirty little Mexican girl.' Seein' how you're not really so carin' and all."

Lisha ached to strangle the laughter from his throat.

Sloan pulled the girl up onto the block. She stared out over the sea of faces, wringing her hands among the folds of her skirts. The proprietor of the Spider's Web clinked a spoon against a glass, and the room quieted.

"Now, what am I bid for this lovely, innocent young girl?"

"Ten dollars," a man roared out.

"I said she was innocent, not insane! Now, gentlemen," he continued after the laughter had died down, "we can do better than that? Who'll start the bidding at twenty-five dollars?"

"How can we bid if you don't show us her wares?"

"Probably 'cause she ain't got nothin' ta show us."

The men succumbed into another fit of drunken laughter, and the proprietor raised his hands to calm them. "Now, gentlemen, that's not the way to treat a visitor to this fair city. So let's have a little bit of decency." He suddenly reached over and ripped open the girl's bodice, displaying her budding breasts before she frantically scurried to cover herself, "See, gentlemen? We have a rose here in the beginning bloom of womanhood. Now . . . what am I bid?"

Lisha watched the tears flow down the child's face, splashing onto her hands, while she gripped the torn material of her bodice. Lisha's heart went out to her. Always, she'd carried the hope that at the last minute everyone would be set free, but now she knew this thinking to be childish. Now, she fully understood the reason behind this awful place. Once an unprotected fly is snared in the sticky web, there is no releasing it.

The bidding stopped, and the clamor ebbed. Lisha strained to see who had outbid the rest. The buyer stood, and she recognized the scalp hunter from the marketplace.

Anguish and fear numbed her body. She couldn't think, and she was long past praying for help. She had to look away as the man dragged the hysterical child out the door.

"Told ya you'd like ta know."

Lisha's breathing became shallow. The blood pounded in her temples. She never knew she could hate a person as much as she hated Lago. His smile grew.

"Come on, Nurse Lady, it's your turn."

"I thought you were saving me for Chavez."

"I am. But that don't mean we can't appreciate a little of his bought goods."

"I bet your mother weaned you much too soon . . . *if* you ever had a mother." She knew she'd hit a painful cord when his smug look changed to one laced with contempt.

"I ain't never had no use for my . . . dear . . . mother, an' she ain't never had no use for me," he blurted out. "Not since I was six." Instantly his manner changed from hot to cold. "Come, you have an audience waitin'." He clamped hold of her arms and started to propel her through the men.

Bending forward, she slung up her arms, shrugged from his hold, and whipped around to face him. "I don't need your help, thank you. I am a lady, and I demand that you treat me like one.

I'll not be hauled up before these men like a common whore."

Lago shrugged and gave an exaggerated bow. She swept past his extended hand. As the men caught sight of her, the murmur died, then expanded into a thunderous roar. She carried her back ramrod straight and her chin up. The bidders' shouts and whistles grew louder the closer she got to the auction block. Men pinched her, grabbed at her soiled clothes, and caressed her buttocks and thighs, but she didn't lose a step.

"Hey, Lago," one man called out as she turned to face the cheering crowd, "why did yah wait so long ta bring her out? Don't yah know I spent my last dime?"

"She's not for sale."

"Then why yah tormentin' us?" another shouted. "I can't sit straight as it is."

The lewd joke delighted the men, and Lisha cringed at their obvious pleasure in it.

"I just thought you men would like to see what makes her so valuable. And, besides," he muttered under his breath, "I'm paying back a long overdue debt." With a smug look Lago reached out to rip open her bodice.

"I wouldn't do that if I were you," Lisha said.

"And who's goin' to stop me?" Lago laughed at the absurdity of her warning. "You?"

Her pent-up anger finally erupted, and she struck out with her elbow, catching him hard on the throat. He pummeled off the makeshift stage and into a nearby table. The force knocked a drunk from his chair, a liquor bottle fell spurting whiskey, and shot glasses crashed to the floor.

After a moment of stunned silence a voice rose from the back. "I don't know who's paid for her, but he'll sure have his hands full, and I don't mean with tits." That broke the stillness, and the men cheered her with raised glasses.

Lago struggled up, spitting blood. He steadied himself with the back of a chair. "Grab her!" he choked out, climbing onto the platform. At his command two bandits seized Lisha's arms.

"What's the matter, Lago?" someone yelled. "She too much of a woman for yah? Thought you was a great lover. Didn't know yah had ta have help holdin' 'em down."

Like a winter rabbit, Lago whitened, then profusely reddened at the crowd's jeering laughter. He lurched toward Lisha. "For that," he warned softly, anchoring his icy fingers in the material at her collarbone, "I'm going to strip you naked right in front of everybody."

Chapter
❧ 18 ❧

With a hefty yank Lago ripped off Lisha's sleeve and brandished it above his head. A gunshot rang out, and a closely aimed bullet tore the material from his hand. Cursing, he gripped his singed fingers.

"I believe you are tampering with my merchandise." A quiet voice penetrated the room. "I do not like soiled goods. Release her."

Lago stared at Lisha long and hard. Reluctantly he nodded for the men to let her go. She knew she would not like to meet up with him again, especially alone . . . especially after she had made him a laughingstock.

She scanned the back of the room to see what kind of man ordered virginal women with fair coloring and saw him standing just inside the doorway, a smoking pistol in his hands. A broad-brimmed sombrero shaded his face. She knew by the expensive cut of his clothes, by the proud tilt of his head, and by the thrust of his shoulders that he took great pride in his appearance.

The man had wealth. He displayed it with a silver hatband, silver buttons on the snug jacket enhancing his lean build, and silver trim up the sides of his tight breeches, which flared at the bottom. A red sash encased his waist.

He wove his way through the crowd. Lisha could see that his finely chiseled features, almost delicate, belied the tempered steel of his voice. Everything about him seemed neat and tidy, right down to the thin mustache that sloped above his top lip.

He glared at Lago, backing the deserter off, before leveling his almond-shaped gaze on her. She noticed that his thick lashes curled above somber eyes, as dark and mysterious as the man himself.

She refrained from shying away. Not even when he ran a thumb down the side of her cheek or fingered a coil of her hair. She didn't care for the way he surveyed her, like a rancher would examine a possible brooding mare. His actions filled her with hostility.

He muttered something underneath his breath. She couldn't understand what he'd said, but from the tone of his voice, she knew he was pleased with his purchase.

"Let me introduce myself, Señorita Harrington," he said, his Spanish accent seducing the words, "I am Don Esteban Chavez, and I welcome you to Chihuahua."

Bowing over her hand, he brushed her knuckles with his lips. He surprised her with his stately manners along with the knowledge of her name. She wondered what else the Comancheros had told him.

"Ah, Señor Chavez," Javier interrupted, hurrying from the back room. His thick sides heaved from the exertion. "I am just now told you are here. You like what we bring you, eh?" He blinked several times, trying to focus on his patron.

Esteban's dark eyes glittered. "She interests me very much. I am slow in coming, but I see I am just in time to protect my investment. I trust she is everything that I had ordered?" He directed his black stare at Lago.

"*Sí*," Javier joyfully announced with a belch. "She is all you ask for. We go in back room and discuss business, eh?"

"There is plenty of time to discuss business tomorrow morning at my hacienda. For now, I am sure Señorita Harrington would appreciate a restful night. Señors."

Esteban inclined his head at the two Comancheros and motioned for Lisha to proceed him out of the smoky barroom. It was then she realized that he still gripped his pistol in his hand.

Voices rose in the crowded room. Sweeping past her buyer, she made her way through the human obstacles. No one tried to fondle her as they had done before. They didn't dare. Not while Chavez cradled a gun in his hand.

Before she stepped out into the night, she felt an overwhelming sense of dread raise the hair on the nape of her neck. Automatically glancing back, she locked gazes with Lago. She had never seen as much hate coiled up inside one man as she now faced. He must thrive on it. Raising his finger, he briefly touched the brim of his hat.

Esteban handed Lisha up into a richly turned-out carriage. She sank in the leather seat and fixed her gaze through the window. The don sat across from her. His lazy scrutiny differed from the Comancheros in feel. Theirs reeked of lust; his felt more like fatherly curiosity. She didn't know what to make of it.

"Was the journey unbearable?"

Lisha stared at him. Myriad painful emotions played across her mind. *Was it unbearable?* She was jerked from what promised to be a very satisfying job, dragged through the blistering desert, came near to losing her scalp, witnessed the horrible death of a woman she had grown to love as a sister, was almost consumed by thirst and heat, was forced to wear the same clothing without a decent bath, and he was asking if the trip was unbearable. Giving what she hoped was a scathing glare, she turned her attention back to the window.

"I am not like the others, señorita, I am not a beast. I understand what hardships accompany such a journey. You might not think it now, but you will come to take pleasure under my care. I promise you."

Lisha kept her face averted. Esteban said nothing else for the rest of the trip. She didn't know which way they headed. In this land of endless desert, she had lost all sense of direction, but wherever it was, she gloried in the luxury of riding with her knees solidly planted together.

She hadn't realized that she had fallen asleep until the mild rocking of the coach stopped and a hand gently shook her.

"Señorita Harrington, we are here."

Lisha raised heavy eyelids and looked about in a daze. Recognition set in, and she pushed the don's hand away. Her action resulted in his amused chuckle. Irritated, she sat bolt upright.

Esteban climbed down from the coach and turned to help her. With reluctance she gave him her hand and stepped onto a courtyard paved with brick. Moths flitted about oil lamps lighting the way to the heavy paneled doors that led into an impressive mansion.

As they stepped inside the entry, a dour-faced woman briskly walked down the hall toward them. Her heals clicked on the coffee-brown tiles, a set of keys jingled from her belt. Because of her matronly appearance, Lisha thought the woman middle-aged, but as she drew nearer, Lisha noted her youthful skin.

"Margherita, please take Señorita Harrington to her room."

The woman curtly nodded and led the way down a hall. Hanging lamps supported by decorative brackets of iron lit their way. The mansion boasted of the same high ceilings and richly textured stone walls as Granger's ranch house.

They passed the sitting room, and she caught a glimpse of an intense flagstone floor waxed a glossy black. Mesquite furniture faced a fireplace with a deep shell head and a raised hearth of stylized blue and white tile. Shell-crested windows opened to an enclosed patio. Obviously Don Esteban Chavez thrived in extreme luxury.

Margherita opened a door, and Lisha stepped inside her room. The first thing that caught her eye was the iron grillwork encasing the window. What was its purpose? To keep the Apaches out . . . or her in?

In a sudden rise of temper she marched over and yanked the curtains shut. She turned just in time to see the door close and to hear the key in the lock. With effort she controlled her anger at being treated like a prisoner and eventually realized that this wasn't just a bedroom, but a spacious suite.

She stood in a small drawing room. Gray stone walls rose above a black masonry floor veined with dark red. A walnut desk took up half the space while a settee and chairs took up the other. A wrought-iron chandelier with intricate scrollwork hung from the chinked ceiling.

A melody of pink tones played itself from the brass vase of

gladiolus sitting on the desktop to the deeper shades in the sofa and throw rug. A few books and earthenware jars occupied a bookshelf that had been carved out of the wall. It, too, boasted of a shell-shaped top. The don certainly took pains to make her "cell" look anything but.

In the next room a wrought-iron bed rested on a large pink rug. The feather mattress enticed her to stretch out and sleep. On the opposite side of the room, locked doors led to what she guessed to be a patio, and she knew it would be enclosed with a very high masonry fence.

She turned and faced what appeared to be a beggar. The girl's sudden appearance startled her. Her dress, a faded blue, was filthy and torn in several places. Her white-gold hair wildly framed a face touched by the sun. Her eyes held a bleak, almost haunted expression.

Lisha's mouth fell open. She had been staring at her own reflection in a full-length mirror. Drawing nearer, she could make out the smattering of freckles across the bridge of her nose.

Lacking heart to investigate further, her attention passed on to a polished mesquite wardrobe. Curious, she flung open its doors and found the closet full of clothes. Their pastel hues suited her coloring. She wondered how on earth the don could have guessed her size. Then she realized that the gowns were several different sizes and lengths. The discovery made her feel as if she should be on a production table in a china doll factory, a factory that put out nameless faces to fit the don's orders. With a snort, she slammed the doors shut.

Wandering into the third room, she found a porcelain tub complete with claw feet sitting on a raised platform. What a delight! She'd dreamed of soaking in a tub for days and now yearned to slide into foamy bubbles, but a pitcher of water and a set of towels on a nearby table told her the luxury would have to wait. At least she'd be able to change by the looks of the clothing that had been placed next to the soap dish.

A silver-handled hairbrush, comb, and hand mirror rested on a dressing table, and upon further investigation, she found a locked door near a tall chest of drawers. A second door opened up into a chamber room.

Haphazardly she pulled open a few drawers to the dresser and found everything a young woman would need and more, from delicately laced handkerchiefs and underwear to gossamer nightgowns. She had to give the don credit. He'd thought of everything.

After Lisha had taken a sponge bath, she grudgingly slipped the silk nightdress over her head. The material felt whisper soft against her skin, a welcome change from the scratchy horse blanket.

Another delightful change since the past few weeks proved to be the cool sheets she climbed between. Taking a deep breath of their clean scent, she stretched her tired limbs in feline grace. The feather bed enfolded her flaccid body, deliciously working its magic.

As she drifted to sleep, she thought how she'd so readily accepted the hospitality of Don Esteban Chavez. No one had forced her to wear the clothes laid out for her, nor made her climb into the bed. She could have ignored these civilized comforts to protest her treatment, but what good would that have done? She remembered reading about the killdeer in her studies. The mother bird flops about with a wing that appears to be broken and draws any predators away from her nest.

With a drowsy smile she snuggled down into the sweet-smelling sheets and thought of the conning bird. She would copy its natural instincts. She would camouflage her dislike at being made a prisoner by pretending to accept the inevitable. Later, she would fight.

Granger's hat covered his face. Feigning sleep, he lay, listening to the rhythmic snores of the other prisoners. After their buyer had paid for them, they'd started the long trek to the mines.

The number of men sold to dig for silver had surprised him. Javier and his band were not the only ones who profited from their fellow man's misery, and all the victims fell to the same fate that the Comancheros had staked out for him.

At least this experience taught him one thing. The foreman who worked for the man named Chavez considered him worth

a considerable amount of money. Too bad. The man would
soon lose his boss's investment.

Granger slid the knife from his boot. He painstakingly sawed
at the coiled rope binding his wrists. Stopping every few
minutes, he listened to see if the wandering guard detected his
movements. After his hands were freed, he worked on the
bands at his ankles. Then he gathered up his things and waited
by a mesquite bush for the return of the guard.

Finally the man came within a few feet. Granger leapt up
from behind, clenched his arm around the guard's neck, and
clamped a hand to his mouth. After a struggle the man's body
fell limp from lack of air.

Granger dragged him behind a pile of rocks and quickly
stripped him of his clothes. He bound the guard's hands and
feet and gagged his mouth with a bandanna.

As he crept to the tethered horses, the night's sounds
covered his movements. When Saber caught his scent, the
animal tossed his head and nickered softly. Granger quietly led
the buckskin well out of hearing range before saddling him.

No one knew that he rode off into the night, and hopefully
wouldn't know until hours later, when it would be too late.

Chapter
❧❦ 19 ❧❦

The next morning a sudden swish of drapery and glaring light made Lisha press her eyelids tightly together. After a few seconds she hazarded a peek to catch Margherita opening the doors to the patio. The scent of blooming flowers rushed in with the morning air. She could see a glorious array of colors, greenery . . . and the expected fence.

Lisha sat up. Drawing her legs to her chest, she clasped her arms around her calves and rested her chin on her knees. She stared at the beautifully kept garden and table and chairs made of wrought-iron.

"What beautiful flowers. Whoever takes care of them does a marvelous job."

A ghost of a smile crossed Margherita's lips and just as quickly vanished. She picked up a breakfast tray laden with a bowl of strawberries saturated in cream, a plate of sliced sweet bread, and a pot of hot cocoa and placed them on the table.

"Come, eat. I have your bath waiting."

Throwing back the comforter, Lisha leapt out of bed. Her taste buds watered at the rich aroma of cocoa. She'd become accustomed to the popular drink on the trek here because the Comancheros drank it more than they did coffee.

She didn't know which she wanted to do first: ease her craving for food that wasn't rolled up in a tortilla or soak for hours in a tub of soapy water. Unable to make a choice, she decided on both.

"Please bring the tray, Margherita. I'll eat while I soak."

Lisha quickly slipped off her nightdress and slid into the tub.
She found the water to be almost too hot, but she didn't mind,
not in the least.

Margherita silently complied to her request. After setting the
tray on a small table, next to a fresh set of towels and a bucket
of water, she drew it toward the tub and handed Lisha the bowl
of fruit.

"I come back later." Margherita glanced about, as if
checking to see that she had everything in order, then left the
room amid the soft rustle of petticoats.

Lisha didn't mind the sound of the key jangling the lock. She
was too busy savoring her first spoonful of strawberries. The
coarse sugar and heavy cream added to their luscious taste. An
hour later all that she'd left in the dishes were a few crumbs, a
trace of cream, and a ring of cocoa.

For the third time Lisha lathered up her hair. She'd wanted
to rid herself of every trace of the desert, real or imaginary.
Sliding under the water, she tried to rinse out the soap, but only
succeeded in adding to those bubbles already clinging to her
glistening body. She sat up with her wet hair streaming down
her face. As she groped for the half-filled bucket to use for the
final rinse, she heard the door open.

"Margherita, will you please pour the rest of the water over
my hair?"

Lisha heard the clink of the metal handle striking against the
bucket and felt the tepid water splash over her head. She
worked the rinse through her hair while some of it spilled
languorously down the back of her head and over her neck and
shoulders.

"You're too far back."

The bulk of the bucket was then dumped squarely on her
crown. She threaded her fingers through the strands and wrung
them free of excess water.

"Hand me a towel, please."

The words were hardly uttered when she felt the fluffy
material pressed into her outstretched hand. Grabbing it, she
dried her eyes before standing. Hoards of bubbles clung to her
body. Briefly she wondered if she should take another bath just
to rinse off.

Bending forward, she allowed her dripping hair to stream over her face. As she began to drape her head, she glanced down. To her shock, she saw a booted pair of feet. Or thought she had before water blurred her vision. She quickly blotted it away and stared through dripping tendrils to see shiny black leather and wide pant legs with silver buttons.

With a cry of outrage she quickly wrapped the towel around her. She jerked up her head to lock with a pair of black eyes. "How dare you come in here without my permission."

"This is my home. I go where I choose."

She did not like the tone of his voice, nor the way his eyes narrowed. He stared at the edge of the towel lying against her thighs. She gripped the cloth between her fingers.

"What do you want? Certainly not to—"

"Javier and Lago came for their payment this morning. Because I am so pleased with you, I generously paid them for your safe arrival." His wide smile failed to charm her.

"I have no desire to hear of your dealings with those heartless butchers."

"They told me of your friend. I am truly sorry."

She glanced away, biting her lip. "If you're here to chat—"

"I came mostly to tell you that because of an emergency, I cannot spend the day with you. Nor can I the night."

She snapped her head back around. His features remained calm, but his eyes clearly projected his meaning. She raised her chin.

"How long will you be gone?"

"I shall be back tomorrow for dinner. After which we will spend the evening together."

"Any preference to which nightgown I wear?" she bit out. "You bought *me* so many."

A slight smile curved his lips at her outburst. "You object to that?"

"I object because everything you have here could be worn by almost anyone. It makes me feel like a nameless face."

The don eyed her, nodding thoughtfully. "Shall I have a few garments made especially for you?"

"That would be a start."

He sobered. "Am I to believe," he asked, his voice quickening, "that you are resigned to your stay here?"

"What choice do I have? And where, in this desert, would I go if I did get loose?"

"True, Señorita Harrington, where would you go if you did succeed in slipping past my guards?"

"Besides," she added with a haughty tip of her head, not mistaking his hidden warning, "as you said, I will eventually come to take pleasure in being under your care. I realized last night that one of those pleasures would be nice things. I've never had very many nice things."

His eyes took on a triumphant gleam. "And you will enjoy nice things for a long time to come if you make the effort to please me. I would rather bestow gifts than beatings."

He tipped his hat and turned to leave when Lisha stopped him, her heart pounding at yet another one of his seemingly offhanded warnings.

"Do you have to lock me up? Can I look around while you're gone?"

He mulled over her question. "You may have the walk of the gardens. That is all."

"But—"

"That is all."

When he went out the door and locked it, Lisha pulled a face. She'd hoped he would let her have the run of the hacienda, because she wanted to see for herself if there might be any means of escape. But Don Esteban Chavez was no fool. Stepping from the tub, she rubbed herself dry, searching about in her mind for a possible escape.

"Margherita," Lisha later asked as the woman helped her into a lavender frock, "how long have you lived here with the don?" The housekeeper took so long in answering that Lisha thought she didn't intend to.

"Many years."

"Do you have a family, any children?"

Margherita stiffened. Her complexion paled. Except for a spark of pain, no emotion marred her features. With jerky movements she finished tying a purple sash around Lisha's waist.

"Once I gave birth to a child, a son, but he died soon after."

"And you never had another?"

"We all have our crosses to bear." For the first time she looked Lisha straight in the eye. "Sometimes they are strict instructions to obey, no matter our objections."

Obviously Lisha couldn't count on any help from Esteban's housekeeper, no matter how much the woman resented her presence.

After a light lunch Margherita unlocked an outside door, opening up Lisha's private patio to a massive garden that ran the length of the hacienda. She drank in the pleasing view of tropical greenery and colorful flowers.

"It's lovely, Margherita. You must be very proud of your work here."

The woman shot her a surprised glance. A slight smile graced her lips. "Thank you. How did you guess?"

"By the way you reacted this morning when I mentioned that someone had done a marvelous job." She glanced around the garden. "Where do you grow your vegetables?"

"We have other gardens through that door, and fruit trees outside the wall."

The woman indicated the opposite side of the patio. Lisha saw the door but knew it would be locked. She guessed that on the other side of that closed gateway lay the don's private suite. Turning, she saw Margherita's retreating back.

Lisha wandered about, admiring the plants. She delicately touched a red rose, remembering the last time she'd picked one and the consequences. Her thoughts led to Granger and the tingling flush that warmed her whenever he came to mind. She longed for the feel of his arms about her, and she ached with melancholy.

Where was he? Was he all right? Was he, at this moment, on his way to her? Would he be too late? She mentally shook herself. Now was not the time to give in to negative thoughts. She still had to live by her wits.

Following the brick path, she came upon a stone fountain surrounded with shrubbery and lush plants. She sat down beside it, hoping the serene setting would calm her, help her to think.

Much later she realized she held a rose she didn't remember picking. She stared at the limp petals. Did the flower's crumpled state signify what the future had to offer? Would she, also, wilt under the don's smothering care?

Lisha found the following day much the same as the first, except that she came across a quill pen and a bottle of ink in the top drawer of her desk. She searched for stationery and found a sheet. With everything she needed at hand, she decided to write a letter to Tilly. A letter, she knew, that would never be posted.

She dipped the quill, and a drop of ink blotched her paper. Not willing to give up on her fruitless letter, she checked deep in the drawer for another piece of stationery. She felt a sheet wedged in a crack and pulled it out.

There was writing on it. At first glance she noticed that a practiced hand wrote it, but there seemed an urgency to the hurriedly formed letters. At a second look her heart froze. She realized that the former occupant of the suite had written the note. With trembling hands, she read the letter.

Last night he beat me. I cannot count the number of beatings I have suffered at his hand. No matter what I do, I cannot please him. I have begged him to set me free, but he refuses. I do not know how I shall ever survive. I cannot understand why he treats Margherita as he does after all she was once to him. Even she cannot help me. I long for death, even though I shall surely live the eternities in hell for the sins committed in this house. I am lost.

Lisha stared at the letter as if she were privileged a peek into hell itself. The words turned her blood to ice. She felt the girl's anguish, her desperate feelings of helplessness, and wondered what had happened to her. Then the next instant she didn't want to know, to see what could possibly be in her own future. She grabbed the paper and stuffed it back inside the drawer along with the spotted stationery, pen, and ink, and slammed the drawer shut.

By the time Margherita came to help her dress for dinner,

Lisha had composed herself enough that she looked uncon-
cerned on the outside, though inside she quaked.

The woman chose a mint-green frock with yards of lace
gathered at the hem only to swoop up on one side, revealing
frothy pink petticoats topped with a pink bow. The neckline,
modestly low, aligned with the dropped sleeves of lace.

After Lisha donned the gown, the woman fashioned her
curls into a twist at the nape of her neck and added a single
pink rosebud to her hair.

Lisha felt anything but festive, but for the sake of pretense,
she whirled about, seemingly pleased with her reflection.
Margherita led her out the door and down the hall to wait in the
drawing room.

Lisha noticed a statue gracing a pedestal near the fireplace.
She drew nearer, enthralled with the image's delicate silver-
and gold-leafed garments.

"The statue is of San José."

Lisha's heart twisted at the sudden sound of the don's voice.
She felt repulsion at his nearness, and to hide her distaste for
him she quickly turned her attention back to the figure.

"It is very beautiful. Have you had it long?"

"*Sí.* It has been with the family since my grandfather settled
here."

"You mean this house is that old?"

"No. I built this house. Come, Margherita is ready to
serve."

Before she had a chance to ask any more questions, he
showed her into the dining room. A silver chandelier hung
from an arched ceiling of salmon-pink brick. The fixture was
beautifully embossed and incised with pierced galleries, brackets, and delicately wrought chains. The chandelier caught the
sun's rays and reflected beams on the chalk-white walls.

Heavy paneled doors were opened to frame the garden and
fountain beyond. She could hear the wind howling outside the
concrete walls. The lonely sound matched the hollow feeling
she carried inside. Even the luxurious surroundings couldn't
dispel it.

Esteban helped her into a chair, then settled himself in the opposite one. Tenting his fingers, he slowly ran a thumb along his sculptured lips. His gaze never left her face.

"You look very beautiful, Señorita Harrington."

"Thank you. You have a lovely dining room. In fact, your whole house is exquisite."

Not able to bring herself to look at him, she pretended to be enthralled with her surroundings. Margherita brought in the first course. Lisha busied herself with eating the empanada, although she didn't care for the turnover filled with sautéed onions and chile. To keep the atmosphere on a light note she decided to have the don explain the making of each dish.

After soup and rice, Margherita served mole poblamo, the national dish of Mexico. A dark sauce flavored with chocolate and a multitude of chilies and spices covered generous pieces of chicken.

Lisha found the course delicious and was tempted to take a second helping until they were served beans cooked with bacon. After that came orange custard, and she forgot about a second helping of mole poblamo.

"Did you take care of your emergency, Señor Chavez?"

She really didn't care one way or the other, but she had to keep the conversation going, or he would detect her nervousness.

"*Sí.* I had to go to the main house."

"The main house?"

"*Sí.* I received word my wife had started premature birth, and the doctor wanted to talk to me."

Lisha almost choked on her coffee. "You have a wife?"

"I have had two of them. This is my third, and I will keep taking wives until one produces an heir."

She could hardly digest the absurdity of his thinking. "Shouldn't you be with her?"

"The doctor is there. He will send word if the boy decides to come early."

"But what if there are complications?"

"I have left orders that above all circumstances the baby is to survive."

She could not believe what she'd heard. How could he calmly tell her that he had pronounced a possible death

sentence on his wife? Dropping any conversation, she made a
pretense of eating her custard, although it tasted like sawdust.

The don sat watching her over the rim of his coffee cup. His
surveillance caused her to feel uneasy. She refused to think of
the all too near future and again prayed for a way out.

He rang a little dinner bell. The tinkling sound dug into her
thoughts. Margherita immediately appeared, as if she'd been
waiting in the wings.

"Take Señorita Harrington to her rooms and instruct her."

Lisha did not like the heavy tone of his voice, nor did she
care for the haunting glint in his black eyes. Once again she
followed the woman down the hall to her suite. Margherita
helped her out of her gown and told her to rest.

With her mind in a quagmire of thoughts, she jumped at
every sound she heard, thinking it was the don, until she
eventually fell into a fitful sleep.

A gentle shaking woke her, and she pulled away with a start.
Then she realized that it was Margherita who hovered above
her, and she relaxed.

"It is time for your bath."

Without question Lisha followed the stiff-backed woman to
the tub. Lisha still wondered how old she was. Margherita had
a young face yet the look in her eyes told of trials beyond her
age. Because of the letter stuffed in the desk, she had an odd
feeling that Margherita had been a former wife of the don's.
Someone who carried the heartbreak of not bearing a son for
the man she loved.

The hot water massaged away fatigued muscles caused by
worry. Lisha didn't realize she had been so tense. Not until
she'd begun to relax.

"It is time for you to dress. You are to wear the clothes laid
out for you."

While Lisha stepped from the tub and dried herself, Margherita took care of her discarded garments. The tight-lipped
woman said no more, and after Lisha wrapped the towel about
herself, she went into the bedroom to get dressed.

The woman had spread a ruffled pink dress on the bed.
Something about it struck Lisha as odd, but she couldn't figure
out what. As she came closer, she realized what it was. Half as

much material had been used in its creation as was the fashion.
She picked up the frock, pressing it against her. To her
surprise, she found the hem reached just a little below the knee.

Thinking this the type of dress that revealed several inches
of slips, she looked around, but found none save a short
petticoat along with pantaloons, long black stockings, and
slippers.

"This is ridiculous."

She threw the dress on the bed. As she did so she noticed the
high neckline, the cuffed long sleeves, and the ruffles, not
fashioned from lace, but from cotton.

"Why, this dress is more suited for a child," Lisha muttered
aloud. "It's . . ."

Her hand stopped in midair. The revelation stunned her.
Almost forgetting to breathe, she stared at the frock lying in a
crumpled heap on the spread. Her breaths came in stilted gasps.

The man was insane. At this moment his wife might be
giving birth to the heir he wanted so badly, yet he was waiting
on Lisha to clothe herself as a child for his debased satisfactions.

"You have not dressed?"

She whirled around to face Margherita. The woman averted
her eyes. "You expect me to put this on?" Her voice sounded
as brittle as that of a screaming fishwife.

"The don expects it. Hurry, there is little time."

Lisha allowed herself to be costumed in the infantile clothes.
Margherita styled her hair into two long braids, fastening large
pink bows at the curly ends. Lisha leaned forward to view
herself in the mirror. Even nature played a part in this bizarre
masquerade. Freckles, bridging her nose, were the crowning
touch. The sound of the key in the lock told her she was once
again alone.

With a sob she sank down by the dressing table, her head
cradled in her arms. What could she do? How could she ever
get out of this? Her father had always said she lived by her
imagination, and if she ever needed to come up with something, that time was now.

As a child, one of her faults had been listening at keyholes.
She'd learned of many things not meant for innocent ears. One

of them was the interest some men had in very young girls. Not in her wildest dreams would she have guessed that Lago would drag her all the way down into Mexico to face the same type of man that had puzzled her as a child.

She thought of Granger. Her heart ached for him. Two days had passed since she'd last seen him. Maybe he hadn't escaped. Maybe he would never be able to.

Refusing to dwell on that frightening possibility, she turned her thoughts to the night they'd spent together in the dugout, a night enveloped in love while a tempest raged outside. Once again she could taste his lips on hers, feel his caressing hand, smell the wind in his hair.

With all her heart she wished that he hadn't stopped their lovemaking. Not only for delicious memories to relive and cherish, but it would have been great fun and a fitting surprise to announce to the don that he wouldn't be the first after all.

Lisha stilled. She slowly raised her head to stare into the mirror, her brain clicking at top speed. A sly smile captured her lips.

"Who's to say it didn't happen?" she asked the childish image grinning back at her. "In fact, how can he prove that I'm a virgin at all? All he has is Lago's sayso."

A key juggled the lock, and she sprinted to her bed. Her heart pounded furiously against her rib cage. Whether or not her idea worked, she intended to give it her all. After all, hadn't she had the best tutor anyone could hope for?

She heard a soft tread before Esteban appeared in the doorway. He wore a loosely tied robe that revealed a chest of curly black hair. When he saw her complacently leaning back on her elbows with her legs crossed and a slipper dangling precariously from her large toe, his black eyes gleamed.

"Didn't your mama ever teach you not to keep a girl waiting?" she cooed, flipping her slipper into the air, and captivatingly hipping her way to the edge of the bed.

His smile dulled. "What do you mean?"

"I mean," she answered with what she hoped was a pretty pout, "that I've been waiting here for eons."

"I am glad you have decided to make the most of your stay here."

"Oh, that wasn't my problem," she said, slowly rolling down her stocking. She slid it off her foot and let it fly with a flip of her wrist. "The thing I couldn't figure out was what kind of game you like to play."

"I don't understand. What game?"

She moistened her lips with the tip of her tongue, lifted her chin, and gazed up at him through narrowed eyelids. Slowly she began to unbutton her bodice, trying to imitate the mannerisms of the whore on the auction block. Only there was no room full of gaping men here, just one confused man.

"I mean with all my new customers, I try to outguess their needs. I must say you really had me going there for a while. It wasn't until I saw the dress that I finally figured you out."

"Customers?" Astonishment and disbelief rode his face. "What do you mean . . . customers?"

"You know . . ." Grinning, she anchored her thumbs inside the band of her petticoats and provocatively eased them down over her hips. "Men who pay, and—might I add?—handsomely for my favors."

"No, no!" He ran shaking fingers through his thick hair. "You are a mail-order bride from St. Louis. You were checked out!"

"Well, you're partly right there. I am from St. Louis, and I did come as a bride. But your friends don't know the real reason why. In my business you try to get everything you can. A client caught me going through his pants pockets. So-o-o," she added, tugging at the end of the sash, "I had to leave in a hurry."

"But . . . but you are so young. And . . . and you have breeding. You are a nurse!" His voice rose an octave with each statement.

"Honey, I started young. And many a high-class family ended up finding other avenues of business since the war. I just happened to choose one with instant profits. And as for the nursing, I helped the house doctor. You might like to know that you're not the only man who likes little girls, and they can get pretty mean, too." She stepped forward, leisurely sliding the sash across her buttocks.

Esteban stepped back. "If this is true, why didn't you tell me?"

"Are you joking? Tell you"—she gestured with a slight twist of her hand—"and lose all this? If you don't know by now, I like pretty things."

The don gaped at her, his face muscles hardening. "I do not believe you."

"Suit yourself." She chuckled throatily.

Her unflinching eyes traveled the course of his half-exposed body. She trailed the sash up over his shoulder and down his chest, stopping at his bellybutton. In a brazen gesture she twisted a fingertip in the curly mat of hair and tapped at his flat stomach.

"But, tell me, what virgin could stare at a naked man without instantly succumbing to the vapors?"

The horror of what he digested played across Esteban's face. His complexion resembled that of a green tomato ripening to a deep red. He knocked her hand away as if she had leprosy and stalked from the room.

"Get me Lago and Javier!" he raged at his men.

Lisha collapsed against the wall, mentally thanking her father for their countless hours of playacting, and her uncle for his success in thoroughly training her as a nurse. If it hadn't been for the male patients she'd seen, she never would've been able to pull off her little charade in spite of the show the whore had put on or her acting ability.

She could hear a commotion all through the hacienda. Don Esteban Chavez had a violent temper. The knowledge spurred her into action. Slipping from her unguarded room, she stayed to the shadows, inching along the passageway. She saw that someone had left the front doors open and, knowing that would be the first place they'd look for her, turned in the opposite direction.

A door stood ajar, and she peeked in. The room was that of the don's. His discarded clothes lay in a heap at the foot of a massive bed, and she quickly gathered them up. After all, she mused, this wouldn't be the first time she'd had to wear breeches. She tried the patio doors and, finding them unlocked, slipped through.

In the darkness she felt her way along the brick path. Esteban's murderous tirade echoed in the background, and she briefly wondered how he would react when he found her gone.

After a few moments she reached what she had searched for, a door in the masonry wall. A movement caught her eye, and she looked up to see Margherita. Her heart stopped. She waited for the woman to give the alarm. For endless seconds neither moved. Then Lisha inclined her head and stepped out into the windy desert.

Her inbred promptings told her to turn right. She had no idea where she was. All she knew was that she would rather be meat for the buzzards than fare for a man's bizarre tastes.

Chapter
❧❧ 20 ❧❧

As soon as the buildings dropped from sight, Lisha stripped herself of the girlish frock and stuffed it among the rocks. She didn't want Esteban's men to find it and figure out which way she had headed. Putting on the don's clothes, she found them too big, especially his boots, but she didn't care. The going would be easier in trousers than a dress.

Even though the night sounds frightened her, she knew that she would have a better chance of escape if she traveled in the dark and hid during the day.

The chilly air seeped through the material, and she pulled the jacket tighter about her shoulders. Before she always had the horse blanket in which to wrap herself against the cold of a desert night. Wishing she had it now, she steadily placed one foot ahead of the other.

The sun began to rise into the sky before she stopped to rest. She'd been walking down a narrow valley between two mesas since the wee hours of the morning, and she crossed over to sit in the shade of the steep hill. Settling herself near a saguaro, she listened to a woodpecker hammer at a cactus. The steady sound drummed her into an exhausted sleep.

It seemed only moments when a horse's neigh woke her. Glancing about in a daze, she finally realized where she was and why. She peeked over a small creosote bush and saw a group of men canvassing the desert floor about a quarter of a mile off.

Although they were too far away for her to see their faces,

the still air carried their voices. She could make out Esteban's angry words, but she couldn't understand what he said. They spread out, searching the rocky ground, and she automatically crouched down.

It wouldn't be long until they worked their way to where she lay hiding. She had to think of something, or she would be lost. Scanning the steep side of the mesa, she found a crevice that she might be able to hide in. She looked about for anything she could use as camouflage, all the while listening to the oncoming men.

She wrapped her fingers around the limb of a creosote bush, trying to break it off, but only succeeded in releasing its pungent odor. Frantically she cast about and saw a dead one nearby. Crawling over to it, she got a good grip on the stock and pulled, using her feet as a lever. Nothing happened.

Changing positions, she grasped hold of the plant just above the ground, dug her heels deeper into the baked earth, and pulled. Again the muscles in her arms and legs quivered from the strain. With a tearing rip the roots gave, and she dragged the plant over to the fissure.

The men were slowly gaining ground. There was enough time if she hurried. She shimmied up the few feet to the crevice and wedged herself in. Her feet and legs were hidden, but she couldn't completely hide her torso. She held the small bush to her chest, hoping it looked as if the plant were growing out of the mesa and praying it hid her. If no one stopped to take a good look, maybe she would go undetected.

Minutes seemed to linger into hours. The muscles in her arms and hands began to quiver against the strain of holding the branch still. Breathing its odor made her queasy. She longed to ease the dull ache caused from the crevice digging into her back. The morning shadow steadily slipped down the rocky side, leaving the hot sun to glare in her eyes. She tried to rub her face against her shoulder but couldn't completely wipe away the sweat, and she pressed her eyes tightly against the sting.

Each breath she took resembled the rushing wind. The men were almost upon her now. She tried to tell herself that they couldn't possibly hear her tripping heart, but to her it sounded like the constant boom of cannons.

A man said something, and the don spit back an answer. His tone did not invite small talk. Lisha knew she had to hold on for just a bit longer. She couldn't risk getting caught, because he would never forgive her trickery.

A hairy insect scampered across her thigh and down her leg, stopping at her knee, shaded from the sun. She blinked away her blurred vision only to focus on a tarantula. A silent scream welled up inside her. She bit her teeth into her cracked lip, trying to quell the tremors that threatened to consume her. The men were passing her now, but she didn't watch them. She couldn't take her fixed gaze away from the spider.

With every jagged breath she drew, she thought she might upset the insect. Her left arm turned numb from poor circulation, yet she lay breathlessly still.

What a choice! To the left of her rode a man bent on using his violent temper for her destruction, and on her knee rested a tarantula whose very presence made her quake with fear. Which carried the least poison? She suspected the spider.

Soon the men were several yards ahead of her. No one paid attention to the steep sides of the mesa. They were intent upon combing the ground for any sign of her.

Only when the men were well out of hearing did she move. Taking careful aim, she kicked out with her knee, tossing the insect into the air. After it landed, the spider took a second or two before it scrambled on down the hill.

The bush fell away from her fingertips, and she clamped a shaking hand across her mouth. She wanted to cry, but the sound wouldn't come. Her stiff back muscles protested any kind of movement, and a tingling sensation needled her arm. She scrambled from the fissure and onto the desert floor, creating a small landslide of shale. Her cramped tendons made it hard for her to walk, and thirst cruelly dominated her thoughts . . . but she was free.

The late afternoon sun reflected off the naked ground and jabbed at her eyes. She wore the jacket over her head in an effort to stave off heatstroke. The thought of food didn't appeal to her. Thirst about drove her crazy.

From her studies in school, she knew that the cactus pulp held water, but she didn't have a knife to cut into one. The sharp thorns and tough skin prevented her from digging in with her nails. She kicked at a cactus with the heel of her boot and succeeded in releasing a drop or two of liquid, which she rubbed into her cracked lips and the surrounding dry skin.

The wind peppered her face with grit, sand, and fragmented pieces of eroded stone. She wiped her hand across her gritty face and came away with flecks of blood and dirt. Dully she rubbed her palm against her thigh.

She knew she should sleep, conserve her energy to travel at night. But she was afraid that Esteban might come back, and she didn't want to be caught unaware.

With each step the boots rubbed against her feet, and they began to hurt. She knew that blisters formed on her heels, but anything was better than going barefoot. If she had no protection at all, the hot earth would soon burn the soles of her feet. A rush of warm liquid angled down her right heel, and she knew that she had broken a blister.

A few times she thought she saw a cool spring of water in the distance. She hobbled over only to find rock and sand. Her tongue thickened against her dry mouth. Swallowing became steadily harder. The skin on her face pulled tighter. She longed for moisture, the wet climate of her beloved Kingswood.

The sun sank lower in the clear sky until it finally slipped behind a mesa. She gloried in the steady drop in temperature. That is, until the wind took on a chill and bit into her sweat-soaked clothing. Huddling next to a cactus, she hugged herself in an effort to keep warm.

She woke at every sound, thinking that it might be Esteban and his men. Eventually sleep eluded her, and long before dawn, she started walking. Her body was stiff with cold, and her swollen feet burned with each step.

As the day wore on, she fought tormenting visions of water spilling over her hot body and down her throat. The intense heat sucked precious fluids from her skin. Her cracked lips bled. As the dryness crept in, she could feel the moisture leave her hands. Tiny fissures worked their way across her fingertips. Creases in her hands and fingers split open and began to bleed.

The pain became unbearable. How could such small lacerations hurt so much?

A sudden movement caught her attention. She looked to see a mouse scurry across the brittle ground. A shrill scream sounded overhead. She shielded her eyes against the bright sun to see a hawk circling overhead. Then, in one fell swoop, the bird dived toward the earth, grabbed the rodent up in its claws, and flew away. She wondered how long it would be before death snatched her up in its iron talons, to carry her away.

With labored steps she zigzagged her way forward. The jacket kept slipping from her head, and it took a concentrated effort to replace it. Half the time she couldn't blink away her blurred vision, and she saw everything through a filmy glaze. Perspiration angled its way down the gully of her back.

Thoughts of Granger occupied her mind, and she entertained the idea that he would find her before it grew too late, never allowing herself to think anything otherwise. She mentally lived her wedding day, that blissful night, and their future together.

A hissing sound startled her from her musings. She jerked to a standstill. To her right coiled a rattlesnake. Thoughts of ending her torment crossed her mind. It would be faster to die of snakebite than from thirst and exposure. Then she remembered the bodies, animals and humans alike, half buried in the mountains of sand.

"No!"

The ragged cry tore from her pinched throat. She swung the jacket at the snake and took off at a halting gait. While there was breath left in her lungs, she would fight.

The afternoon wore on, and so did the wind. Each gust seemed to beckon, then taunt her when she failed to come. It whipped loose hair about her tender face. The bald-faced crests of the mountains wobbled in heat waves rising from the arid land. Ribbons of sand rustled about her feet. She tried pulling up clumps of grass, to chew for moisture, but it sliced into her stiff hands. Toward sunset she crumpled to the naked ground and sobbed. There was no sound, no tears.

She spent another freezing night drifting in and out of consciousness, unsure of dreams and reality. While underlining it all, the throbbing in her fingers painfully made its presence known.

She held out her arms to Granger and pulled him into her tight embrace, feeling his lips on hers. Murmuring softly, she opened her eyes to look into Esteban's gloating face.

Behind him Tilly clicked her tongue while she nervously twisted her hands. "My dear, you shouldn't have gone, you know. You should have stayed here and married that nice young man, Mr. Clayborne. Now how are you going to get yourself out of this one?"

Beatrice stayed to the side clutching her worn Bible in her hands. A pompous expression etched deeply in the woman's face. "That which ye sow, so shall ye reap." She closed the book with a bang. "You have brought this upon yourself, Falisha Harrington. Whatever punishment you receive, you will truly deserve."

Weston stood at arm's length, not allowing her to come near. He sadly shook his head. "Falisha, you are not the lady I believed you to be. Don't you have any pride in your appearance? Look at yourself. You're a sight."

"No, no!"

She struggled from her dreams to find there was no one to hear her muffled cries, no one to care.

Morning came as unwelcomed as the freezing night. She squinted through puffy eyelids at the sunlight filtering down to her face. It was early, but already the heat gathered around her like the prickly plague. She licked a thick tongue across her lips, tasting gritty sand.

Her cramped muscles screamed for release. She raised herself to her knees only to fall back to the stony ground. Again, she struggled up and lurched forward on wooden legs. With each grueling step, she kept telling herself that once she started moving, the stiffness would ease.

The sun's rays hit the colorless ground and reflected back into her face. Her skin burned. Blisters raised up in watery bumps. The dry air bent her fingers into painful clenches. Her bare head received full assault, and her insides felt as taut and shriveled as her skin. There was no shelter in sight, no relief.

She weaved in and out of rational thinking. Her wandering

steps were noted only by the enormous black birds soaring high above her, but she didn't regret her decision to strike out into the desert. She'd rather end her life in the sweltering heat than live as a prisoner for the don's pleasures. A sob wrenched from her heart. She so wanted to see Granger one last time.

A large obstacle blocked her way. She blinked several times, trying to clear her vision. What she saw made her groan in frustration. A high cliff rose in front of her. She hadn't the strength to climb the steep sides, and as far as she could see, there was no going around it.

Crumpling to the stony earth, she was coherent enough to know she lay dying, and she didn't have the power to do anything about it but pray.

A dislodged pebble from the ridge above rolled to a rest at her fingertips. Raising, she saw a lone rider silhouetted against the sky. She pried open her lips caked with dried blood and sand and called for help. No sound emitted from her parched throat. Defeat crawled over her like a bad dream, and she submitted without a whimper.

"Lisha, Lisha. How many times must I tell you there are no small parts, just small actors?"

The man's voice startled her. She forced her eyes open, then wearily clamped them shut. This was the same as the other dreams.

"Come on, Lisha. You know that once the curtain's up, the show must go on."

She raised her head to see the form of a man. "Papa, is that you?"

"It sure is, Curly-locks."

"I'm coming, Papa. I'll be with you and Mama soon."

"No, Lisha. It's not time for you yet. Give it all you've got."

The figure began to fade. She held out her hand in supplication. "Papa, please don't leave me!" her voice screamed out. Was it only in her mind?

"Remember, a good actor plays to his audience. No matter the size."

Her tormented mind played more tricks on her. A horse's shod hooves stopped a few feet away. She heard the creak of leather, and the crunch of boots striking rock before strong hands turned her over. A cap scraped the top of a canteen, and the container was pressed to her lips. Smelling the wet canvas, she greedily drank the sweet-tasting water until the canteen was taken from her.

This was not a dream—this was real! Relief spread throughout her body. Someone had found her before it had grown too late. All she could do was form the words *thank you*. A face swirled above hers before she focused onto Lago's leering grin.

"I'm glad it's me that found yah"—his taunting voice paralyzed her—"'cause we have some unfinished business ta see to, you and me." She felt herself slip into a darkening gorge. His menacing voice droned on. "Don't think passin' out is gonna save ya. I'm a patient man. I'll wait till ya know who you're dancin' with."

Chapter
❀❦ 21 ❦❀

For Lisha, reality meshed with dreams. She saw herself sitting across a succulent banquet from a man whispering words of love. Instead, she got a broth poured down her throat from someone with a gravelly voice assuring her there would be plenty of time. A taunting laugh chased her back into hiding.

Several more times she fought to stay in her secure web of unconsciousness, but eventually she opened her eyes to a darkening sky and smelled coffee. It took a moment before she could see Lago roasting a rabbit on a spit. The reflection from the fire flickered on his face. She could barely make out his shaggy hair sticking out from underneath his hat, and his pleased expression.

He bent his cigarette butt in half and flicked it aside. Slowly he turned his gaze toward her. She feigned sleep, lying perfectly still, but her mind reeled.

From a distance she heard a horse's whinny. Instantly Lago's backbone stiffened. He cocked his head, listening. A lone rider approached the camp, stopping just outside the firelight. The deserter sprang to his feet, the barrel of his pistol flashing in the light.

"Hey, mister. Can you spare a cup of coffee? I swear, I could smell it a mile back."

The man's voice came in raspy breaths, as if he had a sore throat. Lisha found something oddly familiar about its timbre but couldn't figure out why. The stranger eased from his saddle and walked into the light. A poncho hid his torso, and a sombrero shadowed his face, but she knew his casual stride. A tear rolled down her sunburned face. She recognized the voice from her dreams . . . the voice of the man she loved.

"Well, how about it. Could you use some company?"

"Depends." Lago's hand firmly grasped the butt of his gun.

"No need to worry 'bout me," Granger said, whipping his poncho aside to show the absence of a gunbelt. "As you can see, I'm not armed."

Lago waved his pistol, and Granger circled to show that he wasn't hiding any firearms. With one smooth movement Lago holstered his gun and then briefly gestured for his uninvited guest to sit.

"How come you ain't got no gun?" he asked, not taking his gaze from Granger.

"I've a rifle in my scabbard. I just don't have my Colt."

"Why's that?"

"A man didn't appreciate me taking his girl. His buddies disarmed me and tried to string me up." The stranger laughed at his own folly.

"What happened?"

"They were too drunk to tie a proper lynchin' knot, and it pulled loose."

Lago poured a steaming cup of coffee and handed it to Granger. In doing so, the deserter tried to get a good look at his face, but Granger tipped his head, pretending to savor the aroma.

"Lucky for you," Lago commented dryly.

"It was at that. Except I had to beat it out of Chihuahua without collecting my things. There was a darn sight more of them than of me. . . . Is your partner sick?" he asked, inclining his head toward Lisha.

"Ain't my partner."

"Oh, who is he?"

"Ain't a he."

"Your wife, huh?"

"Say, for a stranger, you ask a hell of a lot of questions that ain't none of your business."

"Just being neighborly."

''Well, I don't like neighbors, an' I'm fastly beginnin' not to like you.''

''Whoa,'' Granger said, holding up his hand, ''I don't mean to cause trouble. I'll drink my coffee and ride out if that'll make you feel better.''

''Somethin' tells me that I'll feel better if I can keep an eye on yah.''

Granger shrugged and sipped his coffee. He nodded toward the roasted rabbit that the deserter removed from the spit. ''Mind sharin' a piece?''

After a slight pause Lago grudgingly broke off a section and handed it to him. ''Yah ain't gonna get anywhere in this desert if yah ain't prepared.''

''Oh, I don't worry none.''

''Where yah headed?''

''El Paso. That where you're going?''

''Ain't headin' anywhere, 'cept to Chihuahua. That is . . . after I take care of some unfinished business.'' His glance strayed to Lisha.

The men quietly ate their meager supper. A few times Lago paused between ripping bits, staring openly at his visitor. After he drank his coffee, he prepared another cigarette and settled back to study Granger.

''You seem awful familiar to me. Have we met somewhere?''

Lisha stilled her breathing. Granger had come unarmed, and he would be in trouble if Lago recognized him.

''I'm sure I've never met you before, leastwise not sober, or I'd have remembered it.''

Lago seemed satisfied with his answer. He took agonizingly long draws on his cigarette, his eyes squinting above the flamed tip. His gaze never faltered from Granger. ''Ever been to the Spider's Web?''

''Once. A few days ago. Do you go there often?''

''Some.''

''Say''—Granger's voice brightened, and he leaned forward—''I think I've figured it out. That's the girl who ran away from some rich don, and you're lucky enough to find her. I heard it would be worth goin' after her for the reward.''

Lago stilled his cigarette halfway to his mouth. He snapped

it in half, dropping it to the ground. "For a stranger yah seem to know quite a lot, which makes me think that yah know more then you're tellin'."

"I just heard the scuttlebutt goin' about town."

Lisha could see their silhouettes playing against the flickering firelight, the ebony night their backdrop. Lago unrolled his long legs and stood. He unsheathed his pistol, lazily leveling the barrel at Granger's chest.

Granger carefully set his coffee cup down. "Friend, I didn't come here askin' for a fight."

"Somethin' tells me that you came for more than that . . . Hawks." Lago laughed. "I heard you'd escaped. Your first mistake was stickin' around. Your second mistake was comin' after her. But it pleasures me to let yah know that I'll take care of her personally, so's you won't have to worry."

Lago cocked his gun, and the sound reverberated in the hushed night. With all the concern of a cat stretching in the sun, he took aim and fired. Granger dived sharply to the side, but not before a bullet hissed through the air to bury itself with a soft thud. Lago chuckled. He stared down at Granger's inert form before turning his scoffing gaze at Lisha.

No! Lisha's mind screamed out.

No one heard the agonized cry but herself. Struggling to sit, she found that she couldn't move. She felt trapped in a body that refused to follow her commands. The few tears she had left rolled down her face as she mentally demanded that Granger get up, that he live.

Through bleary eyes she watched Lago take a faltering step, then another. The bandit began to weave. Wiping a shaky hand across his chest, he looked at his palm. He seemed hypnotized by what he'd found.

Jumping up to face the deserter, Granger whipped off his sombrero. "Take a good look, Lago," he growled. "I want you to remember the face of the man who finally sent you to hell."

With a roar Lago lurched forward, firing his gun. The shot went wild, and he fell at Granger's feet. Granger knelt to roll the man over. He'd done his job well. The Apache's knife had found its mark. Lago wouldn't be tormenting anyone else again.

In three long strides Granger reached Lisha's bedroll and gathered her into his arms. "It's all right," he soothed, "I won't let anyone harm you again."

Granger held her until her quivering body stilled, and she slept. He then stretched out alongside her, unwilling to let her go, even for a moment.

Chapter
❦ 22 ❦

Anger flushed Weston's face. For what seemed like the hundredth time, he and Jackal had searched Kingswood, but they still came up empty-handed. They'd dug out fence posts, pulled brick from around the fireplaces, scoured every foot of the grounds, and thoroughly searched the abandoned well looking for the gold. All with no success.

They had been so sure Harrington had hidden it in the old well. No other place would've been so perfect. A few years before, a skunk had fallen down the shaft, fouling the water. The animal and its stench had to be covered up with rocks and dirt.

Weston would've bet his future that the old man had buried the gold in the bottom of the partially filled cavity. He hadn't. At least, that's what Jackal had said. Weston had ordered the bounty hunter to search the well because he couldn't stand the thought of lowering himself down into that filthy, bug-infested hole.

They'd done most of the ransacking during the evenings and early mornings, and Weston knew they'd gone as far as they could without arousing suspicion. Already people whispered about how blockade runners had used Kingswood as a base, and there might still be contraband laying about. He'd always known he couldn't keep a whole crew quiet. So, eventually there was bound to be talk.

What he didn't want was people snooping about. It'd just be his luck that someone would stumble onto the hiding place. He needed an excuse to make a full-scale search during the day. And his excuse had vanished right out from under his thumb.

Once again Weston thought of Falisha Harrington. With swift movements he yanked on his gloves. His jaw muscles tightened, and a familiar dull ache pulled the cords on the back of his neck. Again he thought of her parting letter. His pulse raced, and his head throbbed.

When he couldn't find any trace of her beyond the Arkansas Territory, he took his anger out on Etta. Weston smiled inwardly. He liked to hear her whimper under his punishing hands. He liked to force his attentions on her when he knew she feared and hated him.

Weston pictured Etta's face growing white with alarm. He relished the vision. Without warning, another image of a gaunt woman with thinning iron-gray hair, close-set eyes, and a transparent mouth materialized as it had done so often of late. Weston sucked in his breath with a ragged hiss. He shaped the fingers of his hands . . . as if gripping a scrawny neck . . . and squeezed, once again dispelling the hated figure of his grandmother. Couldn't she stay in her grave and leave him in peace?

To calm his trembling limbs, he forced his mind into other channels. The spiteful old crone wouldn't be allowed to rule his life anymore. He had decided that long before he'd reached puberty.

It took all of Weston's energy to marshal his thoughts to the problem at hand. Finding Falisha. He'd gone to see Tilly several times, but the half-witted woman would not give out Falisha's whereabouts. Well, he intended to go back again and persuade her to do so.

His lips curved into a grim smile. Maybe the gossip floating about would be just the kind of break he needed. Given time, he would turn everything about to suit him. He always did, he always would.

Weston climbed up into his buggy. The springs creaked under his weight. With an impatient flick of the reins he guided the horse down the spacious drive flanked with live oak trees and left Kingswood behind.

* * *

"Mrs. Ward, I hesitate to give gossip credibility, but in this case I must." Weston sat in a high-backed chair, directly across from Tilly. He forced a staid expression to clearly show the gravity of the problem. "Have you heard the rumors concerning Edward Harrington and Kingswood?"

"I don't listen to such talk." The tiny woman denounced the hearsay with an indignant shake of her head. "I think it's all nonsense."

Weston leaned forward. "I'm afraid there might be some truth to the stories." He paused for emphasis. "Since I had been Edward's lawyer, and now Miss Harrington's guardian, the authorities have contacted me for information. Of course, I knew nothing about his possible smuggling and couldn't be of much help."

"The authorities came to you?"

He nodded. "They said a man named Mercer professed to be the captain of the steamer allegedly making the runs. Before Mercer could give concrete evidence, he ended up missing."

"Well, then, if he couldn't give any information, why do they think Mr. Harrington was involved?"

"Because this Captain Mercer had let it slip that he had helped to hide contraband on Kingswood"—his hushed tone added to the bleak mood—"but he was never able to reveal the man in charge."

"My goodness." Tilly pushed her spectacles against her face.

"They have enough circumstantial evidence to argue their case, but they won't entrust it to me. However, they did say they are also investigating Miss Harrington."

Tilly's eyes grew wide. "Dear, dear me."

"Mrs. Ward, I'm sure you understand the gravity of the situation. If charges are brought up against Miss Harrington, without her here to defend herself, the scandal could ruin her, whether she'd proved guilty or not. This whole ugly business could be put to rest before it gets out of hand, if she could just answer a few questions. It's imperative that I get in touch with her." He thrust his final spear. "They could confiscate Kingswood."

Tilly clicked her tongue. "I had no idea, no idea whatsoever."

"Mrs. Ward—the address?"

"Oh, yes, yes, of course. A rancher by the name of Granger Hawks wanted a bride and—"

"A bride?" Weston shot up from his chair. "You mean to tell me that Fal— Miss Harrington has gone off to marry some backward farmer?"

"My goodness me, no." Tilly chuckled at his loss of composure. "She went to be a governess for Mr. Hawks's little girl."

Weston calmed himself. His heart throbbed in his temples. "Where might that be?"

"In New Mexico, on a ranch near a town called Cibola."

Weston smiled warmly. "Thank you, Mrs. Ward. I'll give that information to the authorities."

Tilly watched him leave. She'd known all along that he was sweet on Lisha. Everything would be all right now, what with Mr. Clayborne helping the dear child and all. He was a good man; he would know what to do.

Jackal walked into Clayborne's office and found him lounging at his desk with his index finger resting lightly on his lips. Mutely Weston stared at the bounty hunter. After a brief pause he straightened and lightly flicked a piece of paper across the polished desktop. Jackal picked it up.

"That gives you the authority to bring our Miss Harrington back to answer questions about stolen goods and treason."

"Is it genuine?"

"Genuine enough. Judge Croft signed it."

"Well, now, if the good judge signed it, I don't have any worries, do I?"

Weston's eyes narrowed. "All you have to worry about is bringing Falisha back here all in one piece. She's with a man named Granger Hawks. He runs a ranch near Cibola, New Mexico."

Jackal folded the warrant in half and stuffed it inside his breast pocket. "Of course you had no part in this."

"Of course. . . . And Jackal?" Weston stopped the bounty

hunter at the door. "I want you to get rid of all obstacles, especially this Mr. Hawks. I don't want any interference, no threads left untied."

Jackal indolently touched a fingertip to the brim of his hat and sauntered out the door. The action smacked of mock respect for Weston's authority.

Weston felt his face blanch, then flush with heat. Jackal would be another one who would meet with an unfortunate accident in much the same fashion as Captain Mercer. The bounty hunter's manner had worn thin with him.

He'd had enough of people's taunts as a child, enough ridicule from other children, enough sleeping in filthy alleys and rummaging through garbage, but more importantly, he'd had enough of cold rooms and an even icier grandmother. He shivered, remembering.

Massaging the back of his neck, he forced his mind into other channels. A satisfied smile curved his lips. He thought how his lifelong plan was close to becoming realized. A few setbacks hampered him, but soon Falisha Harrington would be right where he wanted her.

Weston reached for his Stetson. The afternoon grew late, but he thought he might surprise Etta by paying her a visit.

Chapter
23

Granger hid himself and Lisha during the day, choosing to travel at night. He kept a close eye on their surroundings. More than once he'd spied dark figures on the horizon. Chavez and his men must have found Lago's body, and he was not giving up the search. Granger knew that when Lisha became strong enough, they'd have to push harder if he wanted to stay out of their reach.

His gut twisted every time he thought of the don getting his hands on Lisha. He'd never asked her if the man had taken advantage of her before she'd escaped. He had found her alive. That's all he cared about—that and how she fared.

After he'd heard that she had slipped away into the desert, he had won money in a poker game to buy supplies, water bags, and a packhorse. He also included anything she might need, even a change of clothing. What he hadn't had enough money for, he stole from the Comancheros. Their excessive celebrations had made that part easy for him.

He'd taken the last of Lago's food and water and added it to his. Even with the extra supplies, he knew that they'd have to reach a watering hole soon, especially since he'd taken Lago's horse with them.

When he first set out, he had refused to think anything other than that he would find Lisha alive. He had come across the discarded jacket and assumed that it had been hers, because the rumor was she'd taken some of the don's clothes when she had disappeared.

The next day he had caught sight of low-flying vultures. The soaring black birds alarmed him. He'd hurried his pace, making bets as to who they hovered over. Eventually he'd crossed Lago's path, not long after the deserter had found Lisha, and he had waited until dark to make his appearance.

Lisha now rode on a travois board that he'd fashioned for her from the branches of a nine-foot creosote bush and horse blankets. She slept most of the time. Her body craved the much-needed rest. At first she would jerk awake, fear frozen on her face, then she would settle down as if realizing that his care hadn't been a dream at all.

He kept ointment on her blisters, deer tallow on her dehydrated skin. After wrestling off her boots, he'd bathed her feet in Balm and wrapped them with bandages he'd thought to bring. He had done the same for her hands.

When she became restless from the heat, he sponged down her face, neck, and arms. Even though she was too sick to carry on a conversation, he made sure she knew that he was near whether she lay awake or sleeping. Besides her physical needs, he could see her sagging spirits beginning to heal under his loving care. And it pleased him that he was doing her some good.

Awareness sent a jolt through his heart. *It pleased him.* Was this how Lisha had felt when she administered to others?—this feeling of pure accomplishment? Reluctantly he could see the force of her desire to nurse, even though he couldn't fully agree on her doing so.

When she could stomach solid food, he pounded dried meat and tossed it into boiling water with a handful of cornmeal. As he spoonfed her, she made noises to show her delight in the taste.

He wanted time to feed her nourishing food, time to heal her heat-ravished body, but most of all he wanted time to acquaint her to the ways of love. Instead, he had to drag her relentlessly to the border and hopefully to safety.

As time mounted, so did his fear. As of yet, he hadn't found water, and he wondered if he'd miscalculated the directions. During their trip over, he'd tried his best to commit to memory where the watering holes were located. Their water ran low,

and they needed to replenish their supply. He refrained from
telling Lisha; he didn't want her to worry. There was nothing
for it but to press on at a severe pace.

He glanced back at her. She lay sleeping on the travois. The
sores on her face had started to drain, and the minor ones had
begun to scab over, but he couldn't wipe away the memory of
how she had looked the first time he'd seen her. Because of her
blistered and swollen skin, he had scarcely recognized her. He
had a hard time washing the dried blood from her face and
mouth.

The rage in him pumped his blood. She wouldn't be in this
state if it weren't for men who bought and sold human flesh.
He put everybody at blame. The only satisfaction he had was
in knowing that the man who had started this loathsome chain
reaction now provided meat for the vultures. He grinned at the
fitting way kind met up with kind.

As dawn broke around them, he spotted the small village of
El Carmen. Like a man pardoned from hell, relief shot through
him, and he offered up a silent prayer of thanks. He didn't need
to urge the animals forward. They smelled water, and it was all
he could do to keep them from bolting.

They spent a relaxing day beside the stream, welcoming the
shade of the alamos. He allowed himself only short naps,
always mindful of their pursuers. As Lisha slept, he watched
her. Once in a while, she tossed, and her dull eyes would flash
open, searching.

On one of these times, Granger ran a light finger down her
cheek and around her mouth. "I'm here," he whispered.
"Don't worry—I won't let anything harm you."

A smile curved her lips, then vanished. She tried to stay
awake, but eventually her eyelids would flutter closed. Sometimes during her frequent dreams, she had called out the name
of Weston. At other times she would utter his own name
wrapped in a soft caress. For some reason he didn't like the
idea of sharing her dreams with another man.

Because of the don's relentless pursuit, Granger broke camp
early and headed out before dusk. He hadn't slept as much as
he'd wanted, but he knew that Chavez would push his men and
horses as much as possible and still keep them alive.

He wondered what kind of man this Mexican was to keep on with his unrelenting chase. The reason couldn't be because he wanted to somehow regain the money he'd spent on Lisha, because he lost more with each passing day.

While he was in Chihuahua, he'd heard of Chavez's ruthlessness, and how none dared cross him. Granger gathered that the don had a vindictive nature, and the man could no more rest until he got satisfaction than he could breathe underwater. For such a person as this, vengeance was the force driving him. Because of this, Granger wanted to spend even less time at their second stop, the lake filled with brackish water.

Early the next morning he reined in Saber. There was something about the small lake ahead that disturbed him. Before, when they had arrived with the Comancheros, the ducks were spread all along the water's edge. Now they were clumped in two spaces, leaving a wide berth between. One duck quacked furiously at something he couldn't make out.

Grabbing his spyglass, Granger dismounted and moved in for a closer look, eventually fishtailing on his stomach. He scanned the banks through the glass. Everything seemed normal except for the ducks avoiding the empty spot.

He started to back up when a foot planted itself on the small of his back. Twisting around, he squinted up into the broad face of an Apache. Hearing Lisha's startled cry, he raised only to have a lance pointed at his throat. He lay still, his mind a kaleidoscope of emotions tumbling over a score of questions.

Finally another Indian came over and gruffly motioned for Granger to get up. He found Lisha where he'd left her, on the travois. She was talking to an Indian while several more stood nearby. As he drew nearer, he recognized the Apache.

"Granger, do you remember the shaman?" Lisha asked.

How could he not remember the Indian, along with the circumstances that hastened the violation of Lisha's friend, Flora? Granger wondered how he happened to be here.

He nodded. "I remember."

The shaman looked at him with his fathomless black eyes. "You take care of woman?" he asked, motioning toward his slipshod travois and his medical administrations.

"Yes."

The Indian took Lisha's face in his hand and turned her head from side to side, studying her blisters. He grunted his approval.

"I told him why I escaped into the desert."

"Did you tell him about the don and Lago?"

"Yes, Lago's part of the reason he's here."

"Oh?" Granger turned his attention to the shaman.

"I come for Lago. He live without honor, he die without honor."

"That's just what happened. Take my word."

An Indian who had kept himself in the background stepped up, gesturing toward Lisha and Granger. His lips pinched with contempt. The shaman kept shaking his head. Lisha turned a worried look to Granger. After a frightening moment the other Apache stalked off toward his horse.

"Goyaale thirsts for blood. I tell him of my debt to you. I save your life. Now debt is paid."

Lisha let out her breath. "We are grateful, Shaman."

"Yes," Granger added, "thank you. Sounds like the sooner we fill up on water, the sooner we can leave."

"Is Mexican still after you?"

Granger stopped short of his horse. "Why?"

"Mexicans hide by lake. We watch."

"Oh, Granger, do you think it's Chavez?" Lisha asked fearfully.

"Who else could it be?"

"Is this man, Chavez, man who buy you?" the shaman asked Lisha.

"Yes."

"I have heard of this man. He is also without honor. You go. Goyaale will have his wish for blood."

Granger didn't need a second order to leave. He mounted his horse and urged the buckskin down the trodden road, skirting the lake. With Apache war cries echoing behind them, he wanted to be as far away from the lake as humanly possible. He also didn't want to be anywhere in the vicinity if the Indians changed their minds about him and Lisha. One thing was sure, they wouldn't have to keep looking over their shoulder for Chavez.

He pressed on until the horses drooped their heads. By midmorning they came to the next watering hole, Star Stream, and he prepared camp anticipating a tranquil rest not only for the animals but for themselves. After they bathed and changed their clothes, he scrubbed the soiled ones.

By suppertime Lisha had sat up, displaying more strength than she'd done for several days. She patted at her tousled hair with her bandaged hands. "Do you by any chance have a brush in that saddlebag of yours?"

Granger grinned. "I'll see what I can find."

He made a great pretense of shuffling through his things, then turned up with a small package. Lisha pulled the loosely tied string and found a matching brush and comb set.

"Oh, Granger," she said, her eyes lighting up. "They're beautiful. You're so thoughtful. . . . But—"

"But what?"

"But," she repeated, searching through the wrapper, "you've forgotten a mirror." When he didn't answer, she looked up at him with questioning eyes.

"I didn't forget."

"Why? How can I see—"

"That's just it," he said, barely running his knuckles down her cheek. "I don't want you to see yourself, not yet." Lisha reached a hand to her face, and he quickly cradled her fingers in his. "Don't, you're not yet healed."

Lisha's eyes misted over. "Oh, Granger, do I look that bad?"

With a groan, he pulled her to him. "No, no, you don't. It's just that I don't want anything to remind you of the desert. You sit and brush your hair. I'll be back." He disappeared for several minutes, returning with a secretive grin plastered to his face. With the aplomb of royalty, he bowed.

"Would Madam like this to set off her shining hair?" He held his arm behind his back, then with a wink revealed a yellow flower in the palm of his hand.

"Oh!" Lisha's delighted cry made his smile grow wider. "Where did you ever find this way out here?"

"It belongs here. You've been too sick to notice. It's from a prickly pear."

"It's lovely. Are there any more?"

"Look and see. Cacti are blooming all over the place." He pointed toward the horses. "There are some red flowers over there, and when we camped, I saw some pink and yellow ones. Keep a watch out, you'll find all colors."

Lisha held the flower to her nose. "I see something of beauty can sprout from something spiked with thorns, whether in nature or in people's lives."

"If you're saying there's a lesson to be learned here, I can't see it."

"You will, in time."

"I doubt it. Finish brushing your hair. We leave in a half hour."

In the coming hours Lisha changed from riding a horse, to travois, then back to the horse. Granger stopped long before sunup. Lisha's taut skin had taken on a grayish tone, and he made her lie down while he prepared camp in a nearby arroyo. He saw no other place to shield themselves from the coming sun and wind.

Lisha woke with a start. She smelled coffee, but oddly enough she swore she could smell frying bacon.

"Morning." Granger haunched down by the fire, stirring the sizzling strips of salt pork.

"I can't believe what I'm smelling. I'm afraid I'll wake up and find that I've been living the past few days in a mirage."

"You're not. Not anymore."

He handed her a tin plate of bacon and biscuits smothered in gravy. She took it eagerly. As her strength increased, so did her appetite.

"Aren't you afraid the aroma will bring uninvited guests?"

Grinning, Granger sat beside her. "I thought I'd chance it."

"I'm glad you did," she said, taking another bite. After eating in comfortable silence, she set aside her plate and nestled into the crook of Granger's arm. "I don't know when I've enjoyed breakfast more."

Granger picked up a twig and made sharp angles in the dirt. "Lisha, tell me more about this lawyer friend of yours."

"Weston? What made you think of him?"

"I must admit that I eavesdropped while you talked in your sleep."

"To start with, Weston is a very generous man who, with a little encouragement on my part, would declare himself."

"Oh." Granger unconsciously dug the twig into the ground, snapping it in half. "Why haven't you?"

Lisha caught a hint of anxiety in his voice, and she suppressed a smile. "I hesitated because I didn't know if I truly loved him or his magnitude."

"Magnitude?"

"Weston Clayborne is highly respected in St. Louis for his generosity. He has helped several people by coordinating charities, and he's convinced many to open up their homes for orphans. Of course, Weston's tried to keep this part of his life secret, but word leaks out. We've heard about how he's personally seen to the education of quite a few of the orphans he's sheltered."

"Why is he so concerned with homeless children?"

"I assume it's because he was once one himself."

"And here I thought he came from a wealthy family."

"He does. But he ran away from his grandmother and scavenged off the streets until a lawyer took him in. He's never forgotten the time he spent on his own, and he does anything he can to help the orphans."

Shifting positions, Granger tightened the armhold he had around Lisha's shoulders. He found he didn't care for the soft sound of her voice, or the look of admiration on her face when she talked of her "friend." Why, listening to her, this man Clayborne must be a hair-trigger away from sainthood. How could a hard-working rancher compete with a living, breathing saint?

With a startling blow he realized he was jealous. He found he didn't want her to sound and look like she did while talking about another man, even if she didn't love him.

"Tell me more about Freddy, about your childhood," his words clipped out. Not at all like he wanted them to sound.

"Freddy?" Her face lit up when she said his name. "I must confess that we had gotten ourselves into and out of scrapes as the summers passed, until . . ." Her expression dulled.

"Until?"

"One summer Freddy's father failed to make his usual run down the Mississippi. I never saw or heard of Freddy again." She paused. "I sure missed him. But I didn't have time to dwell on it because that's when my mother turned ill, and I gave all my attention to her. Then we had other problems at home."

Granger encouraged her to go on, and while she unfolded the sensitive parts of her character, he saw her in full dimension, realizing that her life hadn't started when she'd come to take care of Rena. His pride in her filled his heart.

For some reason he felt possessive toward her. He hadn't shared that part of her life, and it surprised him to find out that he didn't like it. Oh, he knew he didn't begrudge her her past. He just wanted to be there in her future. He wanted to experience more with her than their harrowing trip down into Mexico and back again. He wanted to be her life, her love, her main reason for living.

An enormous feeling of tenderness enveloped him. He could see for the first time what Jackson had tried to tell him. He could see that he loved her, cherished her, adored her. Studying her in a new light, he thought of the past few months, and his reactions since she'd first introduced herself.

Hell! I loved her the minute I saw her standing beside my wagon, and I was too pigheaded to see it.

He remembered how she'd looked that day with her disheveled clothes. How the dust smudged her lovely face and how her unruly curls poked out from underneath her hat, and he smiled.

"Granger?"

"Yes?"

Lisha had twisted around to face him. "I asked you a question, but I don't think you heard me."

"Sorry. What was it?"

"I asked if I looked that bad."

"What do you mean?"

"You were staring at me so strangely, I must look worse than I thought."

His tender glance roved over her upturned face. Even though

blisters still marred her skin, her unusual beauty shone through. He gazed with awe and wonder at the woman he loved.

"Granger?"

He heard her sharp intake of breath. "The reason I'm looking at you so funny," he said, searching her face, "is that I'm just beginning to realize what a fool I've been. I knew you were a thief of hearts when I found you in my garden that night. Now I realize that you've stolen mine. Maybe that's the good thing coming out of all this. I know now that I love you. That I've always loved you."

Lisha blinked several times, as if she could hardly believe her ears. "Oh, Granger! I have loved you, too, almost from the beginning." Her voice choking on the words, she balled up her mittened hands. "And I could just beat you!"

"Beat me? Why?"

A tear rolled down her cheek. "Look at me!" she moaned. "I have long dreamed of this moment when you would say those words to me. And now, when you do, I look as if I could be the main exhibit in a peep show."

He gingerly placed a big hand on the side of her head and whipped away the tear with his thumb. He bent down and gently kissed the tip of her nose, careful not to hurt her. "To me you're the most beautiful sight I've ever seen. I love your battle scars. They're proof to me of what kind of woman I've chosen to become my wife and the mother of my daughter.

"Now," he said, gathering her close to him, "I want to know what you did to Lago on the auction block. I can hardly believe the gossip going around town, but somehow I know it's probably true. Not only that, I want to know how you outsmarted Chavez." He chuckled. "Take your time. I've the feeling I'm going to enjoy every minute of it."

He didn't have to possess her body to know that he owned her heart. There would be plenty of time for that later, when she fully recovered. For now he contented himself just to hold her close, to feel her breathing beside him and know she belonged to him and him alone.

Later, as he got a good look at the black thunderheads gathering in the far distance, his satisfied smile dimmed. His

brows bunched. By the looks of things, he'd better start
breaking camp, and the sooner the better.

Lisha woke from her short nap. She stretched, taking a deep
breath. For some reason the air smelled purer, and the blue
expanse over her head seemed brighter than before. And . . .
She stopped her musings. Looking to the north, she could
swear it was raining, but the rain seemed to evaporate before it
hit the dry ground.

A noise drew her attention from the sky, and she found
Granger tying the supplies to the packhorses. As he bent to
retrieve his saddle, he glanced up to find her watching him. He
winked and smiled. A shiver of delight wiggled through to her
heart.

"I see you're finally awake." He hefted the saddle onto
Saber and cinched the belt. "I thought I might have to throw
you over the horse like a sack of wheat and tie you on."

"You did not."

"Well, I must admit that I didn't, but the thought sure gnaws
at my mind. In fact, the more I think about it, the more it
appeals to me." He turned toward her, wringing his hands in
villainous glee. She squealed, scooting back on her buttocks.
Executing a perfect leap, he pinned her body with his. "Ha, ha!
My pretty maid. I've got you."

Dramatically placing a hand to her forehead, she lowered her
lashes. "Please, kind sir, let me go. My father ran off with the
schoolmarm, my mother took to her bed in childbirth, and I'm
the only one who can feed my twelve brothers and sisters."

"My, my! Twelve siblings, and your dear mother has taken
to her bed? Seems to me that she's never left it." Suddenly his
eyes darkened. "Although"—his voice lowered to a husky
timbre—"I must admit that the idea sounds exceptionally good
to me. I'd like to get you to bed, too, and keep you there."

His words worried her. "I'm afraid you'll soon tire of me."

Granger kissed her eyelids, her cheek, then the whisper of
space was gone when his lips lingered softly on her mouth.
"When I tire of you, my sweet," he said gruffly, "they'll be
laying me to rest, and even then my hunger for you will live
throughout the eternities."

"Oh, Granger!"

She wrapped her arms about him, holding him close, feeling his rapidly beating heart thump against her chest. Here was a man who truly loved her. She could see it in his eyes, and the knowledge written there made her soul sing with joy.

Without warning, a gun roared and a bullet furrowed the earth inches from Granger's chest. He whipped over, automatically slapping at his side only to realize he'd left his rifle with his gear. Cursing, he pulled Lisha to her feet. They faced a Mexican astride a black stallion, forty yards away.

Don Esteban Chavez favored his left arm. The material at his shoulder matted deep red, and dust covered his clothes. At the sight of him, Lisha felt as if she'd been crushed by an avalanche.

"I must thank you, señor, for taking such good care of my property. Now, may I please have her back." It was not a question but a command.

Lisha stared at the don, her mind too numb to think. Something farther on down the arroyo drew her attention. She clutched Granger's arm until her knuckles whitened.

"Granger, look!"

"Señorita Harrington, I will not fall for such a—"

A thunderous roar interrupted him. He turned to face a flash flood rumbling down through the gorge toward them.

Chapter
❧❧ 24 ❧❧

Lisha's feet seemed to take root, anchoring her to the ground. Powerless to do anything, she kept her eyes glued to the rushing tide. She heard someone yell her name, but she couldn't drag her gaze from the hypnotic wave and the leafless trees and bushes that rolled at its base. The distinct smell of water striking dry earth filled her nostrils.

The don whipped his frantic horse on up the opposite side of the arroyo. The stallion sidestepped, slid in the rocky dirt, then gained shaky ground. Fright widened the animal's eyes, his nostrils flared a bloodred, and his shrill whinnies ripped through the air.

She barely noticed a movement alongside her and scarcely heard the nervous snort of a horse. Then Granger gripped her under the arms and lifted her, setting her crossways in front of him. The saddle horn dug into her hip.

Saber quaked beneath her, and she gripped her arms about Granger's neck, knowing their lives depended on the strength of his horse. The animal shook his head, jerking at the taut reins. Granger guided him on up the side of the arroyo, urging him with soothing words and the pressure of his knees. The horse calmed and took solid steps.

Glancing over Granger's shoulder, Lisha saw Esteban and his stallion war with death. She couldn't force herself to look away, for the closer the flash flood, the more frightened the horse, and he started to backslide.

The don jerked on the reins, whipping his mount's flank

with a quirt. Letting out a shrill scream, the stallion reared. His black tail and mane flared as he pranced on hind legs. In the next instant he lost his footing and fell over backward. For several seconds horse and rider hung suspended in time, then plunged downward to be swallowed up by the boiling water.

The horrifying scene branded itself on Lisha's mind and heart. Would they be next? The flood churned just seconds away, and she buried her face against Granger's shoulder. She could feel each laborious lunge that Saber made as he steadily forged his way up.

Suddenly the buckskin slid backward, dislodging rocks and shale. Lisha's stomach lurched. A scream died on her lips, and she tightened her grip. Granger sucked in air. She could feel his blood pound alongside his neck.

"Easy, Saber, easy," he crooned. "You can make it, boy. Steady now, steady."

Lisha prayed with all her heart. One false step could send them hurtling down into the arroyo. She opened her eyes to see the edge of the gorge give way to the swirling water a scant ten feet from them. The thunderous roar drummed in her ears.

Granger dug his heels into Saber's flanks, and the buckskin lunged. He planted front hooves on firm ground while the flood ate at the crumbling rim under his hindquarters. Little by little the earth steadily gave way. Lisha held her breath. Her chest ached. They would surely be sucked under.

"Granger?"

His grip around her tightened. "We're almost there."

Once more she felt the bunch of Saber's muscles. He jockeyed about, found a solid footing, and scrambled over the edge.

As fast as the flood moved upon them, it was gone. Lisha could no longer hear the deafening rumble, only the rapid beating of her heart. They had come within inches of being swept down the arroyo along with the debris. In vivid detail she remembered how the don's stallion pawed the air, lost his balance, and toppled over. She tried to close her mind to the terrible scene, but it played back time and time again.

Granger stepped down from his quivering horse and reached up to pull Lisha into his arms, hugging her tightly to his chest.

He acted as if she might somehow disappear, and he'd never find her again. "Lisha." He breathed her name over and over.

"Esteban is gone," she choked out, clinging to Granger. "I s-saw his horse fall and—"

"Shh," he admonished, smoothing her hair. "Don't think about it, honey. It'll drive you crazy if you let it. I don't feel bad for Chavez, but I sure feel sorry for that stallion of his."

He led her over to the jittery packhorse. It was then she realized that the other animals had made it out of the arroyo on their own. Granger uncinched his saddle and put it on her horse.

"I'm afraid we've lost the travois along with the rest of your riding gear. I'll ride bareback and let you use mine. When we get to El Paso, I'll trade Lago's horse in on another saddle and replenish our supplies. In a few weeks we'll be home."

"Home! The word sounds so good to me. When I pass through those arches, nothing but an earthquake will get me to leave for a long, long time."

"An earthquake? What about our wedding?" Granger teased, skillfully prodding her to think of something else other than the flash flood.

"The guests and the preacher will just have to come to us."

"And the honeymoon?"

"Honeymoon? I've done enough sightseeing to last a lifetime. Haven't you?"

The corner of his mouth twitched. "Seems we differ on what we think a honeymoon consists of."

"You know as well as I that newlyweds usually travel and see the sights."

"Oh, I plan on taking in the sights, all right, but I've no thoughts to traveling."

"No thoughts? How then . . . ?" Her cheeks flushed at the twinkle in his eyes. "I wasn't thinking of . . . I mean, that part never . . . well, I can't say never, I . . . Oh, dear."

"Come, before you finish burying yourself," Granger ordered. He helped her onto her saddle and swung up on Saber, all the time blocking Lisha's view from the swollen gorge. "Now, tell me, Miss Harrington," he said, urging their mounts forward, "what kind of shindig would you want for our wedding?'' Talking wouldn't completely take away her thoughts of the don, but it'd keep him in the background.

Lisha tired sooner than she thought she would, realizing just how nice the travois had been. Every time Granger thought she needed rest, he'd dream up some outlandish excuse as to why they should stop. She had to smile at his mothering.

The flood had washed away her hat, so he tied his extra shirt on her head. And because he was concerned that she stay out of the hot sun as much as possible, he still chose to travel at night. Sometimes he had to throw a blanket between two bushes for shade, making it a crude lean-to, but it worked.

Early one morning they passed through the shifting sands. Lisha kept her eyes averted from the carcasses strewn about. Granger took the going slow, not wanting their animals to end up with broken legs. When they finally reached the stagnant pool, Lisha knew El Paso was not far away.

Granger wiped the sweat from his brow and scanned the sky. ''It's time to break for camp.''

''Let's keep going. It's not much farther.''

''It'll soon be the hottest part of the day. Besides,'' he said, slapping his hat against his thigh and raising dust, ''I could use some shut-eye, couldn't you?''

''No,'' she shot back. ''I'm not the least bit tired.''

Granger grinned. ''Well, I am, and so are the animals.''

He fashioned her a bed, changed the dressings on her hands and feet, nodding at their healing progress, and went about preparing camp. Annoyed, she lay down. Despite her resolve to stay awake, her eyelids drooped, and she soon fell asleep.

Dawn was just breaking through the ashen sky as they passed through a broken country, perfectly barren, and descended a ridge covered with greasewood and mesquite. When they struck into the valley of El Paso, Lisha reined in her horse to savor the sight of vineyards and orchards.

Was it only last month when she'd first passed this way? To her it seemed like a lifetime ago. She had experienced more in a few months than most people do during their entire lives.

By the time they rode into El Paso, a few of the townspeople had started to stir. A man in the local feed and grain store

appeared in the shop's window and stared after them. The
bartender of a saloon swept his boardwalk, apparently not
caring if he sent dust flying over a man slumped against the
hitching post. A half-empty bottle of whiskey lay wedged
between his thighs. Another of the establishment's customers
lay prone where he'd fallen the night before in a drunken
stupor.

Granger watched three men on horseback advance toward
them. Their sullied appearance rivaled that of the Comancheros. They seemed to take too much interest in Lisha, causing
Granger's hackles to raise. When one man came abreast of her
horse, he opened his mouth to utter something, but Granger's
murderous glance silenced him. Granger pulled Saber in closer
to Lisha, as if in doing so would keep her safe.

She glanced up at him with eyes the color of the early
morning sky and just as languid. A whisper-soft sigh escaped
through her throat. She stretched her back muscles, trying to
relieve the ache.

Guilt washed over Granger. He'd wanted to complete his
trade and leave before the street became too crowded. The fear
of someone else grabbing Lisha waxed strong. But even though
every nerve screamed hurry, he knew he had to let her sleep in
a real bed, between clean sheets. If there were such things as
sheets, clean or otherwise, in this town.

Directly ahead of them was an adobe house with a cross
firmly attached in its roof. The modest building had the
appearance of a church, except that odors of percolating coffee
and frying pork wafted out through the paneless windows.

Then again, maybe it was one of those Protestant sects that
established missions to fed the sinner while trying to save him.
And if they fed them, would they be so apt to provide clean
lodgings?

He sure could down some real food in a *safe* atmosphere and
knew Lisha could, too. And if anybody looked as if he needed
a bit of saving grace, Granger did. Besides, maybe all his
problems could be solved in one place, for he couldn't shake
the feeling that if Lisha carried his name it would somehow
protect her. He reined Saber to a halt and dismounted.

"Are we going to stop and eat?" The gleam in Lisha's eyes matched the hopefulness in her voice.

"We're not only going to stop and eat, we're going to rest a spell," Granger said, securing the reins. With a broad wink he helped her down.

Lisha glanced warily back the way they'd come as if she expected Lago or the don to jump out at them at any moment. "Do you think it's safe?"

"As safe as can be around this town. But I sure could use a good night's sleep on a bed. How about you?"

A smile lit her face. "I sure could at that."

Granger grasped her mittened hand and escorted her through the door. It took a while to get used to coming in from the bright morning sun. The smells of food, almost but not quite, muted out the age-old odor of the house. There were no pews and pulpit to fill the small room, just a hodgepodge of tables and chairs making it look even less of a church. Two old men glanced up from their plates long enough to see who interrupted their breakfast, then went back to work on their food.

"What can we do for you?"

Granger turned to face a large woman who looked as solid as a cannon, just as tough, and twice as old. She'd pulled her hair back into a tight bun, wore men's logging boots, and rolled the sleeves of her dress to her elbows, baring arms the size of a hub from a wagon wheel. Everything about her was big, from the size of her feet to the shape of her nose.

At first glance he knew he wouldn't want to face her across a wrestler's ring. There wouldn't be any question as to who'd win the match. Feeling like a slacker with the schoolmaster bearing down on him, he whipped off his hat.

"I was hoping you could help us, ma'am—"

"The name's Faith, Faith Percell." Her voice even sounded as if it were shot from a cannon.

"I'm Granger Hawks, and this is Miss Falisha Harrington. We are in need of a meal, a bath, a room, and . . . a priest. We want to get married." Lisha took in a sharp breath and squeezed his hand.

"We surely can get you something to eat, but a room . . ." The woman's stern look had swept over their travel-weary appearances and zeroed in on Lisha's dressings. "Laws, child!"

she exclaimed, taking Lisha's hand in a meaty palm. "What in heaven's name happened to you?" She slanted an accusing glance at Granger.

Lisha sighed. "It's a long story. Granger—"

"I found her in the desert. She'd been captured by Comancheros."

"Comancheros?" The woman's face hardened at the name. "Say no more. I've had some run-ins with a few myself. They got the short end of the deal." She smirked at a job apparently well done, then straightened her back and gave Granger a baleful gaze. "I don't know the how of it where you come from, but I'll not allow you another second alone with this young lady without the proper words. You'll find the chapel that way." She pointed to a hall behind them. "My brother Matthew's the minister. I'll find him and meet you there."

Granger stared after the woman. "Well, I guess that's that. Lisha, do you mind not having a wedding with all the trimmings?"

She looked at him, her guileless eyes wide. "We have a bride, a groom, and our love. What more do we need?"

He gave her a quick squeeze and led her to the chapel.

"What God has wrought, let no man put asunder."

The chapel filled with the preacher's voice. For Lisha's sake, Granger wished it were filled with roses and forget-me-nots. Only the minister and Faith attended the ceremony. He wished they had family and friends here to witness their union. Lisha stood beside him in a pair of men's trousers and a flannel shirt three sizes too big. He wished she wore satin and lace befitting such a beautiful bride.

"I now pronounce you man and wife. . . . Well," Reverend Percell boomed out, "aren't you going to kiss the bride?"

For a moment Granger couldn't comprehend what the man had said, then he swept Lisha into his arms and delivered a resounding kiss.

Seconds later Faith pounded him on the back and gave Lisha a swift hug. She dabbed at her eyes with a corner of her flour-splotched apron. "I do so love weddings. I guess you'd call me a pushover."

Granger cocked a brow at that, and Lisha gave him a warning nudge. Already she was acting like a wife. *Wife.* He liked the sound of that.

"Come, come," Reverend Percell interjected into his thoughts, "we've had something prepared for you to eat."

They followed the pair into what Granger guessed was their private quarters. A table had been set with a red checkered cloth and mismatched pewter plates and utensils. A half-burnt candle, nestled in a tin cup, listed to its side.

Granger wished he could have presented his bride to a table dressed in linen, graced with china and silverware, and bedecked by a silver candelabrum and long white candles.

He seated Lisha, and Faith brought them plates piled high with strips of pork, tortillas and beans, and a pot of coffee. Then, almost before he knew it, they were alone. From somewhere in the house he heard a woman humming a tune. It wasn't the violins that Lisha deserved, and it wasn't a magnificent feast that she had due. But he'd make up for it. Even if it took him the rest of his life, he'd see to it that his wife got everything she was entitled to.

"Oh, Granger, isn't this lovely?" Lisha thought she'd never been so happy nor so content in her life.

"What?"

"Everything Faith and Reverend Percell have done to make this time special for us. Isn't it lovely?"

"You mean . . . you're not disappointed?"

"Disappointed? Why would I be disappointed with such loving care—and you by my side?" She poured them each a cup of coffee. "They were right," she announced.

"They?"

"Those who profess that a wedding day is the happiest day of a woman's life."

"Care to venture what part makes a man happy?"

His lips held a casual smile, but his eyes glistened. He gazed at her from over the rim of his cup, and she read the meaning there. Her heart tripped.

The simple meal turned out to be excellent, but she wasn't as aware of it as she was of the man who sat across from her. She observed as much as she could about him; the funny way he tilted his head when he laughed, the way his voice lowered when his words carried dual meanings, and the way his eyes deepened in color when he looked at her.

He made her laugh, blush, thrill, but most of all he made her yearn for the time his arms could be about her. His touch sent her senses spinning. His boyish grin warmed her. His green-flecked eyes promised her of things yet to come.

An impassioned spell wove about them, fusing their souls, capturing their hearts. She made a token effort to consume her food, but she longed for the taste of Granger's kisses instead.

In the action of crossing her legs her sandal fell off, and her bandaged toes brushed against his shin. As if in an unconscious habit, she massaged her toes alongside the inner part of his knee and leg. His voice trailed off.

Taking another bite of beans, she glanced up to face the hunger her aimless actions caused. Granger looked for all the world like a wolf who was about to pounce on a stray kitten. Quickly withdrawing her foot, she stared at his besotted expression, barely remembering to swallow. Their growing hunger craved something other than food. Granger shifted uncomfortably in his chair.

Just then, Faith brought in a cake fresh from the oven and handed her a knife. "It's not the fanciest job," she said, indicating the shrunken middle and shriveled sides, "but our hearts were in it."

"Thank you, Faith. I think it's the most beautiful wedding cake I've ever seen and the most appreciated."

Faith grinned her satisfaction as she headed toward the door. "I'll be back when your room is ready."

"Mrs. Hawks, would you be so good as to cut our wedding cake?" Granger asked, warily eyeing their pastry.

Taking the knife, Lisha sliced a small piece. She picked up the spicy wedge and held it out for Granger. He took a bite, his teeth nipping the tips of her fingers. After he swallowed, she pushed the rest of the cake into his mouth, placing her index finger against his lips while he chewed. She started to draw her hand away, but he snatched it up and kissed away the remaining crumbs.

Someone cleared her throat, and they reluctantly turned to

see Faith filling the doorway. "Your baths and room are ready."

Baths? Room?

"Shall we, Mrs. Hawks?"

Granger gave Lisha a lopsided grin that tugged at her heart. "A . . . bath does sound heavenly."

He leapt up to assist her and planted a warm kiss on her earlobe. "Milady, your . . . bath awaits."

With her heart thudding against her rib cage, Lisha walked beside her husband to their wedding chambers.

Chapter
25

After telling them about a tub in the men's quarters of the mission home and showing them one in the room where they were to sleep, Faith left them to their privacy.

Wordlessly Granger went to Lisha and clutched her to his chest in a hard embrace. "Did I ever tell you how beautiful you are?"

His breath fanned her ear. Her heart tipped dramatically. "In this git-up?"

"In anything. You'd look beautiful in anything. And I love you."

"I love you, too. Oh, how I love you."

His mouth sought hers, moving gently across her lips, then becoming more insistent. She pressed against him, wanting, demanding more. The beat of her pulse in her ears tripped up its rhythm. In shaky motions he tore his mouth from hers and held her tight.

"As I mentioned before, milady," he said, his voice husky, "your bath awaits."

He stepped back, reached for her hand, and began to unwrap her bandages. As the strips of cloth fell away, his unfathomable eyes searched hers, delving into their depths as if he studied her soul. Freeing her hand, he took the other, all the while never taking his gaze from her.

The dressings dropped to the floor, and Granger dragged his perusal from her face to take a look at her injuries. The blisters had changed from raw open sores to angry, new skin. Bringing

256

her hands to his lips, he gingerly touched the sensitive palms with featherlike caresses. Shivers skipped down her spine.

"Too lovely to be impaired."

He set her on a nearby chair, removed her one remaining sandal and unwrapped the bandages from both feet. Here, too, the blisters gave way to new skin. He held her feet, rubbing the sides of his thumbs along her insteps. Giggling, she pulled away. He held fast.

"Ticklish, huh?"

"Very."

"Well, well. Now I know how to punish you when your impulsive nature becomes the best of you."

"Impulsive?"

"Okay, let's go for just plain bullheadedness."

"Bullheadedness?" Lisha retorted, acting offended. "I don't have a stubborn bone in my body." He cocked a brow. "All right, I plead guilty. But you must admit I've been very clever at times."

"Honey, after witnessing your . . . flight . . . out of the barn loft, I'm sure you have talents I'm not even aware of."

He unbuckled her belt, set her on her feet, and pushed her trousers to the floor. Then he started unbuttoning her shirt. She could feel the warmth of his fingers through to her skin and took a calming breath.

"You don't have to, you know." Her voice sounded as jumbled as she felt.

"Have to what?"

"Help me undress."

He stopped his actions and looked at her. "I'm seeing the pleasure you take in helping people."

"Then . . . then it's all right for me to be a nurse?"

He enveloped her hands in his and held them to his cheek. "I lost one woman I loved," he choked out, "and I almost lost you. I couldn't bare going through that again."

"But you didn't almost lose me because of nursing."

"I know. But the fear is there." He buried his face in her hands. "Promise me you'll never even allow yourself to be called a nurse, much less—"

"Shh," she admonished, tilting his chin. "Let's not think of

that right now. Let's just think of the here and now.'' Her
fingers framed his jawline, and she raised her mouth, working
her lips across his. Granger kissed her back, kissed her long
and hard. He crushed her to his chest, as if to convince himself
that she was really here and finally his.

Eventually he let her go and with clumsy fingers slid her
shirt from her shoulders, unlaced her corset, and discarded the
rest of her clothing. Next he unbraided her locks, fanning out
her hair.

He stared at her then, drinking in every line, every curve.
Suddenly she realized she wasn't embarrassed. It seemed
natural; it seemed right. He reached out, cupping her face, then
slid his fingertips along her neck and shoulders and onto her
arms. Leaning over, he planted a kiss on her collarbone.

"You're supposed to be taking a bath," he murmured
reluctantly. In one swift motion he swept her up into his arms,
crossed over to the metal tub, and slowly lowered her into the
soothing water. "Lay there and soak until I get back."

For several moments Lisha thought of her newly wedded
husband and the marital bed. In the past she'd heard things,
caught elusive whispers. Was the complete union between a
man and a wife really as bad as some women had hinted at?

How could it be when every part of her body had tingled
when Granger stared at her? Deep inside she knew that that
part of marriage was something wonderful, something to
anticipate. A thrill raced from her abdomen to her stomach.

Lisha had washed her hair and started the final rinse when
the pail was taken from her hands.

"Here, let me do that for you."

Granger's low voice thrilled her. She bent forward, and he
poured out the water, working it through her hair. At the nape
of her head, around her temples, and across her forehead, she
felt his caressing fingertips and yearned to feel them all over.

Ending too soon, he then wrapped a piece of toweling
around her head and reached for the cake of soap. Before she
knew it, he held one of her feet, working up a good lather.
Carefully, precisely, he rubbed his hands up and down, sliding
his fingers between her toes, and massaging the pad of her foot.
That done he reached for the other.

Nothing was said during his loving ministrations. Nothing needed to be said. She stared at him. His freshly washed hair glittered; his chest, broad and tanned, swelled with muscles; his towel, tied loosely at his waist, exposed a taut stomach dusted with sandy curls.

Again he soaped up his hands, then positioned himself behind her. He washed her neck, shoulders, and back, drawing little figures as he went. Warm water rinsed away any evidence of his explorations. He lathered a trail from her shoulders, down her arms, and onto the backs of her hands, working gingerly around each finger.

With his hands he created a magical friction along her flesh. With his lips he nipped a burning path down the side of her throat. Glistening bubbles burst as he worked one hand down and around to the swell of her breasts, while he slid the other along her abdomen to the inside of her thighs.

Her eyelashes fluttered closed; her head moved limply on her neck. Instead of stroking the sensitive parts of her body that took flame, he deliberately teased the nearby areas. Sensations spread, emotions whirled. She laid her head against his chest, languishing in his touch. It felt good. Oh, sooo good.

He rinsed her off, swishing water over her heated skin. Ever so slowly he drew a washcloth across her chest until water ran down her breasts and angled to her midriff. Gently he slipped his hands through the crooks of her arms and kneaded her hips and waist, tantalizing his way up.

Her stomach tightened. Her flesh burned. Her senses clamored for . . . what? She didn't know. All she knew was that his touch left fire in its wake. Then, in one heart-catching moment, his fingertips brushed across those sentient spots. Desire shot through to her core.

She moaned, and his lips captured hers. Without breaking contact, they stood. She wrapped her arms about his neck, her thighs about his hips. Towels dropped to the floor, and her wet hair fell like a curtain over their shoulders.

His mouth was hot and heavy on hers. She felt the heat of his kisses, the reaction of her senses. Their breath mingled; their tongues dueled; their bodies fused. He carried her to the bed

and carefully laid her down. A heady languor licked along her
veins, filling her with an intoxicating excitement.

Jumbled thoughts vibrated in the silence. She became
acutely aware of every muscle and inflamed nerve ending,
aware that the rapid beating of her heart matched his. She
nibbled at his lower lip, capturing it between her teeth. His
body shuddered its response, and she strained shamelessly
against him.

He claimed her then, slowly, surely. At first there was a
spurt of pain, but it was soon overcome by the intense flow of
hunger. His passion built until it consumed her in its blaze. She
felt herself rise higher and higher, until everything peaked,
until everything ignited, and a flame, hot and searing, burst
through her loins. She cried out her ecstasy, her craving, her
pleasure . . . until her thudding heart calmed.

Instead of returning the way they'd come, Granger preferred
to travel along the western flanks of the Sacramento, and the
Sierra Blanca Mountains, then turn northeast toward home.
They crossed paths with a regiment from Fort Stanton, and
Granger explained their circumstances. The captain agreed that
when the next dispatcher rode to Fort Sumner, he would see to
it that word of their safety reached Cibola.

When at long last Lisha finally viewed the ranch house, an
overwhelming feeling of peace settled over her. The whitewashed building offered solace and a chance to heal her
wounds, the invisible ones.

After reining her mount to a stop, she wearily climbed down
and leaned her head against the saddle. She heard someone
open the door to Granger's home, her home.

"Lisha! Granger! You don't know how I've worried over
you two!" Martha joyfully bounded down the steps and
hugged Lisha. Tears reddened her close-set eyes. "I prayed to
God that Granger would find you and bring you safely home."
She tucked an arm around him, not minding the red dust on his
clothes. "I knew my prayers would be answered."

Lisha smiled. She, too, was glad to see the energetic woman.
Her salt and pepper hair was pulled back into its usual bun, and

her clothes still boasted of their starched appearance, but to her, the woman couldn't have been more beautiful.

"When that army dispatcher brought word to the hotel about you two, I could hardly contain myself. I packed some provisions and came straight away. I gave the house a thorough dusting and almost finished a long overdue quilt while I waited for you. I can't tell you how glad I am to see that you're both safe and sound."

A pesky buzzing droned in Lisha's ears. She could hardly hear Martha or focus on her smiling face. A tremendous weakness invaded her body, and she sagged. A familiar pair of hands gripped her waist. She was lifted up and cradled against a broad chest. Fragments of conversation drifted in and out of her consciousness. "Poor dear, she's plum give out . . . gone through a lot . . . hot water to wash the dust . . . to her room."

She felt the give of a feather mattress under her outstretched body, and she physically and mentally sank into its rich softness. Granger proceeded to slip off her boots and stockings. He unbuttoned her shirt and gently lifted her to pull it from her shoulders.

"Here, what do you think you're doing?" Martha commanded, choosing that moment to bustle through the doorway. She plopped the basin full of hot water down on the nightstand. Its clatter underlined the astonished tone of her voice. "You know as well as I what's proper and what's not."

"It's all right, Martha. We're married. We got married in El Paso."

Martha's eyes widened. For a few moments the news rendered her speechless. "Well, glory be!" she exclaimed, giving Granger a swift hug. "I couldn't be happier." She gave Lisha's hand a quick squeeze. "No, sir, I couldn't be happier. But married or no, it's not seemly for a man to take on nursing duties. I'll see to Lisha. There's hot water for you on the stove." With that, Martha shoved Granger out the door and proceeded to give Lisha a sponge bath.

Lisha smiled to herself. Granger was so accustomed to taking care of her that he automatically started to do what needed to be done. What would Martha say if she knew that he

not only had changed her clothing, careful to keep her dignity
intact, but had bathed and dressed her wounds? A hot flush
swept through her when she remembered how thoroughly he
had helped her bathe. A lot had passed between them,
cementing their hearts, making them captive.

Martha helped Lisha into a flannel nightgown scented with
lavender, and she slept. Built-up tension, caused by the events
of the past months, demanded payment. Hours blended into a
day, then two. Lisha woke for short periods of time, long
enough to eat, wash up, or chat with Martha while she worked
on her quilt, then she returned to her exhausted sleep. Martha
sat at her side, not Granger. The woman said she'd sent him to
his bed because he looked almost as bad as she.

After a while her dreamless sleep evolved into fragments of
the past. The tormenting shards soon developed into nightmares, and she woke up screaming. She found herself standing
against something cold and hard, and she frantically tried to
claw her way out.

Suddenly she was held tight. "It's all right, love. It was just
a bad dream. You're safe now. I'm here. Nothing bad will ever
happen to you again. I'll make sure of it."

Granger's comforting voice broke through to her, and she
sank into his arms, sobbing out his name. He swept her up and
carried her to the bed, all the while talking to her in soothing
tones as if she were a child. She wouldn't let go of him, and he
stretched out alongside her. His tender stroke assured her that
everything was indeed all right.

Martha stood in the doorway, listening to Granger's consoling words filled with love. At first she'd chastised herself for
leaving Lisha alone, but now, after seeing what transpired in
the moonlit room, she was glad she had. The girl's sobs turned
to occasional whimpers, then steady breathing rhythmically
attuned with Granger's. Martha smiled, quietly shutting the
door. She knew she left Lisha in good hands.

Lisha woke to the morning sun. Rays filtered spun sugar
across the room, leaving delicate webbing in its wake. She
yawned and stretched, grateful that the previous night's dream

had dimmed. The shuddering nightmare had been outweighed by Granger's cradling arms.

The door swung open and the object of her loving thoughts walked in, carrying a breakfast tray. Granger smiled his pleasure at finding her awake. She scooted up against the bedstead, eagerly anticipating what the combined aromas promised. He laid the tray across her lap and sat beside her. With a flourish he whipped off the towel, revealing crisp bacon, scrambled eggs, and toast.

"Are you going to join me?"

"I've already had mine."

Granger poured Lisha's coffee and settled back to watch her eat. He could see that the few days' worth of bed rest had produced positive results. Her pallor had changed from a gray cast to a becoming suntone shade. Her blue-gray eyes were bright and full of life. The silvery mane, which Martha had recently washed, curled profusely about her face. The only tattling reminders of her ordeal were the fading blisters and the way her eyelids darkened to a deep mauve. In spite of everything she presented a provocative picture.

Lisha grew warm under Granger's scrutiny. "I must look a sight."

As Granger slowly shook his head, a teasing grin played on his lips. "On the contrary, you look most appealing. Makes me remember how you looked under . . . other . . . circumstances."

"Granger Hawks!"

A wicked glint sparkled in his eyes. "Martha went into town."

"She did? Will she bring Rena back?"

Granger chuckled. "Yes, and no. We thought you still needed rest and decided not to bring the girls back for a few days."

"Girls?"

"You were right. Juanita needs our forgiveness. Besides, there's Maria to think about."

Lisha gazed at him. Water dampened his sun-streaked hair. A ruddy hue darkened his clean-shaven face. The elements had whitened the ridges at the corners of his eyes as well as the hairline scar. This made up part of his handsome exterior. But inside . . . inside, there was strength, courage, gentleness, and love. And that's what really counted. Her heart filled with joy, and her eyes glistened with tears.

"I love you with all my heart. I don't ever want you to leave me."

Granger removed the tray from her lap. He cupped her head with his hands and bent over to lightly kiss her quivering lips. She threw her arms about his shoulders, drawing him closer, and the kiss deepened, quickly swirling them in heated passion. When she thought he couldn't affect her any more than he already had, he teethed her lower lip, her throat, her earlobe. She hadn't felt this much desire, this much yearning, not since that long ago stormy night when they were secreted away in the dugout . . . not since their wedding night.

"We'll always be together," he choked out against the hollow of her throat. "Only death will separate us, and then only for a short time."

She whimpered her longing, and Granger once again played havoc on her senses, sending the blood pounding through her veins. Eventually he lifted his head. His love, devotion, desire, shone in his face.

"I hadn't intended for this to happen. I've been trying to restrain myself."

"Why work yourself so hard?"

She ran a fingertip along the ridge bowing his lips and raised her gaze to his. Could he see the craving deep inside her, the desire to, once again, bind their love? Groaning, he pushed himself upright.

"Before Martha left, she made me promise that I'd mind my manners today." He sighed. "Why did my parents have to pound into me that a man honors his word? It's a lesson hard to forget."

"No one will know," Lisha commented wickedly.

"*She'll* know. You can't keep anything from Martha. She knows I have to check on the remaining cattle and replace some fence posts. Besides, once I start loving you the way I want to, I'll be hard pressed to stop." His gaze locked with hers. "Like watching the early morning sun rise over the mesas, I intend to savor every beautiful moment."

Thoughts of Granger's leisurely lovemaking fluttered in her stomach. She, too, wanted it to be special. And a short romp in bed wouldn't satisfy either one of them.

"You promised Martha you'd mind your manners today," she said, raising a brow. "But I gather nothing was said about . . . tonight?"

A slow smile spread across Granger's lips. "Why, Mrs. Hawks, are you trying to tempt me?"

"I don't think I'll have to *tempt* very hard."

His thumb stroked the fullness of her breast. "You're right. Nothing was said about tonight." Giving a deep sigh, he pushed himself away from her. "You lie here and rest. I'll be gone for a couple of hours, but I'll be back in time to get us something for lunch."

He stared long and hard at her, as if trying to decide whether or not he should chance giving her a parting kiss. Then, thinking better of it, he left her alone.

A few minutes later she heard Saber's whinny. Throwing back the covers, she hurried to the veranda to watch Granger ride off, remembering the last time she'd seen him ride away. Only this time he would be coming back, back to her.

After admiring the beautiful morning with its earthy smells, she turned to see the forgotten tray. She knew Granger had told her to get back to bed, but someone had to take the remains of her breakfast downstairs. And if she had to do it, shouldn't she take time to rest, say on the porch, before making the arduous trip back up to her room?

With an impish grin she rummaged through her clothes and pulled out the ivory dress dotted with blue flowers. It was the same day dress she'd worn when she had eaten dinner with Granger the afternoon she had arrived in Cibola.

Grinning, she shrugged into the frock. The gauzy folds swirled around her. After wearing men's clothes, it felt good to wear a dress again, even if it was a little loose. She looked more like a woman, all curves wrapped up in delicious femininity. After securing the blue sash, she picked up the tray and, feeling like a truant child, headed downstairs.

* * *

Lisha dozed on the porch while a breeze playfully tugged at the loose strands of her hair. She had thoroughly enjoyed the New Mexico scene spread out before her, and now the lazy morning had successfully hummed her into a hypnotic trance. A fly buzzed around her head, but she was too drowsy to shoo it away. She felt warm, and comfortable, and content.

A horse's neigh broke into her lethargic state. Sighing, she roused herself to meet Granger. But instead of a lone horse-man, she saw someone driving a buggy into the courtyard. It couldn't be Martha. She hadn't had time to reach Cibola, let alone return.

The horse stopped just two yards from the steps, and a man easily stepped to the ground. White-blond hair hung almost to his shoulders. His long, drooping mustache gave his mouth the appearance of a perpetual frown. She'd never seen him before, and she sensed that she wouldn't like his purpose for coming.

The man paused with the bulk of his weight thrust on one slim hip. A holstered gun accentuated his stance. The pistol's low position spoke volumes.

"Are you Miss Falisha Harrington?" It sounded more like a statement than a question.

"I'm Falisha," she answered in a guarded tone.

He retrieved a folded piece of paper from his frayed breast pocket and sauntered over to her. "This is for you."

Hesitantly taking the stained document, she opened it up and scanned the words. "What exactly does this mean?"

"It's a warrant."

"A warrant? For me? What on earth for?"

"For questioning. The government thinks your father used his land to stash smuggled contraband brought in by blockade-runners. They want to find out how much you know about it."

"I-I don't believe it. It's not true!"

Even as she protested, several things added up in the back of her mind. This might explain how the money her family had desperately needed had suddenly shown up. Her father couldn't have gotten all of it from stripping Kingswood. She knew in her heart that a grain of truth lurked in this man's allegations.

"I see by the look on your face you know there's something to this. I've been sent to bring you back."

Part of her wanted to protest, to refuse. But she couldn't let things go as they were and allow her mother's side of the family to believe her dear papa was a traitor. He'd been many things, but not a traitor, never a traitor! The ugly word hung grotesquely in her thoughts.

She knew she had to go back and straighten things out, clear the Harrington name. Granger could help her. "How soon do you want to leave?" Her voice sounded as deflated as she felt.

"As soon as you pack. To make it easier on you, I've hired a buggy till we catch the stage. Then we'll take a train."

To make it easier? Ha! Should she tell him that, like a man, she'd spent a month astride a horse? Should she tell him she knew firsthand how deadly the sun can be? No. That knowledge solely belonged to her and Granger. Their experiences were still raw and not meant for a stranger's ears.

She stopped long enough to write a note for Granger before packing. All the while she hoped that if they left before he showed up, he could catch up with her. He had said nothing could separate them. Nothing except death. A tremor scaled her spine.

By the time the stranger hefted her valise up into the buggy, Granger rode in, reining Saber to a stop. He cautiously stepped down, carefully taking in her drawn appearance and the rangy man standing beside her.

"What's happening here?"

Lisha ran to his comforting arms. "This man has a warrant giving him the right to take me back to St. Louis for questioning. It seems they think Papa was involved with blockade-running during the war."

"Is what she says true?" Granger never took his eyes from the man.

"Says so right here." He fished the document from his pocket.

Granger took the paper offered him and read its contents. "It looks real enough."

"It is."

"Then you wouldn't mind if we take this into town and let our sheriff see it."

"Wouldn't do no good. She'd still have to come with me."

"Well, there is where we differ." Granger's tone hardened. "If Lisha's to be taken back to St. Louis, I'll do the taking."

The man's lazy stance stiffened. He centered his weight between his legs. His arms hung loosely at his sides. "Seems we have a disagreement, Mr. Hawks. Money's riding on this. I've been hired to take the lady back, an' I mean to do just that."

Money? Was the man a bounty hunter? And how had he known Granger's name?

Disquiet filled the air. She could taste it. Feeling pressure from Granger's hand, she stepped aside. The knowledge that the bounty hunter wore a gun, and Granger didn't, turned her mouth to sawdust.

The men faced each other, sizing each other up. They could nearly reach out and touch. Almost in the same second the bounty hunter drew his gun, Granger lunged forward. The momentum knocked them both to the ground. Granger's hands clamped tightly over the man's wrists. They wrestled for the weapon, each trying to gain control of the gun, each exerting his strength to the limit.

They twisted, rolling over and over on the courtyard. Suddenly a shot shattered Lisha's soul. Both men lay still. Moments later the stranger confirmed her worst fears when he pushed Granger off him. In a trance she stared at the blood rapidly soaking his shirt. The man rose to his feet and coldly leveled his gun at Granger's heart.

"No!"

She vaulted forward, pushing the man's gun arm up the second he squeezed the trigger. Granger's body jerked once. Blood appeared from nowhere, spreading into his hair and dripping onto the brick. An anguished cry caught in her throat. She stared mutely at Granger. Balling her fist, she pressed it to her quivering mouth.

Curses filled the air. In a rage the bounty hunter swung out and knocked her unconscious to the ground.

Chapter
26

Lisha woke with a start. The steady sway of the train had worked its hypnotic effect on her as well as most of the other passengers. An older man, who had covertly watched her when he thought she wasn't looking, slumped against the cushioned seat, snoring with his mouth open. Wind whistled through his great beak of a nose.

Turning her attention to her skirt, she brushed imaginary particles from the material's soft folds. She looked out at the rolling hills and wondered briefly where she was and why this lead weight in her chest? With a crushing blow, she remembered. Vivid memories of Granger lying in a pool of blood forced the breath from her lungs as surely as if she'd been thrown from a horse.

She placed a pale hand to her face. There were moments when she'd forget, then Granger's struggle with the bounty hunter would all come rushing back to her, and she would vividly live it all over again. The choking pain that suffocated her felt as great as it had when she'd first seen Granger's stilled body.

Would she ever be able to erase the picture of her dead husband from her tortured mind? She knew she'd never be the same again, never be whole.

Men had ogled her all along the trip back to St. Louis, but they'd kept their distance. Even if they'd thought about striking up a conversation with her, the disquieting presence of Jackal, the bounty hunter, was bound to stop them. But all the same, they'd kept a wistful eye on her.

She caused no trouble for Jackal, speaking little and docilely obeying his orders. Her subdued character continued to stay with her, even when they finally reached their destination.

Jackal showed Lisha up the steps to Judge Croft's office. Depositing her in the antechamber, he muttered something about waiting outside. He left her in silence, except for the ticking of the wall clock. The drab room, with its poor lighting and dark furnishings, emitted an unfriendly atmosphere. She much preferred the lighter tone of Weston's office.

The judge's secretary busied himself with paperwork, the quill pen scratching across the page. His leather chair creaked with every move. From time to time he would peer at her from over the rim of his glasses. His annoying glances added to her anxiety. The tedious waiting compounded her apprehension. She wondered if criminals felt this way just before meeting a man who could decide the paths to their futures.

The secretary cleared his throat, and she jumped. He turned his head and carefully studied her before continuing with his work. She knew she had to gain control of her nerves if she expected to convince the judge that she knew nothing about the alleged smuggling.

The door to the office finally swung open, and a portly man emerged. Puffy circles darkened his eyes. His shoulders slumped under an unknown weight. He avoided eye contact.

"Miss Harrington, would you come in, please?" He harshly clipped the words.

She followed the judge and took the chair he indicated. Lisha sat upright with her hands folded on top of her handbag and gave the impression of, she hoped, self-assurance. The man shuffled through some papers, hardly glancing her way. A frown creased his brow. His abrupt actions, and the way he overlooked her, caused her to think him an uncaring man. The thought made her heart freeze.

"Miss Harrington, we have information here that connects your father with a group of blockade-runners. Do you have any knowledge of this?"

Miss Harrington? She had no strength to inform him of her recent marriage . . . and widowhood. "No."

"In the time you spent at your home did you notice anything unusual going on, unusual activities among your staff?"

"We haven't had a staff, not since my mother became ill. And I don't remember ever seeing anything out of the ordinary."

"You mentioned your mother. I understand that your father had financial problems. Then suddenly he came up with the money to pay the creditors. Can you explain that?"

His monotoned questions reminded her of the way her uncle sounded during a flu epidemic. The judge clearly wanted to be done with the interview. Not only that, he hadn't seemed at all surprised by her answers.

"It had been my understanding that Papa sold off parts of Kingswood."

"Do you know this for sure?"

"Ask Weston Clayborne. He's our lawyer."

"I've already contacted him."

"Then he must have explained how he was able to work things out."

The judge's ring finger had a nervous twitch. She hadn't noticed that before.

"He did, but he also said he had no knowledge of your father's activities."

"And just what exactly do you propose my father did?"

"We think that he masterminded a smuggling group and hid the contraband on Kingswood until the goods could be sold."

"I assume you have proof?" she asked, her temper growing. "Proof that a grieving man, who had been half drunk out of his mind since the loss of his wife, ran an enterprise of this magnitude?"

"That part is speculation. What we do know is that your property had been used as a base."

"Then with this great amount of evidence are you planning to make formal charges of treason on a man already in his grave?" She could not disguise her contempt.

"We'll know that better when the investigation is finished.

You're free to go now, but I would admonish you to stay in St. Louis until the matter is cleared up.''

"Is that all?"

"Yes. For the time being." He stood abruptly. "Thank you for coming back to help with the situation."

"I had no choice . . . as you well know." She turned to leave, then thought of something. "Where did you get the information that implicated my father?"

"From a Captain Mercer."

"Could you tell me where I may reach him? There are a few questions of my own that need answering."

"I'm afraid that's impossible. He agreed to talk for payment, and we set up a meeting at the stockyards. When we arrived, we found him trampled to death in one of the pens. He'd been drinking, and we figured he got in there by mistake."

She raised a brow in mock surprise. "Doesn't it seem a little odd to you? This . . . untimely mishap . . . before Captain Mercer could tell all he knows? It makes me think there's more to this than my father's involvement. To me, he seems to have only provided temporary storage. So who, Judge Croft, was the real man in charge?" With a curt nod of her head she swept from the room.

The judge watched her go. A rush of air expelled from his chest. Oh how he hated to play out this farce! He stared at the sheets of paper before him and crushed them up in a fist. The disgust of what he'd been forced to do curled his lip.

By the time Lisha walked out into the afternoon sun, most of her anger had dissipated. She hadn't the stamina to hold on to any kind of emotion for long.

"Falisha, I was hoping I would catch you here."

Turning, she saw Weston taking the cement steps in his long stride. She didn't realize how much she'd missed him until she saw his impish grin. His expression dissolved into concern when he got a good look at her. He took hold of her gloved hands and peered into her eyes.

"Falisha, are you all right? Have you been ill?"

She forced a smile. "I guess I'm not used to traveling. And this matter about my father . . ."

"Yes. It is a nasty business, but it will be cleared up. I promise you that."

The warm pressure of his hands felt foreign to her. Instinctively pulling away, she almost missed the flicker of annoyance. Was he disappointed that, after all this time, she hadn't shown him more affection?

"How did you know I was here?"

"Judge Croft sent word when you would be arriving. I missed you at the station, so I came straight here. Falisha, I had no idea he would send someone after you, much less . . ."

He paused, glancing toward Jackal. The man leaned against the wheel of a rented buggy. She followed his stare and quickly turned away.

"Weston, would it be possible for you to take me to Tilly's? I don't think I can bear any more of that man's company."

"I see no problem in that."

Weston stepped over to her recent escort, muttered something unintelligible, grabbed her valise, and showed her to his buggy. She was grateful for his assuring smile, his comforting presence, when grief ruled her life. But she was afraid his knowing gaze saw more in her fatigue than mere travel.

"Falisha, what's bothering you?"

"Can you charge a man with murder if I swear to it?"

Her question surprised him. "Why do you ask that?"

"I saw someone killed, and I want to press charges. I want Jackal hanged."

"Jackal? That bounty hunter who brought you here?"

"Yes. Have you met him—I mean before today?"

"I've only heard of him. He has quite a foul reputation. Did he harm someone you know?"

"He . . . he shot a . . . friend . . . of mine." She choked on the word.

When Weston had looked over at Jackal and caught his confirming nod to a job well done, satisfaction filled his heart. But not so much as now when he heard love underlining the word *friend*. All along, he was afraid that something like this would develop between Falisha and the rancher. Now he needn't worry. Given time, he would make her forget she even knew him. Given time, all his desires would come to pass.

"Falisha, I hate to ruin your hopes, but everyone knows how a bounty hunter works, especially this one. People are willing to overlook the way things are handled just so long as the work gets done. You can file charges, but it would be your word against his. And in view of what's surfaced—"

"The word of a Harrington doesn't hold much credibility," she finished for him.

Weston placed a hand over hers. "I'm sorry. If there's something else I can do, you can be sure I'll do it."

"I'm afraid there's nothing anyone can do."

They rode on in silence until they came to Tilly's boarding-house. As soon as they pulled to a stop, the little woman scuttled out the front door.

"Lisha, I'm so glad to see you! Mr. Clayborne said you would be coming. Everything's prepared." She practically pranced about in her excitement, waiting for Lisha to step down from the buggy. "Dear me, I'm beside myself." She dabbed at the corners of her eyes with a handkerchief. "Come in, don't just stand out here. You must be tired from all that travel. I have tea ready and those pastries you're so fond of."

Lisha followed Tilly through the front door. Weston took her valise up to her room and quietly left before she realized that he'd gone. Once again his thoughtfulness impressed her. He somehow knew she was in no condition to play games that social pleasantry demands.

Tilly busied herself with setting the small cakes and pouring the tea. All Lisha wanted to do was go up to the silence of her room, but the woman had gone through so much preparation that Lisha couldn't disappoint her."

"Now, my dear," Tilly said, settling herself into a soft chair opposite Lisha. "Tell me all about New Mexico. Was Mr. Hawks very angry when you showed up instead of Elizabeth? What did you tell him as to why she didn't come?"

Lisha's mind flashed back to the first time Granger had set eyes on her. She thought of other times when he lovingly gazed at her. An ache began to grow. She dispelled the vision, dulling the pain.

"Granger—Mr. Hawks—wasn't too happy to see me, but I eventually persuaded him that he needed me."

Tilly clicked her tongue. "My, my. I've been so curious. I've imagined all sorts of things."

Lisha knew that Tilly would never have guessed what had happened in New Mexico. No decent woman would ever dream it. "There's so much to say, but right now tell me about all that's happened around here. How's Uncle John? Did Mrs. Wagner finally have that little girl?"

Skillfully Lisha turned the attention from herself, and in the next half hour Tilly filled her in on everything of interest, though carefully skirting her father's problems. The woman was talking about her uncle when the doctor strode through the door. Lisha let out a squeal of delight and ran to his open arms.

"Clayborne suggested that you might need me. I came as soon as my last patient left."

Lisha gripped her uncle tight. He'd never ceased to be a comfort. "Uncle John, I—"

"Say, what's this—tears? Here, let me take a good look at you."

The doctor teasingly pried her arms from around him. The laughter left his eyes as he searched her face. "Lisha, you have a sickly pallor, and you've lost weight. I want to know what happened to cause this."

"My, dear me," Tilly interrupted. "With all my excitement I didn't realize how poorly she looks."

Lisha avoided looking at them. "I can't talk about it right now. It's too painful."

"Balderdash!" her uncle exploded. "You've had at least a month getting here to dwell on whatever it is that's eating you. Now it's time to get it out in the open. Tilly, help her to bed while I prepare something to calm her nerves."

Lisha did not refuse Tilly's assistance. Soon she laid her head on the downy pillows, and the woman tucked a quilt around her. Her uncle walked through the door holding in his hand a glass of some concoction she knew she wouldn't like. Being the stern doctor that he was, he made her swallow every last drop before giving her a quick exam. He frowned at the rough texture of her hands and the smattering of freckles on the parts of her body that had been exposed to the harsh sun.

"What did that rancher use you for, a field slave?"

"He had nothing to do with this. I . . . ." She faltered, biting her lower lip.

Her uncle studied her face. "Lisha, I really think you need to talk. Don't bottle things up. I've seen some bitter people in my time because they've kept too much to themselves. Don't become like them."

Sighing, she began to tell them about Granger, his daughter, and his ranch. Once she started, the words tumbled out of their own accord. When she recounted the terror she'd felt at her abduction and her living conditions with the Comancheros, Tilly gasped. Unable to stop herself, she told of Flora, the auction block, the don, her flight into the desert, and Lago's rescue.

John Calder cradled her palm in his. Sometimes her hand lay limp; sometimes she gripped his until her knuckles turned white. He sat still, never uttering a word, and let her reopen her wounds. Wisely he knew healing came with pain and tears, but he didn't know if he could stand to hear any more.

He knew by the looks of his niece that this Granger Hawks had taken good care of her blisters and sunburn. He searched and found telltale remnants of those few days Lisha had wandered unprotected from the sun.

She told of the trek home, their marriage, Martha's care, and Jackal's unwanted visit. Then her voice faded in a tormented whisper. Silence smothered the room. He listened, sensing that the worst was yet to come, and he dreaded what he knew in his heart she was going to say.

"Go on," he prompted.

"Granger tried to stop him even though he didn't have a gun. They wrestled for Jackal's. The gun went off. Granger was hit. The bounty hunter tried to shoot him again, but I pushed his gun arm up. I wasn't fast enough. Because of me, Granger was shot in the head. Because of me . . . he's dead."

Her staccato breath wrenched out the words. Words that she had never allowed herself to think, much less say.

Her uncle gripped her by the upper arms. "Lisha, Lisha, you must stop this. Jackal killed him, not you." His words held no impact for something she was so sure of. "Tilly," he barked.

"Get my bag and bring me that bottle of ether and a wad of cotton. Hurry."

The woman quickly complied. The last thing Lisha remembered was Tilly's ashen face and her uncle's haggard one.

During the weeks that passed, Lisha either sat, staring out her window, or aimlessly walked in the flower gardens. Each day brought its own brand of strength, but she still couldn't bare to leave the solitude surrounding the boardinghouse.

Even the elements seemed to mirror her emotions, and rain beat down in glassy sheets. The charcoal-gray clouds entrenched a deeper depression into her being.

She knew she'd have to see to Kingswood, to take care of unfinished business, but she had no desire to do so. She hadn't the desire to do anything. Tilly bought her a lacy shawl, then a mint-green dress, trying to bolster her spirits. Neither worked.

Uncle John came to see her every day. He tried to make her realize the folly of her reasoning that she helped in Granger's death. But she knew in her heart that if she'd been faster, the shot would have gone wild. Or if she hadn't pushed so hard the bullet would have hit his shoulder, and he could have lived. No, it was her fault, and her beloved uncle couldn't make her believe otherwise.

For the first few days Tilly brought her meals up to her room. After that she ate in the dining room, mainly to satisfy her uncle. He'd threatened she'd get no more food if she couldn't come down to the table. She didn't care one way or the other, for she had very little appetite.

Uncle John had told Weston a little of her experience, omitting her marriage to Granger, and the lawyer stayed away. Instead, he sent her flowers, candy, and encouraging letters. One day a theater ticket arrived. The note attached to it read that the ticket could be redeemed for an extravagant night out, any night of the lady's choosing. His thoughtfulness warmed her. She knew he realized she needed time alone, and he wanted to give her that time.

One morning she woke to the sun filtering through her sheer

window curtains and to the smell of geraniums. Her heart lightened. This was the first time she'd noticed the fragrances of the flowers that Weston had sent. With the sun glinting on the petals, she suddenly realized how beautiful they were, and she knew her senses were beginning to thaw.

"Good morning, Tilly."

"Oh, morning, dear."

Hardly glancing about from her work, Tilly continued to sort through her mail. Instantly her coiffured head shot up. She pushed her glasses back onto the bridge of her nose and stared openmouthed at Lisha. Her gaze swept over her neatly groomed appearance and the new mint-green frock she wore, to her fashionably gloved hands.

"My dear, don't you look lovely."

"Thank you. For the first time in weeks I feel lovely."

The woman chuckled. "Won't your uncle be thrilled with the change in you." She leaned forward, as if sharing a secret. "He's been very worried about you, you know."

"Yes, I do. That's why I intend on going to his office."

"To his office?"

"And maybe I'll stop in and see Weston."

"Dear, dear me. You *are* feeling better." She placed her hands on her rounded hips. "It's about time you put the past to rest. You need to think about your future. That nice Mr. Clayborne is sweet on you, you know."

Lisha smiled. She did feel better, but not enough to encourage Weston. She had no intention of marrying again. Her love for Granger proved too great to settle for what would be second best.

"Lisha dear, have you had breakfast?"

"No, I just came down."

"Then come eat with me. From the sounds of things, you'll need some nourishment to help you through this day you've planned out for yourself."

After they'd eaten, Tilly saw to it that her horse and buggy were readied for Lisha's use. She watched the girl drive away, then went about her various projects with a lighter heart.

A short time later the bell rang. Annoyed at the interruption, she hurried to the door and found a tall man on her porch. By the cut of his clothes, she guessed he came from out West. His drawn look told of his fatigue. A jagged scar slashed angrily across the left side of his forehead.

Chapter
27

The bell to Dr. Calder's office jangled the minute someone came through the door. Concentrating on a page in his medical book, he dragged his thoughts away long enough to wave toward a worn chair.

"Please have a seat. I'll be just a moment."

Reading further, a smug look crossed his face. He nodded his head, shut the book, and turned around. "Now, what seems to be the—" He caught sight of Lisha sitting primly across from him, and his face lit up. He reached her in two strides and grabbed hold of her hands. "Lisha, I couldn't have asked for a better beginning to a day." His role of an uncle changed to that of a doctor, and he quickly scanned her appearance. "You look wonderful, but don't overdo your first day out."

She laughed. "I promise I won't."

"I don't want to question a gift horse, but what brought on this pleasant change?"

"Flowers."

"Flowers?"

"This morning when I woke up, I smelled the flowers in my room, and I realized that the worst part was over. I decided I had to make an effort to get on with my life. Even though I'll never forget . . ." She made a conscious effort to push down the memories.

Her uncle placed an arm about her shoulders. "You don't want to forget, not about this man Hawks. I haven't forgotten the woman I loved years ago."

"Uncle John, you never told me. I thought you were just too busy to be bothered finding a wife. What happened?"

"Her family found a more suitable husband. But that's a different story, and I don't have time to tell it. Now, what reason did you come in for besides to bother a busy old man?"

"That was the reason, but now that you mention it, when can I come back to work for you?"

"Maybe in a couple of weeks."

"But I'm ready now."

"You may think you are until you're caught up in one of those extremely long days we can have around here."

"Can't you find something for me? I don't want to be idle for too long. A person can do too much thinking that way."

Her uncle glanced toward his file. "Maybe there is something. You know how I hate to do paperwork."

"Don't tell me that no one has kept the ledgers since I've been gone."

A sheepish grin crossed his face. "I've more important things to worry about."

"All right, I'll take care of it, if I can start tomorrow. Sitting at a desk can't be very taxing. Agreed?"

"Agreed."

She planted a kiss on his weathered cheek. "You old codger, I'll see you in the morning, and you'd better be here to help clarify your entries."

John Calder watched his niece go out the door. His heart ached when he thought of the pain she'd gone through because of this man Jackal. He didn't know until just before she'd arrived that the bounty hunter had gone after her. He would have done it himself if he'd known that the government wanted to question her. Then Hawks's death could have been avoided. Rumors, that's all they were. Nothing to warrant sending an animal after her.

"Falisha, you look absolutely ravishing."

Weston showed her to a chair and sat in the one next to her. He'd forgotten how beautiful she could be, even though her smile didn't quite light up her eyes. When she first returned to St. Louis, her condition had fallen severely short of his standards, and he had to admit that he'd been more than a little upset. Now he was truly delighted at her progress. Her coloring wasn't so pasty, and her silvery hair sparkled with new life. Yes, he was very pleased.

He searched her face and came away satisfied that the sun had not permanently blemished her flawless complexion. A wife of his could not be marred in any way. He wondered briefly if she still held on to her virginity but pushed the thought from his mind.

The reputation of the Comancheros had spread as far as St. Louis, and he knew what those bandits were capable of. He couldn't take time to worry about what more than likely had happened—not yet, anyway. But, for her sake, she'd better be clean.

Weston thought of the plans he'd so far executed, and his heart raced. Everything he'd done since the age of twelve had been geared to his goal of power, and here beside him sat the woman he'd chosen to share the prestige brought about by his genius. She blushed under his frank gaze.

"Please excuse me, Falisha. I hadn't meant to make you uncomfortable. It's just that you have such great beauty, I can't help but admire it." He grinned mischievously. "In the future I'll keep my glances covert, until such time you'll allow me to make public—"

"Oh, speaking of public," Lisha quickly broke in, "reminds me of one of the reasons why I came here. How much are people giving credit to the rumors about my father?"

His mouth twitched. He could tell she wasn't ready for him to talk of marriage, even in a lighthearted manner. If she needed time, he would give her that. He settled back, careful not to unduly crease his pin-striped gray pants.

"Unfortunately, there are those who will believe anything about anybody. They thrive on it. Then there are those who will wait until all the evidence comes in before they pass judgment."

"What can we do about it?"

"Nothing except try to find our own answers. I'm sorry to say that your father was involved with smugglers. To what extent, we don't know." He paused long enough for her to make a comment. When she didn't, he pressed on. "I want you to think very carefully, Falisha. Did your father say anything to you that might give any clue to this mess?"

"I've thought about it a lot, and I haven't come up with anything."

"What about the last thing he said to you?" he asked, then held his breath. He'd brought her all the way from New Mexico for the most part to find what might be hidden in her answer.

"All he did was call me by my childhood nickname, Curly-locks."

"Are you sure?" he asked, dumbfounded. "Maybe you missed something."

"Curly-locks was all he said. I'm sure of it."

He rubbed his neck. His thoughts tumbled in a chaotic frenzy, and he made an effort to piece them together. It would've been easier to find the gold if Edward had told his daughter where he had hidden it, but since Harrington hadn't, he'd have to continue as he was already doing.

"Weston, are you disturbed about something?"

He quickly drew his hand away from his pinched muscles. "I was hoping he had told you something that could prove he wasn't the man behind these runs. You see, I think he had information somebody wanted."

"What makes you think that?"

"I don't want to needlessly upset you, but remember someone beat your father to death, probably for answers."

Falisha blanched. His words seemed to hang painfully in the air. "I can't imagine what Papa knew that could possibly result in his death."

"I can't, either, but so many things point to it. Now, think, did you see your father with any new acquaintances before he died?"

"I've only seen him with his drinking friend. And then only a few times."

"Who did he see? Where did he go?"

"I don't know," she said, waving her hand in distress. "He didn't have any friends to speak of, and he spent most of his time in the saloons. He couldn't have been a traitor, Weston, he couldn't have been, not knowingly.''

He grabbed one of her hands and brought it to his lips. ''Don't worry, Falisha. I'll take care of everything. I'll clear your father if it's the last decent thing I do.'' She relaxed her stiff posture, and he decided to broach another subject. ''Have you heard that I'm hosting a charity ball for the war orphans?''

''Tilly mentioned something about it.'' She laughed. ''In fact she never misses a chance to point out your qualities. I think what you're doing is marvelous. Do you really intend to build an orphanage?''

''I do, and I have enough pledges right now to break ground. But we still have a ways to go. That's why I'm giving the ball. People tend to part easier with their pocket books if they're enjoying themselves.'' He sobered and searched her face. ''I would deem it an honor if I could be your escort.''

''Well, I—''

''I know what a trying time you've had, and I would understand completely if you declined, but all I'm asking is that you think about it. You've made great strides so far. Who knows how you'll feel by next Friday?''

''All right, Weston, I promise I'll think about it.'' She stood.

''That's all a man can ask for. Would you like me to see you home?''

''You needn't bother, I can manage.''

Weston saw her to her buggy. He had wanted to propose marriage and formally announce it at the ball, but he sensed that he shouldn't bring up the subject, not just yet. Not only did he want their engagement to become common knowledge that night, he wanted people to start thinking of him as their candidate for state senator. The charity part was only a ruse to gain support from the gullible residents.

Lisha guided the horse down the broad drive to Kingswood. She hadn't intended to come, but she was compelled to do so. The leafage, dressing the enormous live oak trees that canopied the road, had begun to turn. A few leaves had already fallen, dotting the drive with a mixture of red and green. They reminded her of the many leaf fights she'd had with her father.

The recent rains gave everything a clean, waxy look and lent a fresh scent to the air. This time of year had always been her favorite.

She reined the horse to a stop in front of the wide, curving steps that led up to her home. For a few moments she couldn't move. She just sat and stared at the massive double doors.

Insects hummed under the warm schooling of the sun. From somewhere on the river she heard a sharp blast of a steamboat whistle. How that sound brought back childhood memories and fanciful dreams. Giving herself a mental shake, she jumped down and forced herself to climb the stairs.

One door opened easily, and she stepped into the foyer. The gloomy, dank atmosphere hit her full in the face. Shadowy corners seemed to taunt her until she grew accustomed to the dim light. There were no more oils hanging on the walls, no more lamps to light the way.

Without hesitating, she made her way to the parlor. The only furniture left in the house occupied that room. She had spent many happy hours there, most of them with her father.

As she looked about the cloth-covered room, the chair by the window drew her. Pulling back the dustcloth, she ran her hand across the printed material. Once again she was a child learning her stitches, with her father teasing her in that theatrical voice of his.

Curly-locks, Curly-locks, wilt thou be mine?
Thou shalt not wash the dishes, nor yet feed the swine;
But sit on a cushion, and sew a fine seam,
And feed upon strawberries, sugar, and cream.

His voice droned on. *Sit on a cushion, and sew a fine seam . . . sit on a cushion . . . cushion . . . cushion.*

She threw the dustcover over the chair and ran from the mansion. It was not until she slammed the doors behind her that her father's voice faded. She leaned heavily against the hard wood. Each slow breath soothed her nerves.

I don't understand, Papa. I don't understand what you're trying to tell me.

After an unmeasurable amount of time, she walked out onto

the sweeping lawns. The grass had grown long and thick, and weeds had overgrown the gardens. Fighting back tears at the dejected condition of her beloved grounds, she made her way to the family graveyard.

Here, too, weeds had strangled out the flowers she'd so carefully planted. She dropped to her knees and began to pull the noxious plants.

"No, you can't take over. I won't let you!"

Hot tears brimmed over and rolled down her cheeks, taunting her of yet another lost battle. The faster they fell, the harder she worked, until she frantically ripped away at the wild plants. She didn't care that dirt stained her dress and matted her gloves. The only thing that mattered now was clearing her parents' graves.

When her strength vanished, she collapsed on the bare earth, sobbing out her anguish, her fingers kneading the ground. She hadn't realized someone else had followed her to Kingswood, not until strong hands lifted her.

"It's all right, my love, it's all right."

The soothing voice released a flood of memories before its owner gently turned her around. Numbly she lifted sodden eyes to Granger's face.

Chapter
28

Lisha stared at Granger. She told herself that her mind played tricks again. Too many times she'd thought she'd seen him. Too many times she would turn, expecting to find him, only to be faced with nothing but emptiness. Too many times she would wake, contented, only to realize her lover was nothing more than a blissful dream. No, she wasn't going to succumb to these unmerciful illusions again. Determinedly she squeezed her eyes shut.

"Lisha, it's really me. The bullet wasn't fatal."

Her eyes sprung open at the litany in his voice. Before, her visions had never spoken so clearly, nor with such a tone of supplication. She noted the dark circles around his eyes, the red skin at his hairline, the slight curve of his mouth. Afraid that he would disappear, she hesitantly reached out a trembling hand and touched the angry scar, smudging it with dirt. Reality sank in.

"It. is. It's really you." Her hoarse whisper was barely audible. "Oh, Granger, it's really you!" With a choked sob she threw her arms about his neck.

His unyielding mouth came down on hers. He kissed her with such forcefulness that she grew dizzy from the wild pulse hammering in her temples combined with the heady sensation of sheer happiness. He kissed her quivering lips, her cheeks, her eyes with such frenzy, she thought she'd faint from the mere pleasure of it.

They hugged, they laughed, they cried, they kissed, then

hugged again. They clung to each other, desperate to alleviate the pain of the last two months. Each fed on the other's presence. Each couldn't hold the other tight enough.

"Oh, Granger, I can't believe you're really alive," she murmured between kisses. "If I'm dreaming, I pray I never wake."

He nuzzled her throat. "You're not dreaming."

"But I saw you in a pool of blood. Your head . . . your chest. I thought . . . I thought you were dead."

"Shh, my love," he said, kissing her forehead, "don't cry. I might have died, but Martha took care of me."

"Martha? How could she? She was on her way to Cibola for supplies."

"She was, but she'd forgotten that quilt of hers and the money, so she had to come back. If it weren't for her showing up when she did, I might have bled to death, mostly from the wound in my side."

Tears scalded Lisha's cheeks, and she brushed them off with the back of her gloved hand. "And if it weren't for my being so slow, Jackal wouldn't have shot you in the head."

Granger peeled the gloves from her hands and used a clean spot to try and wipe away the dirty stain she'd left on her face. "Lisha, look at me." When she refused, he forced her chin up. Her self-appointed guilt made her avoid his gaze. "Listen to me. He was aiming at my chest. If you hadn't acted as quickly as you did, he would have put a slug through my heart, and no doctor on earth could have saved me."

"But if I'd been faster, the bullet could have gone astray . . . or a little slower, it would have grazed your shoulder."

"Then he would have shot me again. No, Lisha, as it happened, this . . . Jackal also thought I was dead. So it worked out for the best."

She let the words soak in. What he'd said made sense. Feeling as if she'd narrowly escaped from a rabid animal, she laid her head in the hollow of his chest, content just to hold and be held. She craved nothing but this closeness, this bonding of souls.

Granger buried his face in her hair, and his arms tightened, drawing her ever closer. She felt the rhythm of his heart, the pressure of his hands, the urgency of his embrace.

"Oh, Granger," she whispered, lifting her chin, "I—"

His mouth slanted across hers, his thirst consuming her. Pleasures, hot and unbridled, instantly spread throughout her body, and she strained against him. It had been so long . . . so long.

With a guttural sigh he swept her up and carried her over to the privacy of a grove of trees. Leaves crunched under his weight as he dropped to his knees and carefully laid her down. For a few heart-catching moments he gazed at her, his love clearly evident in his dark brown eyes.

Then his lips were once again claiming hers, his hands once again freeing the barriers that separated them. His mouth ravaged hers; his touch burned her flesh; his tongue left a trail of fire. The craving deep inside grew until she thought she'd go mad with this intense need. She wanted release, wanted it now.

Pulsating with desire, she guided him to her and closed tightly around his warmth. She matched him stroke for stroke, hunger for hunger. Suddenly all of the agony, the love, and the passion exploded in a shuddering pinnacle. She clung to him as wave after wave of the aftermath shook her body, until her cries were hushed, until the flames were spent.

"How did you know where to find me?" Lisha asked, snuggling deeper into Granger's arms.

"Tilly told me."

"Tilly? But how did you know about her?"

Granger chuckled. "I ordered a bride from her, remember?"

She groaned. How could she have forgotten a thing like that—the catalyst that sent her hurtling into Granger's arms and four horrifying months.

"I just haven't been thinking straight lately."

"I can tell. Tilly said you walked about the house as if you were half asleep."

"It sounds as if you two had quite a little chat."

Granger caught a leaf that had floated down to them and secured it in her hair. "We did. I would've gotten here sooner, but you know how talkative she is."

"I do. What else did she say?"

"She mostly filled me in about your father, and of course the charity ball hosted by your lawyer friend. Were you planning on going?"

"No. I have no desire to go."

"I think you ought to."

Granger's words and how he said them made her pause. "Why?"

"Because you need to face down the scandal about your father. If you don't show up, people will tend to believe the worst. And . . ."

"And?"

"I've a gut feeling that this fellow Clayborne knows more about the blockade-runners than he's willing to admit."

"What on earth makes you say that?"

"Mostly because I'm not blinded by his sterling reputation, and I've had time to think about all the possibilities. On a hunch I had wired for information and found there are no records of the supposed land sales involving Kingswood."

His words stunned her. "You mean that Weston never really sold off parts of Kingswood?"

"That's what it looks like."

"But where did the money come from?" He didn't answer. She saw the accusation in his eyes concerning Weston's guilt, and she groped for a logical answer. "Maybe he took it out of his own pocket."

"Maybe."

She could tell by the lift of his brows that he didn't believe in the likelihood, and it forced her to look at things in a different light.

"But why would he lie about something like that?"

"That's one of the questions I hope to find the answer to at the dance."

"You? I didn't realize you intended to go." Thoughts of dancing all night in Granger's arms excited her.

"Of course I'm going. A man can find out a lot of truth from idle gossip. Besides, I'm not leaving you alone with the likes of Clayborne or any other man who might get any ideas." He pulled her closer. "We've been apart far too long."

Knowing how he felt, she luxuriated in Granger's new streak of possessiveness. She, too, was reluctant to leave the private lands of Kingswood, because she didn't want to share him with anybody, not just yet. Their new beginning was much too tender.

Once again they made love. Only this time the urgency was no longer commanding, just the tenderness and the desire to please each other.

Lisha lost track of time, reluctant to let Granger go. Finally he clasped her hand and stood, pulling her to her feet.

"Come, my sweet, it's time to get you home. Tilly will be wondering what happened to you—to us."

"I suppose you're right," Lisha muttered as she did her best to right herself. "But I hate to end it. Granger, why don't we just leave and go home?"

"As much as I'd like to get you out of here, you know I can't. I don't relish the thought of this man Jackal coming after you again. And I have a feeling he would. He knows where we would be. No, we have to stay here until we find some answers."

She knew he'd say that, but she had to at least ask. Granger tied the horse he'd rented to the back of her buggy and leisurely drove her home. When they were within sight of St. Louis, he stopped.

"I don't want anyone to know right now that I'm here," he said, answering her silent question, "or that I'm your husband. That's why I took a room at the Banion Hotel. I want a chance to nose around before anybody finds out who I am. I've already sworn Tilly to secrecy, and she promised to make your uncle do the same."

"I'll bet that was a job."

He gave a lopsided grin. "It was at that. Tilly was all but broadcasting the news to the other boarders. The only way I could pacify her was letting her spread the news to your uncle."

A smile curved her lips, then faded. "When will I see you again?"

"Oh, I'll pop up when you least expect it, so you'd better be on your best behavior." When she refused to smile at his attempt to lighten her mood, he placed a reassuring hand over hers, and she relaxed. "Don't worry. I've got my guard up, and that's half the battle."

"I hope you're right."

"I know I'm right." He kissed her soundly before leaping down from the buggy. "I'll see you tomorrow."

The second Lisha reined the mare to a stop in front of the boardinghouse, Tilly flung open the door and bounded down the steps. Happiness crinkled the corners of her eyes until they were almost shut.

"Lisha, Lisha, I can hardly believe your good fortune."

Lisha hugged her. "Neither can I. I literally have to pinch myself to make sure I haven't been dreaming."

"You haven't. I saw that dear boy myself, remember? Now come in, I want to hear all about it." Tilly hesitated, casting an amused glance at Lisha's soiled appearance. "Well," she muttered, pulling the leaf from Lisha's hair, "maybe not *all*."

Laughing, Lisha gave Tilly another hug and followed her into her office.

The dance was little more than a week away, not much time to sew herself a dress, yet Lisha had to have a new gown. Nothing seemed to excite her when she glanced through her clothes, and she wanted so much to look beautiful for Granger. He hadn't seen her dressed in a ball gown. For that matter, because of the war and her stricken mother, she'd never gone to a ball before.

Quickly making up her mind, she donned a pert straw hat, grabbed her shawl and gloves, and headed for Rebecca's Dress Shoppe. Rebecca was the only dressmaker she knew personally, first meeting her when Rebecca's mother came down with consumption. She had sat with Mrs. St Clair in the last weeks of her life in order to give Rebecca a rest. Rebecca had said she'd never forget her thoughtfulness.

Most of the upper crust traded at the more elite shops where they could boast of gowns practically stitched on their bodies. While Rebecca filled specific orders, her specialty was ready-made frocks.

When Lisha stepped into the little shop, Rebecca peered

over a rack of clothes. A smile lit her angular face. "Goodness, what a surprise," she said, maneuvering around her barrier. "You don't come in often enough."

"I don't often have an invitation to a ball."

"The charity ball given by Mr. Clayborne?"

"The very one. Have you had to fill many orders?"

"Enough to keep me hopping, but not enough that I can't help you."

"Are you sure? I know how busy you must be."

Rebecca shushed her words away with the flick of a bony wrist. "For you, anything. What did you have in mind?"

"I'd hoped you could help me in deciding that."

Rebecca fished in her pocket and slid a pair of spectacles onto the bridge of her pointed nose. She rolled down Lisha's glove and studied the back of her hand. "I don't know what is it with me these days." She sighed, her brows creasing. "It seems my eyesight's getting worse by the minute." She pulled her glasses to the tip of her nose and peered over, then pushed them back again. Sucking in her breath, her gaze flew to Lisha's face. Her jaw dropped in shock.

"Why, it's not my eyesight. What have you done to your beautiful skin? You're . . . you're as brown as a little heathen."

Brown? What would Rebecca have thought if she'd seen her two months ago? "I've spent the past few months in the territory of New Mexico."

"Don't they believe in wearing hats and gloves?" Shaking her drab-brown head, Rebecca went about her inspection. "Mauve," she finally muttered to herself, "and I know just the piece."

"Have you a dress in that color?"

Rebecca's eyes widened. "Goodness, child. I'm creating a gown especially for you with the quality Worth would be proud of. Step into the dressing room." She paused, eyeing Lisha over her glasses. "I assume your measurements haven't changed since you bought that blue dress?"

The mere mention of the blue dress brought scores of memories to mind. "Maybe a little. I'm thinner now."

"Yes, I see. But no harm done." Turning on her heel, Rebecca disappeared into the storage room.

By the time Lisha had shed her day dress, Rebecca was back with rolls of purple satin ribbon, ivory lace, and a bolt of mauve silk, threaded with silver. Lisha gasped when she caught sight of the shimmering cloth.

"I've never seen anything so delicate or so beautiful."

"I've been keeping it aside for something special," Rebecca said, draping the material over Lisha's shoulder and adding the ribbon and lace. "Now, take a look." She turned her toward the full-length mirror. "What do you think?"

The glistening effect highlighted the silvery gleam in Lisha's blond hair. Because of the purple ribbon, her blue-gray eyes took on a violet cast, and the ivory lace complemented her skin. Her heart tripped.

"I think I can hardly wait for . . ." A blush burned her skin all the way to her hairline.

Rebecca gave a knowing smile. "I knew there was a special young man involved. And for him you will be a vision."

"Do you think so?"

"I know so. He won't be able to take his eyes off you. Now that we've decided on the goods, let's decide on a pattern."

A half hour later Lisha emerged from the dress shop. She tried to balance several packages containing accessories that Rebecca had insisted she take. Blindly she walked into a solid wall, with feet no less, and dropped the cumbersome wrappings.

"Excuse me, ma'am," a man drawled, swooping down to gather up the parcels, "I wasn't watching where you were going."

A delicious tingle spread through her. When she took the packages from Granger's outstretched hands, her fingers slid caressingly across his. "No harm done. I'm sure."

Granger raised a brow at her throaty response. "Is this your buggy, ma'am?"

"It is."

"The least I can do is help you with your purchases."

"The least."

"Then allow me." With a flourish he took the bundles,

deposited them in the buggy, and helped her up. "I wanted to tell you that you might not be seeing me for a while," he said, lowering his voice.

"Why?"

"Because I'm going over to Jefferson City to talk with Governor Hall. I want answers that nobody seems to know or is willing to give here."

"When will you be back?"

"In plenty of time to take you to the dance, but we'll have to go in separately. I still don't want Clayborne getting any ideas as to who I am. Not just yet."

She forced her attention from his bold gaze to see the man mentioned headed their way. "There's Weston."

"Where?"

"Down the street. He just passed Mortimer's Mercantile."

Granger glanced about, making motions as if she'd just given him directions. "Oh, do you mean that overstuffed peacock dressed in black?"

"Granger! Granger"—her chastising tone turned to admonishment—"please. He'll be here any second. He'll see you."

"I'll go as soon as you help me with a perplexing question."

"And what is that?"

"Why is it that you take twice as long to disrobe for your dressmaker as you do for me? Ma'am." Winking, he doffed his hat and turned away just before Weston reached the buggy.

The lawyer warily studied Granger's casual stride. "Who was that?"

"A—ah—stranger to St. Louis."

"Was he bothering you?"

"He was just being helpful after he accidentally bumped into me."

"I see." Weston instantly dismissed the man but made a mental note to impress upon Falisha that, as her husband, he would not tolerate her talking to men in his absence. Turning his full attention to her, her flushed appearance made him frown.

"Falisha, are you feeling ill?"

"Not in the least. What makes you say that?"

"You look . . . feverish."

"I do?" Her hand flew to her cheek. "Maybe it's because I've been in Rebecca's Dress Shoppe all morning." His gaze flickered from her and the packages to the shop. A sense of accomplishment filled his being. "Then may I assume that you will accept my invitation to the charity ball?"

"You may."

"Wonderful, expect me around nine."

"Well," she hesitated, "do you think that wise?"

"Wise?"

"To take time to chaperon me to the dance when you are the host? How would it look for you to be absent, even for a short while, when your important guests arrive? It could be disastrous."

"But who would take you?"

She shrugged her exquisite shoulders, shoulders that soon he'd have the pleasure of caressing. He could almost feel her pliable flesh beneath his fingers.

"There're so many people I know whom you've invited, I'll go with one of them. The most important thing is collecting pledges for the orphanage."

He thought over what Falisha had said. She not only had beauty but brains. Just what he needed in a wife. Somehow she knew from the start that he and his project came first. He liked that.

"You're right, Falisha. I'll look forward to seeing you next Friday."

Lisha drove off feeling a little guilty. She hadn't lied, not really. She just didn't tell the whole truth.

Toward evening a boy delivered a bunch of sky-blue forget-me-nots. She knew whom they were from, even before she read the card that simply stated the words, *Love always, G.* Every time she looked at them with their colorful yellow centers, she thought of Granger. But that didn't help the days go by any faster.

Because of her insistence combined with her growing restlessness, her uncle let her help him in the office. Even on the morning of the charity ball, she came in to work.

Sitting at the desk, she completed her corrections in the

ledger. She could hear her uncle's low tones as he talked to a patient in one of the examining rooms. Another patient sat across from Lisha, stiff-backed, waiting her turn. Lisha tried to ignore the woman's impatient glances at the timepiece pinned to her waistcoat.

The bell tinkled for what it seemed to her the hundredth time that morning. "Have a seat, please," she said, beginning to add the same column of figures again. "The doctor will be with you in a moment."

Instead of sitting in a chair, the patient sat indolently on the edge of the desk.

"Excuse me, sir, but you'll . . ."

She looked up from a muscled thigh to a broad chest and a tanned face. Her words trailed off. Granger perched in front of her with a twinkle in his eyes belying the serious expression on his face. A white handkerchief bound his index finger. He held it up, much the same as a child would to his sympathetic mother.

"I need attending to."

"Dr. Calder can . . ."

From the corner of her eye she saw the woman square her shoulders, as if preparing to do battle if Granger got in to see the doctor first.

"You'll feel a lot better, Mrs. Hays," her uncle said, taking that moment to usher his patient from the examining room, "if you'll just follow my directions."

After he saw her to the door, he turned to see who was next. He looked from the irritable patient now standing, to Granger and his bandaged finger. A ghost of a smile flickered across his face.

"Lisha, why don't you see to this man's injury, since it doesn't seem too bad, while I look after Mrs. Ashmorton."

With a victorious snort Mrs. Ashmorton swept into the examining room followed by the doctor.

Lisha showed Granger into the other room. No sooner had she shut the door than he twirled her around and pulled her into his tight embrace, pressing his lips on hers. She responded instantly to his growing appetite, and for an infinite amount of time rapture fused her to him. Her heart beat a wild tattoo against his.

Reluctantly he lifted his head and stared longingly down at her. "I don't think I'll ever get tired of kissing you," he murmured before nipping at her earlobe. "I lay awake every night this week just thinking of holding you like this."

Guilty pleasure left her breathless. "What took you so long in Jefferson City?"

He stopped nuzzling her neck and raised his head. "I couldn't get in to see Governor Hall because of his full schedule, so in desperation, I stepped out in front of his coach and—"

"You what?"

"I stepped out in front of his horses and *pretended* to get hit. He insisted on taking me to the doctor. When I got in the carriage, I apologized and told him what I really needed to know."

"Was he irate?"

"No, he turned out to be a pretty decent fellow under the circumstances. He knows nothing about an investigation, nor has he any knowledge of blockade-runners using Kingswood. So this inquiry has nothing to do with the government. Because of our little talk, Governor Hall is very curious and said he'd look into the matter."

"Now where does that put us?"

A wicked gleam lit his eyes. He pulled her closer. "Well, that puts us right about here."

Once again Granger's lips met hers, devouring all thoughts of lies, smuggling, and treason.

Chapter
❦ 29 ❧

On the evening of the charity ball, Lisha studied her image in the mirror. With each movement the gown she wore deepened from silver to mauve. The upper skirt of mauve, caught up on the sides and draped back with purple ribbon and lace, revealed an underskirt of ivory embroidered with purple and mauve crescents. Ribbon and lace trimmed the low neckline, the off-shoulder sleeves, and the sash at her waist.

The various hues of the gown lent a rosy glow to her face and brought out the silver in her hair. She swore her eyes had more of a violet tone than a blue. Curls framed her face, and Tilly had braided forget-me-nots in her hair.

"You are absolutely beautiful, my dear!" Tilly exclaimed, lacing her fingers together in delight. "Looking at you brings back memories of my youth. I used to be quite a gadabout, you know."

"Tilly, you're still a gadabout."

The little woman waved the remark away. "Here's your shawl, dear. You've let that young man wait long enough."

Putting on the lacy shawl and knitted silk gloves, Lisha took a deep breath, trying to calm the giddy feeling that tickled her stomach. When she neared the top of the stairs, she caught sight of Granger standing at the foot.

His white dress shirt stood out in contrast with his black waistcoat, which seemed molded to his wide shoulders. The cut of the trousers accentuated his flat stomach and long legs. He looked as born to the finery as he did the saddle. Silently he turned and stared up at her.

A dazed look of wonder settled on his face, to be replaced by utter bewitchment, then immense pride. He swallowed hard, jolting his Adam's apple. The naked emotions flickering across his face caused her heart to skip a beat. She descended, placing her fingers in his outstretched hand, and he drew her to him. All the while his eyes never left hers.

"I cannot begin to tell you how beautiful you are, my love." His throaty voice furbished the thrill ricocheting in her heart. "You seem to shimmer with each movement. Tonight, you will undoubtedly put every other woman to shame."

"And you will far exceed the men."

He brushed her lips with his own. The kiss was light, yet told so much. She belonged to him and no other.

Lisha and Granger followed another couple and mounted the steps to Weston's elegant mansion. While their host welcomed the pair in front of them, Granger slipped unnoticed into the growing crowd.

"Mrs. Tanner, don't you look lovely tonight," Weston said, charming the woman, who took on the likeness of a bloated sheep in yards of white muslin. "I'll have to remember to claim a dance."

Lisha couldn't help but notice his meaningless flattery and hollow words. She realized how false he sounded, how false he must have been all along.

The couple stepped into the ballroom, and Weston turned his full attention on her. As his gaze swept over her, his eyes widened with gratification, then blazed with desire. She knew the look, having experienced it enough times in the hands of the Comancheros. Yet she detected something different, something deeper in his probing stare, and she shivered inwardly.

"Ah, Falisha, you are the most ravishing vision here." He took her hand and pressed the back of it to his cool lips. "I insist upon having the first dance before every other male sees you and claims one for his own."

Nodding, she forced a smile. "I'll look forward to it," she said, making way for the guests coming behind her.

He eyed her closely, pleased indeed to see her in such high spirits. Maybe she hadn't been in love with this Hawks fellow, as Jackal had reported. His hopes rose. Before the night was through, he would ask for her hand. No, demand it.

The orchestra struck the first chords to a Viennese waltz, and instantly Weston was by her side. He took her arm and swept her onto the empty dance floor.

To her, his arms resembled iron bars staking out his personal dominion for all to see. She strained to see Granger, but she saw nothing except a sea of swirling faces. Eventually other couples joined them, and she didn't feel so conspicuous.

She felt Weston's hard stare boring into her face, and she glanced up. For a second an unfathomable mask hid his usually calm features. Through his eyes she caught a glimpse of his malicious soul and a shiver ran through her. She'd rather face the Comancheros. They made no pretense. Weston, on the other hand, had lived a lifetime of lies. His dark look cleared instantly, and he smiled.

"Falisha, you don't know how pleased I am to see you in better spirits. Especially tonight."

"Thank you. I'm feeling much better."

"Then I trust you are able to put this summer's painful experience behind you?"

"I have, for the most part."

"Good."

"Envious"—he nodded toward their audience—"they're all envious. The women of you and the men of me. We make the most striking couple here."

She didn't know how to respond. Luckily the music stopped, and hopeful partners besieged them. Scheming mothers wanted to reintroduce their daughters to Weston, and unattached males vied for the next dance with Lisha. At least the persistent young men prevented Weston from insisting on another dance. A circumstance she was most grateful for, until she realized that Granger hadn't claimed one, either. She fully expected to see him at every turn but was disappointed.

She lost count of the dances, and the men who whirled her about the floor. Preparing to decline the next offer, she heard a honeyed voice at her ear.

"I believe this is my dance."

She turned to look up at Granger. Her irritation had grown with each dance he'd missed, and she had intended on staying that way until she saw his childlike grin. She couldn't help but smile back. Granger took her arm and expertly guided her onto the floor.

"You've been gone an awful long time."

"I know."

"You weren't going to let me out of your sight."

"I know.

"I had determined to stay angry at you."

Granger chuckled. "I know, but I'd hoped that after I told you what I found out, you'd forgive me."

"Did you hear something important?"

Granger twirled her off the floor and showed her out the patio doors. He didn't utter a sound until they were in the gardens, and only then, a sigh escaped his lips when he kissed her.

"I've been wanting to do that for a long time." His husky voice began to weave its spell.

"How would you know? You've been too busy spying."

He pulled her closer. "But you're always in my thoughts. Forgiven?"

Coyly she pushed away and pretended to pout. "I don't know. You haven't yet told me what you found out."

"That's because when I'm with you, I lose all track of sensible thought."

"Granger."

"All right. When this fellow Claybeard—"

"Clayborne."

"When Clayborne danced with you, another man standing beside me made a snide comment under his breath about our host. I could tell he was a little in his cups before coming tonight, and not such a stanch follower of Clayborne's, so I struck up a conversation and suggested another drink. Guess who he was?"

"Who?"

He smiled at her rapt attention. "None other than Judge Croft."

"What did he say?"

"I was most interested in what he *didn't* say. As far as I can tell, during the war, Clayborne found out something about the good judge, and he has been dancing a lively tune ever since. I also found out that Kingswood had been used for a dock. What better way to secretly unload smuggled goods than to use a new passage through private property made by the flood?"

His words dulled her happiness. "Then Papa really was at the head of all this?" Even as she asked, she knew in her heart it wasn't true.

"I didn't say that, and neither did Judge Croft. All he would admit is that your land had been used."

"And in the eyes of most of the people around here, that means my father had a hand in everything that went on."

"What do we care what people think as long as we know the truth ourselves?"

"They already call him a drunk. I just didn't want the title of traitor following him to the grave."

Granger rubbed a thumb along her cheekbone. "I know. That's why I intend on breaking this thing wide open." She gazed up at him, and he groaned. "Do you have any idea of what the moonlight does to you?"

He roughly pulled her against him and kissed her soundly. The stimulus he succeeded in arousing took the edge off what he'd told her. She marveled at his soothing effect and delighted in the thoughts of a whole lifetime of his magical cures.

Slowly he raised his head. His fingers rippled down the pearl buttons aligning her spine. "One of these days, Mrs. Hawks"—his husky drawl told of his turbulent emotions— "I'm going to have the time to undress you, button by button."

"Just *one* day, Mr. Hawks?" she teased. "You disappoint me, sir. I thought you were good for at least *two*."

Granger chuckled, but that didn't erase his growing desire; it just seemed to enhance it. "What say we find a cozy little spot and discuss this situation further?"

She traced a fingertip around the sensitive part of his mouth. There was nothing more she would rather do than hide away with him. She wished for the hundredth time they could be done with this ugly business of treason.

"As much as I'm inclined to agree, I think we'd better be getting back. I know Weston will be watching for me."

"Somehow, I knew you'd say that. But one can only hope." He leaned down and softly kissed her lips before taking her hand and walking her to the veranda. "You go in first. I'll follow."

Without so much as one person looking her way, she stepped through the French doors and kept to the back. From the corner of her eye she saw Granger walk in and calmly saunter off. She waited a few minutes, wishing she could somehow avoid the group of men that had clustered around her since she'd shared the first dance with their host.

She looked up to see Weston angrily striding her way. Her heart quickened. Had he seen her step out onto the veranda with Granger? Was he outraged because she'd been gone so long? Well, what if he was? He had no right to be so furious when she was with her own husband. Even though Weston knew nothing about it.

Squaring her shoulders, she readied herself to do battle if need be, but then her host walked past her and disappeared through the doors. The look on his face made her cringe. What had happened to cause this extreme reaction? And who was he so enraged with? But most important, why hadn't she noticed this side of him before?

On impulse she followed him into the night. Weston glanced about, with jerky motions full of anger. A man stepped from the shadows . . . Jackal.

"I thought I told you never to come here!" Weston hissed, his words barely audible.

"We have to talk."

Weston turned and walked on down the veranda. He yanked open a door and stepped in, leaving the bounty hunter to follow. As Lisha watched their disappearing backs, troubled thoughts left her uneasy.

Her guardian had lied about knowing Jackal. He had lied about selling off Kingswood. What else had he been lying to her about? Unable to stop herself, she hurried to listen at the door.

Chapter
❧ 30 ❧

". . . is not a reason to be here." Weston's tight voice drifted through the closed doors.

"What's the matter? Don't ya want your stuffy friends to know we work together?"

An object fell to the floor with a splintered crash. "You push me too far, Jackal."

"Maybe, but I want what's rightfully mine."

". . . yours is in the same bottleneck as mine. I can't do anything about the gold . . . Kingswood . . . Falisha . . ."

". . . remember I'm the one had to go . . . Because of that, I deserve more of a share."

"You'll get . . . nothing more. . . ."

Lisha surmised the men moved about the room because she heard less of their heated conversation. She could definitely tell Weston's agitated voice, driven almost to distraction, from the venomous feel of Jackal's.

"Jackal, you . . . trouble from the start. . . . work hard . . . crumble around me. And no one, not even you . . ."

The rest of the warning and Jackal's response were muffled. Lisha heard scuffling, heavy breathing, and a series of loud thumps. A space of seconds passed before the door opened, revealing Jackal. She pressed against a shadowed corner and held her breath.

"Just remember, Clayborne, no matter how long it takes, I intend on getting my full share of *all* that's buried at Kingswood. Take it as a threat.'' He crossed the patio and instantly disappeared into the night.

Lisha focused on the open door. Her heart hammered against her chest. She now knew of Weston's deep involvement with the blockade-runners. But what's worse, she might be found hiding outside his quarters.

She strained for a sound, a movement of some kind to warn her that the lawyer was still inside. Had he gone back to the ballroom through another door? Because she could not be sure, she stood completely still and waited. Her harrowed breathing seemed to give her away.

After what felt like eons, she decided Weston had gone, and stepped out. Suddenly he emerged and shut the door behind him. She pressed back into the shadows, hoping the darkness would conceal her one more time.

Weston straightened his clothes and smoothed a hand across the sides of his hair, too preoccupied to take any notice of his surroundings. He made a conscious effort to lighten his grim mask and headed to the ballroom.

Her breath came out in a rush. She realized the danger she'd put herself in. Anybody would think that after this summer she would have learned not to be so impulsive. Neither Jackal nor Weston would appreciate the fact that she had overheard their little ''discussion.'' Taking a deep breath to gain control of her nerves, she once again joined the throng of people.

A crowd had gathered in front of the orchestra, and she saw Weston, facing the audience. She found no fault with his meticulous appearance. Nobody would ever guess Jackal had bested him in a scuffle only minutes before.

''I want to thank all you good people for your kind pledges. I'm told that we have not only enough money to put the roof over the children's heads but enough to start supplying the home.''

Applause met his announcement. Some called out his name combined with a few cheers. He waited for just the right amount of time before he raised his hand for order. ''You people should applaud yourselves. We wouldn't have been able to make our goal if it weren't for you.''

''Yes,'' a voice rang out, ''but if it weren't for you, there wouldn't even be an orphanage." The guests enthusiastically agreed.

After a moment Weston made an effort to subdue the crowd. "Come now, if I hadn't started it, one of you good people would have."

"I don't know. It takes real leaders like yourself!" someone yelled. "Leaders who have the people's interests at heart."

"Hey, Clayborne, have you ever thought about becoming mayor?" another chimed in.

"Why stop at mayor? Why not governor?"

"Why not go all the way to the presidency?"

By this time Lisha saw that excitement ruled the audience, taking over like a chain reaction. Someone had pointed out Weston's leadership quality, and the crowd ate it up. He looked a little dumbfounded.

"You people forget. We're building an orphanage here. I have no time to run for mayor or any other political office."

"Don't worry, folks!" a man shouted. "We'll work on him."

"I've never seriously entertained such an adventure, but I promise I'll think about it."

Lisha saw through Weston's little charade and couldn't believe how gullible the people were. How could they have missed anything so obvious? Yet, she had to remind herself that if it weren't for Granger planting the seed of doubt, she would probably have been just as aroused as the others.

Weston's performance was superb. She had to give him that. His calculated pauses were perfectly timed. He knew enough not to quiet down his audience too soon, or it would squelch their growing excitement. On the other hand, he never allowed them to reach the limit of their enthusiasm, for he intended to leave them wanting more. Papa would have enjoyed Weston's production, extremely so. He always had appreciated a good act from fellow thespians.

Granger found his way to her side. "Are you swept up in all this?"

"No. Not anymore."

Weston motioned the orchestra to begin playing and tried to

make his way toward them through a sea of congratulating hands.

"Looks like we're in for some unwanted company." He pulled her into his arms and whirled her onto the floor. "I've decided I've left you alone long enough."

"Granger, Weston has been working with the blockade-runners."

His expression grew dark. "How did you find this out?"

"I overheard him arguing with Jackal. I must admit I eavesdropped at Weston's door."

For a few moments Granger didn't say anything. "Remind me to reprimand you tomorrow"—his voice held a penalizing tone—"but for now tell me what was said."

"They were arguing. I only caught parts of what they'd said, but they talked about gold. And Jackal said he intended to get his share of *all* that's hidden at Kingswood."

"I guess it wasn't just jealous gossip I heard."

"What did you hear?"

"Some guests think that Clayborne was really the man in charge of the smuggling. I found more than one enemy of his here tonight. What I'd like to know is, why they came at all."

The music ended, but before Weston could reach them, Granger again whisked Lisha into the next waltz. The lawyer stood at the edge of the dance floor watching their every move. A black scowl twisted his normally handsome features. His manner prevented those guests close to him from striking up a conversation.

"Granger, do you think there could possibly be gold buried at Kingswood?"

"The more I listen, the more I'm beginning to. Lisha, I want you to think about not only what your father said to you the day he died, but also what he said several days before that. Then tomorrow we're going to look over Kingswood. We know Clayborne hasn't been too successful. Maybe we'll come across something he's overlooked."

When the music ended, Granger, much to her surprise, brought her to a standstill right in front of their simmering host.

"Wonderful party, Mr. Clayborne. Those orphans will be eternally grateful."

Lisha mentally ducked at Weston's icy look. His cold stare moved from Granger's amicable face to linger on his hand that rested possessively against her arm. Granger casually slipped his arm about her waist. The bold action made Weston gape.

"I don't believe we've met."

"Excuse the oversight. Name's Hawks." He dragged out each syllable. "Granger Hawks, Lisha's husband."

Weston blanched, then reddened. The muscles tightened in his neck. A vein throbbed wildly. He held his hands together as if gripping something and squeezed.

"Now," Granger said, lifting Lisha down from the buggy and placing her on Kingswood soil, "I want you to show me the grounds and talk about anything that comes to your mind. Even if it seems unimportant."

A saucy grin shaped her lips. "Even my climbing tree?"

"Especially your climbing tree. I want to see if it is as big as you say."

"It is."

Arm in arm, they strolled about the lawns. "My great-great-grandfather built Kingswood. He was an eccentric old man who believed the Second Coming of Christ would be in his lifetime. So he constructed the mansion to withstand the changes prophesied. Anywhere he could, he used brick and stone in place of wood. I've been told he often bragged how his home would never be taken by fire or earthquake."

"Nice bloodline."

Ignoring his comment, she showed him her father's favorite spot to sit during the evenings, the gravesite, the old boathouse the river had left tilting precariously in the mud, and the summer kitchen.

With Granger, she inspected every knothole imbedded in the trees, combed the shoreline of the river for natural caves, checked the barn, and examined the rock paths. Nothing was found except the remnants from someone else's hurried search.

She talked of her father and recited the poem from which her nickname derived, and Granger could not mistake the love in her voice. He vowed he would never tell her of his suspicions concerning her father's death.

When he had found out the night before that Jackal worked with Clayborne, he realized who really sent the bounty hunter after Lisha and why. He also suspected that the lawyer gave Jackal orders to kill Granger. Knowing to what lengths Weston Clayborne would go to get the hidden gold, Granger knew in his heart that Weston was responsible for Edward Harrington's death.

Nothing on the grounds triggered a clue, and Granger ushered Lisha inside. She showed him the drawing room and pulled the dustcover from her chair.

"See, this is where I sat when Mama forced me to learn my stitches. Every time, without fail, Papa teased me with the poem. I liked the name Curly-locks. It was something special between Papa . . ." Glancing up, she saw the strange look on Granger's face, and her words trailed off.

"This is where you sat to do your handwork?"

"Yes, I . . ."

Suddenly she knew what he was driving at. She picked up the cushion and slowly turned it over. The seam had been torn, and someone had done an amateurish job of restitching it. With shaking fingers, she pulled loose the thread and discovered a packet tucked inside the stuffing.

Granger gave a low whistle. "Your father certainly had an imagination."

"He did."

She opened the yellowed parcel and, among other things, found an envelope addressed to her. The loss she had felt at her father's death washed over her. The message he'd left her would undoubtedly answer all her questions. She didn't know how long she sat holding her letter, and she was vaguely aware that Granger had started to go through the packet. Finally she opened the envelope and read the contents.

My dear little Curly-locks,
    I know that if you are reading this, I am dead. Sweetheart, please forgive me for the pain I've caused you. I apologize. I didn't know what Clayborne was really up to until it was too late. He had said he wanted to use Kingswood as a base for the Union. Only I found

out different. Take this packet to the government. They'll
know what to do with it. Remember, the show's not over
until the final curtain.

Your loving Papa

Curly-locks, Curly-locks, wilt thou be mine?
Thou shalt not wash the dishes, nor yet feed the swine;
But sit on a cushion, and sew a fine seam,
And—

"Feed upon strawberries, sugar, and cream."

"What?" Granger could hardly drag his eyes from the
documents he held in his hands.

"Papa left another clue."

"He left more than that. Here—read this."

Taking the paper, she began to read. The further she read,
the more astonished she became. During the war, Weston had
corresponded with someone who called himself Renfrew, and
who wore disguises while he acted as a secret agent for the
Union. Someone who was a Southern spy. Someone who
actively denounced the Union, its leaders, and especially
Abraham Lincoln. Someone who acted upon his deranged
views to the point of murder . . . John Wilkes Booth.

Stunned, she laid the paper down. She blinked several times,
as if trying to fully understand what she'd just read.

Granger placed a hand on her shoulder. "Are you all right?"

"I can't believe it. Weston knew about Booth's plans, and
he didn't even try to stop him."

"From what I gathered through these other letters, Clayborne encouraged him. In fact, he paid an assassin himself to
stop some powerful men who opposed him."

"Why? Why would Weston do such a thing?"

"Maybe he figured with them gone he would have an easier
ride to the presidency."

"I never would have believed it of him."

"You, and hundreds of others"—he held up some more
documents—"except for those he made a habit of blackmail-
ing."

"What?"

"Take Judge Croft. Clayborne found out that while acting as company clerk in his regiment, Croft had the habit of stealing supplies and selling them to the highest bidder. I'm sure the rest of these are about the same."

With a sigh she touched a cool hand to her temple. "How did Papa get hold of all this?"

"I don't know. Maybe that's why Clayborne . . ."

"Yes?"

Granger looked as if he could gladly bite off the tip of his tongue. "Never mind, stupid thought. Did you say your father left another clue?"

"It's more like what he didn't leave." She gave him the letter.

He swiftly scanned it. "What's the last line?"

"Feed upon strawberries, sugar, and cream."

"And that means food. Show me where you kept your storage."

She took him to inspect the empty pantry, search the food bins, and finally explore the root cellar. The moment she saw the rows of shelves, she knew something was different, but she couldn't put her finger on it. She cringed at the cobwebs hanging from the rafters, all except those on the end. They'd been virtually wiped clean.

She studied the odd-shaped bricks that held up the shelves. They hadn't been there before. "Granger." Her voice trembled.

Granger looked up from his concentrated study of the stone floor. He glanced from her to the row of shelves. Slowly he straightened. On closer inspection, the shelving looked newer than the rest, the construction different. He found an old nail and scraped away the dirty reddish-brown paint to reveal metallic ore. She hadn't realized she held her breath until it expelled from her lungs.

"I guess we found it," Granger uttered quietly.

"What do we do now?"

"Take a sample of the ore and those documents to Governor Hall."

He struggled with the top shelf. A layer of dirt fell on him, and he wiped his face with the sleeve of his shirt. "Your father thought of everything, even to the point of making these shelves look old. Here, help me with this.''

"No use putting yourselves out." A cold voice came from the doorway. "I'll take over from here on in.''

Lisha whipped around to see Weston standing behind them with a pistol in his hand. "Weston?"

"Of course. I knew if I waited around long enough, you would oblige me by finding where Harrington hid the gold. I never could. He refused to tell us. No matter how much we tried to persuade him."

His words stung. She flinched from the biting pain. "You? You killed Papa?" Her voice bore the numbing weight of her question.

Weston shrugged. "We hadn't planned on it, but—"

With a scream she rushed at Weston, but Granger quickly reached out and grabbed her. "Careful, he's got a gun.''

"Yes, and it would be in your best interest to remember that." He waved the weapon toward the door. "Now what say we go up to a more pleasant atmosphere?"

She led the way up the stone steps, her movements purely mechanical. The memory of Weston standing over her when her beloved Papa died added to her growing fury. She remembered how he took her into his arms, uttering words of solace, remembered how safe she felt. All of that had been a lie. Worse than a lie.

Weston forced them out to the river. Concentrating on nothing but thoughts of revenge, she almost missed seeing a shadowed figure slip behind the slanting boathouse. She didn't blame Jackal for wanting to keep an eye on his partner. Maybe she could help their relationship along.

When they were almost abreast of the wooden structure, she stopped suddenly and sat on an upturned rowboat, ignoring the uncomfortable ribbed slats.

"I'm not going any farther, Weston, not until you answer some questions." Turning slightly, she faced the sluggish river.

Seeing she meant what she said, Weston eased past them, careful to step on the tufts of dry grass. "All right, Falisha, what do you want to know?"

She looked him square in the face. "I want to know who beat my father—you or Jackal." Granger put a restraining hand on her shoulder, and she gave it a hard squeeze.

Weston shrugged. "I guess it won't hurt for you to know. I did."

She felt suddenly drained of blood. Granger stood near her. His closeness gave her courage. "I'm surprised, Weston," she said, making an effort to keep her voice calm. "I thought you had Jackal do all your dirty work. In fact, I'm surprised he's not here to take care of us."

"I don't need him."

"You don't? Is that what you told him before coming out here?"

"I didn't tell him anything. And I don't plan to."

"You mean you're not going to let him know that we've found the gold in the root cellar?"

Weston grinned. The smile lacked his usual charm. "I don't see any reason to. As far as he's concerned, the gold doesn't exist."

"Did you ever intend to give Jackal his share?"

The lawyer laughed. It held no humor. "I intend for that bounty hunter to get everything he deserves. Just like Captain Mercer."

She stood. "Weston, you're going to regret saying that."

From somewhere close behind him, the lawyer heard the unmistakable cock of a gun. His back stiffened.

"Well, *partner,* I see you've been busy."

"Jackal," Weston growled, turning sideways, "I thought I told you to make our usual collections."

"I got to thinking that following you would be more interesting. I was right."

"Not as interesting as it's going to get."   •

Each man stared unblinking at the other. Each waited for an edge. Granger's fingers pressed a beckoning signal against Lisha's shoulder. She inched back, keeping a wary eye on the deadly game playing out before them.

To her distress, Granger stepped on a dried piece of wood. The loud crack startled Weston. That was all Jackal needed. He lunged for the lawyer, knocking him to the wet ground. The force sent Weston's gun flying.

"Run!" Granger yelled at her. Instantly he sprinted forward, scavenging the area for the discarded weapon.

In the background Lisha heard the men wrestling for ownership of Jackal's gun, and she knew Granger had precious little time.

"I said, run!"

Gathering up her skirts, she spun on her heel and jumped across a few rotting boards, landing on the spongy ground beside them. Suddenly the earth began to give way under her feet. Too startled to scream, she furiously clawed away at the rain-sodden ground, trying to grip anything stable. She clutched onto a large rock protruding from the ragged edge of the abandoned well, halting her descent down the miniature slide nature had carved out.

"Granger! Help me. I'm slipping!"

Granger jerked around at Lisha's terrified screams. He saw her struggling at the rim of what he could tell was a deep hole. His heart plummeted. He raced toward her, landing on his stomach. Before he could get a solid hold on her wrist, she slipped from him.

She frantically grasped hold of an exposed root a little more than two feet down. It held, for the moment. In muted horror he watched her dangle at the end of the wooden stem. Her face beaconed a ghastly white against the blackness swimming beneath her.

"Granger?"

Her panic-stricken voice pierced him. "Stay calm. I'm going to reach down for you."

Before he had a chance to reposition his body, in order to get a better grip, a booted foot ground down on his hand. Startled with the sudden pain, he twisted up to see Weston's snarling face and a smoking gun in his hand. Vaguely Granger remembered a gunshot.

"Leave her."

"But it's Lisha."

"If I can't have her, no one else will. Least of all you."

"Granger," Lisha barely squeaked out, "Granger, I don't think it will hold me much longer."

Weston leaned over the hole, momentarily blocking the sun. "Hang on if you like. For all the good it'll do you."

Granger bellowed a roar. Ignoring the gun Weston held, he yanked his hand out from underneath the lawyer's smudged boot and knocked him over.

The impact jarred the already weakened ground. Loose particles rolled down over Lisha, choking her, irritating her eyes. In horrified suspension she heard more than watched the men contest their strength. They wrestled for the gun at the edge of the well. Each jolt shook loose more dirt and pebbles. She didn't know if her heart beat at all. Maybe it had stopped like her breathing.

Her palms began to sweat, making her grip more slippery than it already was. She knew she couldn't hold on much longer, even if the root held firm.

Please, Granger, please hurry!

She knew the instant her lifeline began to give. Her heart leapt to her throat, and a shallow scream followed her drop down into the black pit.

Chapter
❦ 31 ❦

For a few moments Lisha lay at the bottom of the shaft, dazed. She didn't know how far she had fallen, but the well wasn't as deep as she had thought it would be. She'd landed with a soft thud and wondered why. Then she remembered about the heavy rainfall the area had recently had and realized that the unseasonably high moisture must have soaked up the dirt-filled bottom. Shoving her loose hair from her face, she squinted into the dark, trying to become accustomed to it.

She pressed down with her palm in order to right herself and mud quickly oozed over her hand. With a sucking noise, she pulled it free. The sludge clung to her skirts, making it harder to right herself. With difficulty she maneuvered a handhold against the rough wall of the pit and struggled to her feet.

Her ragged breathing echoed against the crumbling walls. The stifling air threatened to smother her, and the dank smell made her nauseated. But she was all right. A little bruised but no broken limbs.

She decided to explore her dungeon to see if she could climb out, but she found she couldn't move. Her feet were planted firmly in the mire, and she couldn't remove them. The mud sucked at her skirts, turning them into a cotton prison. Her heart bolted to an abrupt stop, then with a staccato beat raced on. She was slowly sinking in the quagmire. Fear formed a lump in her throat. It tasted as bitter as bile.

"Granger! Granger, help me!" Her screams bounced eerily about her.

Granger had heard Lisha fall, and for an instant he relaxed his hold on Clayborne. The lawyer immediately struck out with the butt of his gun, scraping Granger on the temple. His vision blurred. He shook his head trying to clear it, trying to remember where he was.

Lisha's terrified cries brought him from his stupor. He staggered up after the lawyer. Before Weston could level the gun, Granger knocked it from his hand. Weston violently shrugged from his grasp and lunged for the weapon. Just as his fingers gripped the cold iron, Granger leapt, landing across him. Rocks, sticks, and other debris dug into his back as they spun over and over, stopping on the muddy riverbank. He pressed his arm down on Weston's windpipe while he groped for the man's flinging gun hand.

With a sudden burst of energy Clayborne flipped over, pinning Granger to the ground. Exertion puckered his face. He had already fought one battle, and it showed. His muscles quivered like jelly.

Granger wedged a toe under Weston's abdomen and kicked out, tossing the lawyer over his head. In one fluid motion he pushed to his knees, then onto his feet. But Clayborne was seconds faster. He cocked the gun.

"This is where we finally part company."

Weston carefully aimed. The sound of a gunshot shattered the air. Granger dived to the side, expecting to feel the hot slice of a bullet, but he felt nothing. He looked at Clayborne. The man stared at him in muted surprise before looking up. Following Clayborne's gaze, he saw Jackal hunched against a dying willow tree. Smoke curled from his gun. Weston placed a shaky hand to his chest and drew it away covered in blood. It seemed to mesmerize him.

"You're wrong, Clayborne," Jackal rasped out. "This is where *we* part company."

Shocked, Weston pitched forward, falling facedown in the gooey mud. The mire seeped inside his collar, trickled into his cuffs, and oozed between his clawing fingers. He raised his head, plastered with a ghastly mask of mud. Before he died, a look of absolute horror rode his face.

Granger struggled to his feet. He saw Jackal tumble over, but didn't stop to see if the bounty hunter was dead. With a sinking feeling that he was too late, he stumbled toward the well. The silence coming from within the pit ripped into his soul. His rising fear almost suffocated him.

"Lisha, are you all right?" His prayerful voice wavered.

"Granger? Oh, Granger," her voice broke on a sob, "I'm sinking. Mud . . . the well's filled with mud." Her lungs forced out the words. She hardly spoke, as if she were afraid talking would make her sink all the more.

Relief shot adrenaline through him. He quickly wiped at his eyes. "I'm here now, love. Everything is going to be all right. Stay calm."

"I'm trying."

"Tell me how far you've sunk."

"It's up to my hips. Oh, please hurry!"

Her voice wobbled like a child after a hysterical cry; its tremor ricocheted on the shaft's walls. The hollow sound tore at his bowels.

"Lisha, I want you to think. Where can I get some rope?"

"There's some in the boathouse, but it's old."

"It'll have to do."

As he started for the rickety building, he realized that if Clayborne had done such a sloppy job of putting everything else away after his search, then it would stand to reason that he would just cast aside the rope he'd used to check out the well. As if on cue, he spied a piece, attached to a plank of lumber, no less. The length of rope also had several knots tied in it for better handling. He briefly wondered why Clayborne failed to add wood for steps.

"Granger, hurry."

Lisha's panic echoed to the top. Her terror spurred him on. He checked the knot before throwing the board across the hole. The tie didn't fully suit him, but he hadn't the time to construct another. He quickly fed the rope down the well.

"I can't reach it."

"Don't worry, I'm coming down."

He stepped onto the plank. The sturdy piece of wood held firm. He gave no thought about it holding him, and he also refused to consider the consequences of Lisha's added weight.

Knot by knot, he carefully lowered himself down. Supporting his toes on the last half hitch, he teetered above Lisha. The sight of her up to her waist in muck made him sick to his stomach.

"Now, love, when I drop down a little more, grab hold of my legs, and I'll pull us out."

Lisha barely nodded. She watched Granger leave the sanctity of the last knot. His swinging feet almost clubbed her on the side of her head. When his legs came within reach, she wrapped her arms tightly about his shins. Praying silently, she waited for him to lift her up. She felt him strain, trying to reach the knot above him. Suddenly, his hand slipped, jarring them both.

"What's the matter?"

"I can't lift us," he panted. "You'll have to strip."

"What?"

"Take those blasted skirts off. You're too heavy covered in all that mud."

She felt sure the hardest thing ever asked of her was to let go of Granger's solid support. If she could hold on, she wouldn't sink to her death. She knew, however, that he couldn't pull them both to safety if she didn't do what he had asked.

Taking shallow breaths, she dropped her arms. For a few seconds she struggled with her bodice and ended up ripping it open. Next, she burrowed her hands underneath the material and found the bow securing her slips. Giving it a yank, she pulled it apart. The quagmire now cupped her breasts. Knowing time was running out, she reached up and once again clutched hold of Granger's legs.

"I'm free."

"I'm going to raise you out of the mud, then I want you to get a better hold." Granger exerted his strength. He climbed the rope, drawing Lisha up until he felt the suction give way with a slurpy wrench. She definitely felt lighter.

"I'm out. Oh, thank God, I'm out!"

Beads of sweat stung Granger's eyes. He wiped his forehead

against his shoulder blade. "Now, Lisha, see if you can get a better hold."

"It would be easier if you'd just hold still."

With cumbersome movements Lisha climbed up Granger's legs. She circled her arms around his waist, anchoring her thumbs in the front loops of his jeans. After wrapping her legs around each of his, she clamped her eyes shut.

"I'm done."

"All right, hold on . . . and pray."

Hand over hand, Granger inched up the rope. His muscles strained against the exertion. Sweat rolled down his face. Only this time, he couldn't wipe it away. The rope burned his hands, and he knew he left splotches of red on the scratchy braid. As he neared the top, he could see that with each swing of the rope the plank gnawed away at the coil.

He watched a cord fray, then another and another. Until they all snapped in rapid succession. With a surge of energy, he clamped an arm around the board, then the other just as the rope broke free. He heard Lisha's breath catch.

"Lisha, listen carefully. I want you to pull yourself up."

"Granger, I—"

"You can do it."

Lisha hesitated, and he silently commanded her to obey him. Inch by inch she climbed, using him as a ladder. Her fingers and toes dug into his body as she made her way up his back. When she threw an arm over the plank and laid her breasts on the rough wood, he hefted himself up and pulled her to her feet. She was safe! Speechless, he guided her to solid ground.

She sank in a huddle to the earth. He dropped to his knees in front of her and raised her chin. Shock glazed her eyes. Mire crusted her face, arms, and legs. He fingered a mud-sodden curl and lightly touched the silt that smeared the lace edging of her chemise, leaving a trace of blood. She grabbed his hands, staring at his bleeding palms.

"Oh, Granger, look," she choked out, "look at your hands!"

"That's all right . . . I know a great Nurse Lady." He gently cupped a hand to the side of her head, and she dissolved into tears.

Drawing her up, he clutched her tightly to his chest. Fear, exhaustion, and tremendous relief warred for dominance inside his body. He desperately clung to her, barely conscious that the edge of death yawned three yards away.

Epilogue

As the New Mexico dawn struggled to cast its light into the adobe ranch house, Lisha relaxed on the bed, curled in the protection of her husband's arms. Again, she thought of the events that had sent her hurtling toward a sensitive man and his future . . . Granger. A change had occurred in her since then. Now she carried an air of maturity, a fine tuning, that she had lacked then.

Again, her thoughts turned to Weston, and a sadness engulfed her. She mourned for the loss of a man who in actuality never existed. Granger had taken the documents her father had hidden to the government and related the whole ugly story. Later, he had warned her that the information and the gold they'd found would probably never come to the attention of the public. He was right.

And again, the past few months tried to resurrect itself, but Lisha squelched it. That was then, this was now. Besides, she had a new daughter to think of . . . and her loving father.

Loving?

Lisha chuckled. The word lacked the intensity and emotion that Granger regularly brought to their marriage bed. An intensity and emotion that she eagerly accepted.

Warm embers of pleasure seethed through her body, and she stretched. A wicked smile curved her lips. She'd been warned not to play with fire, but Granger had successfully committed arson in the primitive regions of her soul, creating a smoldering blaze never to be extinguished, only restrained.

Granger stirred, and she turned a saucy expression toward him. Grinning, he nuzzled her neck.

"You are fast becoming a gifted temptress," he teased with a throaty chuckle, "a nymph who isn't content with just one session of lovemaking."

Lisha smiled. Once is not enough, no, never enough!

FREE
Romance

(a $4.50 value)

Send in the Coupon Below

To get your FREE historical romance and start saving, fill out the coupon below and mail it today. As soon as we receive it we'll send you your FREE Book along with your first month's selections.
